AF192409

Andrew Wells

PEOPLE ON THE EDGE

novum pro

This book is also
available as
e-book.

www.novum-publishing.co.uk

© 2022 novum publishing

ISBN 978-3-99131-111-9
Editing: Hugo Chandler
Cover photos: Stevanovicigor,
Valeria De Martini | Dreamstime.com
Cover design, layout & typesetting:
novum publishing

www.novum-publishing.co.uk

Climate neutral
Print product
ClimatePartner.com/16547-2201-1002

PROLOGUE

Five and a half weeks had passed and Raya knew something was wrong. Sunlight streamed through the inadequate curtains, billowing slightly in the breeze and she desperately wanted to jump out of bed and wrench them aside. She yearned to throw open the apartment window and gulp in the fresh early morning air before the traffic in the almost touchable street below stirred up its daily dose of acrid pollution; but something seemed to be holding her down, like a great hand on her body, and so she lay timorously inert, unable, or maybe not daring to move until the feeling in her stomach subsided. She had experienced this yesterday and almost convinced herself that the feeling was simply caused by tiredness and too much lonely, late night red wine, but in the end, she had had to sprint to the bathroom where she had very inelegantly succumbed to the demands of what was politely called 'morning sickness.' Would it be the same today? She hoped not but suspected gloomily that it might.

She chose not to think of the future. That could wait a few minutes longer, at least. Instead, she allowed her mind to phase backwards to happier times, as if the mere thought of the past would undo what she dreaded might be happening to her. Memories flooded into her brain as she recalled her first sight of Gerald at London airport when she had landed. He had been the same tall, smiling, lean faced, well-dressed professional she held in her mind's eye, with his windswept straw-coloured hair flopping seductively over one eye. Looking relaxed and sophisticated in his own surroundings, he was completely in his element as the immigration and customs officers rushed around to process his young VIP guest. She had been treated like royalty, in a quiet office very separate from the madding hoards who were queuing up in their hundreds to push to the front of the impossibly long 'others' line in the terminal building.

Gerald had arrived first after his three-year tour of duty in the Libyan deserts and had managed to pull some long strings in the British Embassy to help her visa application along. She had been nervously impatient, waiting for the process to be completed but then pleasantly surprised that the forebodings of her sister Hasna, about the British propensity for refusing entry to unmarried young women from unusual countries, had proven unfounded. She had simply done as Gerald requested and paid in advance for a run of the mill language school course. Then, waving the receipt at the embassy visa desk all manner of normally closed doors had been magically opened. She knew that Gerald had orchestrated this, and she would be forever grateful to him for that.

Raya now spent her daytime hours happily studying while Gerald went about his mysterious foreign office business. Occasionally, he travelled, often for days on end. She had no idea where, although his capability in Arabic, Italian, French and Swahili probably gave her an indication. Mostly, he stayed at her apartment in Earls Court, after all, he had paid for it, but he apparently still kept his own apartment elsewhere in London. She did not know why, and she had never been invited to visit him there. When she asked to see it, he politely demurred, citing vague national security reasons. Her upbringing had taught her not to question government officials too much and so she had pushed this to the back of her mind. There were more urgent and exciting things to entertain her thoughts.

Their nights together were the times she looked forward to most. She realised that inventiveness came second nature to her, and they rarely spent more than a few hours asleep before luxuriating again in intimacy. Every surface in every room in their tiny apartment had its own special memories and she pondered these when Gerald was away, like now. Raya found that she pined for his touch to such an extent that she seriously wondered whether she was simply addicted to sex. This idea of physical pleasure went against her childhood education so much that the thought had at first startled her, but her newly improved English and her ventures into the London libraries had calmed her concerns. She concluded that she was normal after all. Her research proved il-luminating and she became an avid devourer of all things to do with erotic arts; so much so that she doubled the number of bor-rower's tickets she held and set herself the challenge of educating her ever-willing Gerald.

The past few months since she had arrived in London had been a whirl of dazzling nightlife, from the London theatres to curious restaurants and weekend breaks in the country. She had visited his parents' country estate twice but had never actually stayed there. For some reason she had not been able to fathom why, they had always moved on before nightfall and found some delightful out-of-the-way village inn with splendid food and a huge four-poster bed; but she was deliriously happy and saw no negative motives in anything her handsome lover might do.

As she lay there in the brightening daylight, her attention refocused on the second visit to his family's estate. She had met his father then and the memory still made her shudder a little. Gerald had introduced her as a friend, rather than a girlfriend, but otherwise, there was nothing specific she could put her finger on. However, she recalled his cold looks and the limited conversation that had taken place, and it had scared her. Gerald had dismissed her concerns as being nervousness on her part, but in her heart she knew there was something wrong. Like today, she thought, there's something wrong; and as if to prove the point she threw off the quilt and sat up quickly. Immediately she felt the urge to be sick and only just managed to reach the bathroom in time. After a few minutes to recover she managed to crawl back to bed, and into a safe horizontal position.

Gerald was due back that evening and she thought back care-fully, to the crazy time they had had in Paris only a few weeks ago. That had been another display of family influence, in get-ting her a tourist visa at almost no notice, but that wasn't the thought that occupied her at that moment. She realised that, of late they had become casual and lazy about contraception and had been taking ever more risks. It had become an exciting game to see how long they could engage in erotic play without actually reaching an orgasm. She realised too, that it was almost certainly her own pushing that had prompted this change in behaviour and her thoughts began to turn more towards regret. She wondered if another change of pace was needed although every erogenous zone her body argued for more, not less. She had no wish to disrupt their idyllic lifestyle and had fond hopes that one day soon they might be able to make their relationship legal, although she dreaded the obstacles that her family would raise to block her way, so she decided that some sort of plan was necessary. Firstly, she needed to be sure of her condition; no point in worrying unduly, she thought. Her stomach seemed to be behaving at last, so she forced her thoughts towards nearby pharmacies and looked up the English words related to pregnancy tests in her dictionary.

On the other side of London, Gerald was on a high. He had just completed a difficult negotiation to open the way for an exclusive oil deal in the Middle East for British companies. He regretted the fact that his recent three-year tour of duty in North Africa had not been as fruitful, during which he had been amazed at how little could be achieved when policy outranked money as the official language between governments. He was in a taxi from the airport and looking forward to seeing Raya. It had been nearly two weeks since they had been together, and he smiled in anticipation at the thought of their imminent reunion. Their parting was still burned into his brain, coming as it had a few days after their wonderful Paris holiday. It had been an emotional, if not completely exhausting occasion and he mentally urged the chattering cockney in front to drive faster.

He closed his eyes, and his near photographic memory captured her image and subconsciously catalogued his thoughts. Beautiful (of course, he thought), twenty-two years old, tall, slim, with an oval face, olive skin, and long, long black hair. How he loved the feel of that hair, and she knew exactly what to do with it too. He relaxed into the grinding cab and daydreamed his way back to her apartment. Memories of the tiny hotel with the huge bed near the Louvre, the cafés where water was more expensive than wine, and the romantic river trips all flooded back. He had been surprised, and pleased that Raya had taken such an interest in the Crazy Horse show, as if she was trying to see whether there was anything to be learnt. It certainly seemed there had been, as he found out late that evening back in the hotel. They had finally fallen asleep at eight o'clock the next morning before a wake-up call for the airport taxi dragged them back to reality two hours later. Happy days, he thought.

Gerald climbed the stairs eagerly to their second-floor apartment and pulled out his keys. He made a display of rattling and banging them against the lock, while he deliberately fumbled his way into the slot. Finally, he pushed open the door in the full expectation of having Raya fling her arms around his neck, shrieking joyously as she normally did when she heard him at the door; but she did not throw her arms around his neck, and there was no shriek, no sound at all. In fact, she wasn't there.

He looked around the two small rooms quickly, searched the tiny kitchen carefully for signs of habitation but only found a few empty wine bottles, so with an almost audible intake of breath, he carefully pushed open the bathroom door. It was empty too. He walked to the fridge and opened the door, but everything was normal. His stack of beer was untouched, and the only other food was a stray orange. Raya was not the world's most adventurous cook. He found a glass and poured a beer, then sat down to think. Maybe she'd mixed up the date, or maybe she'd gone to meet him at a restaurant, and he'd not got the message. He looked around the flat one more time, but found no notes, no messages, nothing. His disappointment sapped his energy. He kicked off his shoes, gulped down his beer and rested his head on the sofa. In a few minutes tiredness overcame him, and he slept.

Raya was sitting in the park, watching the children playing after school. Their mums were attentive to their charges but clearly relished the chance to chat together. Raya felt a little out of place but wondered what she might be doing herself in a few months' time. Her mind raced as she tried to stop herself jumping to conclusions. Her trip to the pharmacy had allowed her to buy a couple of test kits but the pharmacist had reminded her that she ought to wait until the following morning to use them, otherwise she might get a false result. She felt betrayed by technology and her plans to do this, or that, depending on the outcome of the test were in complete disarray. She had no idea how long she had sat in the park but as she enjoyed the calm of the evening sunshine and the quietening scene in front of her as the mums and children wander homeward, she suddenly remembered that Gerald would be coming back today.

She glanced at her watch and in horror, realised that she had been sitting daydreaming for nearly three hours. But she was rooted to the spot. Her confidence had evaporated and, without knowing, she felt completely at a loss. She must 'know' she thought, and then it came to her, like a bolt from the blue. She looked hastily round and walked quickly to the nearby copse of trees. Another glance around but the few remaining mums were too busy rounding up their offspring. She went further into the shelter of the trees, took out one of the test kits, lifted her skirt with one hand and, holding the fragile spatula in the other, she crouched behind a holly bush, said a prayer, and peed.

A few minutes later found her running, running as she'd never run before. Her mind had slotted into gear and begun to function again. She wanted to see Gerald, now. She wanted to throw her arms around him as she usually did. She wanted to shriek happily as she normally did. So, she ran. It was not far, but it seemed to take forever to reach the main road, and forever to wait for the traffic to slow enough for her to dart between the cars, and then the pavements were so crowded. She pushed and shoved her way forward until at last she turned the corner of the road by the bank and ran up the steps to the large porticoed front door. She punched the entry code, pushed through and kept running, up and up the seemingly never-ending stairs. Their apartment door opened easily to her key, and she burst inside.

Gerald stirred on the sofa and blinked open a bleary eye to find Raya's face almost touching his. Not a word was spoken but within seconds they were kissing and tearing at each other's clothes as they searched and found, again and again. They eventually progressed to the bedroom where they collapsed, almost steaming in the cool of the early evening. Raya nuzzled Gerald's shoulder and pulled the quilt around them. They dozed for a while.

But Gerald felt something was different. Despite her energy, Raya was not her usual relaxed and happy-go-lucky free spirit.

"What's the matter?" he asked.

Raya nuzzled deeper. He pushed her gently away and looked carefully at her face. She refused to return his gaze and after a few seconds, prised herself away and reached for her bag of books, where she had thrown it on the floor. Gerald was wide-awake now, his senses telling him something was wrong.

Raya delved into her bag and pulled out a white spatula, no longer than her middle finger. The small blue patch near the end caught the overhead light and flashed ominously. She handed the spatula to Gerald. His eyes widened and a look of shocked horror came over his face as the consequences of this tiny patch of blue ripped through his brain. He physically backed away from Raya, until he was almost falling off the bed.

"How could you?" he shouted.

Raya's world fell apart.

1

Irrigation seemed such an obvious need. The dusty sand blew lazily in snake-like rivulets across the sizzling, soggy tarmac leaving a pristine surface in its wake. The few trees that had struggled through the dunes were now gnarled and shrivelled sticks, long polished by the blown sand and dried to tinder by the relentless sunshine. They appeared in the overpowering heat like ancient statues of wizened old travellers, tramping through the desert and frozen in time. In the distance, the outline of the airport shimmered like an oasis in the afternoon desert air, its verdant welcome of featured fountains surmounted by waving palm fronds; a forlorn attempt to give the necessary good impression to newcomers. In the surrounding environs there was nothing, no farms, no buildings, no people, and no water. A solitary camel waded sulkily through the spiky undergrowth, nibbling occasionally from the unappetising meagreness. Between the road and the camel was a rusty steel mesh fence that looked as if it was designed to keep out an army, rather than a few grizzled animals.

Dale Connors had imagined he would change great prairies of dusty desert sand into swathes of rolling greenness like the East Sussex Downs of his youth. Dale was Business Development Manager for Global Infrastructure Ltd, a large multi-country, multi-cultural, multi-services company that specialised in the creation, design and management of large projects around the world. If people needed infrastructure, airports, roads, dams, offices, palaces, parks, railways, schools or hospitals then Dale and his colleagues were interested. He had arrived on his first visit to Libya full of optimism that he could make a difference and change just a small part of the world for the better. He often wondered at his own gullibility, hesitating to call it naivety and preferring the description 'optimism.' After all, he thought, without optimism and courage there would be no progress.

But this place was tough; much tougher than anywhere else he had worked, and he had already been to every continent in the world in his fourteen-year career, which seemed to specialise in working in the more unusual parts of the world. In the time since he had been coming to Libya he had learned emphatically that nothing was ever as it seemed. The whole country was run by committees. In fact, it was more correct to say it was run by committees of committees, all monitored by further committees of security officials. Everyone was represented by someone, somewhere in the multiple machinations of the cumbersome system, and everyone was watched and reported upon by someone else; and so the great stage settings of committee work plodded their tedious way around meaningless work targets and endless reports of artfully created results. They dwelt relentlessly on bureaucratic topics and yet insisted on recording suggestions for improvement with a sense of purpose that belied their ability for change. The ill-informed chairmen listening half-heartedly to the representatives of the people who, had they been there themselves might actually have had something useful to say. Dale and his team found the process intensely frustrating. Obvious solutions were, for obscure and unrecorded reasons always relegated to second place behind political interests, generally of the personal, vested interest variety. So, they learnt to match the whims and cover the foibles of ministry officials with some of their irrigation project's aims; and in this way, they managed to at least appease the demands of both, whether they be voiced, clearly perceived or merely hinted at. It was enough to make slow progress.

The Ministry of Agriculture was housed in a forlorn looking building, some nine stories high. Its windows were shrouded in impenetrable grime and dust, its doorways uninviting and its security staff unbending to all but the intensely persistent. The ministry's remit nonetheless governed the lives of the vast majority of the population. Simply put, they had to feed the nation, striving to grow any and every possibly crop on the mountains of sand and dust, which formed the hinterland to the coastal cities, or cultivating the endless salty flatland close to the sea. Equally simply put, their resources to achieve such a task were close to zero and their obstacles considerable.

They needed water, but there was none within practical reach of the coastal cities. So, Agriculture had to deal with the Ministry of Power, as most water came in concert with electricity from the fearsomely expensive desalination plants installed in bygone years. The plants ran on oil, piped over huge distances from the country's interior. The economics of these two staple utilities was a well-guarded secret, except that most knew that they had made a select few of the ruling group extremely rich in illegal offshore funds.

They needed equipment and pipelines to transmit water to where it was needed, but sanctions forbade their import. So, they resorted to cannibalising the country's older oil fields for their basic necessities. This took time, of which they had plenty, and influence with the Ministry of Oil, of which they had very little.

They needed economic scale but there was none. The farming communities were deliberately divided into small tenant plots where a single family could supposedly survive. Equality was the political watchword. Small families, small plots, small-scale farming, large-scale administration and bureaucracy built on committees. It was the politics of people-empowerment and certainly kept the population employed, or at any rate occupied, although in such an inefficient manner that Dale wondered inwardly how long it could possibly last. Each family was allocated a part share in a tractor, and they had to plan and argue for their use of this with several other families in the co-operative. The fuel was free but rationed. In fact, there were more officials dealing with fuel allocations than there were mechanics looking after the tractors and their various antiquated attachments. So, getting things done was slow, painfully slow, and in the meantime, water was scarce to non-existent. The families laboured under the sun to bring up their children with whatever produce they could grow, in addition to the quota needed for the common good.

They needed a means of getting produce to market, even though prices were fixed, and the food supply was centrally directed and rationed; but the lorries used to transport produce were the responsibility of the co-operatives and the small holders would queue in vain to ensure that their produce was collected on time. Refrigeration was a thing of the future for these families and so the daily battle against the system was fuelled by the ever-imminent threat of rotten crops. As spoiled crops meant no pay, the families' efforts were focused on beating the system, rather than efficiently growing food.

Dale's project was to get irrigation water to the small farms and to make it safe for their families to use. It had started amidst what he jokingly termed an environment of militant apathy among the ministry officials who openly admitted that they knew all the answers, had had endless studies done before and all they wanted was the wherewithal to get on and implement something. More to the point, they wanted someone else to provide the money, enough money in fact that someone else could do the getting on and implementing and leave enough for them to participate in rich pickings too. Dale's team nonetheless included an agricultural expert whose job had been to advise on crop selection and water optimisation.

Winston Stanford was an experienced dry-climate specialist who knew his stuff and always found, as he found here, that the clients already knew what they needed to know, just like they told him every day. They simply needed the means to do it, just like they told him every day too. Winston was an unusual Brit, a 'character' who insisted on wearing one of a colourful collection of sarongs when not actually working. He claimed it was a habit he had picked up in India and would appear at the hotel bar or pool wearing one of his frail and precarious garments. The way it was tucked into itself beneath his now ageing belly and hairy torso defied both gravity and physics as it clung tenaciously to his lower body.

No one ever knew what he wore beneath but his assistant, Marlena, a solid and sombre German girl who didn't know a great deal about soils but did speak excellent Arabic, would hint in her rare moments of humour that he was really Scottish at heart. To the local lads in the hotel, this news was not especially enlightening and so Dale entertained them with lengthy discussions explaining the history of Scotsmen, kilts and underwear. For good measure, he told them stories about the haggis, and would have them believe in this mythical animal of the past, to the point where they constantly sought more and more of his seemingly never-ending tales; but all this tongue in cheekiness confused Marlena and offended her logical mind. She would raise her eyebrows in abject resignation at his so-called British sense of humour.

Dale was not altogether sure where Marlena had appeared from. His boss in the UK, Jim Westead had suggested her as a team member and had assumed that his suggestion would be adopted. There really had been no discussion, but her linguistic abilities made up for any perceived inadequacies and in the endless meetings with the co-operatives' committees, she was invaluable. She was also a ferret for facts. They had sat with several families, always chaperoned by a collection of committee representatives and when questions about farming were raised, the official figures were trotted out, but at such evident disparity with the facts that Dale and his team ended up with two sets of notes. One was official for the files and one as real as they could tactfully manage. This generally stayed out of sight on their project computer hard drive. Everything they printed was scrutinised by their security chaperones. Everything they said was listened to for hidden innuendo. Everything they did was commented on and discussed by the small group who were allotted to them. It became a game they learnt to play quite effectively, and in time the local watchers grew tired and bored, and then careless.

In the Ministry of Agriculture, the technical staff were all Egyptian. They worked as expatriates for Libya's national staff who were their senior managers. They were a dusty, large and ambling bunch, generally amiable but nonetheless a group who knew how to get things done, albeit slowly, without actually doing anything themselves. The people who ran around at everyone's beck and call were Palestinian. They were not expatriates but a people in exile, and without them, the place would have fallen apart.

Kept on short leashes through an under-the-table system of visas and work permits that made them completely servile to their ministry managers, the Palestinian workers were willing, intelligent, underpaid and very under-fulfilled. They were however, as one young worker told Dale one evening, "alive." "And when Palestine is free" he had mused, "we will return there with our families." The young fellow had a six-year-old daughter who had been born in exile. There was no obvious end in sight.

Their visas could cost them half their pay and their accommodation, without long term papers, was expensive. They were indeed a people on the edge of existence, exiled westwards along the southern Mediterranean shore until they could be exiled no further. Without homeland, nationality, passport or rights, they were nonetheless part of a people bound together by such patriotic strength that it seemed to Dale that their very souls provided the life force on which they thrived. The country accepted them for what they were, people with a cause, but also competent and uncomplaining workers. It exploited them for what they could provide.

Dale's project needed maps and here the Ministry of Security came into its own. When he had fought his way through layers of officials in explaining exactly why he needed the maps and that it was nigh impossible to plan anything engineeringly orientated without them, he was then faced with the inevitable negotiation of the fee. In vain, he explained that their contract stated that maps and government information would be issued free of charge. In vain, he attempted to bargain the astronomic price downwards. The only concession he obtained was that he could pay out of the local currency fee component of the project.

But in the Ministry of Agriculture, he came up against the ultimate barrier.

"Your money's in the safe" advised a cautious Sulaiman, the large forty-year-old Egyptian in charge of procurement and contracts, "and we can't open the safe. It's stuck," he added sheepishly.

Dale asked to see the offending chunk of metal and found that the safe was indeed closed. It was a circular combination lock with tumblers. "But surely you have the code?" he asked, "it can't be so difficult to open."

"Well, yes" pondered an embarrassed Sulaiman, as if not sure how to admit the real story, "but the instructions are in a strange sort of language that we can't understand and so we aren't able to open the safe." He spread his hands expansively. "The fact is we don't usually close the safe. It sort of closed itself."

Dale did not believe his ears but offered to try and help, and Sulaiman handed over the instruction booklet and code with an obvious sigh of relief. After a couple of minutes study Dale could see the problem. The instructions were indeed long, running to some six pages and written in that form of instructional shorthand so beloved of board game manufacturers. He persevered through the demented dungeons-and-dragons-like literature, until after twisting and turning the reluctant, clunky tumblers backwards and forwards, he finally managed to open the door on the third attempt.

"La voila!" he exclaimed.

Sulaiman leapt into action and, retrieving an old tennis shoe from beneath his desk he stuck it firmly in the doorjamb of the safe. His wide face beamed his happiness and in short order, he had paid Dale the whole of his local currency fee and invited him round to his house for dinner on the following day.

"Does Fatimah know where you live?" asked Dale, thinking of his ministry-provided driver.

"Oh yes" chuckled a still happy Sulaiman, "no problem there."

The safe door remained visibly propped ajar. Dale's payment had hardly made a dent in its contents.

In due course, the maps were delivered personally by a Ministry of Security official. Fuad Asmi himself had done the honours and brought the bundle into their project office as if it contained the crown jewels themselves. After much signing and rubber stamping of papers the team carried their prize away and opened it up in anticipation. To their surprise, the maps were full of holes, huge gaping holes cut out by hand in the most unlikely places. It was as if a gigantic moth had feasted on their maps while in transit. It was a bizarre sight and only Marlena seemed to take this turn of events in her stride. She pointed out that every sensitive security risk, every official building, and every piece of officially secret land had been simply excised from the map. She also pointed out that some other countries' agencies blackened sensitive areas but not many went to the trouble of cutting them out. It was as if the administration wanted to broadcast the locations rather than hide them from sight. Marlena also warned them that Fuad was the Deputy to Fayez Shakari, the chief of the country's secret police. Her implication was clear. "Be very careful," she added.

Dale wondered how she was so knowledgeable but let it pass. It struck him that Marlena was maybe not just a simple agronomist. Sure, she knew her stuff in an academic sort of way but lacked the fire and enthusiasm exhibited by Winston. She was also decidedly vague about her past experience in this type of work and her face was always a masterclass in inscrutability.

But for now, the team could at least make progress. They also knew where not to tread and although the holes were more representative of a giant colander it was comforting to have their limits shown clearly.

2

The two bearded, dark-complexioned men sat in the departures lounge at Heathrow. Their destination was Frankfurt but their route to reach their present location had been tortuous. Their travel plan had taken them first to Milan, then Paris by air, and then on to London by cross channel train, where they picked up a hire car. With the car they had visited Stanstead and Manchester airports.

Jamil Shakari was more interested in the cities and the night-life. He was the only son of Fayez Shakari, whose capabilities and successes in charge of the secret police were legendary and whose contacts were impressive. Unfortunately, Jamil only appeared to have inherited his father's size and propensity for food, drink and women, while attempting unsuccessfully to cover his lack of professional abilities through general vindictiveness and ordered-up brutality towards his luckless suspects. He was however careful to only allow others to indulge in any thuggery he demanded. His hands were kept spotless.

Jamil was over-fed, over-privileged, arrogant and impatient. He had money to burn and intended to treat himself well. In Milan, they had blown quite a considerable sum in the upper end clothing shops, followed by the bars and nightclubs around the back streets of the Duomo area, before finally parting company in the early hours. His companion Hussein pleaded tiredness and had headed back to their hotel, but Jamil wasn't to be deterred and wended his way to an almost deserted Corso Sempione to find a girl for the rest of the night.

The girls were exceptionally well heeled. It was a cold April night and fur coats were very much in evidence. This was the serious red-light district in Milan, not like one of the infamous areas out towards the stadium where anything and everything was on display. In the cut-price areas, the girls wore very little all the year round, sometimes burning old tyres in an effort to stave off the cold, so desperate were they to show off their assets to full advantage in the competitive street environment, but not here. Corso Sempione was where you didn't ask the price. If you did, you probably couldn't afford it. This was for men with serious money only.

Jamil surveyed the girls arrayed along the roadside. Several lounged against upmarket cars and he walked purposefully towards a tall dark-haired beauty. Without speaking, she scooped him into her Porsche and then said something in Italian to him. He was overawed, completely enraptured by the girl and simply said "Yes." He had no idea what she'd said and had been too awe-struck to pay attention anyway. He struggled with rapid English, let alone Italian, so he hoped his pocket full of dollar notes would do the talking. The girl was stunning and murmured something further in Italian. Jamil simply nodded. She was so unlike any of the girls back home.

The girl slowly drove off and Jamil was surprised when they pulled into a tiny pensione only two hundred metres away. He looked around him and noticed that all the cars in the packed parking area were either very fast, very sporty, very luxurious, or all three. The old pensione owner spoke perfect English and was a paragon of helpfulness, although he met Jamil's request for a room for the night with quiet amusement. "We rent the rooms by the quarter of an hour" he told them, "how many quarters would you like?" Jamil's girl looked suitably impressed at the wad of dollars he handed over.

"Send us up a bottle of your special champagne," she smiled knowingly at the owner who looked her straight in the eyes and nodded in response. She pulled her fur around her elegant shoulders and smiled. Tonight, she would have no trouble earning a good fee.

Hussein walked towards his hotel and when he was sure that Jamil wasn't following he dived down a side street and into a phone booth. For ten minutes he grappled with his memory, but it was no use. The credit on his phone card was almost gone and so far he had failed to find the right combination of digits. He struggled again to remember the sequence. Why hadn't he written them down, he wondered. Of course, he knew why. It was much too dangerous to carry such numbers around with him. His last attempt to connect was answered and he shifted his attention to the voice, but he immediately knew he had failed. The phone has been answered by an unfamiliar, angry voice, clearly not happy at being woken at such an antisocial hour of the night.

Hussein gave up and threw away the card in disgust, angry at himself for his stupidity in forgetting the number and brooding about what his new lords and masters would have to say. He stumbled back to the main road and turned his attention to finding the hotel. He pondered for a moment on what Jamil might be doing but put that from his mind too. He didn't care for Jamil and certainly didn't want to compete in his games.

On the top floor of the pensione, the girl carefully emptied the wallet of its remaining banknotes, wondered why there were no credit cards nor in fact any identification at all, and then replaced it in Jamil's jacket pocket. She picked up the half-finished bottle of wine, opened the door quietly and slipped carefully out of the tiny room. Jamil slept on peacefully. His energy quickly spent, even quicker than his dollars, he had collapsed before the first quarter of an hour was over, and although the room was paid for until morning, the girl clearly had other things to attend to and had no compunction leaving her now unconscious and impecunious client to his own devices. She descended the stairs and tipped the pensione owner, handing back the bottle as she passed his desk. When Jamil asked him in the morning what had happened to the girl, the old owner would tell him she had just left. He had 'just missed her,' he would add. But Jamil wouldn't be waking up for some hours yet, not with the extra sleeping draught he had unwittingly taken. The old man tucked the extra money away in his pocket and went through to the small bar to wash out the bottle.

As they sat in departures, Hussein was worried, and voiced his concern for what must have been the tenth time to Jamil. "Our tickets are traceable" he said, "and our hire car is traceable. If anyone puts two and two together they will trace our entire route."

Jamil turned to face him. "Listen," he warned, "we started with false papers and changed the whole lot again in the UK. By the time anyone catches up with us we will be long gone."

But Hussein was a worrier. "Jamil" he continued, "how are we going to get enough information? This is our fifth airport in as many days, and we've not been able to get behind the gates of any of the cargo areas. There are cameras everywhere and we simply don't look like most of the people here. We are very obvious. Since 9/11, every time an Arab travels anywhere half the world's security staff are looking over his shoulder, especially at airports. I don't understand how we can get the information we need."

Jamil knew he was right but was not about to lose face in admitting it. He had already concluded the same thing and would have to face his father with the reality of modern airport security when they returned. "Don't worry" he mumbled, "we have a plan," although he had to admit that the current plan was not working, and he had absolutely no idea how to do better.

Hussein was right to worry. Their movements had already been noticed. In fact, from the time Jamil had been off on his night's wanderings in London they had been marked men. They had stayed in a medium-priced hotel in Gloucester Road and Jamil had spent a happy two hours collecting hookers' flyers from the local public telephone boxes before sitting down with the hotel telephone and notepad to do some serious research for the evening. Hussein had not seen him again until morning, when Jamil had appeared in the lobby late, with a happy glazed expression on his face.

"No sleep, no money," he announced to the desk clerk. Hussein paid the bill.

What Jamil had not known was that the two girls he favoured with his London wad of dollars were informers who were paid to be on the lookout for high-spending Arab gentlemen of no discernible occupation. Jamil and Hussein's exit from the Gloucester Road hotel had been telegraphed to a room in Whitehall and they were now targets of the British security services. Their names had thrown up nothing in any record, but Hussein's photo had raised serious alarm bells. It exactly matched a known asset of British Intelligence, supposedly not in the UK at the time.

Somewhere in the labyrinth of buildings next to London's Vauxhall Bridge a very senior intelligence officer looked at the file in front of him. The name didn't match of course but the face was remarkably similar. The computer scan had given it fifteen points of similarity, but he ignored that and looked at the trace. The two Arabs had hired a car in London three days ago and returned it with nearly five hundred miles on the clock. So far, he didn't know where they had been, but it evidently was not driving round Hyde Park. The officer placed a call to Russell Clark. He needed a second view on the picture of Hussein Al Baz and if it was the same person then Russell should know. After all, he had recruited him. There was something he did not like about these two. He made a note to call Frankfurt, the pair's next destination, later. Meanwhile he had more of the men's photographs run through the database. Better give the system a chance, he thought.

As the plane landed in Frankfurt, Hussein looked out of the window. There seemed to be an awful lot of police cars busily circling the plane. He was frightened. He was still kicking himself for forgetting the UK telephone number but even that had been an afterthought, a belated act of conscience. He knew his correct path should have been to forewarn his London contact about this trip before it happened but, he kept telling himself, there simple hadn't been time. Of course, there was always time, but Hussein was seriously concerned for his safety. Back home, he knew his turf. Here he did not. In his darker moments he imagined that the Brits must have noticed him in London. After all they had cameras everywhere. Why had they not picked him up? Then he rationalised, even if they recognised him they would probably keep it quiet, because it was unlikely that they would want to publicise what they were doing in his country. He brooded on and on. Jamil was snoring at his side, despite the landing.

Their plan had been to leave Frankfurt airport using their current false ID and then to revert to their previous identity as soon as they returned to Libya. Jamil had a theory that immigration officials never cared who left their country, only about who arrived, so if someone disappeared after arriving then that was a fair way for them to play the game. Hussein's view was that Europe was now much more co-ordinated. He was worried.

As they entered the terminal building they realised how large the airport complex was. To even walk around was a problem as they had no tickets or boarding passes. To approach the cargo areas looked impossible unless you were German and at least two metres tall. They clearly were neither.

"How about going to the nightclub district," asked Hussein. "We can think through our plan there."

Jamil had no trouble agreeing. They grabbed an old Mercedes taxi at the airport entrance and, as it sped them to yet another seedy hotel, they carefully stuffed their passports under the greasy rear seat cushion and reverted to their previous false identities. To Hussein it seemed a complicated way to achieve not very much. But at least the trip was nearly over. Only two more days to worry.

3

Dale and his small team were driven everywhere by their willing Fatimah, and it was with some difficulty that they persuaded her to drop them at a street-side café, rather than the hotel. She had become agitated and concerned, both for their safety and also about her job, and her usually stilted English became determinedly non-existent. So, in the end they compromised and had her drive past the hotel on the way to the coffee shop they had in mind. It was only a ten-minute walk back to the hotel and she could at least say that she had taken them back to their official residence. Honour had been satisfied.

The café had an Italian name emblazoned in faded grandeur across its front window. Who Marco had been, and why he had started a café remained a well-hidden mystery as there was certainly little sign of the owner's former foreign influence anymore. The tables were cracked pieces of laminate mounted precariously on bent, flimsy metal supports and the wooden stalwarts which served as chairs were so old that their legs had long since given up any attempt at staying level. It was a hangout for young and old, but curiously served no middle-aged customers. The old sat and sipped their sweet coffee or tea. They would play cards or chess and had been there for years. The young preferred the local brand of cola. Either way they knew how to make a glass of something last all day. How the owner made any money from his ramshackle, open-fronted establishment remained a mystery.

Dale, Winston and Marlena squeezed around a tiny corner table out on the pavement. To their left two gnarled and turbaned old men were playing some variant of chequers. The two huddled over their dog-eared board and communicated in asthmatic grunts while a small crowd of onlookers muttered their comments as the game progressed. To their right, a group of students studied their books, a mixture of seriousness and wariness on their faces. A young Palestinian appeared instantly and in commendable English asked them what they wanted to drink. "My name is Raheem. Tea okay?" he continued, and then he departed before they had chance to utter a sound.

The glasses of hot, sweet amber liquid appeared quickly. The bottom two fingers of each was a sea of grainy grey sugar and a solitary bent spoon accompanied the tray of three.

"If you only want it sweet, rather than incredibly sweet, then don't stir" warned Dale, but Winston was already whisking the concoction with vigour.

The waiter dragged up another apology of bent sticks and sat down. "Hi," he proffered his hand. "My name is Raheem" he introduced himself again, "are you new here?"

Dale took his hand. "Hi" he said, "nice to meet you. I'm Dale. We're starting a project here. An irrigation project."

"In Al Samudra?" quizzed Raheem.

"Yes. How did you know?"

"They're always in Al Samudra!" Raheem beamed. "There have been three projects there already, but nothing ever gets done. What they really need is some large-scale irrigation work out in the desert but there's no money for that sort of thing."

"You seem very well informed." Winston put down his syrup and paid attention. "How come?"

"I've been here eight years," Raheem was disposed to chat. "I have a job with the ministry in the mornings and then work here in the evening. The Ag Ministry is pretty poor. It has no income and so the Minister can only make money from doing projects which get special funding. That's additional to the money he makes from hiring us Palestinians," he added ruefully. "He has his fingers in everything."

"He makes money by hiring you?" Dale was curious.

Raheem paused, as if he wasn't sure which story to tell. Then he made up his mind and in an instant was off down what was obviously a very well-trodden path. "We are welcomed here, unofficially, and liked by the people, I think" he began his tale, "but officially we're refugees and under threat of repatriation without cause and without notice. Some of us have sometimes been shipped off in trucks and have ended up back in the West Bank without homes, families, jobs, nothing. In fact, I believe they ship a few back every now and again to keep the rest of us under control," he added.

"To stay I need a visa and a work permit, and to get them I must have a passport and I have to come here legally. But, I don't have a passport and I didn't come here legally. So, I'm stuck. The only way is to have a sponsor, and I think that the sponsors have all been to the same training school. They say, 'trust me – I understand your situation – rely on me' and then they go off and talk to their friends. The next thing you hear is that they can't get you a normal visa but, because of their influence they can get you a short-term, two-month permit. Of course, you have to pay, and every two months you have to pay again, and again and again. If you don't pay, you find yourself on the truck back to the West Bank. That's not a good option, so you keep paying."

Raheem drew breath. "So" he said, "you become a slave, because all your money has to go towards staying here. You are living on the very edge of life with your sponsor holding you by your wallet to keep you from falling over the brink."

"And you can't simply apply for a longer-term visa, or maybe a passport?"

"As I said, I have no passport. I don't officially exist. The only place I could apply for a passport is back in Palestine, and the chance of getting one there is zero. They are not kind to people who run away."

He paused. "I'm luckier than most, as I'm now quite useful at the ministry, especially for the Minister himself." Raheem looked sombre, "so I don't have to pay him so much now."

Dale could see where the conversation might be going. He wondered whether it was all part of a carefully orchestrated story for a good tip. "Expensive?" he asked politely.

"Now only 50% of my pay" said Raheem, "and my pay isn't much anyway."

Dale's eyebrows raised a notch and Raheem saw he had his attention. "Anyway" he shrugged, "we have to live and that's just part of the price."

Marlena picked up on the 'we.' "You have a family?" she asked.

"Wife and two children" was the prompt reply, "my daughter is six and my son is four. We live on the coast" he explained, "which is cheaper but a long way to travel."

The three foreigners said nothing, and Raheem leapt into the silence. He had jumped to his feet and was waving his hands vigorously to illustrate his speech.

"We live at the old Yanbu Beach Resort, in one of the guest villas. The hotel is closed now and so there are no services, and no guests of course, but there are still a few staff. The manager's a friend of mine and he lets us use the villa for a small fee. It's a bit broken down, but we manage. We can do our own cooking there too," he continued as the three sat mesmerised, watching his hands stirring an imaginary pot.

"Before we found this place it was terrible. Everywhere was so expensive and none of the landlords really cared about us. The only problem now is that it's right out of town, in the old tourist resort area and it takes a while to get there and back."

"Where did you learn such good English?" Marlena was as ever determined to be precise about her facts.

"At school, at work and from talking with the students" Raheem admitted, "and also your famous World Service radio. I listen to the news and the weather forecast! I'm trying to teach my children English."

"Why?"

"Because it's the international language of the world and I want my children to be brought up in the world, not here. We have suffered for so many years that I want to either go home to a proper country or take them into the international world. You can help me if you like." He cocked his head into a cheeky grin.

"How?"

"I need English books and story tapes so my children can read English and hear it spoken properly. This is very important please. My wife doesn't speak English much, hardly at all really, and so she can't teach my children. You see, my time's very busy working. I thought these books might help. I don't want a gift" he frowned, "I can pay"

Dale could only be impressed. Raheem's clear determination was infectious and before long the three of them had promised to come and meet the family, and also to search out books and story tapes for their next visit. With further promises of eternal friendship, they paid their modest bill, left a sizeable tip, and started their short walk up the main street towards their hotel. It didn't occur to any of them that there was no traffic. Usually there wasn't much, just a few cars and trucks rumbling by, but now there was nothing. The street was completely and eerily empty.

As they turned the first corner a lump of broken concrete thudded into the column beside them. It was the size of two or three house bricks and was followed by another smaller missile, a hooked, evil looking piece of steel reinforcing bar with the end shrouded in more ragged concrete. Dale and Winston dragged Marlena down behind the column. The rocks kept on coming.

Dale peered out and saw that they were on the edge of a makeshift battlefield. Youths had appeared, as if from nowhere and were now frantically hurling construction rubble at each other across the street. The leader of the nearby stone-throwing crowd glanced in their direction and waved them agitatedly to stay down. His attention was then grabbed by the activities of the other crowd of youths across the road who were clearly the object of their barrage. Through the dusty fusillade of concrete remnants Dale could see that the two gangs were well seasoned at hurling rocks at one another, although it was the buildings that seemed to be suffering the most. The nearby group looked smaller in number but rather better organised whereas their opponents across the road were already resorting to returning fire with the same concrete shrapnel they were receiving. Windows shattered as smaller stones were hurled by the less talented throwers.

The noise showed no sign of diminishing and it was becoming scary. Dale thought about returning to the café but to even think of deserting the sanctity of their column seemed madness. They were at least safe, for the time being. They huddled.

A camouflaged lorry roared up the street behind them and, without regard for the stones and concrete it ground to a halt in the centre of the crowd and disgorged a dozen or so seriously dressed riot police, with shields and rifles and the whole paraphernalia of street warfare. A shot ricocheted off their column and they scrunched lower and tighter behind its sandstone comfort. They didn't dare to raise their heads.

Then a frantic hooting came closer and closer until its source, a dilapidated Mercedes taxi, pulled up less than a metre away with its rear door open.

"Get in!" shouted Raheem, his face grinning feverishly in the open front window, "quick as you can!"

They needed no further encouragement and dragged themselves into the back of the Mercedes where they huddled in a dishevelled heap on its capacious floor. Marlena hated smelly taxis, and this one stank.

"Don't worry about them" Raheem waved his hand airily towards the rear window and tried to sound reassuring, "they're just having a bit of fun. You're safe now."

Dale sat up and straightened himself out. Marlena was quiet but Winston looked as if he had seen a ghost. They didn't recognise the road but were sure it was not in the direction of the hotel.

"I'll take you home for a while," Raheem was a mind reader too. "You can meet my family" he explained. They continued with Raheem directing the driver and twenty minutes later he ushered them out of the taxi and pointed through the side entrance of the Yanbu Beach Hotel. "Follow me!" he commanded and set off at a swift trot.

Dale stopped to pay the taxi. "You wait here?" Dale was always cautious about taxis, but the driver seemed happy enough to slump down behind the wheel and sleep. He was in no hurry to be paid and so Dale repocketed his money and ran to catch the others.

Raheem was as proud as a peacock as he led his charges through the once ornate gardens of the famous hotel. Now all was dust and barrenness as the trees had long since given up any struggle at life in the arid environment. The grass must have died within a day of the water being turned off. But the guest villas had at least been sturdily built and as Raheem moved a large piece of plywood that served as their outer door, Dale wondered how many of the others were similarly rented out to the manager's friends.

Inside was gloomy but cool. The pleasantness of leaving the torrid heat behind was palpable. As their eyes accustomed themselves to the lack of brightness, it seemed that the villa was empty. It comprised two largish rooms plus two bathrooms and a maid's quarters. The décor was standard hotel fare, and it had aged much over its few years of life; but no services meant no electricity, no water, nothing. Raheem called two names and from behind a sofa two small children rose like tiny phoenixes. When they saw Raheem, they jumped over the sofa and sprinted towards him, arms outstretched. He beamed and turning to his guests introduced his daughter Naomi and her brother Ibrahim.

Marlena crouched down. "Hello Naomi," she said in Arabic. "My name's Marlena, and how old are you?" Naomi shrank behind her father's scruffy shirt and said not a word. Ibrahim was even quicker and dived for cover behind the sofa again.

They became aware of another presence in the room. Raheem looked round and waved his wife forward. She was dressed in jeans and a faded Coca-Cola tee shirt and was somewhat shorter than Raheem. She looked worn and pensive, and much older than her likely years.

"Salma, we have guests," Raheem was in his element. "They are going to help me with the children's English education," and then he lapsed into Arabic and Dale was lost. Never mind, he thought, Marlena will bring me up to speed later.

Dale and his colleagues sat and drank tea and eventually the two waif-like children found their voices. Raheem went to help his wife while Marlena chatted to the children in a mix of languages that Dale could only admire.

Salma produced a mini feast. Where from they didn't know, but Raheem was clearly serious about his books and tapes and Salma was under orders to assist. They felt that they must have severely depleted Salma's kitchen stores but there was little they could do except accept the offered hospitality, gratefully.

"Where did you two meet?" asked Dale.

Raheem was the spokesman. "We are both from Palestine" he said, "from Gaza originally. I came with my uncle when our village was bombed. My parents were both killed, and I had no other family to turn to. The two of us were all that was left after the bombs."

"Why was it bombed?" Dale pressed.

"Retaliation. They thought we were Hamas. The whole apartment building was demolished and those inside died. My uncle and I were out at the café and so we escaped. We fled first across the border to Egypt and then worked our way along the coast. There are a lot of us in this part of the world, all escaped and wanting to go home."

"What was your job in Gaza?" Marlena was as ever keen on accuracy.

"Hospital Administrator" was the prompt reply, "but after the bombing there was no hospital to administer anymore." He paused as if some memory haunted him. "Salma was a nurse" he said, "I met her first in Egypt. We became friends there and after I had been here for two years, I managed to find a way to bring her here too. Naomi was born later that same year. We had no money, but it was a happy time." He stopped to look at his daughter. "One day Naomi will be a doctor" he announced, "and Ibrahim will be a lawyer," he added with finality.

His face beamed. "We shall all work in the same hospital" he explained, "and Ibrahim will make it all possible."

Dale wondered whether Ibrahim was aware of the awesome responsibility resting on his shoulders but said nothing. Raheem's path was clear, and he was obviously determined. "Okay, I will see what we can do about books" he grinned, "although I'm not sure they write legal books for people so young."

Salma sat at Raheem's side and held his arm. Her eyes shone with pride.

They spent a further two hours with Raheem's family, ate well and enjoyed the rambling conversation. When they came to leave they were overwhelmed by a feeling of inadequacy, and by their inability to do anything more tangible than promise to bring a few things for the children next time. Marlena in particular had softened considerably from her normal rather brittle state.

"It reminds me of when I was a student," she said as they bumped their way back to the hotel in the ancient taxi. "The Palestinian community in Cairo was very united too."

"You were in Egypt?" This was news to Dale, one of the rare snippets he gleaned occasionally about the mysterious Marlena. "Why was that?"

Marlena looked as if she'd just remembered something and for a moment Dale thought she was going to ignore him. "I studied there for a while," she said. "It's where I learnt Arabic," she added firmly. Dale knew there would be nothing else forthcoming today.

4

In the calm of the Ministry of Security Fayez Shakari was debriefing his son Jamil about his travels. A large man with a pockmarked, battle-scarred face, Fayez had a feared reputation for short temper and brutality. He was a man who hated many things in life and anything that crossed his chosen path was removed, if not instantly, then always most assuredly. He was a secretive man, dedicated to his job as a committed anti-insurgent, although there could only have been imaginary ones remaining by now. Fayez was also determinedly anti-foreigner and despised the apparent ease with which they won their superior wealth. He used whatever power he could muster to relieve them of it whenever possible.

His deputy Fuad Asmi sat quietly to one side. Whereas Fayez was lazy and quick tempered, Fuad was diligent, active, thoughtful and scheming. Tall and thin, he was a weasel of a man, always managing to squirm his way around and out of any discussion and never expressing his own opinion on anything. He was Fayez's man, and everyone knew it. They treated him with the softest of kid gloves, at the maximum distance possible and never, ever, commented on anything controversial in his presence. He personally controlled the large and very effective group of watchers who kept track of local people and foreigners with equal vigilance. The group was huge, a small army in reality, and Fuad filtered and reviewed a massive amount of the gathered information himself. Anything, absolutely anything, was brought to his attention, on pain of the watcher finding himself out of favour; and out of favour with Fuad was bad news for the watcher and his extended family. He was the primary link between Fayez and the entire intelligence network, his eyes and ears and his trusted advisor. But he feared Fayez. He had seen what the man could do, violently and completely without compunction and he knew that he must tread a careful path to maintain his privileged position, and to keep control of his information stream.

Hussein did not rank highly enough to join the meeting and in any case, he had to get back to his seconded role in the Ministry of Agriculture. Jamil had not had an easy time explaining to his father what he had not managed to achieve. By the time he had left out the detailed references to nightclubs and girls his mind struggled to make much sense of the remainder. He wished that Hussein could have been there to take some of the pressure. With his father, he couldn't simply ride roughshod over the conversation, as he did with his own subordinates. He couldn't lie to his father, and he certainly couldn't bully him. Fuad sat quietly and suppressed a smirk from his face as he listened to Jamil struggle. Although Fayez and Jamil looked remarkably similar they were no match intellectually. So Fuad concentrated on looking unimportant and severe and, especially, absolutely still. He didn't want to draw attention to himself, and he certainly wasn't about to miss the interaction between father and son, not for the world. He sat rigid and held his breath.

"In effect," Fayez was brusque, even with his son, "you achieved very little, except to confirm that the cargo areas are well protected, which is what we might have expected. What we need …" he continued, almost talking to himself "is someone who can move freely inside the airports."

"Maybe we could infiltrate the security staff?" Jamil looked hopefully at his father. There was a pained expression on the older man's face.

"In the current security circumstances, I am not sure that would be very practical," he answered. "You said yourself, we all look like terrorists these days. No, we have to use the Europeans themselves. Actually, I am thinking more along the lines of them bringing the airport to us."

"How?" Jamil looked confused. "How can you bring an airport into the country?"

Fayez paused, as if unsure whether to continue to spell things out for his son's benefit. Then he made up his mind and continued.

"It's really very simple," he explained. "You recall the attack on the Atlanta basketball stadium?"

Jamil nodded.

"You remember when we built our own university basketball court?"

This was a little before Jamil's time, and although he had heard something about this, he did not want to be put centre stage in the discussion again. He was silent.

"No matter. The way we planned that exercise was to invite tenders for a new basketball court from foreign companies and to make sure that the winning company had also built the Atlanta Olympic court too. It was relatively easy to ensure that the courts were almost identical. And once we had the copy built, we were able to plan and train without preying eyes and without the need to send anyone in advance to the actual facility."

Jamil frowned. "But doesn't that approach need to be thought out a long time ahead?" he asked.

"Ah" smiled his father, "you have no patience, my son. If something takes five years or more in the planning, then by the time we decide to act, the chance of the original import of design details being matched against the event becomes quite remote."

"So how will we gain plans of the airports?"

"Well, I admit it is rather trickier as we can't simply invite foreign companies at the moment. Sanctions do form something of a block, and even our Italian friends have their limits, so I have an idea to recruit one of the new consulting firms that is currently working here on a totally unrelated topic. Their projects are sanctioned by the UN under the humanitarian aid programme. Irrigation, my son, irrigation. Who will link irrigation to airport security?"

"But father, if it is so difficult to link how do you plan to do it?"

"Camels." Fayez was emphatic.

Jamil stared blankly "Camels?" he almost shouted in disbelief.

"All in good time. First, we get our research done for us, then we have our plans almost brought to completion, and without a stain on our hands. These foreign companies can wander around

Europe as if they own the place. They're immune from security in their own countries and will do almost anything to keep their business here with us."

"And the end target?"

"Of course, we will deal with that ourselves, at the right time. We can't have foreigners doing everything for us."

"But what is the end target?" Jamil persisted

Fayez smiled. "That" he said, "is something you will find out at the right time too."

5

The Ministry of Construction was housed in a straggling series of buildings that had once served as the Public Works department of the city. Despite the huge amount of construction work that was on-going and needed, all work was done using state-controlled groups where control and profits belonged largely to the people who ran them. Truly private companies were unheard of. The result was slow, laboriously planned construction where materials were limited to what existed in the country, rather than what was available on world markets. The level of quality was uniformly poor.

In years gone by, many of the prestigious projects had been completed by overseas companies, with Eastern Europe and Italy taking the lion's share. The US and UK companies had also done extraordinarily good business, especially in the development of the oil fields. In those days, the ministry had directed and managed, from its tall marble clad skyscraper headquarters, which now lay in abject emptiness because of the sea-sand scandal. An infamous local supplier of materials had made a fast buck by providing unwashed sea sand, which had promptly corroded the steel reinforcement. Many buildings had been affected, but when the ministry's own pride and joy had alarmingly sagged on its second floor, the embarrassment to all concerned had been total. Of course, the kickbacks in the process had been some consolation.

That was all a thing of the past. The Ministry of Construction had been reduced to renovating poor quality buildings and revamping basic infrastructure, most of which had been shot to pieces in the many political purges that had ravaged the heart of the city. Politics had spread its detritus of broken structures like a vulture scatters the broken bones of its victims. The ministry was but a poor relation to the Ministry of Security, and Ubaid, the long-standing Construction Minister knew it. However, he also knew that the Ministry of Security needed him, as he was still the only contact with the overseas consultants and contractors. He needed to keep the initiative, which was tough, as he was not privy to what was behind Fuad's suggestion that he, the Minister should meet with the Agriculture consultant's project leader. His phone buzzed. He rose to meet his guest.

"Mr Connors," he beamed at Dale as he was shown into the capacious office. "My name is Ubaid Abu Namur. Welcome to the Ministry of Construction."

"Dale Connors, I'm very pleased to meet you." Formalities begun, Dale relaxed into the massive sofa and accepted tea. They sipped. He waited for the Minister to continue. After all, he hadn't sought the meeting. Let him make the running, he thought.

"It's good of you to come. I try and meet all our overseas colleagues." Ubaid was effusive, his use of English scrupulously correct and formal. "Our country is very appreciative for the work your company is doing here. I hear excellent reports," he continued. "What you and your company are doing today will benefit our people for many generations. You should be proud of that. I believe in developing good working arrangements with my overseas colleagues and I am especially keen to build a long-term relationship with your company. If there is anything this ministry can do to help please let us know."

Dale waited patiently for the set speech to conclude and thought of the agonies they had gone through in order to secure the maps they needed. Even though most were in the Construction Ministry it had been the Security Ministry that had called all the shots, and presumably cut the holes. The construction people had bureaucratised and prevaricated and generally been completely ineffective. Despite the problems, Dale felt it was not the occasion to criticise and did his best to keep the meeting very formal. "Thank you Minister" he said, nodding his head slightly, "and similarly, if there is any way we can help your ministry we shall be only too pleased to do so."

"Well," Ubaid smiled, "I'm not sure we have safes to crack every day but there is something on which I would like your advice please.

Dale again noted the very correct English and wondered where the Minister had been educated. He coloured somewhat at the mention of his safe opening exploits. Their grapevine must be very effective, he thought, although opening safes was definitely the sort of story to fly quickly. He waited in anticipation for what must presumably be the reason for his summons to the meeting. Pleasantries and courtesy calls were all part of the business game but generally you were not invited to meet a minister unless he wanted something.

"Actually, there are two things." Ubaid noticed the discomfort over the safe. I don't see why he should be embarrassed, he thought. If the stupid fools in Agriculture had half a brain between them they should have managed it themselves.

"Do you have children?" he asked, although he had seen Dale's files and knew the answer.

"No," said Dale, wondering where the conversation was heading.

"Very wise." Ubaid mused for a moment. "I have three. The youngest is my son Shafiq. He has just finished an engineering degree here and I am keen for him to go overseas to carry on his studies and improve his English."

Dale let out an almost audible sigh of relief. University assistance was fairly commonplace, and he was well experienced in dealing with this type of request. His mind flipped back to Ubaid's own very correct use of English. He took a small gamble.

"Were you at university in the UK yourself?" he asked.

Ubaid looked up. "Yes, and school too. Winchester and Bristol. I read politics and played rugby. Wonderful game," he added.

"And what does your son want to read?" Dale paused. He wasn't sure about politics courses anywhere in the UK for foreign students, let alone from here.

"Management," pronounced Ubaid carefully. "Engineering management, project management and business management. I want him to return and take over the management of rebuilding our country's infrastructure. Once these sanctions are gone, we will be busy and will need good management, and good use of English if we're to set our country straight for the future."

This sounded almost like heresy to Dale's ears, but he was relieved that the request was fairly straightforward. One troublesome thought crossed his mind, but Ubaid's next statement banished that too.

"We aren't looking for financial help." Ubaid could almost read his concern. "Money is not the issue, but we cannot simply ask for a prospectus and apply. These sanctions tend to block the postal service and raise other application issues."

Dale's thought process was already well ahead. "How old is your son?" he asked.

"He was twenty-two in March, last month. What I want for him is a good engineering school where he will learn something. From what research I have done, maybe Southampton looks a good place?"

"Okay, how about this? I'll be back in the UK in three weeks' time and will contact one or two professors and heads of engineering departments that I know. Southampton is certainly a very good school and I know the head of department there. Give me a month and I will let you know what I can do. Do you have any more details about your son and his academic background? Is it possible to meet him before I leave?"

"Of course." Ubaid pressed the ubiquitous buzzer and spoke rapidly in Arabic, "I had foreseen that you should meet him. He's waiting outside."

Dale felt he was part of some pre-orchestrated plan but stood to meet the tall, clean-shaven young man who entered the room.

"Mr Connors," Shafiq's English sounded perfect to Dale.

"I hear you're keen to come and study in the UK?"

"Actually, it's my father's wish that I study English correctly. I would have preferred to go to the US, but politically it is very difficult, and my father wishes me to learn what he calls 'correct English' first, before becoming linguistically adventurous." Shafiq smiled and inclined his head towards his father.

Dale smiled. "Your English sounds excellent to me" he said. "Mine's been sabotaged by too much travel and so I find it refreshing to listen to correctly spoken English for a change."

Ubaid beamed. Dale noticed and mentally patted himself on the back. Everyone has his pride about something, he thought.

Shafiq produced a folder of information, exam grades and CV in Arabic, along with a beautifully presented English translation. Dale wondered about its veracity but nonetheless took it gratefully.

"I offered to get back to you within the month," he said.

"So my father said. That's very kind of you. Now, if you will excuse me please." And with a very proper handshake, he turned and walked smartly from the room.

Ubaid was almost bouncing with agitation. "What do you think?" he asked.

Dale was not sure what he was being asked to think about. "An accomplished young man," he plumped for Ubaid's soft spot again. He was right.

"I'm so glad you think so. His education means everything to me."

Ubaid suddenly shifted seats and sat opposite Dale, across the low table. "Now," he said, "it is time for me to help you. What do you know about camels?"

Dale stared. "Camels?" he queried, "Actually very little."

"Well, no matter, camels are rather like water. When you release them they wander about and collect in the lowest part of the land. I thought this might be a good project for you. We need a proper camel ranch."

"A camel ranch?"

"Yes, nothing elaborate, but at the moment our camels are herded around the desert and cause all sorts of problems. We need something more secure where they can be bred more effectively and used as part of our future tourist development. Go and have a look this afternoon. Hussein and Fatimah can take you and I will arrange for some survey assistants from this ministry so that the agriculture people don't complain about us using their staff all the time."

Dale brightened a little.

"Do you have any idea of size?"

"Oh, I'm sorry, I should have mentioned. 40,000 hectares is what we had in mind. Can you give me an estimate for fees and construction by say Saturday?"

Dale felt a little dazed. As he took his leave and left Ubaid's office, he took stock of the situation. Hussein was a helpful guy but had no apparent authority to act on his own at all. Meanwhile his other brain was churning over 40,000 hectares. The size had caught up with him. If a hectare was 10,000 square meters, then 40,000 hectares was … wow … 400 square km. 20 km x 20 km. He fled back to the project office. Maybe Winston had ranched camels before. Hopefully, somebody had, otherwise he was in trouble.

6

The café was decayed, dingy and dirty. Its walls were ragged, unplastered brickwork, or rough bare concrete, decorated with overlapping and half torn posters for events long since relegated to history. The cracked and cobwebbed windows filtered the remote sunlight to the colour of murky mudstone, while a solitary light bulb hung in the tiny kitchen. A tired window-mounted ventilation fan did more to create a background noise than to stir the torrid air. The alcoves at the rear of the main room were shrouded in even greater gloom. It was not a place for strangers.

Two water filled hookahs glooped peacefully, the Shisha tobacco coming today from Abdullah's own home where the molasses and indeed the old recipe itself were kept safely out of harm's way. The Minister of Security, Abdullah al Khayr and Fayez sat in silence in their favourite corner alcove, enjoying the peace of old comrades sharing a couple of pipes. Privacy was enhanced by the shabby velvet curtain which half covered the opening to their small preserve.

They were both big framed, powerful men, with large stomachs, tough looking faces and reputations to match. But there the similarity ended, and both knew it. Abdullah was old school, ruler's family in fact, and his connections and his ability to make things happen were impressive, even to Fayez; whereas Fayez had to take care, plan, scheme and often cover his tracks as head of the country's secret police, Abdullah simply had to raise an eyebrow, murmur into his assistant's ear, or maybe imply casually what was required. Fayez envied him his power but knew that he was invaluable to Abdullah when it came to finding and reporting reliable information and particularly when it came to deniable action. The two men complemented each other's abilities and, although it was never discussed, they respected the status quo and used it to their advantage.

Abdullah's own family extended to sons in the Ministry of Finance and the Military. His youngest was temporarily in the Ministry of Agriculture.

The two men would soon start their discussions, and for this topic they valued the privacy. The café was run by an old relative of Abdullah and in return for keeping the place free of intruders he was paid handsomely, for an old café owner. Abdullah also had the old man's file. He had files on most people, but the old café owner knew that his life depended on the contents of this particular file never reaching his wife. A woman of direct views and simple virtues, she had borne him five children and then declared that sex was off the agenda. She had insisted that this meant he too must take a vow of celibacy. That had been over twenty-five years ago. She had never known about his evening companion at the café, and he intended it to stay that way. He shuddered at the thought of the photos in Abdullah's file. A single glance at them all those years ago had pledged him to the man forever. He had always been good at secrets and safety, but his allegiance now knew no bounds.

Abdullah and Fayez were happy to use the café. They eschewed the official safety of their Ministry of Security office building where the rooms were swept every day for devices but so many people were always watching and listening they could never be sure they weren't the target. The two of them relaxed in the smoky gloom.

"How's your mother?" Fayez broke the silence.

Abdullah frowned at the thought. "Difficult," he said slowly. Abdullah was an extremely well connected and powerful man but his mother, Raya Al Khayr was in a different league entirely. Fayez always asked after her, knowing it was a slight vulnerability in Abdullah's otherwise impenetrable hide.

"She has better access to information than I do sometimes. I've no idea where she gets it. I've traced her calls, recorded her movements, tailed her friends, everything, and yet every time I meet her, she comes out with some little gem that shows she knows exactly what the ministry is doing. She can almost quote me the file reference. It's as if I have no independent life" he complained, "she's not a docile old lady, and at seventy-five she should be."

Fayez smiled. Abdullah was undoubtedly well respected, impeccably connected and was seen as the feared and suitably tyrannical head of the most powerful ministry in the country. His family connections to the ruler set him apart from people like Fayez in a way that Fayez could never hope to match, however hard he worked, schemed or plotted. But Fayez knew where the real power lay and he also knew how to feed that power, just enough, to keep himself and his secret service team in control, and indispensable. He mostly had no need to refer to Abdullah, certainly not for permission, but today's discussion was international, and he could not afford to be caught isolated. His face didn't alter as he listened to Abdullah, but inside, he silently praised his own man Fuad. Everything Abdullah saw and heard came through Fuad and everything Fuad divulged was approved by Fayez. Information was indeed power, especially covert information.

Raya might be difficult in Abdullah's eyes, but she was a remarkable woman and her ancestry linked her to the ruler's family 'roots and all' as she put it. She was more powerful than Abdullah and certainly had better and broader connections. Her age was no impediment; in fact, she was a mere youngster alongside her ninety-year-old sister, the ruler's grandmother.

Raya and Hasna met every week to discuss the state of the country and their families. The elder woman's son had been killed in the political turmoils and although her grandson, now in his early forties was still considered a young and headstrong ruler, full of revolutionary principles and unproven ideas, his grandmother's support ensured that his power structure remained intact. The two old ladies had long memories and needed no files to maintain their grip on people and events. Their relatives and particularly their grandsons held them in a respect that bordered on the terrified end of the spectrum.

"On this issue I have clear orders" Fayez said, implying the ruler's own hand behind him. Abdullah knew that no one ever crossed the ruler's will, or even thought to question his motives. Secret police aside, the ruler's personal bodyguards were all drawn from his extensive family and their information network was as far-reaching as that of Abdullah's ministry. A few years before, Fayez had offered to combine the two networks under his own leadership. But the ruler had merely looked at him and then, while he voiced the opinion that the single entity may be a good idea, he made it clear that he thought Fayez not old enough to retire, not just yet. Fayez had taken the hint and had never let loyalty or control ever again be an issue of doubt between them. He had also made sure that a suitably spun version of the meeting quickly reached the ears of Raya and her sister.

"We are looking for something dramatic against those who have belittled our country," he continued, looking carefully to see Abdullah's reaction. But if he had any, his face showed nothing.

Abdullah finished his pipe and coughed his lungs clear of debris. "How many overseas companies do we have on the hook?" he asked hoarsely. It irritated him that these international ventures were deliberately kept out of mainstream ministry business, but he knew it made sense. The fewer people who were involved the better.

"Five, although three are worse than useless. They're paranoid about legal correctness and won't think for themselves at all. Everything is run past their lawyers in some remote headquarters or other. All five are susceptible to various sorts of pressure, and all are basically driven by greed. We need to see which will work out best, but it is amazing, you only have to dangle a contract in front of some of these managers and they'll give you almost anything in the world for free."

"Do you think they know they're under surveillance?"

"My guess is that they all think they're being watched but none of them really care. It must be something about being brought up in this modern Europe, especially the UK. There are so many cameras everywhere in the UK that no one gives a damn. It's ironic when you think that they claim to be the land of the free, with demonstrations against big brother intrusion and yet they're probable the most watched nation on earth."

"These companies are such fools too. They all use the ticket agency scam to export cash, and they all think that the guy behind the desk actually works for the airline."

"Well, he is on their payroll." They laughed. Fayez and Abdullah were both beneficiaries of the well-proven method of using local currency to buy air tickets and then redeeming them in foreign currency in Italy or the UK or other foreign airline direct destinations. As the local currency was not exportable it was the only way foreign companies could shift their spare local cash. Of course, the old-timers had long ago realised that the best way was to negotiate more foreign currency, and up-front too, but new companies were too eager to win contracts and the currency export business was just another pitfall they fell into. The redemption discount was huge, but companies were happy to transfer the remaining 60% of their money out of the country. The airlines never cared, they could use the currency to buy fuel and the ministry officials were happy with the cut that came back to them. One amusement in the whole exercise was the expressions on company officials' faces when they opened their bags of cash in the tiny ticket office and asked for several hundred return tickets. The airline clerk wouldn't bat an eyelid, as if people came to him every day for this number of tickets. He would look carefully at the cash and then simply ask "and what are the names of the passengers please?" It always produced a smile for the watchers, viewing the tortured look of disbelief on the foreign faces through their camera lens. If all else failed, airline employees had been known to lend a ticket buyer his own airline employee phone book. It was after all the only phone book in English. Failing that, the companies usually brought their own phone book. It was a time-consuming business.

A similar discount principle was applied with all overseas contracts, although here the Ministry of Construction had to have a reasonable share of the fee as they generally administered the contracts. The Construction officials seemed to think that they were really selecting companies on merit, but it was the Security Minister who always made the decisions. When the contract finally came up for signing, the Construction, Finance and Security Ministers all had their mechanisms in place to capture their agreed shares.

The same magic number of 60% would apply; this being the amount of the total contract value that finally went towards actually building something. The ministry leaders gobbled up the rest. Construction and Finance were necessary players, but it was Security that really mattered and only Security knew the true background to the company's selection. When it came to agriculture, the general view of the others was that this ministry's people were only farmers and therefore didn't count. Although Mohammed would fight his corner, he had to accept that the bulk of the commissions would end up with the big three. He would grumble about his smaller share, but only for appearances sake. He had his own ways to make money from foreigners. Even less of a contract's value ended up improving the land.

Abdullah continued his questioning. He was a well-organised, methodical man and generally had a list of something or other in his mind. Fayez knew him of old and waited for the questions to come. "How's this new consulting company doing? What is their name? Global something or other?" Abdullah always feigned an apparent lack of knowledge that was never merited.

Fayez accepted the topic and mentally checked what information Fuad would have passed on to Abdullah. He replied, saying, "they are new here, friendly, keen, willing to please and so far not interested in much, apart from getting their job done. Of course, in time they'll be very keen to do other work as their current project will be delayed and they'll need to stay here doing something more productive for us, while their first project's problems are resolved." Fayez paused while he thought through the various ways his staff could delay a project. The need for security approval on all invoices made this so easy, but there was all manner of bureaucratic nonsense that they could impose on almost anything when there was a need for interaction between the team and government staff.

He turned to something more interesting. "They also operate throughout the world with a series of local standalone companies and so are not legally affected by sanctions as much as others. It's an offshoot of their Italian company that is working here," he added, "so they can easily provide consultancy services for irrigation, under the Italian humanitarian programme. If they were working under the guise of the UK parent company, there would have been problems."

"Do they really work all over the world?"

"Most places, and they do most things too."

"And how agreeable do you think they would be to helping us provide a new cargo handling area?"

Fayez considered his response carefully. "Their manager has met Ubaid" he said, "I suggested to Ubaid that Dale Connors may be able to help his son with his university placement and apparently they got on like a house of fire. I also suggested that Ubaid should ask him to look at his camel problem."

Abdullah nodded. "Maybe camel security is only one step away from cargo security," he said. "Does this Dale Connors have any other pressure points?"

"Oh, I'm sure he does." Fayez already had his ideas. "All in good time," he added.

7

Fatimah waited patiently in the big Peugeot. It was a welcome change to be able to use a properly air-conditioned official ministry car rather than the project's beat-up VW. Hussein was fussing with a file of notes and the two young security assistants were lounging in their Toyota Landcruiser. Dale hadn't yet appeared. Fatimah pondered her luck at driving the foreign team around. The hours were not onerous, and the people were polite and really very civilised. The only thing she worried about was their constant wanting to visit old tourist sites and meet local people. They liked to sit in a street café on their way back to the hotel in the evening, and she was anxious about ensuring that her own managers not hold her responsible for any indiscretions they might get up to. Her job doubled as an informer to the security committee, and, despite her poor English, she was assiduous in her duties. Her report covered the time when she was at work but not the time outside working hours. She was happy with this balance of loyalties and had no wish to cause disturbance for her foreign charges.

When Sulaiman had invited Dale to his house she had played along in her role as driver until they had arrived and then had taken great delight in disappearing briefly, only to reappear in tee shirt and jeans to join Dale and her husband over the inevitable sweet tea. It had proved a good ice breaker and she had chatted happily, mainly through Sulaiman, whose English was much better then hers, although Dale wondered how much he translated her views and how much he imposed his own as they rambled through the evening. Dale had discovered that it was a very 'government service' sort of family, with her parents both working in the Ministry of Security.

Dale surprised her by coming up to the car from a completely different direction. These Englishmen always insist on walking everywhere in the heat of the day, she thought. They headed off towards the south, taking the airport highway initially as the surface was better. It was about an hour's journey which Dale spent mostly in conversation with Hussein, whose English was near perfect. Hussein Al Baz was short, energetic and helpful. His role was supervisor of engineering projects for the Ministry of Agriculture, but Dale had already fathomed out that Hussein didn't ever make a decision himself. He appeared to be some kind of intermediary. Everything was passed back to one of several committees. This had been irksome at first, but patience and planning had proven his saviour and now, as long as he wrote down his needs and remembered to add a 'need-by' date, his system of getting ministry approval, or 'endorsement' he found was easier, worked pretty well. He had discovered years before that it was usually almost impossible to get someone to approve something but equally easy to secure their endorsement. Endorsement had a suitably nebulous quality about its meaning, or as one official once explained it, 'Endorsement infers agreement in principle without responsibility, whereas approval means the opposite, responsibility without necessarily agreeing to what is being done.' Dale was an expert at getting through systems. Creative use of procedures was one of his acknowledged strengths.

The desert road was straight and almost without incline. The super-smooth and remarkably non-sticky tarmac seemed wasted on the sparse traffic of government Peugeots, old Mercedes taxis and dilapidated trucks, interspersed with a few camel carts. Fine, dusty sand blew across their path in waves of rivulets and yet never hung about long enough to block the carriageway. Dale often wondered why. No one he knew ever had a plausible answer. About twenty km from the airport, they turned inland and immediately faced a different landscape. The tarmac disappeared and the hard gravel showed imminent signs of impermanence. Another twenty-five km saw them climbing a shallow mound, at the top of which Hussein called a halt. The Toyota screeched dramatically to a standstill alongside and the two occupants jumped out. Dale had the impression they were there to see what he did, so he adjusted his sunglasses and extracted himself from the coolness of the car to join the two men in the instant, overbearing heat. It was four o'clock and the hot sand whipped around them with jagged teeth that bit into their skin like razor blades. The horizon was an indistinct haze and there was not a tree, or camel to be seen.

Dale pondered on Winston's words about camel ranching.

"All you need is a big fence" he had sagely advised, "camels will eat anything. They're worse than goats so you have to protect the new trees from being eaten and ration their access to the older trees so they can't destroy them too quickly. The problem is that they'll eat the fence too unless it's very big and very strong."

Dale stared at the barren hinterland. He even peered over his sunglasses, but that merely hurt his eyes. There was nothing, absolutely nothing in sight. He turned to Hussein. "Is this the ranch?" he asked.

Hussein pulled out his file and showed Dale a drawing. It was little more than a square with a few smaller squares inside. He pointed to a black smudge halfway along one side of the large square. "This is where we are," he announced proudly. "Of course, nothing is built yet, but this is where the main gate will be."

"And these?" Dale indicated the smaller squares. The smaller of the two Toyota youngsters leaned closer to hear the conversation.

"Nurseries for new trees," said Hussein, turning to look the Toyota youth straight in the face.

"And water?"

"We thought you might be able to help with water."

"Maybe. Have to think about that one. How do you know where the camels are?" he asked. "Do they stay in one place?"

Hussein tugged at his beard. "That's something else we want you to look at," he said. "In the old days we used to have camel boys, one for each camel, and their job was to stay with their camel and look after it. Now the Minister wants something more up to date. He wants to farm the camels and also introduce a stud for camel racing. He was a great traveller in his youth and used to travel to the Middle East. They race camels all the time there."

Dale nodded. He had once been privileged to accompany a group from Abu Dhabi to a camel race where the host Sheikh had insisted that Dale join him in his Range Rover. As the camels started their race, a second race of Range Rovers took off in hot pursuit of their animals, their owners driving, shouting and generally having a great time as they hurtled round the desert track in their upmarket four-wheel drive steeds. "I guess there are a few ideas we could look at," he said, narrowing his eyes against the overpowering stinging of the wind. "Maybe we could use the same technology as we do for rail cars?" he thought aloud. "If we tagged the camels, that way we would know when they pass through any gate."

"Don't forget they eat anything" warned Hussein, "and wander everywhere."

"Well maybe a GPS tracking system?" Dale was inclined to be flippant. How could anyone in their right mind imagine building anything in this environment?

"Ah, now you're talking," Hussein beamed. "That sounds expensive and that will be what the Minister would like."

"Will camel racing be held here?" Dale shouted against the wind

"Oh yes!" exclaimed Hussein. "I'd forgotten to tell you. This will be a big tourist attraction for our future economy."

Dale looked at the wilderness, its barren sand and howling wind and wondered at the madness of it all.

"Tourists? From where?" he asked.

Hussein didn't answer. "Come," he ordered. "We must take your photograph at the site – show the Minister we've been here and are taking action."

The larger, more menacing of the attending duo detached himself and produced a small camera. "Please," he pointed to the top of the mound, "please."

Dale and Hussein dutifully stood against the background of dust and haze. Duty done, they climbed gratefully into the cool of the Peugeot. Fatimah turned the car and they sped back towards the city. Their site visit has lasted no more than three minutes. The Toyota followed at an indiscreet distance, almost bumper to bumper. Dale wondered how its driver could see in the storm of dust thrown up by his own car.

8

Fatimah was right in that the foreign members of the team were keener to roam the cafés and bars than stay a minute longer than need be in their hotel. It became a habit for her to drop them off somewhere between the project office and the hotel, and then leave them to find their own way back after that. Dale was trying to find somewhere else for them to stay, cheaper and more private, but as yet, nothing had materialised. They all hated long stays in hotels and preferred to while away time in a local café rather than use the hotel bar.

Marlena was proving to be the surprising find in the team. Resourceful rather than technically expert in an academic sense, the mystery about her was her Arabic. Its Egyptian origin remained a dark secret. Dale had several times tried to explore her past but always drew a complete blank. It was almost as if she were under orders to remain silent, or maybe there had been some terrible experience in the past which she refused to admit. Her linguistic abilities carried her everywhere and he had accepted that without her, he would be much less effective.

When Marlena suggested a visit to the university Dale had been cautious. He recalled his visit there the previous year when he had been exploring work opportunities. The discussions then had been lively and the teaching impressive and worldly. He found the practical topics interesting, but the hypothetical theorising left him rather cold. He recalled discussing the merits of various political ideals related to agriculture and irrigation and had even struggled through an evening on economics with a couple of professors whose knowledge of world affairs had been surprisingly comprehensive, if not daunting to an international engineer such as himself. He hadn't been in the country during the recent purges but had heard much about them. The university had been turned into a people's court and sentencing and punishments were meted out there and then in what had been the students' union building. The withering effect on initiative and free expression had been dramatic and he was not especially keen to see the physical reminders that scarred the buildings. Nor was he keen to be taken again to the hanging ground, where a gallows had been set up for those not fortunate enough to merit a swift bullet in the back of the neck.

However, Marlena had enthused, and in the end he reluctantly succumbed, more out of curiosity than anything. They entered the university compound to find a worried group of students. Rumours were rife about another crackdown and a shift even further towards mandatory political studies. The union building had been reopened but was considered to be at risk. Accusations of subversion and general political incorrectness abounded and that it would only be a short time before reinstitution of official normality could be expected. They met under the poor shade of an almost leafless eucalyptus tree, and Dale was introduced to an attractive Italian student Emanuella, an Egyptian girl whose name he instantly forgot, and a slightly older German student named Fritz. He was highly curious at the mix of nationalities in what he had thought was now a campus without foreign students. He pondered on the array of girls before him and was aware that he was noticing Marlena as a woman amongst them, perhaps for the first time, he thought. She was tall and broad shouldered, without an ounce of fat on her. He reckoned she was slightly taller than himself. These Germans, he thought, are big people, as if fulfilling some personal preconception or in-built prejudice. The Egyptian girl, by contrast was smaller, cuter, he thought, in fact almost petite. She was slim and hard bodied, almost like a boy until he looked again at her attractive, striking facial features and her long flowing black hair. Neither of the girls wore Arabic dress. Jeans were the order of the day. As he continued to look, he realised that, while the Egyptian girl's face was mobile, friendly and inviting, Marlena's was like a carefully painted mask. He saw the same professionalism that he had noticed before and wondered where she had learnt to fix her features in this way. He was sure it wasn't natural.

He looked across at Emanuella. Like the Egyptian, her skin was olive coloured and Mediterranean acclimatised, although from a different shore and her hair too was strong and long but was tied back in a determinedly casual way, which accentuated her sexuality. He reckoned that she was a little younger than the others and as he gazed impolitely in her direction, his mind came back to the old maxim 'always look at their mothers.' He had been caught out once when he lived in Italy, by a wonderfully attractive girl who in the span of a single year had aged before his very eyes. When he met her mother, he understood exactly where she was heading and, although they remained the best of friends, his mind no longer entertained any route more intimate than an occasional dinner out and an early escape back to the hotel. He guessed that girls had similar views of the men they dated, but he had never explored that particular avenue before.

"Fritz and I were at university together," said Marlena, as if that explained everything. "We also studied together here before I joined your project."

"We?" quizzed Dale. He turned his gaze to Fritz, a tall gangling sort of guy, with short ginger hair and an open naive expression that showed every thought he had in his head. He reminded Dale of a basketball player, all clean and pure and with a never-ending motion of the limbs, a sort of ready twitch for action. Fritz sat with one lanky leg crossed over the other. His left foot was bouncing up and down. Dale refused be drawn by the mesmerising movement and turned back to Marlena.

"We're foreign students here," Fritz grinned. "I study Arabic language and literature, although most of the seminars are about the theory of modern politics."

Dale was dying to ask who was funding them. He couldn't imagine anyone studying here of their own volition.

Fritz appeared to read his mind. "We're all part of a programme called 'International Communication.' It's a programme funded under the UN and sponsored by various subscribing governments. Germany is a strong supporter and helps German students like me and Marlena. That was before she started working for real money with you guys."

"So how long were you here for, Marlena?"

"Oh, for a while." She was not specific.

"And you're from Italy and Egypt?" He looked across at the other two girls. "Are these countries also sponsors?"

"Emanuella is helped by Italy and Basmah is sponsored under a German aid programme to Egypt." Marlena explained in Italian, looking straight at Dale while she spoke.

Dale didn't react. Italian was his second, and almost only other language and from his years in Italy he was reasonably fluent and enjoyed the language. But it seemed that Marlena was testing his knowledge in some way, and he didn't want to be drawn too much at the moment. He had worked for some of the German aid-funded projects but had never heard of this language-focused programme, although its name seemed entirely feasible. "Basmah," he smiled at the long black haired Egyptian girl, "how long have you been here at the University?"

"About eighteen months, on and off?" Basmah responded in Italian. "I'm sorry," she added "my Italian is much better than my English."

Dale smiled. "No problem," he responded in kind, "I can manage well enough in Italian. Just please don't ask me to speak Arabic!"

Italian seemed to have become the de facto common language for the group. "We heard you used to live in Italy. Whereabouts was that?" Marlena was as ever the seeker of facts. It struck Dale that she was relentless in worrying away at an issue, until she had satisfied herself that she understood it completely. She was also meticulous about detail and inconsistencies, a trait that the project team blatantly relied on when proofreading their reports.

"In Milan," he said, dragging his mind back to the topic, "I was there for about three years, and I've visited a lot since. In those days it had rather a chemical atmosphere, but it's improved hugely now. I used to say it was great place to escape from at weekends, but I think that now I'd be quite happy to live there again. I think Italy was where I really learnt to drive. The weekend traffic was so bad you had to very creative to avoid the jams." Dale was rambling deliberately and struggling a little to avoid the obvious questions in his mind about the University. He was always conscious of walls having ears and didn't want to get the student threesome into problems.

Fritz again showed his mind reading abilities. "You were here last year," he said. "People remember you, but things have changed a lot since then. The university was purged of so-called foreign idealism and most of the teaching staff were sacked if they were lucky. The campus became a nasty mess for a while and was used by the military and the secret police. They set out to make a point and only stopped when there was nothing foreign left at all. The focus now is very narrow and is rumoured to become more so in the near future. Some technical subjects are still taught, but that's about it. There are no humanities subjects, no arts, and no languages apart from Arabic; nothing associated with world events or economics. Most things are overlaid with a theory of modern politics, which is basically a catalogue of the ruler's current thinking. The numbers of true students have of course much reduced, but the numbers of others, the watchers and listeners, have increased hugely. Don't worry" he added, "this tree is a blind spot, visually as well as audibly. There are a few around. The campus was designed to create lots of private discussion areas, not to make surveillance easy. They didn't manage to tear it all down."

Dale couldn't help himself. He looked around him and realised that the bare walls and concrete panels did indeed create barriers on all sides, although there was oddly no air of repression around where they sat.

Fritz paused, as if realising he was giving a lecture and needed to lighten up a little. "You know, the one interesting thing is that, although women must be covered when walking in the streets or anywhere in public, here it's still treated like a single house and so clothing is less restricted. There are some very illogical laws here."

They moved on to more mundane topics and shared hot sweet tea for a while longer. Dale had found the couple of hours interesting but was still struggling to rationalise why Marlena had been so keen to bring him to the campus. Her fellow students had been interesting, but there seemed something else about the group that he couldn't place. There was some bond that was not just student bonhomie and camaraderie. There was something more organised and professional. He filed it away for later thought.

9

The meeting was scheduled for 7.30 a.m., but he had been asked to come fifteen minutes early. Ubaid was keen to learn about Dale's impressions from the site visit. Dale wasn't sure he was able to enthuse about the dusty, hazy, sandy heat, but felt duty bound to try. This time there was no waiting before he was ushered into Ubaid's office and he sat, with his bundle of papers and sketches, and with the inevitable PowerPoint presentation sitting on his laptop. Ubaid was full of nervous energy and insisted that Dale only present the ideas and facts. He seemed extremely worried about costs being discussed in detail.

"Please keep any costs out of the discussion" he said. "I want to make sure that we get enough money for this. Those finance people will cut any figures I give them."

"Sounds the same as everywhere in the world." Dale realised that there had to be more people arriving. "Who else are we expecting?" he asked, indicated the empty seats.

"Oh, the Minister of Finance is coming over." Ubaid clearly held him in some awe. "And a few of the Agriculture and Construction staff, plus a few security people," he added. "They'll be here before seven-thirty."

They chatted about various UK universities for a while as several others arrived. Haddad, the Minister of Finance arrived at seven-thirty sharp. He was a large, expensively dressed man with pronounced Arab features and traditional attire. His beard was immaculate and mottled grey. Dale would have placed him as sixty plus, but he was probably older.

Ubaid switched smoothly into formal meeting mode. He could be impressive as a chairman, and he was not about to lose this project to another ministry. Dale had structured his presentation to cover the likely issues to do with racing camels first. He left things very open-ended and in effect gave them a wish list, from the basic track up to the air-conditioned stables and stands, right through to the Range Rover parking area. He touched on fences and water but not in great detail. There were nods of approval as he drew to a close and Dale thought it time to draw a few lines around the options.

"Let's start with the fence," he said. "For X million dollars you get the fence, and everything else is optional." Ubaid smiled at the X. Time for costs later when he could add all the normal mark-ups. He was thankful Dale had been listening.

Half an hour passed in discussion of ideas and needs. "You haven't mentioned the restaurant yet." Haddad had been quiet but was now leaning forward in his chair, intent and hawk-like.

"Restaurant?" Dale had heard nothing about a restaurant.

"The revolving restaurant." Haddad was specific, "and an air-conditioned observation deck with views over the countryside and over the camel track too. This land is fit for nothing, so we will have to add attractions if we want tourists in the future. This is of course quite separate from the executive boxes in the stands."

Dale's eyebrows lowered again, and he added a revolving restaurant to the list. He was past being surprised at the gulf between rich and poor, even in this officially egalitarian country. If they wanted a revolving restaurant, they could have one, as long as they paid.

"And the President's box?" Haddad spoke again.

"President?" Dale was now confused. Did he mean the Ruler?

"I believe that Haddad means the President of Camel Racing," suggested Ubaid. "When anyone comes to his box, even the Ruler, it will be at his invitation only."

"Maybe we could have a meeting with the President." Dale brightened a little.

"You are meeting with him," a smiling Haddad slightly inclined his head, "but I agree that we should talk some more. Maybe you and Ubaid could advise me on costs in a while."

Dale spent a further half-hour revising his list of options and, with Haddad's pressure, the rest of the assembled group readily agreed. The three of them were left in the room.

"So, my friend, how much do we want to spend on our camel extravaganza?" Haddad had turned to face a contemplative Ubaid.

"If we add in all the options outlined by Dale, plus security and restaurants we think the total project will be between 165 and 190 million dollars. Dale stifled a gasp. His own thoughts had been around the 45-million-dollar mark, although the revolving revelation would add significantly to that. As far as he knew, Ubaid hadn't even reviewed his figures.

Haddad pondered the situation. "Okay," he said finally, "this is a key project for me as well as for the country. I am prepared to support a budget of 120 million dollars, but I would like no more than 50 million dollars to be in cash, the rest must come by trading new oil."

Ubaid didn't move a millimetre. "50 million dollars would be tough," he said, "but I think we could perhaps manage with about 60 million, as long as we have 60% of that in foreign currency."

Dale could see the frowns deepening all round.

"Let's stay with 60 million dollars in oil, and 60 million dollars in cash, but no more that 50:50 in foreign/local funds, and completion in time for next year's race season"

"You drive a hard bargain," Ubaid slumped a little and hardly moved as Haddad rose to conclude the meeting 'but we'll see what we can do." Haddad inclined his sculptured face again and swept out of the door.

Dale bit his lip in an effort to remain silent. Ubaid watched the door close, waited to make sure it didn't reopen and then looked at Dale and beamed a conspiratorial grin in his direction.

"I guess you can manage with about 60 or 70 million dollars?" he said, "including your fees of course. We have a few other things we need to do on this project, but they don't concern you. Can you let me have a summary, with fees by tomorrow?"

Dales began to breathe again. "The capital costs will be okay," he was awakening rapidly from his stunned state "but fees might take a while to work through."

Ubaid was not in a mood to wait. "Maybe we can agree on a percentage?" he suggested, "but don't be greedy. Anything less than 20%, including project and site management, I will be able to agree to, and not all in foreign currency please," he added with a smile. "You will have to visit your travel agent friend again for the rest."

"Okay, tomorrow morning first thing." Dale almost jumped out of his seat "Must get going now" he said, his mind already thinking through the news he would have for his firm. "One last thing," he turned to face Ubaid, "when does next year's race season start?"

"October first, so you have sixteen months."

10

It was Dale's third visit and the year had sprinted into early September. The camel project had started, and he was pleased with the team he had put in place. Grant was an excellent project manager and they had managed to obtain a healthy down payment. It was a pity that it had to go through their Italian branch as the Brits were now trying to extract the cash from their Italian office without too much being held back for services, in support of their northern colleagues. The irrigation study had encountered a few blockages and was entering its 'how to get the client to endorse the findings' stage, and of course, 'how to be paid'. It was proving frustrating, and Dale felt that it was time to revisit the ministers and sort out a few glitches. He was going to be busy for the next few weeks but overall, he considered that things weren't going too badly.

The curfew was announced the day after he arrived. Armoured cars screamed purposefully around the streets and the population hid. The rest of the foreign team was now in a rented villa but there was no room there for him too, and anyway they felt he should be in the city centre, not camping in the suburbs. He had spoken to them by phone, and they were treating it like a typhoon party in Hong Kong. They jokingly told him to expect a Number 8 curfew, so they thought they might be stuck there for a few days. The hotel staff advised him to stay in his room for the evening. He was not inclined to argue. Officially, the night curfew only lasted until seven in the morning but he couldn't find anyone who could tell him exactly what it was for, and how long it was likely to last. Was this a one-off event or a daily activity? No one knew. He resigned himself to a book and a beer.

The next morning, Sulaiman called from the ministry. "I have been speaking to the Construction Ministry and we have obtained curfew day passes for all your foreign staff. It means you can travel during the day but not of course at night."

"Does that include all our foreign staff?"

"Of course."

"Including our Egyptians and Palestinians?"

The pause was almost palpable. "Let me see" said Sulaiman. "I think the Egyptian staff will be fine, but the Palestinian staff may cost a little more."

"Can you bring my permit here to the hotel?" Dale was anxious to get moving. "I need to come in to talk to the Minister."

"Yes of course. Hussein will bring it with Fatimah later this morning. Maybe she can then take the others down to your staff villa"

Dale was a little alarmed at the apparent forethought and organisation. It was not normal and in fact was highly unusual for Sulaiman to exert himself at all.

He waited. The pass and car came at eleven-thirty. Not much time to do things today, he thought and sped off to the Ministry of Agriculture.

Minister Mohammed was in jovial mood. "Your passes for the camel project are free of charge!" he announced. "I'm under orders to look after you and your team, all of them," he added. "You should be able to move about unhindered but please keep away from the university."

"Why?"

"We had some problems with a number of foreign students. They've been subversive it seems. Anyway, the buildings have been taken over and put under tight security while the students are questioned." Mohammed was looking straight at Dale. "Didn't you have a German student working in your team?"

"I'm sure we don't have any current students," said Dale carefully, "although I guess we were all students once upon a time."

"Well, be careful" Mohammed closed the subject. "Now, how can I help your irrigation project?"

"We're having a few problems getting paid." Dale was in no mood for small talk and if Mohammed had invited him to air his problems, then he would do so. "It isn't this ministry, in fact, the Agriculture Ministry is very efficient." He paused while Mohammed visibly gathered his shoulders together in pride. "But the approvals for payment seem to need an awful lot of signatures from other ministries and Security and Finance are very slow. In fact, they've stopped approving our invoices and we can't find out why."

"I know that foreign currency is tight. The sanctions mean that we can't sell our oil in the normal way, and everything takes much longer to process."

"But our fees are tiny in comparison to other payments." Dale was used to all the arguments. Government staff in most countries regarded project funds as their own personal money and judged their success on how long they could delay payment.

"Okay, let me talk to the other ministries."

"Thank you. I was planning to talk to them myself, mainly about other things. Maybe you could let me know what their reaction is regarding payments?" Dale was anxious to keep Mohammed on his side.

"Yes, let me talk about money with them. Maybe there's something we can do to help. Perhaps if we transferred some payment from foreign to local currency?" Mohammed asked, grinning.

"A year ago, I would have considered that" said Dale, "but extra air tickets are difficult now. The airlines have reduced their flights."

"Okay, it was worth me asking. Let me ask Sulaiman to join us so I can understand the payment situation properly."

11

The two men were eating a leisurely lunch. Their table on the large airy balcony was shaded by vines and overlooked the waterfront. It was an idyllic spot where they could savour the excellent Italian cooking but also intoxicate themselves with the spectacular view over the lake. To the south lay the ancient city of Como and across the water to the west clustered numerous tiny villages, clinging to the near vertical far shore. They seemed to hang in mid-slope, spilling into the water with their rooftops a riot of multi-coloured tiles, interspersed with battered window shutters and tiny wrought iron balconies, many with precariously balanced window boxes crammed full of still more colour. The whole countryside had a timeless quality that they both appreciated.

McGuire pondered that it was probably one of the most expensive areas of real estate in the entire world, where people paid fortunes for tiny properties on minute plots, with terrible access and no parking. All for the view, and perhaps the occasional restaurant. McGuire was the UK based Regional Chief. Winchester educated, he was a likeable old school type, and impressively connected. From school he had become a Cambridge maths scholar, not as good as he should have been as he had a tendency for laziness, but he was still an exceptionally intelligent man. He had been recruited to the service while at university, admittedly with his father's influence, as he wasn't a linguist at all. He knew an awful lot of facts about an awful lot of people, and not only in the UK.

His colleague Russell Clark, on the other hand, was an accomplished linguist. Although British, he thought of himself as European and so, although he spoke six languages well, he didn't view it as unusual. Most of his European friends spoke at least four. Maybe his Arabic was unusual, coming from his days as a field hand in the Middle East. Based in Milan, he lived out of town in a tiny apartment high on the slopes of Lake Como, commuting all too regularly to London's South Bank headquarters. Now single again, his wife had died eight years previously, in a mysterious car accident that was widely thought to have been meant for him. He was a worrier who saw shadows everywhere and ulterior motives behind every expression. He was a professional through and through, who had little other life.

Dale wasn't the only person using an Italian front to work in the country. The British Foreign Office and its associated services had for a long time, enjoyed a useful relationship with their Italian cousins, and it was truly symbiotic. The Italian services were based in Rome, but the English staff preferred the north around the lakes of Coma and Garda. So, they had set up a small office in Milan, which was about as far south as they liked to venture. It worked out well for both parties. The Italian service could keep the Brits at a reasonable distance and the British office was able to remain sufficiently low key, so as not to raise eyebrows in Italian political circles. In any case, the Brits were focused on agents on the ground. So were the old-style Italians, although McGuire considered that the younger generation had been watching too many American movies and were more inclined towards whizzy widgets than real people assets. He was sure that it needed more than a glass of red wine and a computer to play mind games.

McGuire had struggled long with the US propensity for near-total reliance on technology. After all, how can you learn what a man is thinking by watching him from a satellite and relying on good weather, and even better eyesight? He had argued the point on many an occasion. Computer enhancements and automated listening and sifting techniques were all very well but there had been some spectacular failures. The famous fiasco over Hainan Island in China was one. The amount of raw noise that had been trawled out of the ether was so great that it was almost impossible to separate information from data. He much preferred to have his own men on the ground.

"When do you travel?" McGuire asked.

"Next month. I'll time it to coincide with Dale's next visit. We need to get some arrangements in place with Wafa first so we don't raise alarm bells at the airport."

"That fellow, what's his name, Naiem Fahoud, is an excellent operator, one the few I have any time for over there." McGuire's encyclopaedic memory was legendary, he was said to remember not just the name but also to the position on the page where he first saw it. The only downside was that he had to see it written down. But once written, it was there forever. "And you're taking Miles with you this time?"

"Yes, he's a good pair of hands." Russell raised his head and levelled his eyes at his boss. "There isn't anything else I need to know about Miles Cameron is there?"

McGuire was coy. After what seemed an age he merely said, "No, I don't think so."

Russell was now even more convinced that his hunch was right. There was something about Miles that was not all it seemed. The guy was thirty, some fifteen years younger than Russell and he spoke perfect Arabic. 'Learnt it when I young' didn't entirely add up, although he knew his father was in the oil business and worked in the Middle East. But never mind, he was well thought of, energetic and intelligent.

"If there is, please tell me." Russell persisted, but there was no response. McGuire was deep in thought and gazing out into the distance.

"Tell me about Bertelli." McGuire suddenly changed subject. "He's still there, isn't he?"

"Yes, still running his contractors' association. He trips in and out without any problems at all. It's almost as if he's welcomed there on official business. It amazes me how the Italians have the cheek to navigate around sanctions so effectively."

"Very creative people, and they've been doing it for a long time too. Bertelli makes contact pretty easy for us really, although we must not become too dependent on him as a single route. Tell me," he jumped topic "ever met a girl called Emanuella?"

Russell's face must have shown its shock. McGuire noticed and smiled. "Look after her, she's the daughter of a good friend of mine."

"And what about these airports?" McGuire was expert at the non-sequitur.

"Well, we know that Hussein did visit six European airports with Jamil Shakari, and we now know that their path matches with the passports we saw. He says that all he knew was that they were looking at airport security, both passenger and cargo. They took some photographs but not much else. He says they didn't meet anyone, apart from Jamil's night-time exploits in virtually every city. The story is that they want to redo their own airport security."

"And?"

"And, it doesn't make sense. Their airport security is very good, as we know. Naiem Fahoud is an excellent operator and yet he wasn't involved."

"So?"

"So, maybe they're planning something at one of these airports and they are visiting them all to see which would be easiest, or maybe they've already decided and so they visited the others simply to confuse the picture, or maybe Jamil just likes the girls in London."

"Maybe. We need to find out. I think there's clearly something going on and we need to understand exactly what, when and who."

12

The camel project had a problem and Ubaid was agitated. "Haddad's lost a camel" he explained. "It ate the fence-post and escaped. I know it's a temporary post and that the proper steel ones will be camel-proof, but it was one of Haddad's best camels." He frowned. "The other problem is that the ranch is so huge that we don't know where Haddad's other camels are!"

Dale was patient. "Camel tracking was one of the options we suggested," he said, "but it was ruled out by Haddad if I remember rightly."

"Yes, I know, I know, but I think you'll find that Haddad's changed his mind. Now he'll prefer to know where his camels are himself, rather than worrying about others knowing where they are, and not being able to do anything about it. He's paranoid about them being slipped something harmful to eat."

"Well, we can certainly do something, but the equipment will have to come from overseas and we still have the payment problem over the other foreign goods. The contractors have not been paid and that is why the temporary fencing is still being used. Even Haddad can't expect to contain hundreds of camels with a length of barbed wire."

Ubaid was thoughtful. "If the equipment is regarded as security equipment then we can import and pay for it in hard dollars, no problem. Sanctions won't bother us too much as there are plenty of companies willing to find a way around them for small items such as this. How about adding this equipment to your contract directly and paying you in foreign currency to cover this and also your fees. We could adjust your contract and the extra would cover both items."

"And Haddad?" Dale was sceptical.

"No problem, he'll do anything for his camels."

"And Minister Abdullah? How will the Security Ministry react?"

Ubaid laughed. "It was actually their idea. Of course, you might have to help them out with some other problems they have, but overall you would be paid, paid well in fact, and in foreign currency."

Dale was sometimes quick off the mark. He held out his hand. "Then I accept" he said, "we'll roll up the whole of the remaining unpaid work into the new security equipment and accept payment in foreign currency. But I'll need a 50% up-front payment before we can start." He held his breath as Ubaid's frown deepened.

"Forty" he muttered, almost as a reflex action.

"Thank you," Dale breathed again. He would have settled happily for twenty-five.

Ubaid still frowned and Dale sensed that this was not the main point of the conversation. There was clearly a story behind the offer. He didn't have to wait long.

"The fact is we are planning for the post-sanction era."

Dale waited again.

"We need a new airport and especially need a new cargo handing facility. Modern trade is relying less on shipping and more on air cargo, and ours here is really old and small."

Dale nodded and waited some more.

Ubaid thought of his recent conversation with Fayez. He had been specific about the need for Dale to be helpful if they provided the approvals for the extra camel security work and had outlined the project they had in mind. He knew these men never did anything without reason and he sensed that it would probably not be in his best interests to know exactly what their reason was. Although the cargo handing area was small, the passenger terminal was not very old and with Naiem Fahoud in charge of security the place ran like clockwork. He ploughed on.

"The long and short of it is this," he looked up to see Dale's reaction and was treated to a knowing grin. Dale's appreciation of his English phrases helped their relationship a lot. "We appreciate the way you and your firm are working here. You have an ability to get things done. We trust you, and I and my other ministers" Ubaid sat up straight and did his best to sound pompous, "would like to extend the relationship we have with you, for our mutual benefit."

"In short" he went on, "we would like to appoint your firm to programme manage the new airport facility." His voice gathered pace as he entered familiar territory. "We would like to do it in three phases. Research and concept design, then detailed design, and finally of course, construction. We would want to have a lot of input into the concept and approve this and the designs before they are built."

Dale smiled at the lack of any reference to such words as study, or feasibility, or cost benefit analysis, or even cost estimate. Technical feasibility was a forgone conclusion in their eyes and the need for it to make economic sense never entered their minds at all. If they wanted it, it would happen. They had the oil; therefore, they could generate the money.

"I understand the need to approve designs" he said, "but tell me what you mean by research."

"Well, we don't want to reinvent the wheel" Ubaid grinned again, "so we thought maybe the first step might be to look at designs from some other airports and see which ones we prefer. There must be dozens of consultants who'd be keen to provide old drawings if they have a chance to join your team."

Dale could now see where the conversation was going. Taking responsibility for others' work was a risky business unless you were paid for the risk. He decided to be formal.

"Firstly, let me say that I appreciate your trust in us." He thought of the unpaid bills and delayed payments, but this was not the time to raise them. "However," he began to talk while he thought, "I will have to discuss with my company as airport design services are definitely not humanitarian and I doubt whether many firms will want to play at the moment."

Ubaid's frown hadn't left his face. "My colleagues would be very disappointed if we aren't able to agree a deal." He let the silence hang. "We estimate that the research and concept stage is worth perhaps 20 million dollars and I am authorised to pay 50% in foreign currency and 50% in local currency, with a reasonable down payment within the next seven days."

Dale didn't flinch. "50%," he mused. Was the foreign/local split immutable he wondered?

Ubaid misunderstood him. "I guess we could manage 50%," he said.

Dale realised that he meant a 50% down payment. For a service contract this was very good indeed. These people must want this badly and in a hurry, he thought. We can do it, but we wouldn't be the first choice on the international stage at the moment.

He decided to increase the pressure a little and see just how much he could improve the offer. "My real worry is the foreign currency element," he brooded. "I am under a lot of criticism back home about the lack of payments and I am not sure I could take on any more without real cash on the table. The camel project's also showing poor foreign currency payments. It's really becoming a big problem."

Ubaid sighed. "I will be open with you" he said, "I cannot change the split. 50:50 is the maximum that Haddad will agree to. However, I can increase the fee and the up-front payment. How about we settle on 25 million dollars, 50:50 foreign/local currency and a 60% up-front payment; but that's as far as I can go. If you want the job, then it's yours, otherwise we will have to approach others."

Dale remained silent for as long as he dared. He managed a big sigh, wrung his hands and shuffled in his seat. In trying to look uncomfortable, he hoped he wasn't showing his excitement and astonishment at this amazing offer. Finally, he held out his hand. "Okay" he said, "what did you say to Haddad? You drive a hard bargain. I'll speak to our head office today."

Ubaid's face changed instantly. He recalled the meeting with Haddad very well. Maybe Dale was not quite so crestfallen as he appeared. Anyway, they had a way forward. It was within Haddad's limits and the Security Ministry only cared about product, not price.

Dale managed a grin. "How's your son?" he asked.

Ubaid visibly relaxed. "Started last week" he said proudly, "I must thank you again for your help."

"You're very welcome. Let's hope he turns out as well as his father."

13

The two old Arabs relaxed into their hookahs. "So how did it go" asked Abdullah, although he'd already had feedback from Ubaid.

"I think we have the makings of a good deal all round." Fayez was not in the mood to chat. He had listened to their conversation and although he admired Dale for squeezing the price upwards, he knew that the negotiation would have gone on much longer if he had been party to it. "The next step is to protect our interests," he added. "I intend to step up our surveillance of Mr Dale and find a few more pressure points. Just to be sure."

"When do you think we'll see some results?"

"Product? Maybe when he comes on his next visit. I understand that this one was only a short trip to sort out payment delays. He should be coming for longer in October."

"Pressure points?"

"Similar time, I guess. I'm going to throw some temptations into his path. We already have some minor things, like evading customs inspections and fraudulently exporting currency by buying and redeeming air tickets. And of course, we have all this on tape."

"Minor things though."

"Yes," admitted Fayez, "although he does do the customs trick very neatly. Apparently, they use the video for training the security staff."

Abdullah smiled. He was not about to stop someone exporting currency when he and his fellow ministers were getting such a handsome profit for the scam.

"By temptations, I suspect you mean some of our young ladies?"

"All things are possible," Fayez was not going to be drawn.

14

Arrivals and departures brushed shoulders across a flimsy barrier in mid-terminal. The difference in pace and the expressions on the two lines of passengers told all. Arriving was always a gloomy affair, but leaving was different, as you could imagine yourself amongst friends or fellow conspirators at least. Departures almost ran, clutching their smiles in case they vanished, hoping that their flight was on time but reassured by the evident camaraderie of their fellow travellers. Arrivals were grim faced, with a million thoughts behind their set expressions. The first timers, and especially non-Arabic speakers had the toughest time as this was probably the only airport in the world where no concessions were made to an international language, not even little pictograms, and definitely not any announcements. The Arabic signs had arrows, but most people simply followed the crowd and hoped. The only English writing appeared in the political slogans.

Dale was no longer fazed by this and in any case was now expert at speeding his way through customs. He had two basic approaches, and if one failed then the other hadn't let him down yet. But it was risky, he could never be sure. He checked the piece of chalk in his jacket pocket and walked deliberately to the longest line of passengers, already waiting patiently at one of the six customs benches. He joined the tail end and mentally geared himself for at least fifteen minutes.

He turned his mind to the next few days of meetings and stood passively in front of two garrulous German salesmen, who were comparing brochures and business cards. They were large, incongruously leather coated for desert climates, and uniformly dishevelled. He strained to listen and try to understand their conversation and from the smatterings of talk about Leipzig he guessed that they were East German, and had something to do with chickens, though he could not make out anymore. His German was not up to eavesdropping. Either way, sanctions clearly did not concern them, or maybe chickens were not on the current hit list. They shuffled closer to him until he was almost suffocated by their hot garlic breath. He tried to move away and turned his attention back to the customs officials but one of the East Germans put a large sweaty hand on his forearm.

"Excuse me." The large man had clearly been drinking on the plane. Dale looked into his face and then down at the restraining paw on his jacket sleeve. The German made no sign of removing it.

"Excuse me," said the German again, "didn't we meet here last month?"

Dale winced. "I don't think so," he said disinterestedly. "Whereabouts?"

The German ignored him. "I knew it was you," he said, his fat face broadening still further into a moon shaped grin. The hand on the arm relaxed a little. "The Alambra," he slurred. "I knew it was you."

Dale pulled his arm away. "I'm sure you're mistaken," he said, and moved away from the two men, almost reaching the customs desk in the process. The German was not to be deterred. "You gave me this card," he said, pulling a bent business card out of his leather coat pocket.

Dale glanced at the card and smiled. "That's not my name," he said, visibly relieved, "and anyway, I'm English, not Italian."

The German blinked and turned to his colleague. "But you said this was the guy," he mumbled.

Dale turned his attention back to the customs queue and leant down to pick up his computer bag and briefcase. The computer bag had gone.

Overlooking the customs hall, in a room guarded by slanting one-way mirror windows, a technician inserted a small transmitter into the small computer chassis. Naiem Fahoud, the airport security chief watched while his man completed the delicate task. A justifiably proud man, Naiem regarded his job as being the driver of fine piece of machinery, something like a Ferrari sports car was how he described it to others. In fact, he kept a picture of a shining red Ferrari posted in his locker, along with a range of confiscated magazine centre pages which he assured himself were his only vice. Others could never understand his sports car logic, but they did accept that he ran the airport security system better than anyone in its chequered past.

Every move was orchestrated, and the beauty of it was that most passengers never realised it. They saw only a frustrating set of apparently illogical events and stupidities whereas Naiem knew, and his staff knew, that everything had a purpose. In the quiet times, they would often review the security footage and track some poor unassuming punter through the system. Naiem called it training. Some of his staff simply enjoyed the voyeurism. Either way, Naiem was intensely proud of his work. Today Dale was the man in their sights.

The technician finished and re-zipped the bag. They looked through the one-way window at Dale below in the hall. He was still trying to explain what had happened, to one of the security staff, with some difficulty as the man's English proficiency was close to zero. Naiem admired Dale's persistence. He hadn't panicked but had merely accepted the loss of the bag as something that might simply occur anywhere.

Naiem nodded to his man to start the next step in their carefully choreographed process and a minute later the man appeared in the hall below, holding up the bag. Next to him stood a young woman interpreter. He raised his voice above the commotion.

"Does anyone own this bag?" he shouted in Arabic, still some way away from Dale. The interpreter repeated the question, first in Italian and then in English. The pair moved a little closer to Dale. The double act raised its voices again. "Anyone own this bag?"

Finally, Dale heard the voice and looked around him. His expression told all. "Over here!" he shouted, "it's mine."

The security man looked unimpressed but walked over to Dale. "Do you have any identification?" he asked. The woman repeated the request in English. Dale fumbled for his passport and ticket and offered them to the official. He grunted. "Come with us," said the woman. It was not a suggestion, more of a command. Dale followed.

The room was small, bare and quiet. A metal table and two chairs were the only furnishings. There was no window. Dale sat where he was asked and waited for the man to speak.

"He asks if this is your computer?"

"Yes." The man and woman conversed again.

"He asks how you know this is yours?"

Dale blinked and then remembered. "On the base," he said "there is a company inventory label. Global Infrastructure Ltd. The same name as on my business card."

"He says can you turn it on?"

Dale pressed the switch and the screen flickered briefly and then turned itself off. The battery was almost dead. "Sorry," he said, looking round for a power point. "Needs charging."

The official frowned. "Okay," he grunted and another conversation in Arabic took place. "He says they saw someone pick this up and stopped him outside. He says he is glad that they were able to return it to its owner."

"Thank you." Dale was more relieved than he cared to show. "My whole life is in here," he added. "Can you please thank him for me? Can I go now?"

"Please," offered the official. "He says he is sorry you were delayed," added the woman.

Dale rejoined the queue. He failed to notice the tall official looking man who had also switched lines to stand a few places behind him.

Bertelli was thin, grey haired and sported a short goatee beard. He carried the remains of a stylishly slim, leather-bound brown briefcase, something akin to the black plastic sort that went out of fashion years ago but refused to die, with aluminium edging along the join and a cracked handle long ago worn smooth and ancient. He wore a long, high collared camel coat and although clearly from a fashionable European city, he had a studied blankness to his face that could have placed him anywhere from Paris to Prague, or maybe Milan to Munich. A smart, blend-in-anywhere, city sort of a man, his eyes did not match his expression. They were alert and active behind his gold-rimmed glasses. If Dale had been more aware he might have seen this man sitting waiting, studying a newspaper, just like a dozen others, when he disembarked from his plane. He might have seen him casually following Dale from near the air bridge, always at a respectable distance. He might have even seen him murmuring into his mobile phone or might surely have seen him quietly switching lines to be close behind Dale. But he did not. Dale missed all this. He had been attentive only to his customs hall plan, and now was absorbed in thoughts about his agenda for the next few days.

His previous experience proved right. One after another, the shorter lines ground to a halt as their respective customs officials disappeared to change shift. Changing shift could take anywhere between five and twenty minutes, while the uninitiated fretted and swore and hopped between queues in a desperate attempt to beat the system. He hoped his official had only recently come on duty, and that this was the reason for the longer line. He was banking on his customs official working his way through his line of passengers, at least as far as himself, without vanishing. So far, he was right. Then, with only two passengers in front, disaster struck. The official simply walked away and abandoned his bench; leaving it in the charge of the lazy security guard. A babble of swearing rose around him like a dam breaking its banks. Dale ignored that and moved across to the heap of luggage.

Plan B involved the chalk. The routine at the customs desk was that you had to identify your baggage in the heap behind the officials, and then they would inspect your luggage, mark it with chalk and let you pass through, more often than not. There was always a small crowd of people hunting for baggage when they reached the front of the lines while the officials waited placidly. Time had no meaning for them. And so Dale simply joined the crowd, soon spotting his bag amongst the chaos and, while he leant over ostensibly to check the luggage label his other hand carefully made a chalk mark near the lock, using the same sign he'd seen being used by his now missing official. With a casualness he did not feel, he simply wandered around through the melee for a while and then headed for the barrier. The exit guard glanced at the chalk mark and waved him through. He heartbeat stepped up a notch, but he was home free. He grinned at the tall, camel coated goatee man walking beside him, an acknowledgement of someone else who knew the system.

The camel coated goatee turned slightly and opened his mouth as if to say something but then checked himself. He frowned instead, touched his hat brim lightly and strode purposefully away. Dale looked after him but then turned his attention to more pressing matters. Where was his driver? He recalled Fatimah as a round, friendly girl, late twenties but seeming older. She was nowhere to be seen.

He scoured the heaving crowd and worked his way along the row of shifting, handheld signboards. As he moved past them several were thrust enthusiastically in front of his face with hopeful smiles hovering above. 'Mister, Mister' was the common cry. Shouts of 'Taxi, taxi – here, here – special rate!' also rang around him as shady characters with scruffy name cards tried to catch his attention. He recognised nothing and slowed his step, reluctant to be engulfed in the crowd too quickly. The illegal taxi drivers crowded round and redoubled their efforts.

He clung to his bags, keeping one hand firmly in his side pocket, wrapped even more firmly around his wallet. But still nothing, so he humped his computer bag higher on his shoulder and tugged his Samsonite across to a corner of the arrivals hall from where he could survey the masses. He noticed the camel coated goatee chatting to one of the many black veiled girls near the door but passed them by while he scoured for anything resembling his name or the company logo. He thought he would give them a few minutes before digging out their phone number from his computer and made a mental note to put the damn thing into his mobile. The last time he'd resorted to opening up his laptop in an arrivals hall four security guards had jumped him with commendable speed and determination. It had taken an hour out of his day and at least three years off his life to work though the anti-terrorist heavies and reclaim his computer, and keep his body, unscathed.

He walked around the nearest column looking hopeful for a power point, as he would need one to fire up his dead computer battery if he had to retrieve the phone number. Damn things, he thought, why don't we just use paper anymore!

The only power point he could find was one already occupied by the sulking Coke vending machine, and he was pondering on the advisability of hijacking it for a few minutes when a small card with his name, neatly handwritten in blue, was pushed towards him. Dale followed the arm to its owner. It was not Fatimah but a taller girl, dressed entirely in flowing black, maybe older but somehow looking younger. What made him think that he wondered? She held her head-dress carefully to shield her face.

"Meester Connor?" She muttered.

"Hi," he smiled. At the back of his mind, she looked somehow familiar. Why?

"Driver," she placed a hand on her chest. "Come pleeease." Her English was accented and stilted. She had already turned away before he could reply.

So, he simply followed, computer bag on shoulder, dragging his trusty suitcase and briefcase with one hand, while the other stayed in his pocket, wrapped resolutely around his wallet. As he walked into the blinding brightness of the outdoor sunlight he wondered which of the various beat-up VWs blistering in the heat would be his. The tarmac was sticky and stank of cheap contractors' profits. He tried to keep the Samsonite out of the worst patches while he struggled to keep up with the rapidly disappearing driver.

15

Dale's sleight of hand with the chalk had been smiled at. Naiem silently commended his ingenuity and audacity but really couldn't give a damn what he brought in through customs. Why make a scene at the airport when the hotel room was so much easier and convenient to search? This was Dale's fourth visit and ever since he had arrived on his third he had been a marked man. People were allowed to come twice, as if they were playing out some unfinished tourist ambition. Maybe some of the sights had been closed on the first visit, maybe they had some special offer in the souk to take up. But two visits was the limit. Two visits merely warranted a record in the log, the sort of coincidence that was given the benefit of the doubt. But three was different. Three signified purpose, and purpose signified an agenda and overt reasons were rarely all that they seemed to be in this country; and so the three-timers were investigated in an organised and brutally efficient way.

They knew a lot about Dale Connors. Maybe not inside out, but much more than Dale would imagine. Thirt-five years old and as fit as they come, despite hating sports and never gracing a gym in his life. Maybe it was his incessant travelling, developing business for an international engineering services firm. He was wedded to his work now, after six years of marriage which had oscillated haphazardly between the tempestuous and the boring, before settling into a bland urbanity that made him scream with impatience and frustration. They concluded rightly that he enjoyed life, especially when travelling and on the move. They also rightly concluded that he hated staying in one place for long. Must have been born on a Thursday, 'far to go,' they surmised. They had a list of the girls he knew and kept in touch with. Maybe it was a form of escapism, they hadn't worried too much about reasons, just facts. They documented and data-based many of the people he worked with and met. They had pages on Dale and from every angle their lords and masters in the Ministry of Security concluded that he was perfect for their needs. And the beauty of it was that he had no idea that they knew.

He had been their special target today. They had been worried about using the East Germans to divert him but in the end it had been a master stroke. He had suspected nothing and had actually thanked them for their efforts. And now they had the laptop wired. Excellent. They had tracked him all the way from the energetic walk up the air-bridge to his carefully assumed casualness in the customs hall. They could tell the fitness-driven foreigners apart from the local lads. Generally big and purposeful, the visitors always marched smartly off the plane as if in mortal fear of their legs never working again. They had remarked positively on his patient wait at immigration, very calm and no sign of agitation there. Then they had nodded appreciatively at his careful selection of the longest customs queue. They had admired the fact that he had a system for dealing with the customs officers and they had taken childish delight in waiting until the line in front of him was down to two people before whispering into their colleague's earpiece. Sometimes power was sweet indeed, especially if measured in small victories.

They had also noted the Italian goatee's movements. They knew him well from the old days, before sanctions had caused the closure of most of the foreign missions. He was not seen as a threat, more a dinosaur from a past era. Naiem mentally checked out the details. Antonio Bertelli, ex (probably still) Italian Intelligence when they had an embassy here, used to be commercial attaché and communications expert in those days; forty-seven years old, born in Milan, still based in-country representing an Italian contractors association. Naiem pondered that sanctions did not seem to worry the Italians. Bertelli acted as local agent for Italian suppliers and contractors, dealing officially in goods that strictly speaking were not on the banned list. What's in a name, he thought.

Naiem prepared to call it a day. He had made sure that Dale was en route to his hotel but as usual, he had paid no attention to the driver. That was someone else's job. He made a note to check when Bertelli next contacted him, although that too would be someone else's problem. He mentally filed away his ordered thoughts, made sure that his cache of magazine photos was secure and turned his mind homewards.

16

When Bertelli had spoken briefly to Nadia she had been in a crowd, but he had been careful to keep her back to the cameras. He knew that women attracted virtually no suspicion from the security staff, but he still did not want to cause unnecessary problems. He had almost succumbed to the temptation to speak to Dale in the customs queue, but he had a healthy respect for Naiem Fahoud and his airport staff. It was the one place he was always doubly careful. Contact could therefore wait for an easier time, when only the regular Ministry of Security people were on duty, and events were less likely to catch the special interest of Jamil Shakari.

Bertelli knew Jamil Shakari of old and by tacit agreement Jamil did not pry too closely into Antonio's dealings. Bertelli kept some cards not played and Jamil knew it. They were stronger that way.

Bertelli assumed that someone, somewhere in the ever-present security organisation knew all about his past life and indeed his current activities, and so he was careful to lay only visible trails which fed the agreed legend. Security organisations, more than any others, existed on records, files and a surprising amount of paper. So, he was careful and played his role as the local rep of a large association of contractors in as believable a way as possible. He planned to limit his public meetings with Dale to construction and supplier meetings only. This would give him more than enough access as Italy's history in the country was long, their contractors the most active of all foreign companies and their politicians the most pragmatic when it came to balancing the niceties of international trade, or non-trade, against self-interest and profit.

17

In the dusty, grey-brown Ministry of Security building, the routine checking of incoming foreign names against the computer record had been half-heartedly started. But it was late and so the task had been shelved until tomorrow, when the paper originals arrived from the airport.

Naiem's staff had already meticulously recorded the number of visits against each name and their recommendations for anything unusual. Against the name Russell Clark the tally stood at '3', and an asterisk noted that he should be put on the investigation list. His profession was noted as being an academic, a historian writing a book about the region. In total there were seventeen names marked with the number '3' written casually in Arabic script; but by the time the list reached the shelf, the total would be reduced to sixteen. Wafa smiled to herself. This time it was easy to change the Arabic '3' back to a '2' and by the time this passenger made his next visit she would have his bogus file in place, with a summary already sent to the airport, the investigation system neatly bypassed. When Naiem and his staff checked against the fourth time visitors they would see that an investigation had been completed and they would suspect nothing. The ministry investigators would think simply that another of their number had done the investigation, if they checked, and Wafa could guarantee that they would not.

Wafa knew Russell from years ago and had met him in a single hurried meeting on his previous visit, but she had never seen the other name travelling with him. A number '1' sat against this new name, so no action was needed yet, but she was sure that Russell would be asking her. Maybe she would have the chance to meet him. She reviewed the newcomer's passport scan carefully.

Tall, thirty and unmarried, and something about his appearance that hinted at a mixed nationality background to her experienced eyes. She liked his photo and began to imagine what meeting him would be like. He looked a little older than his years, maybe a little older than herself, which would be a good thing indeed. Perhaps, her long held ambition to find a good foreigner to take her away from all this might be on the cards after all. Wafa was ever optimistic about escaping but so far, had always been disappointed. She wondered whether she would be destined to be a hopeful spinster for the rest of her life. At thirty-two she definitely thought she was past the magic age when girls can find husbands. One of her 'targets' had been very blunt to her. "Girls of thirty are scary," he warned her. "You don't look thirty-two, so I suggest you don't admit to being so old." She had thanked him politely for his wisdom before doctoring his file to make sure he never set foot in the country again.

She had started working for the Brits when she was a young student in Hull, studying English and Communications, which turned out to be a mix of PR and media skills. She was surprised that Hull even rated a mention in the British Secret Service vocabulary but then discovered that the Service actually targeted the lesser-known colleges and universities, as they reckoned that the girls worked harder and were more susceptible to being recruited. She had been to London and was interviewed there in a supposed language school in Earl's Court. That was as close to the razzle-dazzle as she had managed to come. She had also found out that her English accent was peculiar to the North and instantly recognisable as 'Yorkshire.' She had tried tapes and movies to try and soften the vowels. Russell had told her it had worked pretty well.

In her years working for the Brits, she had seen the full cycle of diplomatic paranoia in action as the UK, in common with its neighbours and cousins, firstly remonstrated with the Libya's powers-that-be and finally disowned them for their purported support of third-party terrorists. Sanctions had taken their toll but as in everything, a closed door for some is an open door for others and a handful of countries had done surprisingly well from the situation. Business with Italy, Egypt and the Eastern bloc had grown significantly.

Wafa packed up her desk and pondered the text message invitation on her mobile phone. Russell was keen to see her. Maybe tonight she would meet her white knight. She drifted off towards home, a romantic haze washing over her as she walked.

18

The highway stretched into the distance. There were no other cars in sight, just a couple of broken trucks minding their own business while their drivers waited for divine intervention. The desert sand howled and eddied across the carriageway from the dirty, tan coloured dunes to the south and west. The port straggled along to his right, almost empty, as the wrath of UN sanctions took its heavy toll. Beyond the port lay the Mediterranean and further along the coast he knew, from past visits, that there were modern multiple star resort hotels, as the coastline turned due west. With water sports long since a thing of the past, the waterfront hotels lay forlorn, empty and decaying, abandoned to the political edicts of the government. But with the advent of sanctions there were few visitors anyway.

Dale pondered what this place must have been like in the old days; definitely a tourist magnet along the North African shores, a playboy's haven maybe, probably a sophisticated gambling resort for the rich and determinedly-not-so-visibly famous. Across the sea lay Italy, and despite the UN sanctions, or maybe because of them, it remained the county's biggest trading partner. Even today the second language here was Italian. Small boats plied the straits and he recalled how easily it had been to use this mode of transport when the airport had been closed, three visits ago. The only problem had been the Italian customs authorities. They had been unimpressed by his attempt to hide a stash of local dinars from their inquisitive gaze. He had used the argument that, as the currency was not tradable in the rest of the world then it had no value, and being worthless, it did not need to be declared. He had pointed out that the only time he could spend it was when he returned, and it was only by chance that he had it in his bag anyway. Like true Italians they had enjoyed the argument but in the end they hadn't cared, merely treating the issue as entertainment in an otherwise dull afternoon.

His mind flipped back to today. As they passed the university, brash, colourful slogans in flamboyant Arabic script fluttered from every spare wall. The accommodation blocks were more or less intact, promoting a stylish version of Islamic architecture that had the look and feel of a sympathetic, if somewhat idealised Westerner's view of local design. The courtyards were deserted, a change from previously when he had met and discussed the political merits of agricultural irrigation on the local economy with a group in the Al Bahad students' common room. However, now was different. The Union building was shot to pieces, literally. He had heard about the shootings and hangings from the remaining occupants. Bullet holes drilled into the courtyard building were the lasting proof. But now the lectures were stereotyped, the curriculum more political than practical and the professors had long ago escaped. To where? No one could tell him.

His eyes remained fixed to the front, as he peered through the grimy windscreen, partly to avoid the glare of the sun on the sea and partly to contemplate his agenda for the next day or two. It was his fourth visit and already he had a feeling that things were somehow different this time, yet he could not put his finger on any particular reason behind it.

He shifted his attention to the car. It was the same dusty, grey, battered VW Beetle he'd used previously, and as it bounced along the pot-holed highway, its driver seemed intent on finding every hole and testing the shock absorbers to the full. When he first visited Libya all the drivers were men, mostly young boys it seemed. He recalled hurtling through tiny streets on one occasion with an enthusiastic lad at the wheel of a huge Mercedes. They had skimmed door handles and dodged imaginary chase vehicles as 'my uncle's car' Hussan stood on the pedals in order to both reach them and see out of the windscreen at the same time. 'My uncle's car' Hussan claimed to be eighteen but would have passed as a pre-teen at any fun fair back home.

More recently, female drivers had become common. They were invariably from some obscure military background but driving now seemed to be an acceptable, even encouraged occupation for women. It was an odd mix of Arab and Western equality in this country where traditional practices were regularly being redefined. He recalled how his last visits had been guided by Fatimah, whose driving skills were fine but whose conversation in English was equal to his in Arabic. Their limited vocabularies were devoid of overlaps and so their long car journeys had been largely silent. He recalled being taken to her house once and discovering that her husband was none other than Sulaiman, their contract supervisor, a beaming, fat and lazy government official whose only purpose in life seemed to be to browbeat his wife constantly but in an almost friendly way. You could not dislike the guy, despite his constant harping.

He had expected Fatimah to meet him again at the airport. It was not like the Ministry of Agriculture to spring surprises; but this driver was very different. She had introduced herself in fractured English and even though fully shrouded in the traditional black abaya demanded by political and religious correctness, he could see that she was different. Her body was taller and slimmer than Fatimah's, even shapely, and her face alive. He was puzzled as her facial characteristics indicated a non-Arab, mixed background, but the fleeting glimpses he was able to obtain of her behind her headdress were not enough to give any further clues. What he had noticed was that her large, dark eyes blazed with purpose.

From his privileged seat in the rear right hand corner of the VW he decided to test his linguistic ability over the racket made by the old rear engine driven car.

He leaned forward. "Excuse me," he shouted, "My name is Dale, do you speak English?"

The girl didn't shift her attention from the road ahead. Silence ruled, apart from the raucous rear-mounted engine and complaining gearbox, so he tried again in his best, and almost only Arabic.

"Min fadlak, ismi Dale," he paused to remember the phase, "hael taetaekaellaem ingilizi?"

The response was immediate, brief and incomprehensible, from which he assumed that the simple answer was 'no'.

The car appeared to have a homing instinct as they bounded towards the city, which now loomed on the near horizon. As they passed yet more bullet-ridden buildings he wondered what the poor souls there had done to deserve such a pummelling. It was a discrete area of the city only, not widespread but almost completely destroyed for maybe six blocks by four. People nonetheless seemed to live in and around the ruins and at a street corner an argument raged between police and a group of youths. Passers-by stood shouting encouragement and waving vigorously and fiercely but he had the impression that they would vanish at the drop of a hat if the police attention shifted.

A glimpse of his client's headquarters focused his mind and as they flew past the ministry building, he wondered whether they were already aware of his journey from the airport and arrival time. Informal communications here were remarkable and it was not unusual for a reception committee to be waiting at the hotel. He pondered the day, Sunday, just a normal working day here, although the ministry's official hours were brief starting at some undetermined hour but always finishing promptly for the day at 2.30 p.m. His mind added up the hours. With time off for breakfast and lunch there didn't seem a lot of time for work, but he knew, as they did, that the real action happened not during the set period of administrative convenience, but later, after a siesta, into the evening and well into the early hours of another day. Siestas! Noel Coward's lines had come to mind – Mad Dogs and Englishmen were indeed the only visible occupants of any hot climate in the middle of the day.

Today it was nearly four-thirty, a civilised time to arrive. He stretched a little at the thought of a shower and a cold beer. Travel was not so tough after all.

The main street broadened into a plaza, surrounded by the ubiquitous bullet ridden buildings, mainly from a development boom in the last century but interspersed with more modern, partially completed concrete framed constructions, definitely in no particular state of urgency from the appearance of the jobsites. The hotel was the only building without bullet holes, and he knew from his past visits that this was firstly because it was less than two years old and more importantly, because it was owned by the Minister of Security.

The front of the hotel was clad in unexceptional concrete panels and dusty, blackened glass but as he stepped through the door the owner's influence became apparent. The lobby, large by western standards, was ornate to the point of being brash and ostentatious. Complex and expensive-looking glass pieces, no doubt from Venice, vied with gold leaf column decorations and impeccable copper wound Cloisonné ceramics. The effect was startling, as was the evident wealth in such contrast to the poverty of the outside world, that Dale could only shake his head in bewilderment. He had always stayed here since its opening and yet the impression on him never diminished. He still found it rather alarming.

He clutched his carry-on bags as the porter tried to wrest them from him. Experience told him that if he relinquished them he would not see them again for ages. So, he clung on and let the man do his worst with his main bag only. He arrived at the check-in desk. His Samsonite had already disappeared, he had no idea where.

"Fax from Mr Combers," the desk clerk grinned triumphantly.

"Thank you." He nodded, recognising the sender as Mrs Harriet Coombes, his PA. "But this fax is for the hotel, not for me," he peered questioningly at the desk clerk, "confirming my reservation," he added.

The clerk grinned back and insisted that Dale keep the fax. He pushed forward a registration form, completely blank and asked Dale to sign it. "We fill in rest," he smiled. "Please give passport."

Dale pulled the form towards him and filled it out himself. "I'll keep the passport," he said, smiling thinly, knowing full well that the short time out of his hands could turn into a long time and probably a lost passport, while the original made its way into the well-trodden fake circuit. He had long given up the argument that they should have a record of his passport details from last time.

"Room 1801, king size no-smoking", the clerk was unfazed by the reluctant passport holder and handed over a large weighty key fob that could have sunk a dozen small ships in the wrong hands. Dale sighed as he took the monstrosity and dragged away his computer bag and briefcase. He bet himself an extra beer that the main bag would take at least twenty minutes to get back to him. He changed this to two beers and thirty minutes as he rode up in the lift.

The corridor was long and unmemorable and surprisingly devoid of the ground floor's flamboyance. Rounding the final corner, he matched his monster piece of metal with the room number. He turned the key and found that his door opened onto a large corner room overlooking the side of the hotel and the main street. The ostentation almost equalled that of the lobby, the most spectacular item being the bedside telephone, so encrusted with onyx and gold coloured metal that he wondered whether it was really capable of modern function. He was also a little surprised to see that his suitcase had already arrived and was on a stand next to the TV. One catch was open and looking closer he saw that the other was unlocked. He sighed resignedly. Searching suitcases was commonplace. Then the large ornamental ashtray caught his eye just as there was a knock at the door.

Opening the door, the porter who had absconded with his case beamed into the room and held out a large white envelope, embossed with a crest and the Italian flag. "From the front desk" he explained, "they forgot."

Dale took it without thinking. "I thought this room was a no-smoking room," he said.

The porter looked at him quizzically. "No smoking?" he sounded unsure.

Dale pointed to the sign on the door and then to the large ashtray. "Ah!" The porter's eyes lit up with recognition. "No problem," he added and almost sprinted into the room, grabbed the huge offending object with two hands and retreated to the door. "Okay!" he said triumphantly "no smoking now Sir!"

Dale hung the 'Do Not Disturb' sign and locked the door behind him. He had arrived.

He looked again at the Italian envelope. It was from one of the large contractors, and opening it he saw a printed invitation form, inviting him to dinner with their visiting management. Under the invitation was a post-script. *'Hope you can come – it will be good to meet up again. Will send car at 7.30.'* It was hand-written and signed *'Russell,'* an old friend over the years, and almost the last person he expected to see at the moment. To Dale's knowledge, Russell was supposed to be somewhere in Central Asia.

Standing under the thankfully opulent shower he contemplated the message. There had been no telephone number, no address, just the reminder that Russell would pick him up by car, at seven-thirty. In effect the decision was made for him. He would be going, and the evening of preparatory work he had planned would have to wait until later. Maybe he could cry off early when he had caught up with Russell. Dale vaguely remembered the contractor's name from an informal gathering during his last visit. He recalled that the contractor was represented by an Italian named Antonio 'somebody' although they had not actually met. Antonio lived somewhere in the city and acted as the local agent for Italian suppliers and contractors. As sanctions were in place, purchase and sale of many products were banned. So far, this had not affected the service industries from certain countries, including the UK, as the Foreign Office mandarins took the fairly pragmatic view of the need to keep their foot in the door of fortune, as his friend Russell had himself once explained. The whole sanction programme was something of an exercise in futility. Some countries were vociferous in their interpretation of the rules and banned all contact by their countrymen. Others however, were blatant in their flagrant circumventing of procedures so that trade actually increased, despite the official denials. The

Italians were not too concerned about the sanctions. They were so used to operating under flags of convenience to circumvent their own government's bureaucracy that going through a few more hoops was nothing to them. They took it in their stride as all part of life's rich game.

Dale changed into something more appropriate for a printed invitation and, putting his laptop and a few other more liftable items in the room safe, he pulled the room door closed behind him, made sure the 'Do Not Disturb' notice was intact, and set off for the lobby bar. The giant key bounced like a grenade in his pocket, but he had no intention of leaving it at any desk. As he waited for the lift, the corridor room boy quietly noted his time of departure and picked up the telephone from his tiny desk.

The lift laboured on its tortuous journey downwards, stopping for no apparent reason at most of the floors. Suddenly, he heard an English voice echoing up the shaft, its disjointed conversation continuing every time the doors opened.

"Hello … Hello … I can't hear you … what? … you can't hear me either? … how's the car darling? Did you get back home okay?"

The doors closed and Dale winced inwardly at his fellow countryman's efforts to be heard. It sounded like one half of a fairly tortuous telephone conversation. As the lift descended to the next floor, the voice became louder, more animated and obviously Scottish.

"Is that any better? What? No, I can hear you okay now." Again, the doors closed, and Dale prayed for transportation to another planet, as for the caller himself, he didn't care.

The lift reached the lobby as the voice still boomed across the crowd. Dale joined the assembled onlookers and stared towards the phone booths. The lobby was rectangular, with a bar running across one end. The long reception desk curved lengthways from bar to booths and in between there must have been over a hundred people scattered about, all staring in the same direction. In the centre booth an animated, balding, grey haired and bearded professorial type of person was shouting Scottish epithets into the phone for all he was worth. The strange thing was that he was shouting into the wrong end of the telephone, into the earpiece. The hotel manager looked up as the lift doors opened and came running over to Dale, who realised he was probably seen as the only other British person there. The subtlety between Britain, the UK, Scotland and England was not a topic for the moment.

"Can you please do something?" gasped the manager "he's not even a hotel guest."

Dale walked slowly down the length of the lobby, rather hoping that the spectacle would resolve itself before he arrived at the phone booths. He was fortunate that, as he approached, the manic little Scottish professor reached out his hand, gave a last shout into the wrong end of the phone and hung up.

The silent crowd immediately came to life. Some cheered, most clapped and animated discussions exploded around him. The manager was relieved. But Dale was curious and asked the professor what he had been doing.

The professor looked blank. "Ah, the phone," he said "I was having trouble making myself heard and I'd read somewhere that shouting into the ear-piece had the same effect. At least I got through!"

Dale looked querulous.

"It's my daughter's birthday" rambled on the professor, "and I promised I'd call her."

"Then let me buy you a beer" said Dale and led the professor away from the phones before he decided to call someone else. He steered the little man through the still staring and gesticulating crowd and aimed for a table in a corner as far away as possible from the bar area.

The professor looked askance. "But isn't that rather antisocial?" he said. "Why can't we join these two gentlemen over here, I'm sure they would welcome some conversation. I would," he added defiantly.

Dale looked up and recognised the two East German salesmen from the airport. He was not pleased to see them after the computer bag incident and it suddenly crossed his mind that they might have been involved, but he banished the thought. There seemed no logic in it.

It was not surprising to find so many passengers from one plane in the hotel. There were simply not many hotels open and even fewer where foreigners could be accommodated. The Germans had clearly checked in and shed their leather coats and were now doing what most travellers do when they have nothing to do, they sat sipping a cold beer, deep in conversation. Before he could say or do anything, the little professor had marched across to the two, whose expressions had frozen as they looked up from their beers.

The professor started speaking even from a distance. "Mind if we join you?" he boomed, his accent suddenly moving several hundred kilometres south. The ensuing silence was palpable. "My name's Cameron. Do you speak English? Are you here on business too?" he continued.

The slightly thinner German came out of his trance. He pushed forward a chair. "Please" … he mumbled. Dale summoned four more beers. The fatter man, who had grabbed his arm, looked at the floor, unwilling to meet his gaze. Dale's senses told him there was something amiss. He kept his eyes on the man.

The professor was undaunted. He leapt forth with a barrage of questions. The Germans had slow but commendable English and indeed turned out to be from East Germany. They were selling chicken feed. It transpired that they had sold and installed a chicken rearing plant a year earlier and admitted quite openly that they made their money out of selling the follow-on feed at very good prices. After a while, even the larger man joined in the conversation, his airport drunkenness apparently now a thing of the past. Dale wondered how.

The professor clearly subscribed to the principle of giving as well as receiving in a conversation. His speed of delivery accelerated, and he was soon holding forth on the merits of different types of governments, economic indicators, business and international finance. His animated seminar on the economy of the country continued for a while and Dale noticed that both chicken feeders were avidly taking notes. As they touched on currency convertibility and exchange rates, the scribbling became intense. Eventually the professor talked himself hoarse and subsided.

"Please ..." The thinner chicken feeder almost raised his hand to ask the question. "Please ... which bank do you work for?"

Now the professor was silent. "Bank?" He looked puzzled. "I'm not a banker," he finally pronounced, "I'm an engineer!" To ram home the fact, the professor-engineer struck a pose as if in a Victorian photograph.

The chicken men were evidently untutored regarding the historic poses of Brunel. Instead, they simply exchanged looks, raised their eyebrows and, in complete unison, carefully tore up their notes, politely finished their beers and rose to go.

Dale felt he had to find out more. "An engineer?" he quizzed "what sort of engineer?"

The professor spied his new audience with a smile. "Geologist," he said, "and you?"

"So, you're not a professor?"

"No, – whatever made you think that?"

"But all that talk about the economy?"

"Just what you read in the FT!"

And having stamped his QED on the conversation, the professor stood, bowed politely and headed towards the lift.

Dale breathed a sigh of relief and called for another beer.

The watchers were amused. From their subterranean hideaway behind the hotel's kitchens, they had recorded the conversation between Dale and the 'banker' as the East Germans were at the top of their hot list for foreigners under scrutiny today. The two provided much of the sensitive merchandise used by the Ministry of Security and the Minister was keen to ensure he was getting exclusivity, value and above all, loyalty.

The watchers had checked out the professor too. But it was only his first visit to the country, and they were not really interested. Dale too was officially classified as a benign commodity, not on their special red lists, but watched carefully nonetheless, as Fayez seemed to be showing a keen interest in anything he did.

Their files on the two East Germans were extensive. They ranged from the overt business deals the two had been concluding with the Ministry of Agriculture to the less publicised arrangements in ex-Russian weaponry concluded in the Al Hambra. This was the Ministry of Security's own night club, where sound and video recording were part of the interior décor, as indeed they were in any MoS-owned establishment, including the current hotel. Their choice of evening entertainment in the Egyptian quarter was meticulously documented. Nothing too adventurous but they were clearly connoisseurs of Egyptian singing and belly dancing and knew how to entertain as well as be entertained in these establishments.

The watchers switched their screens and tuned into one of the East German's rooms. They were proud of their handiwork, with tiny cameras built onto the ornate controls of each hotel room's TV. If you could see the TV, then the watchers could see you, and also hear you too, and who didn't watch TV in a hotel bedroom, or at least ignore it, as part of the landscape?

The older East German had tuned in to CNN and was watching the pictures on the news. The pace of language was too fast for comfort. Not much exciting there, so the watchers turned their attention to the other. He sounded as if he were taking a shower, just out of picture. They settled in for another long, tedious night, room surfing for amusement when the fancy took them, but nobody seemed to do anything interesting anymore. There used to be a time when they could watch a good argument, even an occasional murder but now it was all single businessmen, and they were generally behaving themselves. Watching had become a bore.

In the lift, the East Germans had compared notes on the little professor. They had had a preconceived idea that the English were quiet and reserved. But this fellow, with his balding head and wild hair sprouting sideways above his ears, was like nothing they had ever experienced before. For so many years, their own country had strictly controlled news and discussion and the sort of topics raised by the little man would have had them all locked away, just for listening.

They were much more interested in Dale, who hadn't really told them anything, not even who he was, nor why he was there. They knew he was working for one of the ministries but apart from that, they were curious as to why he had divulged nothing, despite their gentle questions. Most Englishmen were quiet, but he seemed professionally so, without a prepared story line to tell, as they had. They agreed he was someone to watch. Hadn't they been asked to divert him at the airport this morning? He'd been almost too casual for their liking.

The older, arm-grabbing East German was enormously fat. He lay with eyes glazed towards the TV. The latest request from the Ministry of Security still bothered him and he felt unusually un-settled. It involved some high-tech water treatment equipment, a hotchpotch of steel tanks, piping, pumps and controls, with special filter media packed into long tubes. What it was needed for, or where, they had no idea. And why it was a security issue; again they had no idea, and frankly they didn't care. All that concerned them was that it made a profit.

They would do anything for money. But this time it was definitely different. There was an air of secrecy that most of the dealings did not attract. During their previous visit, Fuad had been insistent that they provide full working drawings of the equipment before they decided to buy. They had given him a list of possible suppliers, always being careful that they could route the final product through Italy, and he had selected three; and just, it seemed, by studying the pictures! What was he looking for? The colour of the pipework? Well, they were not sure whether it had only been Fuad's decision, but they were pretty sure that the ministry people were not looking at the detailed technical specifications, which were in German, Russian or Italian.

He flipped channels a few times but found nothing better than the news. At least the pictures were from an active battlefield, something he could relate to. It had taken much effort to find a source of the detailed fabrication drawings Fuad was seeking, and he still felt that there was something strange about the request, but he had no idea what it was. Getting the detailed drawings had not been easy either. It never was unless you actually bought the equipment or were a big buyer like the oil companies. He had had to pull a few favours from some of his émigré friends in Italy, so he could bring the details on this visit, but they were safe in his bag now and they should be paid handsomely tomorrow. It was a sweet deal, and even more so when they bought the actual equipment, and it was all in foreign cash. Thank goodness these people had oil. He had become used to strange requests from Fayez and his staff, although they usually related to specialised security items, even small arms sometimes. But the more he thought about it, this equipment seemed different. Someone behind it was thinking. Usually they didn't, they just followed the latest trends from the armaments magazines.

He switched off CNN as a talk show had started and he couldn't follow the rapid chatter. Anyway, there were no more pictures of the Middle East war. Heaven help us if peace ever breaks out, he thought. We'd be out of business.

He stretched out as far as his podgy arms and legs would allow. Should he call up his friend and go for another beer? Or maybe they could try the Egyptian nightclub, which had been such a success last time. On second thoughts, he decided to stay with their agreed plan. They had been travelling a long time and were dead tired. He was not one of these travel maniacs who could sleep on planes. He needed a bed, and to sleep he needed to be in bed on his own.

He put out the bedside light and deep in the basement the watchers screen went blank.

19

Her warm breath caressed his ear. Dale blinked his bleary eyes in the brightening room and felt his morning beard scratch across the rough cotton sheet as the shifting rays of early morning light continued their attack on the night's gloom. He twisted his head slowly towards the sound of breathing, struggling unwillingly against consciousness as his eyelids fought a losing battle against the wake-up reflex of his befuddled brain. But as his head turned, her perfume caught him unawares. And then his memory jolted, and he remembered where he was, and who he was with; the Italian girl, Nadia.

His mind paused as he tried to recall the previous evening. It had started well enough, with an invitation for dinner, sent by Russell, car provided, no apologies allowed. There was the printed invitation card, left at the front desk with his name on the envelope. He had been surprised but not alarmed and had suspected nothing, not even as the car wended its way through the backstreets to an out of the way, out of the town, hole in the wall sort of restaurant.

They had driven past endless buildings, all uniformly grey and dusty and most of them shot full of holes, as if a manic machine gun artist had been let loose for the weekend. Occasionally the remnants of another half-destroyed building loomed out of the darkness, its shape defying any common sense concept of gravity. Newton would have turned in his grave. Walls, floors and columns were wrenched apart and yet still the buildings remained, stubbornly clinging to the world as if on a movie backdrop. He saw one pitted lattice of concrete reduced to just a single corner, with floors jutting out like CDs in one of those trendy holders. Another had fallen on its side and the floors struck a near vertical pose, reminiscent of toast racks in the English seaside holiday hotels of his youth. The old Peugeot ploughed onwards, lurching around potholes while he clung grimly to the door handle to save himself from being buffeted across the rear seat.

An ancient timber and masonry bridge teetered perilously over what had long since graduated from being the moat around a coastal fort. It was guarded in a perfunctory sort of way and a cursory police torchlight had been poked through the window and a bundle of documents waved in return. But they seemed to be looking for someone else. His young Arab driver, who proudly called himself 'Me Akbar!' drove with his face almost entirely shrouded in a red and white chequered cloth. Underneath, he boasted a pair of piercing, scary eyes and absolutely no English. He had grunted something to the torch-waver and the light had immediately been turned away. Continuing across the bumpy, narrow carriageway they had met a convoy of camouflage-painted jeeps travelling at high speed and had been forced to pull over, and then over again until they were almost teetering on the edge of the rickety parapet. The driver took it all in his stride, muttering furiously as he extricated his car from the ornate iron railings and non-functioning street lamps.

Random near misses with crazed taxis and ancient trucks carting scrap construction materials added to the eventfulness of the journey but even so, it was not exceptional for this city. As they wound around the suburban hinterland of shattered roads and buildings, the landscape became modified, even mellowed. The cityscape of bulky buildings had shrunk to more human proportions but in recompense, the valley roads had abandoned their covering of patchy tarmac and broken lumps of concrete. They were travelling more slowly, and he could easily recall the sight of smaller and smaller houses, each clinging for dear life itself to their personal patch of hillside territory, and all were dark, private and uninviting. The lengthening evening shadows just added to the forbidding spookiness of the place.

As they drew into the outlying communities, a further change had become apparent. The housing was more inhabited and harsh strips of florescent lighting were visible at some of the occasional windows. They stopped in what seemed to be a small-town square, surrounded by closed shops, a derelict gas station and several dilapidated café fronts. The only inhabitants were half a dozen mangy goats, grazing in the rubbish that overflowed from an old drainage channel.

After scanning a nearly invisible horizon 'Me Akbar!' pulled sharply into a narrow alleyway, eventually coming to a halt beside the remnants of an arch with multi-coloured lights draped around an old doorway. Dale eased himself out of the car and, almost before the door was closed, 'Me Akbar!' took off, navigating the dusty passageway at speed. Dale narrowed his eyes against the swirl of debris and realised that the car had been travelling without lights.

The coloured bulbs around the entry gave the restaurant a vaguely festive look, mixed with the seediness of age and decay. The owner and the interior décor of the restaurant had not done much to dispel this impression. Dale was led into a low-ceilinged, dimly-lit restaurant, which sported a number of soft seat booths hidden behind old columns and dingy drapes. Maybe three or four were occupied and he was prodded towards the large one in the corner. There was no one being served at the few open tables scattered around the small dance floor, but this was clearly where the owner and entertainers gathered as stacks of costumes littered two of the tables and papers and invoices were heaped on a third.

The music was Arabic, probably Egyptian or maybe Lebanese. He was learning to tell the difference, but it was still much of a muchness to his Western-European ears. A small stage area occupied a corner, manned by a silk-shirted young lad, a wannabe DJ whose laconic looks belied his sleight of hand with the discs. The sound during the evening had been loud enough to mask any conversation without completely drowning out the speaker, its volume and tempo had both increased as the night wore on towards the dancing hours.

Russell Clark was with another Englishman. They had risen from their corner table, and he greeted Dale in that way only the

English have when they meet long lost friends unexpectedly. A single handshake, without fuss or emotion and all over remarkably quickly. But then, they had reminisced and drank whisky and talked before the others had arrived. He couldn't remember the other Englishman's name. He was younger and very quiet although he recalled that he spoke excellent Arabic. Did he have a Scottish accent? Maybe he'd not been English after all. Dale struggled to remember. Maybe it didn't matter.

The two Italians had arrived together, late enough to meet the protocol of both their own nationality and the local environment. And with them, the wine had started. Heavy red wine imported from Sicily. How they brought it into the country he didn't know. He recognised Bertelli immediately as the camel coated goatee from the airport and with him was a girl. The Italian girl, and she was quite exceptional. She had entered the restaurant robed in a dusty grey coloured abaya, not the traditional black, but had removed it as she walked to the alcove. Her tight jeans and white crossover top made his eyes water for a moment. She was tall and slim, and her jet-black hair cascaded almost to her waist. Russell introduced her as Signorina Ettori. Dale recalled him saying that there were two or three others still to come but they would not wait for them. So, they started eating, drinking the heavy red wine, and dancing.

And what dancing! It had been a convivial evening, with food and drinks aplenty; and dancing, drinking, dancing, drinking and more dancing. The owner joined them for a while and girls appeared everywhere. The other tables filled, and the place became alive. Dale was astonished, it was not what he would normally have expected in a purportedly Islamic country. But he really enjoyed himself and so the offer, when it came, seemed exactly the natural next step for him to follow.

He became aware of the Italian girl murmuring in her sleep, her long black tresses strewn across the pillows. Suddenly he was wide awake, clear headed with all senses tensioned. His ears tuned in with a rising feeling of inner panic as they picked up an unmistakable rustling near the window. He strained his ears in an effort to interpret sounds but was momentarily distracted as the girl snuggled closer. Maybe the noise was just a breeze after all, fumbling its way through the shutters and blinds. The snuggler showed no sign of awakening as her right arm draped across his chest and her head moved down slightly to his shoulder. The feel of her hair against his face fed his memory and the perfume aroma gave way to other sensations as he felt the warmth of her naked body relax against him.

For a moment he felt reassured, almost safe. His mind drifted back again to the previous evening, a bizarre place indeed to meet his friend from years gone by. He turned over the events, the introductions to the other men, Arabic men, in the dark restaurant as they came and went during the evening, the long and circuitous conversations and their final offer to him, in exchange for his help. It was all very low-key, and the mix of nationalities left him wondering just who was in charge. They wanted so very little from him and it had been played as an easy patriotic game, so that the response for him to say 'yes' was never in doubt.

And then the belly dancer entertainment, interspersed with his favourite Lebanese mezze, and its endless humus and tabula. No black shrouds in the restaurant either. He could have been anywhere in fashionable Amman or Cairo. And of course, the girl, the Italian girl who called herself Nadia! Oh, how he loved being able to speak Italian again. They had finally managed to chat to each other, oblivious of their surroundings. Much had been explained to him in these private tête-a-têtes, but he was struggling to remember what it was about.

His brain fought again for order and clarity. The drinks, the heavy red wine, the talking, the offer, then the dancing, and more red wine, more talking, more dancing, more wine, more dancing, before a car (or was it a taxi this time) and Nadia had wrested him away from the never-ending cycle. He couldn't remember their return journey; not even sure it was the same 'Me Akbar!' who drove. Maybe they'd slept on the way. He did remember trying to clear his head with an open window, so maybe not. But the smiles of the hotel staff now flashed in front of his eyes as he recalled how they'd walked brazenly hand in hand through the lobby.

And then finally the taste of heaven in his hotel room. His mind swam with the image, but it was racing forwards too quickly. It was a good memory, and he decided that he must conserve it and revisit it carefully. His Italian girl, why did he keep thinking of her as that and not Nadia? She had been so unexpected and inventive, and yet seemed to know so much about him. How had she known exactly where to touch him? Perhaps, he thought gloomily for a moment, all men were the same. But he banished the thought as unhelpful, definitely unflattering. Instead, he savoured the recollection and felt an involuntary stirring against her thigh.

Pulling aside the sheet he gazed at her smooth lankiness, slim without being thin, her closeness to him exuding a sexual presence, even in sleep, which he was sure he had never experienced quite like this before. He willed it to continue. Lying on her side her visible breast formed a perfect double curve shape. He remembered an artist friend of his explaining that drawing nudes was actually not so difficult. It was simply a matter of getting these two curves right. His eyes wandered and drank in the scene, pausing at the one nipple he could see, with its dark areola and softness as it too slept peacefully, in perfect harmony with its world.

Then his reflexes again seized back control and the adrenaline and inner panic welled into his head. The noise had returned and shifted pitch somehow. He tried to raise his head, but it rebelled, still confused from last night's memories and wine. So, he lay immobile, listening, imagining, in that terrifyingly lucid state where the mind is acutely aware of its surroundings and knows exactly what the senses are communicating, but the body seems unable to respond. He was sure he heard the crunch of dirt under a boot, then the rap of a leather coat against glass. In his thoughts he could see shadows of men in long black leather coats. But his logical mind fought the image – it had been thirty centigrade last night. No one in their right mind wore leather coats this weather. But the sound was unmistakable. There was definitely someone next to the window. His mind rebelled again. What was he thinking, they were on the eighteenth floor?

Then the rustling stopped, abruptly, and without warning a blinding flash of electric blue-white light shut out his sight and seared into his brain.

20

"Mr Connors, as I live and breathe." Russell stood up from the table to greet his old friend. "Sorry for the cloak and dagger ride here. I hope you survived yesterday evening."

"Mr Clark. Good to see you in daylight. I must admit at being surprised to see you there last night. I thought you were in Kazakhstan or somewhere."

Russell laughed, "I was, but I came specially to see you."

Dale rubbed his head and stretched his eyes open.

"Still suffering, I see. Did Nadia manage to get you back to the hotel?"

"Oh yes, she's an … interesting girl." Dale was wary and fully awake now. It was just that his head didn't know it yet. He wondered how much Russell knew about last night. His head was pounding. When the call had come to the hotel at seven o'clock he had been dead to the world; Nadia too. He had left her sleeping soundly and crept out of the room. "Breakfast meeting!" he said unnecessarily to the floor boy as he left the room. Russell's driver had also been a young woman and had brought him through an extremely circuitous route to this room above a bakery.

"Good, good. I thought it would be a good idea to catch up again as soon as possible and go through the logistics of what we agreed." Russell looked at Dale. "But maybe first another strong coffee?"

"Thank you, I will. My head needs to catch up with the day. Actually, there is something you can help me with first."

"Fire away."

"This morning, at some ungodly hour, although I guess it was only five-thirty, someone climbed along the hotel window ledge, into my room and took a flash photograph. It almost blinded me. We were on the eighteenth floor, but by the time I realised what had happened the guy had gone. I looked out of the window but couldn't see anything. The ledge is about a foot wide so he must have been pretty nimble."

Russell frowned. "You say 'we,' were you with Nadia?"

Dale felt himself turning crimson. "Well, yes. How did you know?"

Russell thought for a moment and then burst out laughing. "Sorry, just listening to what you said. I shouldn't laugh, but this sort of thing happens to lots of us. Actually, I think it shows that the local intelligence people regard you as a good partner for the ministries, so they'll be trying to keep up the … er … pressure points, I think they call them."

"Pressure points? Why?" Dale was uneasy.

"Well, blackmail, that sort of thing. I don't think they realise that you're single again."

Dale began to see through the fog. "I guess being divorced has some advantages."

"I wonder why a photograph was so urgent. It's normally a backup. You must have blocked the TV. I can't believe it wouldn't have been working."

Now Dale was completely confused. "TV?" he repeated inanely.

Russell smiled and moved into a practised narrative style. "Yes, they're very much into surveillance and one of their favourite tricks is to mount a tiny camera lens into the face of the hotel's TV controls. You've probably noticed they are all extremely ornate and covered in shiny glass bits, onyx and so on, all around the edge. Well, don't look specially or they may see you, but if you study them from the side, it should be obvious which one is the camera eye. If you want a good trick to confuse them then turn the TV around so you can see it from the writing desk, and then forget to turn it back to the main room again. I'm sure Nadia knows all this too." He paused and grinned. "She's a relatively old hand here, and she obviously took quite a shine to you. I wonder where she put her clothes. Hung them over the TV perhaps?"

A hundred questions flooded into Dale's mind. "So how did you know she was with me? Just because I said 'we' surely isn't enough."

"Oh, we have our moles, or should I say our Italian friends do."

"And …" Dale stumbled through the ravages of his headache, "does she do this sort thing all the time?"

Russell grimaced. "That sounds a tad chauvinist to me" he joked, and with mock gravity pronounced, "it's okay for the guys to live freely but not for the girls, is that it?"

Dale was not amused.

"Okay, okay, depends on what you mean by 'sort of thing'." Russell had an impish grin on his face again. "But if I read your question correctly, then no, I don't think she's had a boyfriend for some time."

"Look" Russell continued seriously, "this is all good, entertaining stuff but I need to brief you properly, so let's start at the beginning, and you can fire away about the entrancing Nadia afterwards. OK?"

"Okay. Let me have some more coffee too."

"Here, help yourself. Now then, the four of us there, apart from you, were Antonio Bertelli, Nadia, Miles and me. You know that I work for UK intelligence. Well, so does Miles, he's a junior level official from London, here for a bit of training … on his first visit actually. Neither of us is supposed to be here officially so please keep that to yourself. The two local guys who called in later in the evening are both runners for Antonio. These Italians tend to throw a party for everything and everyone shows up. It's not usually our style but we were invited and so we came along. We also have some local assets, but you didn't meet them last night.

Antonio is an old friend. He used to be here as part of the Italian Embassy staff and I'm sure everyone knows he was part of their intelligence operation. They probably assume he still is. He's been very helpful to a lot of people and so now he seems to have pretty much a free run of the place as the co-ordinator for the Italian Contractors' Association."

"So, all four of you are part of the intelligence business?" Dale managed to couch his question about Nadia less directly this time.

"Nadia does some work for Antonio occasionally. I wouldn't say she's a fully-fledged intelligence person. Once you become one of them, or us I suppose, you sort of lose the human touch. Everybody and everything is seen with an ulterior motive. I don't think she's like that, although she's been here a while and you'll find her a good person to have around. Antonio is the key person. He's extremely successful here, commercially."

"How does he do that with the sanctions in place?"

"The Italians have a special exemption for humanitarian projects. It goes back decades. All they have to do is make their projects meet the humanitarian criteria and then they're legally okay, strictly speaking. Your irrigation project comes under the same programme, which is why your firm contracts to do it from your Italian office. Isn't that right?" He raised a querying eyebrow. He was guessing but thought it worth a try to see whether he was correct. Most companies here did that.

"That's right" said Dale, "but I hadn't realised that the Italians are so organised about the whole thing. I mean, to have a contractors' association in a county where sanctions are in place is quite forward looking."

"You mean for when sanctions are ended?"

"Yes, these guys will be in the right place at the right time, with all their friends and relationships intact."

"Well, you're exactly right. Not such a disorganised bunch after all, eh? Anyway, let's assume that our Italian friends are mainly interested in commercial gain." Russell made it sound like a disease. "While the Brits, I'm sorry to say, are not. The fact is, we are more concerned about national security issues."

Dale pondered on the fact that, while Britain was pragmatic, Italy was really creative, but his attention was now riveted on his friend. "Last night you asked me to keep my eyes open about what these fellows are doing about their new airport. We'll be starting our programme management job soon so it shouldn't be too difficult."

"And breaking sanctions in the process," added Russell calmly.

"But it comes under the humanitarian programme." Dale felt trapped by Russell's quiet authority. "They said that they were treating it as an extension of the camel farming project and therefore it should be able to secure a UN no-objection."

"And it will, I mean they 'will' approve it," said Russell, "because 'we' will endorse the proposal. Anyway, if you believe the diplomats, the sanctions will all be over soon."

Dale stopped dead in his tracks and looked directly at Russell. "Why should you guys be involved?" he asked.

Russell became serious, no mocking now, his face grew instantly old, and Dale saw a multitude of lines he hadn't noticed before. "Because you and I both know that they don't need a new airport at the moment, so why are they going to all this trouble to build one?"

"But these projects always take years. Isn't it simply good planning?" Dale felt his answer very feeble. Russell's eyebrows became upwardly mobile again. He clearly agreed.

"Okay, I guess not." Dale hurried on "so how can I help you?"

Russell relaxed. "You're in a very good position to help," he started. "All we would like you to do is to do your normal job. Easy? And then to report to us everything that your clients are doing, especially regarding airports. Nothing fancy. Nothing dangerous. A sort of information specialist if you like. The fact is that your job takes you into contact with all the main players here as a matter of course. You don't need to do anything unusual to gain that access. Your projects and business development work are an ideal cover." Almost as soon as he'd said the word, Russell realised it was the wrong thing to say.

"Cover?" Dale looked alarmed. "Are you asking me to spy?"

"No of course not, slip of the tongue. Typo in the brain. Sorry. All we're asking you to do it to tell us what's happening ... be an information specialist."

"Okay, and how do I tell you?" Dale looked curious. "You're not here all the time are you? I can hardly email stuff to you."

"Ah, that's the nice part, for you anyway." Russell tilted his head knowingly. "Your route for information is Bertelli, who can forward things to me very easily. And your route to Bertelli ... is Nadia."

Dale blinked. "Nadia?"

"Problem?"

"No, not at all. Does she know all this?"

"She will when Bertelli tells her today."

Dale sat for a while, letting this piece of information sink into his brain. Well, he thought, things could be a lot worse.

"Tell me," he said. "how did you pick me?"

Russell sighed. He knew Dale of old and also knew that he rarely let things go until he understood the background. Typical engineer, he thought, probably Type A blood too.

"Well, with the new work you've been asked to do you rather picked yourself. But we've had our eye on you for a while, since your third visit in fact."

"Third visit? Why third?" Dale was back into 'why' mode. "That's only a month ago anyway."

"Everyone is allowed two visits for free, without question so to speak. When you come here three times we … how shall I put it … 'take an interest' … is probably the best way to describe it."

"Meaning?"

"We vet you; positively of course. We check with your friends and your employer, company record, internet accounts, that sort of thing."

"Which explains the strange call my ex-wife received? She gave me hell over that; intrusion of privacy, human rights, wayward ex-husband, all sorts of things."

"Ah … another oversight. My apologies. She was apparently quite clear about the fact that you two were no longer … er … cohabiting. Look, it's no big deal. We do this routinely for everyone who comes here."

"Three times or more"

"That's right. And there's something else you should know too. The local intelligence people do exactly the same thing for visitors, even me if they could. Your third visit here instigated a very similar process to ours, except of course they don't use blind telephone calls to check up on things." Russell began hunting though his pockets. "You may be interested to know what they know about you? I apologise for the lack of prose, but it's only a scratch translation". He pulled a piece of paper from his pocket and handed it over.

Dale read rapidly.

Dale Connors – *Professional engineer. Sheffield University – Engineering degree. Global Infrastructure Ltd – International Business Development Manager. 35. Married 9 years to Fran Connors – no children. Travels extensively. Enjoys life when travelling. Potential pressure points? Likes alcohol and women. 1.73m 75kg. No regular sports. Skis occasionally and climbs mountains. UK resident, ex Italian resident, languages English, Italian, some Arabic. Chalk system for bypassing customs.*

Wife – *Fran Connors – social worker – 33 – married 9 years to Dale Connors – no children. Birmingham University – Sociology degree. Works in hospice. UK resident.*

Boss – *Jim Westead – Global Infrastructure Ltd – Partner in charge of International work – 54. Cambridge University – Mathematics degree. UK resident.*

PA – *Harriet Coombes – Global Infrastructure Ltd – 58?*

"And what did I have for breakfast?" He scowled at Russell. "And I'm not married any longer. They've missed my divorce three years ago."

"This is a summary." Russell continued as if Dale hadn't spoken. "The full version is several pages long and is very detailed, although I'm not sure about its accuracy. As you say, they're better at marriage certificates than divorce court rulings. On a lighter note, it seems that your customs avoidance system has been noticed with some admiration!"

"It's not an avoidance system." Dale was becoming agitated. "It's just that they have this crazy habit of changing their customs staff whenever I get near the front of the queue. You have to do something otherwise you'd be there for hours."

"It's okay." Russell spread his hands. "Don't panic. It's not a hanging offence. I'm showing you this, so you realise that they are a serious bunch of people, and we are worried about them.

Very worried in fact. We need your help to keep us informed about what they're doing. I'm assuming that, in the clear light of day, you haven't changed your mind from last night?"

"No, no. It's just that I'm a little overwhelmed by all this information about me. If all you need is information on what I am doing, or rather what the clients are doing from what I can see, then that's not difficult. I guess if Nadia is the point of contact then that sounds pretty good."

Russell smiled. "Okay, thanks. This is where I formally say thank you and then add that there's just the one thing you need to be aware of."

Dale's heart nearly missed a beat.

"Our Italian friends can sometimes be a little slow in passing things over if it compromises their commercial advantage. You must understand that their main interest is money, construction work to be exact. It's one of their major exports and is linked with oil deals and all sorts of things, sanctions or not. They'll be keen to monopolise your information for themselves to retain their commercial advantage. Of course, it will eventually get through to us, but they do have a history of slowing things down sometimes."

"Ah, the cheese principle." Dale laughed. Russell looked blank.

"When I lived in Milan" Dale brightened at the thought of changing the subject, "the Italians organised a British week and invited all sort of products to be put on display, including cheese. Now, can you imagine an Italian accepting that English cheese is the equal of his own? Of course not, so they arranged for their customs people to hold up the truck at the French border, just long enough for the cheese to go off, then they let it through. The newspapers had a field day showing how awful English cheese really was."

"That's a nice story." Russell was not as amused as Dale would have thought. He'd told the story a good few times and it usually merited a better reception. "Maybe you can send me an email through your boss, Jim Westead. Use some sort of common keyword that won't look unusual."

Dale showed his surprise. "I didn't know you knew him."

"I don't … not yet, but my boss does. Old university chaps, or something like that. We called him once, during the vetting. He was very helpful, in fact very complimentary about his globe-trotting business development manager."

Dale sat quietly. Everything seemed to have been thought through. He felt a little manipulated.

"Okay, maybe if I mention something mundane, like sand? Then you'll know that Nadia has a package for Bertelli," he suggested.

"Sand sounds fine. Everything's full of sand here. We'll make a spy out of you yet! Now, before we go, maybe you can fill me in on what your first discussions have been on the airport project. Perhaps we can help you."

Dale accepted more of the bitter, gritty coffee and then recounted his conversation with Ubaid. Russell listened thoughtfully. "Let me think about this," he said, "but while I do that, I must ask you for a favour. Everything you've just repeated to me, can you please also dictate to Nadia, and let's see whether the Italian connection really does work, as Bertelli's so keen to prove. I'm here for a few days. Let's see how quickly they can react."

Dale trawled through his mental list of questions again. "You did say I could ask about Nadia, when you'd finished," he said.

"Sure, no problem." Russell looked quizzical. "What can I tell you that you don't already know."

"Well, firstly, how does an Italian come to be working in the ministry, and what does she do?"

"And secondly?"

"I'll think of something while you are talking, but I'd like to know more about her background please. She's told me some of it, but I'd welcome your professional view."

Russell thought for a while, his eyes slightly glazed. He'd known Dale a long time since they had met in a ski bar. Neither were great skiers, but they were okay and they'd agreed that the environment was enjoyable and so they'd shared a regular skiing holiday away from their wives, neither of whom enjoyed skiing at all. That was years ago when Dale was first married, and Russell's wife was still alive. Since then, they'd found they also shared a common school background, although they were several years apart and, apart from the occasional family holidays in the past, they now kept in touch and met up occasionally in strange places.

He looked around the room. Bare walls, peeling paint, poor furnishings, filthy rug, broken light bulb … but safe, unlike the hotel bar where you couldn't speak without rattling a microphone. He pondered on what he was asking Dale to do. He had come to respect him for his attention to detail and inquisitive nature and he had noted that when Dale was wrestling with a problem, he would drag it around and around like a dog with an old bone, until he found a logical solution. His colleagues apparently always referred to him as Mr Logical and if they made proposals to him which were ill thought out or poorly researched, they would be subjected to lengthy 'why' and 'how' sessions until the logic was clear, and the facts organised and complete. Overall, he thought, he probably could not have a better information specialist. He deserved to know more about Nadia and Russell decided that a little of what he knew would do no harm.

"I believe she has been here about three years," he said. "Her parents were Italian passport holders. I say were, but in fact only her mother is still alive. She comes from an old Italian family near Genoa. Some old palazzo up in the hills. A beautiful olive grove, so I'm told." He stopped for a moment. Enough about the mother, he thought. "Her father was an immigrant to Italy from here, and was killed in an explosion, an oil storage tank I believe, down in the Port of Genoa. He worked for one of the big oil companies." He stopped again. "So, she has a dual nationality and that's what enabled her to start work here," he concluded suddenly.

Russell looked across at Dale, to see whether his explanation was sufficient. He saw no reason to explain the details of Nadia's parents, or to explain her father in greater detail, not yet anyway, but he did need to tell Dale about the change in arrangements at the ministry. Dale was about to jump into the conversation and so he hurried on with his narrative.

"I don't know when she started working for the Italian Intelligence guy." He looked at Dale again and decided he'd have to do better. "But let me see what I can remember about her. She's thirty, I think … ish anyway – used to work years ago for the UN as an interpreter in New York and apart from Arabic and Italian, she speaks very good English, French, German, Dutch, Spanish and some Russian. The Italians managed to get her employed in the Ministry of Construction, so she has a natural link to Bertelli in the contracting area, which works very well and raises no suspicion. He's always in and out of their ministries looking for contracts, so meeting her isn't difficult. Also, the ministries tend to be relatively bug-free, unless they have meetings. You should see their meeting rooms, they're like sound stages. Be careful!"

Dale's mind sprinted through his recent conversations with Ubaid. He would do so again in more detail later. It had not occurred to him that they would monitor their own senior people.

"Her biggest asset is her language ability and I guess this is why she's recently been switched part time to the Ministry of Agriculture, to be your driver. I also guess that the Security people, Fayez in particular, will have their hooks into her to tell them exactly what you two are up to." He paused and looked at Dale a little slyly.

Dale held up his hands. "Hold on a minute" he said, "just say that again. Are you saying that she will be my driver from now on?"

Russell put on his best schoolboy ear to ear grin. "She already is my friend. You just didn't recognise her when she collected you at the airport. These black abayas are wonderful disguises. You must have heard the story of that BBC news reporter, quite a big guy actually, dressing in one to cross the border. Got away with it too."

Dale was speechless. "Are you saying that the girl who picked me up at the airport was Nadia? But she had such poor English!" he exclaimed.

"Just part of the job to play dumb, and anyway, she would have known that the car was bugged. She wouldn't want to have an open discussion in English there. I thought she would have told you on the way back to the hotel last night." He laughed. "You must have had other more interesting things to talk about!"

Dale was past feeling embarrassed about others knowing of his evening. He simply could not believe what he was hearing. How could a girl look so different? Then he cast his mind back to the airport and recalled the incidents before Nadia had come over to him. Why had he felt she looked familiar, even though he had only caught a glance at her eyes? His mind raked back to the customs queue and suddenly it came to him. Of course, the camel-coated man who he'd met last night; introduced as Bertelli; and Bertelli had stood talking to the girls by the barrier. That must be why he thought Nadia had looked familiar. His logical mind relaxed a little. Order in life was such a comfort. He settled back into his seat and smiled.

"You look as if you've just worked something out." Russell was scrutinising his face carefully.

"I have" said Dale, "Bertelli was on the same plane as me and met Nadia at the airport before she picked me up."

"Well done" said Russell, clapping his hands gently in mock admiration, "but you missed the fact that Miles and I were also on the same flight. I'm afraid we were at the back of the plane. We can't afford to keep up with you businessmen." He paused. "which reminds me," he said, "tell me about losing your computer at the airport."

Dale blinked. "How did you know about that?" he said.

"Bertelli told me." He paused again. "We wondered whether they had doctored it while it was out of your sight."

"Doctored?" Dale looked alarmed. "You mean bugged?"

"Well, could be anything really, probably a tracking device and maybe a sound bug. We should check but not remove it. Better to let them think they have you under surveillance."

"You sound amazingly casual about it!" Dale was beginning to feel a little out of his depth.

"Just par for the course. Next time I see you let's have a look and be sure. A tracking device is okay. They will know where you are anyway, but sound can be tricky. We need to dampen the reception without giving them the impression that it's not working." He smiled. "Don't worry about it" he grinned "you get used to being careful here."

21

Nadia still refused to speak English in the car. Her paranoia about the listeners was absolute and she was reluctant to follow Dale's suggestion that they simply disable the recorder. It wasn't especially well hidden, and a loose wire would not be difficult to arrange, but Nadia's argument was that they should save that ploy for a real emergency.

Italian was their private, non-work language of choice. It was Nadia's mother tongue and Dale's fluency enabled him to match his temperament to her company. He was unhappy to treat Nadia merely as a seconded employee and equally careful not to let his personal feelings spread too much into this work life. Using Italian for private times helped. It was like a secret affair when they switched languages and their mood and demeanour altered perceptibly so that anyone near them could sense the change too; but they didn't care. He wrestled with the fact that no one had had this effect on him for a long time, in fact 'for ever' if he were to be honest. Certainly, his six-year marriage to Fran had never instilled this type of energy and passion, not even when they were courting. It had been a very practical relationship; pure business really, and 'business' was the word he generally used to describe it.

He had hoped that things would improve when they married. Fran had promised that marriage would liberate her, and he had believed her. It had not and when she had started work in a hospice the effect of being with terminally ill people had imposed a further remoteness of her when she was with Dale. He felt admiration for what Fran had chosen to do but it was as if she had finally found her purpose in life and so, in the end they had recognised that they were going in completely different directions.

A couple of days after Dale's revelation about the true identity of his driver he asked Nadia to take him to the camel ranch site.

Hussein came along too. It seemed that there were problems with pedigree camels being chased by neighbouring tribes and the Minister wanted him to see for himself and a first-hand report made, recommending action. Camel security was evidently vital when expensive personal assets were at stake.

As before, visibility was low and the wind stinging. Progress on the fence was good and there seemed to be a better spirit and determination to get things done. The news of the recent payments must have filtered down well into the ranks. It was amazing what money could do. Dale's earlier assurance to the contractors about payment had had no effect on its own. However, the first foreign currency payment of the new deal, struck on his previous visit with Ubaid, had arrived the week before he had departed from the UK, and this had provided inspiration for even the most recalcitrant of contractors.

The first batch of trial camel tracking devices had been air-freighted to the project and already fixed to the guinea pigs, or GPs as the ten chosen camels were called. Dale was looking forward to seeing how they worked. They drove around the perimeter fence and after a while Dale saw the problem. The temporary fence had been flattened, but not by a camel. An ancient red Nissan pick-up straddled the fence line like a poacher's assistant holding down the barbed wire barrier for his boss. Two young lads were chasing a camel with long sticks, trying to herd it through the gap. They looked up as Dale's Peugeot roared up to them. Hussein leapt from the car and screamed in Arabic. The teenagers ran to the pick-up and an old man at the wheel struggled into a sitting position, fumbled to start the engine and attempted to extricate the front wheels from the fence. Hussein grabbed the door handle and tried to pull the driver from the cab, but the two youngsters joined the fray and Hussein was forced to divert his attention. Suddenly he stopped. "What did you say?" he shouted to the old man.

The man repeated himself and a ferocious argument ensued. Finally, Hussein backed away, leaving a torrent of Arabic vitriol behind him for the threesome to digest. The old man crashed the gears, and the pick-up took off into the desert. The camel had stopped to pull at a barren tuft of brown vegetation and Dale saw that round its neck hung a small black box with a tiny flashing red light. This was one of the ten, an expensive one.

"And?" he waited for Hussein to explain. Nadia sat in the front of the car, silently listening.

"He says he is being paid to help camels escape" Hussein said.

"And who's paying him?"

Hussein paused. "He says our Minister Mohammed. I told him to go and drink camel's piss, but he still kept to his story. Anyway, they've gone now. I don't think they will come back. I told them we worked for Fayez and his security bunch. No one messes with them."

Dale sensed there was more to this than met the eye. He first called the contractors on his mobile to come and mend the fence and then asked Hussein what he thought was behind the strange statement, assuming that someone in the ministry was involved, maybe Mohammed, maybe not.

Hussein was reticent about voicing an opinion and Dale didn't want to press him. He mumbled and prevaricated and clearly knew more than he was willing to divulge. Thankfully, the contractors arrived, and Hussein took the opportunity to join their group, to supervise the fence repair. He almost jumped out of the car and Dale was happy to let him go.

Nadia joined the group and spoke in English so that all could hear. "Would you like to visit the old fort on the way back? It's still a bit of a tourist place, although we don't get many tourists these days. There used to be local artisans working there, all geared up for the foreigners to buy things. There are still a few but it's mainly cafés now."

"Sure, that would be a good idea. Maybe we can get some coffee there?" Dale's mind was still a long way from forts and tourist ventures but the chance to spend a few minutes with Nadia had compelling appeal. He needed to think through the revelation about the Nissan trio and sometime in the car would do him good. They tidied up some admin with the contractors and then drove off towards the North, driving through a seemingly interminable dust cloud.

After fifteen minutes or so they saw a sight, on a rise about a mile away, which literally took Dale's breath away. It was as if a medieval king had transplanted his vision of Camelot onto a distant hill in the desert. Its battlements stuck out against the now clear sky and its high stone walls seemed to glow with a reddish tinge. Nadia spoke slowly and in English, describing the fort's 500-year heritage and its more recent conversion as a tourist earner for the people. To Dale's fevered imagination she was not talking to him but rather to some other person sitting in the car. He thought of the tape recorder being downloaded sometime later. They pulled into a disorderly parking area between an old truck and a closed white van and stopped.

"Come," commanded Nadia in an obviously clear and loud voice "I will show you some of our history," and she led Dale on a tour around the outer walls. As they approached the fort she switched to Italian, and their heads moved together in more intimate conversation. "We're now out of earshot" Nadia confided, "I recognised that white van where we parked. They'll be sitting inside with their cameras and directional microphones, but they won't hear anything in this wind. They also won't follow us as it's too open here."

"And all that talk about history in the car?"

"Just for the tape. These guys have gone more techno than is good for them and spend all their time watching and recording, but they lack the proper resources to transcribe the tapes, even less to understand what's being said. They don't have automatic computer transcription yet. I believe it's coming. In the meantime, they rely on good English speakers to produce Arabic summaries of their most interesting targets. The rest are consigned to storage."

"And am I interesting?"

"To me or them?"

"Both I guess."

"To them you are on their new acquisitions list. They've asked you to help with their airport project and they'll want to listen and translate what you say for a week or two, so it's best to keep English conversations above board. After a week they'll become lazy and only sample a few phrases now and again."

"And to you?" Dale persisted.

"I'll show you," Nadia smiled "come and have some coffee."

They wandered around the entire outer walls and entered the old, fortified gateway. The disused gates hung in a dejected state and a few urchins played in the dust. Inside the walls, the ground floor comprised a partly roofed, partly tented annular courtyard surrounding some sort of solid inner core structure and surrounded by columns and crypt-like open fronted rooms which Nadia explained had once been workshops for carpenters, blacksmiths, and other tradesmen, along with stables and storage areas to guard against siege. The old workshops had more recently been turned into tourist shops but were now scruffy caves in the old masonry, inhabited by a collection of ancient local characters who looked as if time had stood still while they grew old.

They completed their inner encirclement of the fort and sat at a small café just inside the main entrance, sipping more of the gritty coffee. "I have something else to show you," Nadia murmured conspiratorially. "The fort used to be an upmarket tourist hotel, very exclusive. There are eight suites and on the roof there's a swimming pool and restaurant. The pool isn't used anymore and the hotel is not open to regular visitors. It's been turned into eight apartments, one for each of the principal ministries."

"And?" Dale was quizzical.

"And, I have the key to Minister Mohammed's apartment. He was insistent this morning that I show you round and look after you. In fact, he suggested it wasn't necessary to visit the camel fence until later today."

"Was this anything to do with the old man at the fence? Maybe Mohammed wanted an extra delay."

Nadia frowned. "There's something else," she said. "I was listening to the old man when he argued with Hussein. You weren't told the whole story. The old man was claiming to be a relative of Mohammed. He told Hussein that Mohammed wasn't getting his fair share out of the financial fees on the project and wanted to increase the contract value. Helping our Finance Minister's camels escape is a great way to get more funds and it also make Ubaid's oversight of the project look poor too. Apparently, it was he who insisted on the type of fence being constructed."

To Dale it seemed all too plausible, too pat an explanation, but then often the simplest explanation turned out to be true. He filed it away for future thought as they rose from the table and walked into the dark interior of the fort, this time heading directly through an imposing stone archway near the very centre of the edifice. They found themselves in a surprisingly spacious circular atrium where a broad staircase wound leisurely upwards around the outer wall. The stone balustrade was smooth and polished by the hands of generations. There were no windows apart from the central skylight, but in the centre of the chamber, beneath the rooftop glass hung a huge, ancient brass chandelier. It was unlit and dusty, and several bats had made it their home.

"Come," Nadia linked arms with Dale and directed his staring eyes away from the cavernous emptiness. Dale followed her up the spiral to the first intermediate landing, suspended in mid-flight, their feet echoing on the worn steps. They paused to peer into the void, which had become darker and darker as they climbed. The two guards at the main entrance took no notice. All was silent. Dale felt his heart pulsing with apprehension. The quietness was uncanny. They continued to the upper landing, a circular corridor behind ornamented columns facing the inner cavern. As they moved around the circle, every so often a stylishly carved but very solid doorway indicated a private suite. Nadia stopped at No 7, a complicated looking small key in her hand. Dale's heart was now thudding so much that he worried that Nadia must hear it. But she was concentrating on the lock. It suddenly gave way with an echoing clunk and the heavy dark wood door swung open.

They almost fell into the apartment and as the door closed Nadia turned, took his right hand, and placed it over her heart. It was pounding too. He laughed and did likewise and for a moment they stood in the semi-darkness of the entranceway in complete symmetry, hands on hearts and eyes locked. Their smiling faces drew together, and Nadia nuzzled her moist lips against his nose, then along his upper lip and finally tugged playfully at his lower lip with her teeth.

Dale suddenly came to life. "Is this place empty?" he asked almost in a whisper.

She nodded.

"Have you been here before?" He mentally kicked himself at asking such an obvious question.

"Only once, and not like this," she spoke hoarsely. "I came with the Minister and some of his guests a couple of months ago. He had a private meeting here. I was his interpreter." She indicated an archway to Dale's right. "Come," she said and took his hand again, stopping only to pull the security lock across the door.

The entrance opened into a spectacular sitting area, large and opulent with outer windows leading onto a private terrace. Dale now understood why the apartments were not visible from the ground below. He realised too that Nadia was gripping his hand with both of hers. He turned and placed his hand on her heart again. "My turn to say 'come'," he said as her face melted into his and they fell together onto the gold coloured, capacious leather sofa. Within seconds Nadia had shrugged off her black shrouds and lay before him in the tightest tee shirt Dale had ever seen. His eyes trawled her body appreciatively, from her perfectly formed breasts and hardened nipples, which pressed precociously against the 'C' and the 'A' of the famous trademark, down to the slim indentation of her stomach. He recalled the night in the hotel and his mind swam through the satisfying memory, drinking all the way.

"No cameras here" she whispered, "and no sound recorders either!" Nadia pulled at Dale's shirt and in a moment they were rolling playfully along the gargantuan sofa, clothes falling and breathing quickening as they explored each other, delighted at the opportunity to indulge themselves, safe in the knowledge that they were truly alone. There was no faking, just pure enjoyment. Dale was in heaven again as Nadia systematically worked her way around every sensitive part of his body. He did his best to reciprocate but felt he was taking part in a masterclass. He nuzzled against her black pubic hair and pulled gently with his mouth. She tasted of honey and poured wetness upon wetness around his passionate tongue. Nadia arched her back and whimpered as her own tongue flitted around his special place. Dale thought he was going to burst as Nadia panted "I want you in me, now, now, now!" They turned and their mad, frenzied coupling culminated in a gasping, energetic climax before they collapsed, drained of adrenaline and exhausted, side by side in the centre of the huge sofa.

"Don't speak" murmured Nadia, "and don't move. Just stay here with me for a moment, please."

22

Grant Andrews looked across the smoky room and headed towards the bar. His eyes and ears adjusted to the dim light while the sultry music beat urgently around him. He knew that the Al Hambra was owned and managed by the Ministry of Security, and he had been told that this was a practice ground for their surveillance teams. Two alcoves were occupied by small groups of Arabs talking in hushed tones, their heads bent forward to overcome the background barrage of sound. A handful of individuals sat around the room. At one end of the bar two foreigners sat on tall stools, jars of beer in front of them on the counter. They were large men and looked mid-European, or maybe Russian. They were deep in conversation and as he drew closer, he realised they were speaking German. He decided to leave them alone and pulled up a stool near the centre of the long bar. He ordered a small beer. After a few seconds he sensed a movement to his right and turning he saw that a young Arab man had picked up his own beer and was moving along the counter towards him.

"You're the new Project Manager for the camel project." The young man had obviously had a few beers already. He swayed slightly and sat down on the adjacent stool.

Grant looked at him. He had no idea who he was. "That's right," he said "I started a few weeks ago. Do you know the project?"

"Oh yes. Part of the Ruler's great new tourism idea." His cynicism was apparent, even through his stilted English.

Grant thought it best to humour him for a while and took him through a rapid summary of progress. "I'm sorry" he said after a while, "I didn't catch your name."

"Jamil, just call me Jamil."

An alarm bell began to ring in Grant's head. "You didn't sound too much in favour of the project," he said.

"It's just another way to spend oil money and recover it from tourists. Who wants tourists? Just a lot of foreigners. Most foreigners are whores anyway. Businessmen certainly are. Sell themselves all the time." With that Jamil called for two more beers.

Grant recalled his briefing by Dale. He decided to make certain. "Aren't you Jamil Shakari?" he asked.

Jamil beamed at the recognition.

"You must find us foreigners very boring people," Grant said. "All we do is work, work, work. Maybe I don't know where to go. What do you suggest for real entertainment?"

"Cairo or Milan" was the instant reply. Grant was a little taken aback.

"Girls!" confided Jamil. "Very good in Milan, very cheap in Cairo."

"Well," said Grant, "I agree about Milan, but I've never been to Cairo."

Jamil put his arm around his new friend's shoulders and breathed beer fumes into his face. "I'll take you," he slurred happily. "I had a wonderful visit to Milan earlier this year. Wonderful place, wonderful girls."

Grant decided he'd better join the party and talked about some of his own exploits in Eastern Europe and the Far East. Jamil was enraptured and pressed for more and more details. Three beers later they had moved to an alcove and Grant had learnt all the sordid details about Jamil's trip to Milan, London, Paris and Frankfurt. Apparently, he had not indulged himself in Manchester as he thought it too poor and the girls too ugly. Jamil had found an appreciative audience in Grant but after four hours, still more beers and various local concoctions he had exhausted his repertoire and had fallen asleep. Grant spoke to the barman and asked him what he should do.

"He has his own car and driver outside. I'll give him a call. Do you want a ride too?"

23

To any onlooker she was merely another woman shrouded in black waiting for the bakery to open. The others in the small crowd were patient too, chattering quietly amongst themselves. In the window above she saw his face again. He had arrived some time ago, but she dared not join him yet.

The bakery finally opened its doors and the women rose as one, in an orderly manner, without the need for a formal queue. Nadia followed the crowd towards the shop but, with a sidestep melted into the adjacent alleyway. A few seconds later she climbed the stairs to the waiting open door. Russell was sitting patiently. "What kept you?" He grinned and held up his hands to stop her response. "Actually, you blend in pretty well."

Nadia closed the door quietly and pulled up a chair. "Why do you live in this out of way place?" she countered, although she knew the answer. The owner was a friend, and friends were valuable these days. "It takes me ages to get here."

Russell shrugged. "Have some tea" he paused, "I brought it with me. You should try some, it comes from Northern India. I became an addict to this particular type when I lived there for a while."

Nadia dutifully tried the proffered tea but tuned out as Russell continued his homily about the tea's origins.

"Your summary to Bertelli was very interesting" he continued, as if not sure where to start. "You have a knack of writing good English. That's something very rare these days."

Nadia was not in the mood for small talk. "We must do some planning, quickly," she tried to kick start the conversation into something tangible

"Okay," Russell could sense her tenseness but still lapsed into his habitual courtroom style. "You say that Dale has been asked to provide plans for certain European airport security systems so that they can update the airport system here."

"That's right. It all seems pretty innocuous so far. It's the sort of copycat engineering that goes on all round the world."

"And you say that the initiative for this came from their interest in the camel ranch security. Seems an odd link."

"Maybe, but the technical stuff isn't the issue. It's the fact that Dale is well regarded and seen as honest and unconnected with your people. So far, they've asked five firms to provide similar sorts of details, for different types of facilities round the world." She added. "From what I see, they're only really interested in Dale's firm at the moment. That was in my report too."

Russell spread his hands again, as if calming the waters. "I know." His voice was at its smoothest. "Sorry to sound a bit slow so let me move on. What I really need to do is to brief you on what we think about all this. We are firmly of the view that, how shall I put it, all is not as it seems."

Nadia's sense of frustration at some of the British phraseology got the better of her. Why do they always beat around the damn bush, she thought, but she said nothing and waited quietly.

"You remember the port incident in Yemen?" He appeared intent on another side-track.

"Yes of course."

"Well, we've traced the source of the explosive. It came through East Germany and two of the CIS states. It was made in Egypt"

"So?"

"The Egyptian connection has a brother who works in the Ministry of Construction. It was funded through there. So, we're concerned" he continued, "very concerned."

He was now in his stride. "This connection proved interesting for some other reasons too. You recall the Olympics incident in Atlanta?"

"Sure."

"Well, the same route was used for the explosive there. In fact, there are another dozen or so likely links which are being followed up at the moment"

"So how does this affect Dale's programme?" Nadia was now alert, all thoughts about beating and bushes relegated to the past.

"All these incidents weren't simply random events. They were wake up calls, and loud ones too. But particularly they were all extremely well researched and meticulously planned. Where did they get the plans for the port? When you look at the port here it bears a striking resemblance to the port in Yemen. Is this really a coincidence?" He paused. "When you look at the sports complex here at the university, it bears a striking resemblance to the basketball venue in Atlanta, before it was demolished," he added. "We simply want to know what Dale is really bringing into the county. Would it have a use? And when? We think the ministry may be using his project to bring in their research as part of an otherwise innocuous engineering package, without him being aware of it himself."

"Look at the target facilities." He spread out a list on the small table. "They're exclusively airports and they are all major hubs with direct intercontinental flights to just about anywhere. We think they're planning a hit on one of these airports and are using the engineering drawings as research material. Moreover, his project here is for the master planning of the whole cargo handing area upgrade, in addition to the security systems. We need to know more about what he's being asked to do by the ministry."

Nadia's mind churned at the possibilities being laid out before her. "But why go to all this trouble?" she said, "there must be an easier way to obtain plans without paying foreign companies to come and build a replica."

"Not really." Russell turned to face her. "Think about it, any visiting Arab nationals are photographed and tracked ad nauseam in Europe, especially around an airport. In short, they stick out like a sore thumb and can't move without a tail. European firms can pretty much wander about at will, and there are enough commercial pressures and vested interests available to secure whatever plans they need."

"And what happens when they come here?"

"Well, although foreign firms coming here are also photographed and followed, it's not by us. We are not here officially at the moment and certainly don't have the assets in place to track our own nationals." He paused. "What we need is to know what is behind these requests."

Nadia frowned. "But doesn't this go against what you told him last time you met? You told him specifically that all you wanted him to do was to report on what the Agriculture Ministry was asking him to do. Couldn't finding out any more place him in danger, let alone his team?"

"So, you will have to find out without him knowing." Russell's voice was chill. "You seem to be very close to him, from what I've seen anyway. I can't imagine it will be too difficult to pump him for more information."

"My private life!" she started to exclaim.

"Is close to my heart," finished Russell. "Don't screw it up, if you'll excuse the pun." He smiled at his own rather feeble joke. "Have some more tea," he said.

24

Fayez thumbed through the photos. Since their initial shot of the couple in the hotel room they had been targeting them systematically. The first few of the new group of prints showed Dale and Nadia at the fort, drinking coffee and chatting in the café. He asked about sound. They had the car's recording and some of the later conversation, but the van had been parked too far away and the recording was indistinct. What they had heard was just work related and personal chatter. It seemed that Nadia had been taking Dale on a tourist visit, and history had been the main theme. Nothing to worry about. But then the photos showed Nadia and Dale rising from the table and wandering off into the depths of the fort. The couple had walked into the dark interior and simply disappeared.

"No more photos?" Fayez asked curiously.

"They went into the old fort, what used to be the hotel" explained Fuad. "We have no cameras working in there. It seems they were there as guests of the Minister. They were using his own personal suite."

"Mohammed?" quizzed Fayez, "Minister of Agriculture?"

"Yes."

"Ah well, at least we know where they were. Was there nothing from the TV camera either?"

"No. The girl seems to be wise to that and covers it with something every time they use a hotel room. That was why we used a real camera the first time they were together. But in any case, there's nothing in the Minister's personal rooms at the fort. He has them swept quite often. All the ministers do. They're some of the few no-go areas we have for cameras."

Fayez settled back into his leather chair, thinking of his own minister's apartment at the fort and the occasions when he had been able to borrow it to impress certain people. He swivelled again in the chair. It had been specially imported from England years ago as an antique. It was his pride and joy and gave him even more of a sense of power than he already enjoyed. He loved information and revelled in knowing the inanest details about people. His memory was like a diary. Even a verbal report was stored away in his cavernous mind, filed according to the messenger and date of its creation. His favourite pastime was to trawl his memory for some long-forgotten piece of minutiae and present it, and its relevance, to his astonished staff. Fuad was used to this and took it in his stride, but it nevertheless raised his own admiration for the old man's abilities.

"Okay, add these to the file," instructed Fayez. "One day soon we will have a little chat with Mr Dale, and I am sure he'll be most helpful for us."

25

Friday was upon them and with it the declared day of rest for the ministries. Dale was keen to visit Raheem again and to take some more of the books and tapes to him that he had promised. It also gave him a reason to travel with Nadia. He saw no reason for secrecy and so they arranged to meet Raheem at the ministry and use the project car for the visit. As they drove to the beach hotel Raheem chatted relentlessly. Nadia listened quietly. A small crowd of children ran from Raheem's villa as the car drew up. Dale recognised Naomi but Ibrahim could have been any of the three or four young lads racing round the scrub. Salma welcomed them into the house, chatting easily with Nadia as they entered. Dale carried a large bag of books and tapes and set them out on the low table in the sitting area. Raheem could hardly contain himself. The books were opened and examined; the children summoned to admire the treasure trove. Even Salma couldn't escape the prevailing enthusiasm and Raheem insisted on reading parts of the books which caught his attention.

"Mr Dale," he hopped from foot to foot, almost overcome by emotion "how can I thank you?"

Dale sat happily reading to Ibrahim. He was determined not to accept any payment. "I'm just happy to be able to help," he said rather lamely. "Tell me how your family's doing in Palestine. Have you heard any more recently?" As Raheem launched into a diatribe about the injustices being perpetrated against his kinsmen Dale listened politely. It seemed that it was a repeat of the previous discussions, but he let Raheem vent his anger in talk. Maybe it would help, he thought. Raheem continued in full flood as Salma brought out food and it was only when she asked him to invite in the children that he packed away his vitriol and changed the topic back to education. All the children joined them to eat.

Dale was anxious to know where they all came from. "Are they all Palestinians?" he asked.

"Absolutely," said Raheem, lapsing into the inevitable political clichés. "These children represent the future for us exiles, and your books will help educate a new fighting force for liberty."

"A fighting force?" Dale was puzzled how the 'Mr Men' series could help produce freedom fighters.

"Of course," Raheem was undeterred. "Freedom is the key for the future. I don't mean that the children will become gunmen," he added hurriedly. "They will fight their cause with words and language. Their strength will be their learning. Ibrahim will be a great lawyer one day."

Nadia was impressed by Dale's obvious empathy with Raheem's family and as the evening wore on and the books were read and re-read aloud to the eager youngsters it became evident that there was genuine warmth between them. But she worried about what her various lords and masters would make of it all. Befriending Palestinians was risky. It could be regarded well or badly depending on the minister involved and her Italian and British masters may well view Dale's sympathies with concern. She pondered on the likely re-vetting that would be necessary but at the same time it was obvious that Dale's intentions were well meaning, genuine and certainly matched the humanitarian criteria set down by the UN.

The dinner was as long and convivial as previously and by the time they had finished the ever-present white van's occupants had long given up listening and were fast asleep. Dale and Nadia headed back for the hotel where they joined the other foreigners in the bar, Nadia leaving her city black inside the car. Inevitably, they gravitated to Dale's room as the evening wore on, being careful to drape clothes over the TV and ensuring all the windows were closed and locked. Nadia didn't stay overnight, not quite.

Fayez listened to the tape they intended to pass on to Abdullah. The microphone must have been close to the corner of the room where Dale was reading from the children's books as the sound quality was excellent. Fayez saw no problem in Dale's allegiance with Raheem's family, on the contrary he thought it showed Dale's concern for people under oppression and therefore that he would be more helpful in ensuring the success of Abdullah's plans. He settled back in his old swivel chair and pondered the outcome of the recent surveillance. This Dale character seemed too good to be true. A real person caring for other real people. If Dale continued like this, he thought, he wouldn't need to maintain the current level of watchers. An occasional random check would suffice.

Bertelli's men also compared notes. They had no tape and no video and had only seen Dale and Nadia enter the villa. To them it looked a suspicious meeting, and they did not like suspicious meetings. More to the point, they had not enjoyed sitting out in the beach area. It was too exposed, and they had had to share their roadside with an old white van that they knew was part of Fayez's empire. Overall, they were inclined to put a negative mark against Dale, if only on the grounds that he made their life uncomfortable. All local liaisons were a problem in their mind and links to penniless refugees could only be cause for grief.

26

It was evening and Dale and Nadia were in the rooms above the bakery. It was three days since the visit to Raheem's family and Russell's face was grave.

"Your Palestinian friends are causing a few ructions." He had decided to play the stern employer for a while. "Or more precisely your visit to Raheem's family has raised a few eyebrows back home."

"So, tell me more," said Dale resignedly, "Nadia warned me this might happen."

"Perceptive young lady. Our lords and masters in the UK are very concerned about publicity and the negative image these sorts of visits can have if the media get hold of things. Fraternising with possible terrorists, that sort of thing."

Dale was incredulous. "Publicity? Here?" he asked, "do they know the degree of paranoia about the media and the depths of non-publicity that exist here?"

"Yeah, yeah, I know; but perceptions are everything I'm afraid. The bottom line is that they think that your relationship with Raheem is high risk, given what we've asked you to do, as it draws the attention of the security people more than we would like. On the other hand, they think it may actually endear yourself to the local powers that be, so on that basis they're willing to let things ride and see what happens. They also expect that Fayez and his boys will likely see it as a good thing that you are supportive of the common man, and especially of poor political refugees at that. So, on balance no real harm done and I guess my brief is now to take you through the potential hazards and provide an experienced warning to you." Russell smiled helplessly. "I know this sounds patronising, especially for someone as widely travelled as you, but officially I have to go through all the possible downsides that could occur, approaches to watch for, all that sort of thing. The trouble is that most are obvious and the people in the UK tend to forget that things are much more immediate on the ground here. You tend to see and react to events without being told. It's all part of working in these sorts of places. So" he added, "as a friend, all I would simply say is, 'be careful not to overstep the mark and think about everything you do before you do it.' Okay, homily over for today!"

But Dale was still quizzical. "All right, I realise the risks" he said, "but tell me more about the individual parties, the Italians for instance, as well as our famous people in the UK."

"Well, the Italians were really quite interesting. Firstly, their field people were pretty upset. It seems they had to share the only available shade under a tree with a couple of Fayez's lads, and it seems that Fayez had sound in place, and they didn't. They felt very exposed, and probably inadequate too; not happy at all and so their report was less than positive, as you might imagine. Fortunately, Bertelli and their people in Italy took a more pragmatic view. They knew that local contacts were always useful and they credit themselves with more local experience than they probably deserve, so they tended to see these incidents as well meant and non-threatening. Of course, Nadia also had the chance to brief Bertelli, so in the end the whole visit was placed in a better perspective."

Dale was surprised. "I hadn't even imagined we were watched at all. Do you people have the resources to do this to everyone?"

"Only the ones our local friends are really interested in, but my guess is that the airport is much more important than we realise. So, they're checking you out, and we're checking the checking, so to speak."

"For what?" Dale was still curious.

"Security breaches, unfriendly contacts, hostile views, inappropriate opinions and of course potential pressure points, opportunities for blackmail if you like. Forewarned is forearmed when it comes to blackmail. As it is, I think your visits with Raheem and his family are being seen for what they are, friendly and generous; humanitarian if you like."

Nadia joined the discussion. "You mean to say that they had a microphone in the beach villa? How could they arrange that? I thought all the remaining hotel staff were Palestinian. They're hardly going to agree to install something there."

Russell was non-committal. "They don't have to. It was probably a give-away, a sort of mini Trojan Horse" he said, "maybe a gift for one of the children, maybe in some food packaging, that sort of thing. These things are very small. Can be stuck to almost anything with a tiny battery to last for days. As I say, be careful. Think before you speak."

"Is there any way of checking, sort of sweeping the room?"

"Sure, but it looks rather obvious if you go around with a box and antenna."

"So how did they know we were going to Raheem's on that day?"

Russell smiled. "Not difficult," he said. "Raheem isn't exactly secretive about his new English friend and the children's books are big news in the Palestinian families. On Thursday he was telling anyone who would listen that you were going there the next day."

"Well, I guess we can use that to our advantage another time," Dale mused.

"Exactly, surveillance really only works when the subject is unaware. As soon as you know, you can play the game right back to them." Russell smiled. "You're learning quickly, my friend."

27

Bertelli was in full flow, both hands gesticulating while the scrambled line in the contractors' association was clamped under his chin. He hated the implication that his judgement was not sound. "No, I don't think for a minute she's sympathetic to the terrorist cause" he shouted, "she has the hots for him and he's being kind and friendly to a Palestinian family. He brought them a pile of children's books. That's all."

The voice on the other end of the phone clearly had other ideas.

"Did I vet the story tapes for hidden messages? What do you think I am, a magician?"

The Italian voice on the phone was curt.

Bertelli launched into more hand waving. "Did the local guys vet the tapes? I have no idea, except that they have recordings of the whole meeting and any extract of tapes that were played will show up. I can't imagine their faces when they listen to stories about witches and wizards. Where exactly are all these crazy ideas coming from?"

Again, the mobile droned in his ear. He held it at a distance before replying.

"Your external consulting firm. I might have guessed. They should come and look for themselves."

The voice was abrupt and short.

Bertelli, frowned before answering, in as measured a way as he could. "Do I think she's fallen for the Brit? Yes, I do. Do I think that this clouds her judgement? No, I don't. Absolutely not. She's professional and I trust her. We've worked together for years."

The phone chattered again.

Bertelli held his hand over his mouth and distanced himself from the handset "Sorry, the line is breaking up. Can't hear you. Have to talk later." He let the Romans ramble on for a while and then quietly broke the link.

"Damned consultants" he grumbled, "they read too many books."

28

Ubaid was in sombre mood. It was mid-afternoon and the heat outside was oppressive. In the conference room the air conditioning chewed at the warm moisture in a vain attempt to make the room habitable. For some reason it had been switched off all day. Ubaid sweated and shuffled about while Dale took him through his report on the fence intrusion before suddenly calling a halt and transferring the meeting to his office.

It crossed Dale's mind that whereas the conference room discussion was certainly recorded, maybe a minister's own office was exempt. Nevertheless, circumspection was the order of the day. His report on the camels had carefully mentioned only that they had found the trio of people trying to herd camels through a gap in the fence. He recounted the old man's remonstrations before disappearing into the desert but had not detailed the conversation with Hussein and even less the added translation provided by Nadia. Ubaid's reaction had been to mumble and curse and then, as Hussein had predicted, he had raised the issue about a more secure structure, going back to the design first recommended by Dale's engineers. Dale was happy to oblige and had the contractor's prices already to hand. Ubaid had clearly done his homework too as he had a pre-approved figure for the extra contract. It far exceeded the contractor's quote and Dale was careful to agree a price where his own management component was identified separately. What the contractors and the ministers got up to in fees and kickbacks was up to them. He had no intention of entering that arena.

"Let's hope this keeps our friend Haddad happy. If there's one thing guaranteed to release his purse strings it's a threat to his precious camels. Why the man is so obsessed with them I have no idea." Ubaid rambled on for a while about his internal financial problems and Dale sat quietly, absorbing the information for possible later use.

"What I really wanted to talk about was the airport," said Ubaid at last. "Your camel team briefed me on the approach you are taking to the Program Management project and things seem to be moving well. They tell me that your airport team will arrive with you on your next visit, to start the project in earnest. You've obviously overcome our bureaucracy's famous inertia. I congratulate you." Ubaid inclined his head but dithered again before continuing with forced casualness. He finally found the topic. "So, how's the research going?"

Dale smiled. It seemed that Russell's paranoia about Ubaid's interest in airport security was well founded. "I leave from here to Frankfurt in the morning," he said. "I shall be meeting a number of companies who have worked on airports, and we'll gather what information we can. The main team will return with me in November.

Ubaid was pleased. "Good, good." He rushed into the conversation. "Maybe you should also have a copy of these papers. They are the UN approvals for the camel project, linked to self-sufficiency in camel ranching and there's reference to the upgrading of certain airport facilities to assist this humanitarian project. Maybe you won't need them, but it may help if you meet officialdom."

"Thank you." Dale folded the papers into the side pocket of his computer bag. It was some reassurance that his and his firm's activities rated official approval.

"One more thing," added Ubaid. "Mr Bertelli has been beating a path to my door. That is the right expression, is it?"

"Absolutely, your English is as impeccable as ever." Dale laughed.

"Good, good." Ubaid relaxed a little and went on, "anyway, he's been badgering me about his Italian contractors being able to compete. I promised to pass this on so that you can make sure they are on the list of bidders later on. It seems some of them have good airport experience."

Dale smiled. Bertelli's credibility as the Italian contractors' association's rep was hard won. "Okay," he said, "anything else we can help with? How's your son getting on."

"Excellent, excellent." Ubaid finally relaxed even more. "He's taking up water sports" he added, "not sure what that means."

"Well, to each his own." Dale threw the curious phrase on the table and Ubaid immediately took off into a discussion of its origins. Dale couldn't help thinking that Ubaid would have been better suited as an English professor at the university, rather than trying to control a bunch of devious contractors. He thought of Nadia waiting in the car below and began to shuffle his remaining papers together.

29

Nadia waited patiently with the engine ticking over and the air conditioning turned up full. When Dale had left to meet the Minister, the car had been partly in the shade of an old eucalyptus. Now the October sun beat relentlessly on the black Peugeot's roof. She recalled a friend saying that black objects radiated more heat than white ones but if that was the case then she presumed that black ones must surely absorb more heat too. The car was certainly proving her right. Despite the air-con it was extremely hot. She turned her mind back to the rest of the day.

Dale was leaving the next morning and had already made it clear that he wanted to spend the rest of the day with her, somewhere, her choice. She was more than happy to share time with him. The two of them had recognised a real chemistry, which was difficult to define, and she hoped that his next visit would cement things further. People always said that relationships that started with sex were doomed to failure, but she was not so sure. The sex was great, but the conversations were better; and his Italian was so beautiful. It was as if he never stopped studying it and was always seeking a more poetic way of speaking to her. It was their private world and she loved it.

She had a couple of places in mind for the evening, but her preference was to take him back to the village where he had met the others in the restaurant and then recreate their first evening and night together. The restaurant owner was an old friend of the Italian community, and she knew a good driver who would bring them back to the hotel. The alternative was a newer restaurant, further out of town. It had the advantage of anonymity but on balance she preferred familiarity. She called Akbar on his mobile and arranged for him to collect them from the hotel in his old taxi, then dozed against the leather headrest and pondered the evening ahead.

As Dale opened the rear door of the car, she turned and grinned. "All set?" she said.

"Yep," he replied, "all done for this trip, so 'home James,' I want to get rid of these bags and bits of paper and then we can think about how to plan the evening."

"Don't worry" Nadia murmured, "everything's taken care of. We can leave at seven. Plenty of time for a shower first."

Dale relaxed back into the project car and smiled. He leaned down and turned up the recording level on the tape recorder under his seat. "Looks like a long evening" he said for the benefit of the listeners, "these reports are going to take several hours to complete." Then he turned the volume down again almost to zero but not quite, so that the background could still register. 'Don't know why we didn't think about this volume control trick before,' he pondered to himself.

30

Marlena was curious to know why McGuire had come over to Frankfurt. He and Russell Clark sat opposite her in the airport coffee shop, sipping slow mochas all round while they killed time waiting for Dale's flight to arrive. To Marlena it was obvious that the importance rating of the airport drawings had been increased dramatically. People like McGuire did not normally meet people like Marlena. They had been talking about her work on the projects and her proposed secondment from the German security services for the next few months. It was obvious to Marlena's logical mind that her own boss had been extremely farsighted when he had suggested that she become an in-country resident on the back of a commercial project once the university closed most of its doors. Marlena had been surprised at how much they had known of her background and the hurried brush up on agronomy in order to be accepted on the irrigation team.

"So, tell me about how you first learnt Arabic." McGuire was always open-ended with his questions. He liked to sit back, watch and listen. Russell remained quietly in the background. He already knew the story and could only surmise that McGuire was just trying to have Marlena do the talking, as he knew his boss had been well briefed on the girl. McGuire also never forgot a damn thing and loved to pick out minor inconsistencies.

Marlena sensed he was expecting her to open up a little. She wondered what their files said about her. "It started with a boyfriend" she ventured, "and then a girlfriend, both Egyptian. Learning Arabic seemed an interesting thing to do." She paused but there was silence in response. "I quite like languages," she added cheekily.

McGuire sat perfectly still; his eyes fixed on her with a quizzical expression on his face. "I know" he said, "languages are not my strongest point, so I have a great respect for those who are multi-lingual, such as you and Russell here. Nadia is pretty multi-lingual too. How well do you know her?"

Marlena blanched as her mind raced ahead to the possible reasons behind his question. McGuire struck her as the type who was never casual with words. Everything he said had a purpose. She opted for the truth. He probably had it all on file anyway. "Only socially," she replied cautiously. "From my briefings I know her background with the Italians and the UN, but we haven't worked together before now."

"Is she part of your university group?"

"No, she's met Emanuella and Fritz but I haven't told her anything about what we do."

"Okay, good." McGuire was still, as impassive as a Buddha. Marlena became obsessed with his eyes, wondering whether he ever blinked. "and Basmah?" McGuire raised half an eyebrow. "Does Nadia know Basmah?"

Marlena's mind instantly froze and then spun round in circles. "Not to my knowledge," she said slowly and with a calmness she did not feel. Her mind racked itself backwards, rebounding off the many private barriers she had erected over the years. How much did McGuire know about her old friend Basmah, the main reason she had learnt Arabic in her youthful days as a freethinking student? How much did he know about their old relationship, before she switched her attention to men? Her life raced before her eyes. Basmah had been her teacher at an enlightening time in her life and she was happy that they could now still keep in contact and work together without the disappointments from the past interfering.

Her mind turned back to her time in Cairo, to the student house she shared with Basmah and three others. Yasser, the reason she had ventured there, had implored her to join him and she had fled willingly from the stuffiness of her Stuttgart University to participate in real life, as she believed it to be at the time. Being German, she had been cautious at first and had secured a grant to study arid agriculture with a view to becoming part of the infrastructure export business from her government sometime in the future, but her mind and spirit had been easily seduced as soon as she landed. Yasser had introduced her to the informal student body in Cairo University whose numbers far exceeded the numbers of registered students attending, and presumably paying for courses. She had been overcome by their intellectual passion, their credibility and their knowledge about the struggle of the Arabs against their perceived oppressors. She had developed sympathy for these people and an empathy she had never thought she could possess. She had shared their poverty in material things and their richness in commitment for change.

Yasser had been abandoned almost as soon as she arrived. He sulked in his corner of the large upper floor they all shared, grimy tatters of curtains strung between the rafters in a dismal attempt at privacy. The sleeping arrangements had left Basmah and Marlena together at one end of the loft, far away from Yasser, while a quiet couple hid themselves amongst packing cases in the middle of the room, too engrossed in their own sexual enjoyment to worry about the rest of the inhabitants. Maybe listening to the nightly repertoire from the centre of the room had been the prompt she had needed when Basmah had cautiously explored her breasts one night.

She had lain there more excited than she had ever been in her life. She had been with many boys, she didn't think of them as men, but the excitement and anticipation had never been like this. That first night her mind had been in turmoil, and she was too scared to make a noise. She had simply remained there in rigid disbelief at the pleasure it brought her. The second night she had dared to reciprocate and before long they were eagerly exploring and touching, kissing and fondling, and arousing and satisfying each other in ways no boy had ever been able to do. The affair, if affair it was, had lasted nearly a year, by which time they didn't care who heard them in the student house and would blatantly indulge their physical affection for each other in front of the others. But out in the streets and coffee houses it was a different matter. There they remained paragons of demure Muslim femininity, so that the male students concluded that they were frigid, sexless creatures, and therefore, paradoxically able to be trusted with male dominated discussions.

By this time, Yasser had long gone and been replaced in the house by two noisy lads who talked revolution constantly but seemed incapable of any practical ideas, let alone action. They drank themselves to sleep most nights and paid no attention to the girls.

When they had parted it was with good intentions to keep their closeness intact and away from preying male intrusion, but both had succumbed to family and social pressures, Marlena from her staid German upbringing and Basmah from the expectations of her family traditions. Marlena often wondered what would happen if the two of them ever found themselves in some situation where the ethos of the old house in Cairo was reincarnated, but it had never happened, and she had never pushed for it. Maybe it really was simply a phase. The girls' secret life together remained secure.

Or so she thought until now. How much did McGuire know of all this? How much was she showing on her carefully orchestrated face? Marlena searched McGuire's eyes for some glimmer of understanding, an indicator to either terrify her or put her mind at rest. She found nothing and, as much as she dared to study, she found no flicker of recognition or change in expression in the emotionless map before her. It was as if he had been caught in a grainy photograph.

"Can I ask you a question?" Marlena was not happy playing the interrogatee and was keen to get to move on to safer topics. "When can we discuss our engineering problem?"

"As soon as we are back at headquarters." McGuire smiled at last, the reverie broken. "When we've had a debrief from our visitor. Speaking of whom" he added, "we should be leaving, and you should be meeting. I see his flight is now on the arrivals board. We'll see you in the city."

Dale almost didn't recognise her. He had a mental image of a tall and solidly built girl when they had chatted at the University, but to see her in the airport arrivals she looked almost slight. Despite her height, the surrounding passengers and waiting crowds were simply so much larger, in all directions. Gone were the trappings of the student and in their place stood an elegant young woman, every bit the fashionable European professional. Marlena waved and began walking towards an exit behind her. Dale followed and matched his pace with hers as they passed through the double doorway. On the far side was another luggage handling area and as they walked down a series of steps into its midst Dale wondered how passengers ever pushed their trolleys around this nightmare of an obstacle course.

Marlena seemed to read his mind. "It's a dreadful airport," she said. "Everywhere you go there are stairs, ramps, and escalators. They've been modifying this place for ever and it shows. To make her point she ushered him towards a pair of doors that had a severe 'No Entry' sign across them. To Dale's surprise Marlena pushed them open and they walked into an empty corridor. No alarms sounded and no lights flashed. Marlena walked purposefully towards another pair of spring-loaded doors, but they opened before they reached them and two security guards, carrying sub-machine guns blocked their way.

"Is this the way to the washroom?" Marlena's voice was one of confused contrition. It had the desired effect as they were shepherded out of the doors again and directed by what sounded to Dale to be an extremely complicated route.

"Why did we do that?" Dale was curious.

"I thought you'd like to see where Fritz normally works," Marlena grinned. "He's on the airport security staff, though not as a guard, more the undercover sort of thing I guess. The fact is that the airport is a mess, and they are going to let a consultancy contract bring the whole thing up to date and unify the security at the same time."

"So, Fritz changes from student to airport security overnight and no one bats an eyelid. Come on" he said, "that can't be the whole story." He was rapidly becoming disenchanted by all the subterfuge. He much preferred things that he could see and certainly things where what you saw was what you got. All this additional interaction with security forces was beginning to get to him.

He still had no idea who Marlena really was or who she really worked for, although he now understood that she was connected to one of other of the security services in Europe. He guessed German, in which case why was she obviously working with Russell? He would have to ask him in a quiet moment. Maybe he could shed light. His mind stalled and he winced at Marlena's next words. "Can you repeat that?" he mumbled.

"And we think you should win the project." Marlena spoke slowly this time and watched for Dale's reaction. She was not disappointed.

Dale literally stopped dead in his tracks. "Who's 'we'? And how can you be so sure I can win a project that I've only just heard about for the first time?"

"Later" grinned an animated Marlena, "first I promised you a ride in a Mercedes from the airport. Remember?"

Dale sighed in exasperation but looked through the next doorway. On the far side was a waiting Mercedes. Just as she promised, he thought. Damn the woman. Then he walked through the doorway and realised that virtually all the waiting taxis in Frankfurt were Mercedes. He grudgingly accepted that she perhaps had a sense of humour after all.

31

The field was laid out with rough wooden tables and long benches. Flags and bunting flapped disconsolately in the cool autumn breeze while beneath the trappings the noise was overpowering. Accordion players competed for attention as they fought their way amongst the cramped tables and jostled the busty servant girls, each hugging armfuls of steins overflowing into their capacious cleavages. It seemed that everyone was intent on out-consuming their neighbour. Table pounding had given way to table stomping and groups of large lederhosen-clad youths were tramping up and down the rough planks of the table tops, arms around each other shoulders and a ready beer to be poured over the unsuspecting. The waning sun cast a golden glow across the festivities, although most people were past caring whether it rained or snowed. The beer god was in his heaven and serious worshipping was underway.

"So how much have you told him?" Fritz was struggling to make himself heard over the drunken racket. They were seated near a corner of the field and were guests of Fritz's brother, who so far had not appeared. A 'fun evening' had been how Fritz had explained their presence. 'Good for Emanuella's education' had also been mentioned. Marlena was used to these events. Emanuella was a little wide eyed and sipped carefully.

"Enough to get him worried." Marlena grinned. "You should have seen his face when I said he was going to win the Frankfurt consultancy!"

"I'm not surprised, it hasn't been announced yet." Fritz was amused whenever he saw this almost frivolous side of Marlena. He had told her once that it didn't match her famous deadpan looks. She had not thought it amusing.

Emanuella giggled. "Where is he this evening?" she asked.

"Meeting his old mate Russell Clark. I dropped him off at their hotel for a debrief. They've got one of their lords and masters over here – Mr Robert 'I can freeze my face longer than you can' McGuire. These Brits give me the creeps, honestly they do. You can never tell what they're thinking."

Emanuella shrieked with laughter. "Coming from you I think that's rich" she spluttered, "you should look in the mirror sometimes, Marlena."

Marlena smiled, for once at a loss for words. "I do" she frowned, "that's how I practice."

The table stomping veered towards them, and the steins bounced and lurched. Beer poured down Marlena's jeans as she jumped up to join the nearby crowd in a hopeless attempt to divert the table lads towards more distant pastures. She glanced at the local police scattered round the edge of the festivities. It would be a while before they intervened in what was regarded simply as good old-fashioned German boisterous behaviour.

It crossed her mind that the policing was not so different from the cafes and restaurants where they sometimes met in the desert. Maybe their guns were less obvious in Germany, maybe not. She looked at her soaked jeans and wondered when she would get time to change. She resigned herself to reeking of beer until late evening. But what the hell, you had to enjoy yourself sometime.

It was Fritz who pulled them back to the main topic in hand. "These engineering drawings" he started to say, "I think I may have found a way of arranging them."

Marlena was all ears at once. She looked hard at Fritz. "Don't bore me," she warned. "We've been down this route several times, and short of doctoring a full set of drawings, which is really like rc-designing them as there is so much cross referencing of detail, I can't see how we can avoid giving real drawings."

"Ah, that's the point." Fritz was smirking with enjoyment. "We do give them real drawings, just that they're the wrong real drawings."

"Go on." Marlena knew Fritz well enough to know he was winding her up a little. "Don't you think that putting a Frankfurt label on some other airport design might be sort of noticeable?"

"Normally yes, but what I've discovered is that the original drawing of the Frankfurt cargo area is already a copy, almost anyway. It turns out that Luton in the UK was used as the basis for its design. It seems that Luton was done first and was considered state of the art at the time. When Frankfurt copied it, they kept the same layout but increased the level of security substantially. Interestingly, they closed off several internal doorways. It needs looking at carefully, but I think we could simply change the title blocks and pass Luton off as Frankfurt. What do you think? Worth a try?"

"Maybe, how do you make sure no one notices the change?"

"Well, the drawings are all on AutoCAD. We would need to reset the computer's internal clock to amend the dates when the original drawings were edited. One problem is that there's no such thing as a simple drawing on paper anymore, although that's what we would give to Dale. There's an electronic trail for each drawing showing when it was changed and by whom. The last change is almost always to update the title block as there are electronic signatures to add. Rewriting the dates would not be difficult. The nice thing is that the company that designed Luton was the one that also did the original Frankfurt. Although the dates are different most of the staff are likely to be the same. My guess is that they could be passed of very easily as Frankfurt drawings. For complete transparency we would expect to give over the electronic copies at some stage, so getting the dates and other tell-tale evidence right will be important."

Marlena admired Fritz's ability to think through the technical detail. Having to change electronic dates and signatures hadn't even occurred to her. She wondered whether it would to Dale. Probably, she thought almost instantly, he had that type of mind, very like hers but more technically focused. She also wondered how much of the subterfuge should be explained to Dale. In many ways maybe the least he knew the better, but then there might be problems down the line if his own people discovered the switch. She was still mulling over his comments when the table took a decisive lurch. The planks tipped perilously in her direction and three jugs of beer slid towards her. She caught two, but the largest tipped dramatically down the front of her shirt. At this point the bench she had been perching on gave way and the two remaining jugs emptied themselves over her as well. Fritz and Emanuella were in hysterics as the roving master of ceremonies dragged an unwilling Marlena up on the stage to join the Best Dressed Frauline competition. She didn't bat an eyelid but was happy that another girl was more liberal, or maybe simply more drunk, when it came to removing her wet clothes and she willingly acquiesced as the popular acclaim was directed towards her opponent. As she squelched back to their corner table, she pondered again on the ways people enjoyed themselves in different countries. She thought of Raheem and his children's' books and wondered how many of the assembled masses would be happy to sit and read to their own children in a foreign language, and regard it as a high point in their life.

"Okay, time to go." Emanuella was suddenly all business. "if only because I don't want to get wet. I haven't any spare clothes! Let me understand where we are. I'll be flying with Dale to Milan tomorrow and can take the time to brief him on where he will get his drawings. Fortunately, a lot of the original equipment came from Milan because that's where the specialist engineering company is based, although I don't think they manufacture there anymore. He'll need to visit them though; in the same way he has been visiting the key firms here in Germany. You and Fritz will talk to the Brits about whether we can work on the Luton plans, and if so, then Fritz will be the point of contact here to act as Dale's source. No doubt our masters will have their own view about what should happen but it's always better to have our own plan."

32

It was only late October, but it was already cold, and the wind howled outside the terminal. The storm had brought an instant darkness and visibility through the downpour was down to about twenty metres. Gate 67 for the flight to Milan was crowded mainly with a mixture of returning Italians and German businessmen. There were also occasional strays like Dale. Outside there was no aircraft in sight and it was already late morning. Suddenly the wind noise increased, and the spattering rain turned to a violent rattling against the glass of the terminal's outer wall. As one, all passengers turned to see an incredible sight as a blistering hailstorm caught the window in full fury. Rain had turned to lumps of hard ice, large lumps of ice, some of them as big as a child's fist. They looked down at the nearby apron where groups of small airline company cars huddled. Their roofs were already pitted like egg cartons while the storm continued around them unabated. Dale had never seen anything so awesome in his life. The whole scene had changed with such dramatic suddenness that they could only stare. Another blast of huge hailstones beat on the sloping glass wall window, but thankfully nothing gave way and the white carpet, now more like a ploughed field, continued to build on the concrete apron in front of them. Then magically the hail stopped, as quickly as it had started, and to their amazement, snow began to fall, slowly at first, but then with greater and greater force until the sky was obliterated and visibility had been cut to somewhere just beyond the glass wall. Simultaneously the wind stopped, and the snow continued its silent avalanche unaided, like a white polar bear suffocating its prey. And it was still only October.

"Ladies and Gentlemen," the tannoy croaked into life. "There has been a freak hail and snowstorm which has engulfed the airport. This has seriously affected our operations and we regret to advise you that Flight 617 has been cancelled. Please proceed to the transfer desk where we will be happy to rebook you on a later flight. As the airport is now closed, any further flights will be no earlier than tomorrow. We regret any inconvenience caused."

Emanuella looked at the heaving masses and then at Dale. "I've an idea. How about the train?" she suggested.

"Train?" Dale was incredulous.

"Why not? Our tickets on the plane are redeemable and we don't have to sort them out now. Let's see what's happening to the trains. Maybe they've not been hit by this storm. It's a fun ride to Milan through the mountains and I much prefer trains to planes any day."

It proved a long wait for their baggage to be recovered and while they sat forlornly with others in one of the several baggage halls, they pondered on the layout and incremental damage that had been done to the design by subsequent administrations. Emanuella was very blunt in her views. "This place is as bad as Heathrow," she said. "No thought given to future expansion. Now if you look at Paris or Rome, there they thought big for the future."

"And ended up with the airport almost in a different city," said Dale. But his mind was already thinking about how to improve the layout. The fact that their project was only for cargo at present didn't worry him.

In the end they still had to retrieve their plane tickets and queue with everyone else to recover their refunds. They learnt too that the airport's snow clearing equipment was currently being serviced in readiness for the winter season and consequently it would be 'some time' before the airport functioned again. By the time they had finished they were eager to escape from the mass of disgruntled passengers.

The railway was indeed unaffected by the snow and by chance there was a train leaving fairly soon. It was an old-style compartmented carriage, with a side corridor running the length of the train. Dale and Emanuella found themselves alone. Few others had considered the train and they blessed their good fortune. It wouldn't arrive until late in the evening but that didn't matter.

The dismal landscape of an industrial city quickly gave way to the Rhine valley before diving into trees as they made their way through the Black Forest to the mountains. Emanuella was entranced by the scenery, but Dale was poor company. He worked his way steadily through phone calls until his battery was exhausted. In the end he had to give up and asked Emanuella if she played cards.

"Cards?" she asked. "Depends on whether we're gambling."

"OK, how about Canasta. You deal. Dollar a point."

"Make it a Euro and you're on."

They played a while and Dale's mind began to wander. He realised he knew very little about Emanuella too and should probably learn more. "So, tell me" he ventured, "how did you become mixed up in all this undercover stuff?"

Emanuella looked at him with her dark eyes and blinked. He realised she had extraordinarily long eyelashes. They made her face even more attractive. And she probably knows it, he thought mischievously.

"My father" he realised she was speaking, "was a diplomat and used to travel a lot. In fact, I was brought up in various parts of Europe. I guess that's why I like languages. It's also why I learnt Arabic originally."

"You say 'was,' what happened?"

"He was killed in that embassy accident in Sudan. Do you remember the one? He was on his way to interview for a new posting at the time."

Dale did remember. That particular incident had been close to where some of his colleagues had been working. "I recall that the reason for the explosion was never confirmed. Isn't that right?"

"That's correct." Emanuella had become quiet, not her usual ebullient self at all. "I was recruited soon afterwards. I guess it's no secret that some of your current clients are on the suspect list for the incident."

"Hence the student role at the University?"

"That's right. Strictly speaking I'm officially only a student but you obviously know I'm a little more than that."

"How much more?"

"A little. You should stop fishing now Mr Connors!" She yawned and moved across the carriage to join him on the seat facing forwards. "How about something to eat? And where's that bottle of wine we bought?"

The train wound slowing up the incline as they picnicked on the seat between them. Afterwards Emanuella yawned again and settled back on the seat with her head against Dale's shoulder. He found the sensation pleasing and turned his mind to when he had first met Emanuella at the university. There had been something of a cause about her. She seemed to be lady on a mission, and he wondered whether her father's death had been a determining factor in her being recruited, or whether she was merely responding to a personal ambition. She had been unusually open when they had talked through the outcome of her discussions with Marlena and Fritz. Dale had respected her openness at the time but was now wondering whether it was all a carefully scripted performance. He was learning quickly about these undercover people as he mentally referred to them and he suspected that he would learn a lot more as time went on.

They arrived late into Milan, and they already knew that hotels were at a premium. Emanuella had called from the train to check whether Dale's booking was secure, but it had been let go. With a dead mobile phone battery, he had no way of checking for himself. She had confirmed the next night's booking while she was on the phone and left things as they were. In the end, Emanuella had offered him a spare bed in her apartment, and he had gratefully accepted.

The apartment was on the second floor in an old eight-storey building near the Fierra. Dale caught sight of Piazza Amendola on a street corner before the taxi pulled up nearby. Late night trams, full of returning spectators from the sports stadium crossed the square, obviously full of the victor's fans, judging from the noisy good humour of their occupants. In fact, all the buildings in the area were a standard eight floors high and Dale wondered in his ever-inquisitive mind whether it was something to do with the influential owners of nearby tall apartments concerned about their view. They had entered through the building's palatial front doorway into a small, dimly lit but spectacular courtyard bristling with plants and a fountain, which dribbled water from a small statue of a cherub sitting thoughtfully on a rock. They entered another side door and, ignoring the elevator, climbed the curved stairs to the next floor. The elevator in her building was clearly an add-on, built like a lion's cage in the centre of what had once been a sumptuously handrailed staircase curving round the outer wall of the well. They reached the apartment and battled through the fortress-like door and multiple locks, but once inside, the rooms were shuttered and quiet, the outside late-night city bustle still audible but much subdued. The apartment was spacious and impeccably decorated with real art on the walls. Dale was impressed and studied a series of beautiful Italian miniatures while Emanuella busied herself elsewhere.

"Help yourself to the bathroom" Emanuella invited, "I'm afraid there's only the one. And then I must ask you a favour."

"Ask away."

"Please sleep with me."

Dale blinked, "I beg your pardon," he said.

"I'm frightened to stay on my own," she said simply. "If you like, we can make love, I'd like that, but I don't want to get in the way with Nadia."

Dale was completely speechless. He struggled for air. Here was a beautiful girl simply asking him to sleep with her, in every sense of the word. In all his travels he had never, ever been faced with such a dilemma. If he slept with her, would Nadia find out? Did it matter? "What if I prefer to sleep on my own?" he ventured.

"I guess there's always the sofa," she replied. "It's a one bed apartment."

Dale looked at the large inviting bed and made up his mind. "OK," he said, "but I'm really tired. I really do need some sleep."

"No problem." Emanuella smiled, tore off her long tee shirt and leapt smoothly and nakedly into bed.

Dale joined her, on the other side, his brain in turmoil. After a while he said "Emanuella?" There was no answer, except the steady breathing of someone who slept as if they hadn't a care in the world.

33

Russell listened carefully. "I need to understand the changes that were made to Luton's design" he said cautiously, "otherwise it sounds a very good idea." Fritz and Marlena had been at pains to cover the angles and had presented a very logical picture to Russell. He had smiled at their Teutonic detail and, while he had no doubts about their research, he mentally searched in vain for any big picture failings. "What if they access the drawings directly via the Internet?"

Fritz jumped on this as if it was a question on his prepared list at an interview. "The simple fact is that if they could have done that they would have done so already. But the drawings are archived in private systems, not on-line, and so they're not accessible. I've tried to hack through the company's files, but their firewalls and security systems are very good. The simple fact is that they're not accessible."

Russell winced at having so many simple facts thrown his way. He always worried about overbearing youthful enthusiasm, especially when brandishing 'simple facts.' "All right" he challenged, "if they ask for electronic copies, you say that it's all covered, but what if they go direct to the company who did the original Frankfurt work. Is there any danger that they'll simply give out a set on demand?"

"I would say not, but isn't that a topic your own security people can better advise on?"

"Probably, I'll make a point of raising it with Marlena's boss." Russell paused and looked straight at Marlena. "So" he said, "what about logistics? How do we transmit these packages to Dale? Which company front is he going to deal with to secure his drawings? He'll have to come clean about where he gets any data and so the company and names had better be real. These are all big companies who plaster their key staff all over their websites. There's no hiding these days. How do we deal with that?"

Marlena held up her hand to Fritz, whose enthusiasm was about to launch him into further details. "When the airport was completed, all copies of drawings were passed to the airport authority, who let a contract for archiving them. The archive company is obliged to provide access to its files on authority from the airport direct, not from the company who did the design. What I was thinking is that Dale could be provided with these drawings by the archive company, for a fee." Marlena knew it was a long shot, but her masters were insistent that she at least try, as this would give them overall direct control of the product.

Russell sucked in his breath. "No, doesn't work" he said, "we need a private route, not an official one. Can you imagine the flak if it ever leaked out that Frankfurt Airport Authority had provided details of its cargo area to some third world adventurer? No, it may be an easy way to do it, but it won't wash. We have to think again."

Marlena was expecting the answer and so simply ploughed on with the script. "The only other possibility is the UK firm who designed Luton. They were the original designers of Frankfurt's plans. Maybe they could be co-opted as sub-consultants."

Russell smiled. "Better" he said, "and not just because they're British, although I do have more control over what they do. Want me to talk to their people?"

Marlena took her turn to smile. "Sure" she said, "but we will still have final vetting of the product."

Russell recognised that her statement was not a question but decided to treat it as such. "Heavens yes! We can't do this in isolation, but I think it best for me to deal directly with Dale, don't you? It sort of keeps the channels clear."

His answer was what her boss had predicted, so she smiled and acquiesced to his plan, silently wondering why they always had to go through these mind games.

34

Jim Westead sat in his comfortable office. It was not large, but it was covered in the memorabilia of a lifetime of international projects. Maps and pictures of people covered the walls, people from the company, people from different countries, people everywhere. Jim prided himself on being a people person and would defend his approach against all comers. He measured his successes in life by the people he felt he had served, in the big picture by way of infrastructure but on a personal basis through the many friends he had gained in his eventful career. At fifty-four he thought of himself as still young and his enjoyment of travel remained undiminished, even though his knees felt the impact every time he ventured onto another plane.

Jim liked Dale and saw in him many of his own strong points. He also recognised that Dale was a better negotiator, and invariable pulled off some marketing coup that he himself would not have thought possible. Surround Dale with good operations people, he thought, and you have a real winner. That was Jim's role, to sweep the paths behind a very talented and valued member of his staff, and to ensure that work won turned into profits realised.

He pondered on the proposal in front of him. Dale's measured enthusiasm was evident, but he also appreciated that the risks were well enumerated and to a large extent more than adequately addressed. Foreign currency payments remained his biggest concern, but Dale seemed to have pulled off nothing short of a miracle in his 50:50 deal, and with such fees, and moreover with the up-front payments, he felt that the offer to sole-source the cargo logistics centre was a good one.

Dale sat in front of his old friend and boss. "What are your worries?" he prompted. He dared not admit it, but he desperately needed the airport security project, partly in order to cover the delays on the previous project payments and partly, he openly admitted to himself, because he wanted to see Nadia again. Having turned down Emanuella's offer, he was even more determined to hook up with Nadia again. He hadn't felt this way about anyone for a long time.

Turning his mind to contractual topics, he flipped through the positives in front of his boss. Firstly, the camel project was going very well and making a lot of money. Secondly the old irrigation project was all done and dusted, apart from some final payments, which he thought now he could swing as part of the start-up of the airport add-on. He waited for Jim to compose his thoughts.

"The contracting is my real concern." Jim finally announced, as if he had been considering the question for some time. "We are a services company, not a contractor and I don't want to get burnt. I like the way you've structured it as a programme management project. At least that keeps us at a distance from serious commercial damage, but I'm still concerned about our liability if contractors don't perform. We'll have the legal mob go through the contracts but it's still my main worry."

"I think it's manageable." Dale was cautious. He had long ago learnt that saying 'no problem' to his boss did not endear himself to him. It was much better to admit to potential problems and show how they could be dealt with. "I've discussed this with Ubaid," he said, "and he is clear about this being a real concern of ours that we're not willing to take on board. The maximum liability he might impose is for us to reselect another contractor at our cost. As we have a full team on site that isn't really a cost issue, it's only if things drag on and on that we might get into problems."

"And what would the maximum downside be?"

"Really not a lot. We get almost all of our foreign staff paid up front and if they reneged on all other payments we would have time to pull our people out in good time, to maintain profitability. I also reckon that we can cover our outstanding irrigation payments in this way, so the overall outcome can only be positive.

Ubaid and Haddad are extremely keen on this project and appear willing to do almost anything to get it moving."

"Maybe that's a worry too." Jim smiled. "I'm just trying to cover the angles, not pour cold water. I guess the link from camel tracking to airport cargo logistics is a bit of a stretch as a humanitarian project, but I'm told that it's all above board at the UN, so why not? Dale, I have to say that overall, I'm very impressed by what you've done, and I hear there may even be more on the horizon in Frankfurt."

Dale was speechless. "How did you hear about that?" he stammered. "I haven't got the details yet."

"Friends in high places, I guess. Your cryptic emails, which I copy to Russell, are not the only communications I have with HMG. Dale" he went on, "I'm fully behind what you're doing. If there's anything I can do to help, you must let me know. I hear you're planning on using Derek McCullen as Programme Manager. I'll make sure he's available. Good choice, that man."

"Thanks Jim." Dale filed away the compliments for later thought when he needed a mental boost, and meanwhile secretly wondered how much Jim had been told about his relationships outside the clients' organisations. Hopefully not a lot, he thought.

35

His face lit up when he saw her, still shrouded in black but definitely not hiding in the shadows like last time. Customs hadn't seemed such a hassle as he played out his normal routine, targeting the same long queues, being forced to use the same old chalk trick and adopting the same bored expression while he waited. Everything seemed as normal. The same illegible signs awaited visitors and the crowd of taxi vendors remained undaunted as usual; but this time, Dale was wary. He looked around him constantly, trying not to be obvious but searching for tell-tale camera positions, blinking like tiny red stars in the night of the shadowy terminal ceiling. He had noticed them before, but only in passing. Now he was surprised that there were in fact dozens of them, almost everywhere he looked. He had fixed his face with his best bored expression when he realised just how many cameras there were, but the sight of Nadia waiting with the other drivers caught him off guard and by the time he realised he was smiling, it was too late. Ah well, he thought, give old Fayez a treat.

Had he been able to see behind the cameras he would have found none other than Naiem Fahoud himself, carefully scrutinising the live feeds and watching Dale like a hawk. Naiem had ignored the normal customs antics with the chalk but carefully noted down that this was his fifth trip to the country. He would have passed over the girl driver completely, they weren't important, but something in Dale's expression caught his eye. He ran the recording loop back in 'instant replay' and saw it again, clearly this time. He smiled to himself. So, he thought, maybe young Mr Dale has something going with his lady driver. He wondered whether this might be one of the pressure points Fayez had asked him to keep his eyes open for. He logged their meeting on his day sheet and turned his attention to the next mass of arriving passengers.

"Hi, you're on your own?" Nadia was brief and coy when they met.

"Yes, the Programme Manager's coming in a few days so that we can negotiate the start-up details."

They climbed into the Peugeot. "Hotel?" Nadia reverted to her normal brevity when being recorded.

"Yes please." Dale settled back into the cool interior and watched her. It was becoming a favourite occupation, but his mind kept turning back to something Emanuella had said. He had not pushed her further, but she'd implied that it was essential to keep Nadia at a distance from their conversations about false drawing details. Dale had already planned to do this, but Emanuella's insistence had worried him. Just who did Nadia really work for? Russell had been fairly open about her past and her present liaison with Bertelli, but he realised that there were huge gaps in his knowledge. Details of Nadia's official employment at the ministry were sketchy to say the least. He mentally pigeonholed the problem until a more appropriate time and looked forward to her company that evening. It's best not to mix business with personal life, he thought to himself well, not too much anyway. He pulled out his mobile phone to clear up his calls before they reached the city.

36

The discussion had been terse and lasted only twenty-five minutes. By the time it finished Russell felt drained. But he also felt much more confident than when the session had started. They had given their blessing and the relevant technical support had been sanctioned. As they entered the soundproof room, McGuire had whispered that he wanted him to lead the main presentation and in his meticulous way he believed he had covered all the obvious bases, leaving a few tactically open for questions.

The review team were used to well-thought-out proposals and a few had complimented him on his forethought, but they were also a wily bunch, drawn from active agents as well as senior staffers. Their concerns seemed sometimes mundane and occasionally completely off the wall, but Russell knew that they all probably came from experience, rather than theoretical 'what-ifs.' He had been completely thrown by a question about Abdullah's links to the UK. 'Were the team sure that these would in no way be compromised?' Russell had blinked a little at the question, but McGuire had calmly assured the questioner and the meeting hardly missed a beat. Russell mentally filed the issue away for future discussion.

A sample of some of the product, which was to be endorsed by the Germans and then developed in detail lay on the conference table. When both agencies were satisfied it would be passed back to Russell for onward transmission to Dale. The modification of the handful of selected Luton designs, carefully re-badged with the same drawing numbers used in the actual Frankfurt construction had not taken long to achieve. There were even post-project photos of some of the features at Luton, dressed up with a background of the contractors employed in Frankfurt and carefully dog-eared and hole punched as if from some archive, all to add depth to the legend. As with all such schemes, the problem was not usually getting the first product off the ground, but in maintaining consistency in future deliveries, and covering the backtracking and checking that the local security experts would inevitably carry out.

The ploy of providing false details was a very obvious one and its success depended on two things. Firstly, the limited ability of Abdullah's staff to cross-check original sources and secondly to ensure that any such checks turned up only consistent information. Occasional minor errors were allowed, and in fact encouraged, to add to the aimed-for reality, but nothing that should have been picked up in the normal course of modern quality assurance programmes. The key point that had not escaped the sharp eyes of the review panel was that the footprints of the cargo facilities and Luton and Frankfurt were identical. Aerial photos showed entrances and principal walls to be the same. In fact, it was only when it came to internal accessibility that things became subtly different. Whereas Luton was built for open access, primarily for fire fighting vehicles, Frankfurt had been altered, to make entry hugely more difficult for visitors unfamiliar with the building.

From the offices on London's South Bank, Russell had taken the package himself to Frankfurt, always ensuring that his fingerprints never appeared on any part of it. The need for deniability was paramount, in the same way that the search for authenticity had led them to use a print machine that was identical to the one still used by the engineering firm who had prepared the original drawings. As he fastened his seat belt in preparation for landing, he pondered on the likely tortuous task he had ahead, taking his German counterparts through the plan and, more importantly, getting their thorough review of the product, both before and after it had been completed.

In many ways, he was pleased that they would be required to be thorough in their approach. Some of his colleagues might call it pedantry but he felt reassured by their methods. Nothing was left to chance. After all, it was their biggest airport. He imagined the numbers of people who would be involved if Heathrow was ever in the same position. He had his own ideas about possible risks, but no one could be sure what was being planned, or how it might be carried out. He turned his mind to his engineering friend. Were they really justified in involving civilians in this subterfuge, even on a need-to-know basis? Dale was being exposed to very real and acute dangers. He had to do his best to make sure things worked out. Dale hadn't been at all impressed that it would take at least a month to produce the drawings, and then there was the Christmas vacation too. Germany and the UK at least shared that in common, even if it shot holes in their work schedules.

37

Ubaid sat at the head the long conference table. On his left sat Dale, with Derek McCullen at his elbow. On his right a number of his own ministry representatives, plus Hussein Al Baz and Fuad Asmi, the unofficial conduit both in and out of the Ministry of Security. They had worked through the contract and settled most remaining issues, but Ubaid was clearly unhappy about something and was not prepared to say what. Dale hadn't seen him so out of sorts before. Fuad was not helping either. He glared at Ubaid expectantly on a number of occasions, as if willing him to make some sort of agreed statement. But Ubaid stubbornly ploughed on until they had completed their agenda. As the meeting broke up, he called the two Brits into his office so they could initial the agreement.

"I have a problem," he admitted when the door was closed.

Dale motioned his colleague to be patient. "Anything we can help with?" he asked.

"Well, the problem is that it will affect you." Ubaid paused to collect his thoughts and then rushed onward. "We have a problem about the choice of contractors."

"But surely we're only doing the planning and concept stage for now?" Dale tried not to sound too worried.

"That's correct, but the contractors will always be putting their noses into things, if only in the name of marketing and that's something our colleagues in Security don't want. Why, I don't know."

"So, what do they what?" Dale began to see a pattern from the camel project.

"They want to use their own local company."

"I see, but I thought we had agreed, at the ministry's request, that the project would be competitively bid in the international market."

"We did agree, and I must apologise. Frankly speaking, I hadn't expected this opposition. My bigger problem is how to deal with our Italian friends. The Security Ministry people are adamant that they don't want them involved and yet I owe them some opportunities at least. You probably saw the look on Fuad's face in there. He was under orders to ensure that the Italians are not involved. For the life of me I can't think why. We would get a much better job with them than any of our local crowd."

Dale breathed a sigh of relief as Ubaid had opened up the very topic on top of his mind. "You raise a good point" he said, "our problem will be that, without competent contractors we will have to put in much more supervisory effort. A lot more in fact."

"And that means more fees, I suppose?" Ubaid was not stupid.

"Yes, I'm afraid so, but as it is way down the track we can't really estimate it at the moment. Maybe we can insert some provision in the contract to recover the costs of supervisory staff, plus a management fee."

Ubaid looked beaten. "I even spent some time with Abdullah on this issue," he confided. "He told me flat out that there were too many foreigners involved and he only trusts you on this project. He even wanted their own government company supervised by you personally." Ubaid looked up at Dale. His version of the conversation with Abdullah was a little off the mark, as Abdullah had also noted that having foreigners involved added a degree of reality to the project. He suspected there were other motives behind Abdullah's comments but he himself was not privy to them and frankly he was not interested. "Look" he said finally, "draft me a clause and let's see if we can get this thing wrapped up tomorrow morning."

"How about we use your conference room now and meet you again in fifteen minutes?" Dale was keen to secure closure on the contact.

"Sure." Ubaid brightened up considerably. "And if you have any ideas about what to say to our friend Mr Bertelli, I'll double the management fee!"

They stood to leave the office. "Don't forget that the conference walls have ears," added Ubaid. "This room doesn't. Why don't you stay here while I take a walk? I need to stretch my legs."

Dale was profuse in his thanks and motioned Derek into the chair alongside him. As Ubaid left the room, he scribbled a note on his calcs pad. 'Ubaid records all his conversations here. Say nothing.' He had already warned Derek about the conference room eavesdroppers in the Security Ministry. He pulled out his laptop and opened up the relevant section of the contract. From his archives he pulled out an alternative clause providing a mix of fixed management fee plus time related establishment charges, plus staff related costs and mark ups. It was actually the original clause that he'd inserted before Ubaid had insisted on a lump sum. Now he was getting the best of both worlds. Jim Westead and he had discussed this particular issue and, while Jim had been more than happy with the level of the lump sum, he was going to be over the moon at the revised arrangement. Derek worked through the numbers while Dale edited; and together, they smiled at the win-win result. It was not often they could reduce risk and also secure a higher fee. Dale finished editing and, looking at Derek, held a cautionary finger to his lips.

"Hmm … these figures are going to hurt unless we're very lucky with Abdullah's contractor," he said gloomily for the benefit of Ubaid's assumed recording, "but I trust Ubaid not to screw us and so I guess we don't have much choice. Much better to get on with the job. I'd feel happier with a contractor from Ubaid's group, but never mind. Time to move on." He turned the topic to English football while they waited, and Derek was extolling the virtues of Man United when Ubaid re-entered the room.

"Well?" he asked. "How are you doing?"

Dale smiled. "If I can borrow your printer in the outer office for a few minutes, you can have a revised section to the contract straight away."

Ubaid brightened. "And our Italians?"

"Well, for starters, why don't we ask them to negotiate all the building work for the camel complex, especially the famous revolving restaurant? We've had a number of preliminary bids, and so we could quite properly enter negotiations if the ministry decides to give the go-ahead." Dale looked at Ubaid to see what mark he had made. "It would save time too," he added.

Ubaid's face told it all. A way forward on all fronts. He could sell the camel contracts to the Italians and make a handsome profit for himself. He much preferred negotiated contacts, especially when he was in control. He couldn't understand Dale's insistence on keeping all his own company's contracts highly visible. It meant there was no opportunity for them both to make extra money on the side. Whenever Ubaid had argued for higher fees, in exchange for part of the action, Dale had demurred and suggested that as engineers, their fees were pretty low anyway, so why try and make them lower. Much better to let the engineers do their job properly, working on the small margins they had. In the end, Ubaid had accepted that Dale was a straight player who wasn't looking for personal gain from the contracts. He'd turned his attention back to the main contractors and suppliers.

"Looks like a multiple win" Ubaid was now grinning, "but let's keep things quiet for a while until I've positioned ourselves with the security people. It wouldn't do to be seen to agree with them too easily!"

38

Derek would have been forgiven for thinking that he and Dale spent all their time in government meetings. He and Dale would spend hours revising proposals to accommodate the latest whim of some minor official or editing reports into the small hours of each morning. As they ran off the last copies and had the Arabic summaries produced, they knew that at least some further progress could be made at yet another tortuous steering group meeting the next day.

Derek was impatient with clients and felt happier when everything was under his control. He was an excellent project manager but not the best person to deal with people. He had managed to contain his impatience with the ministries so far, but Dale knew it was always a potential flash point. He was therefore deliberately philosophical and patient. "Choose your battles," he kept saying. "It's easy to make a few small changes. They add nothing except a lot of good will and detract nothing apart from a good night's sleep for us. If we're seen as helpful then all to the good. As long as we know where to draw the line on changes we'll be fine."

The good news was that their project plan had been accepted and was now with the Ministry of Security for 'rubber stamping,' as Ubaid had indicated was the likely outcome of this morning's meeting. From Derek's jaundiced view in the sidelines, there didn't appear to be a rubber stamp in sight, either literally or figuratively. Ubaid appeared tired and had been a very non-directional chairman, allowing many interruptions and digressions. Although they had ploughed through the agenda it had been very difficult to hold things on course, and to get resolution of the simplest of issues.

Undoubtedly, one reason for the lack of progress was that Abdullah himself was in attendance. He had said little so far but his presence cast a shadow over the participants, who were either silenced out of fear or pushed themselves into the limelight to show their concern for all things linked to security. Abdullah himself had only two topics, which he retreated into at every opportunity. The first was the Italians. His instructions to Fuad did not seem to have been followed and he wanted to know why, although he couldn't raise the issue directly in this grouping of people. He had gleaned that the project was going to deal only with selected local contractors, which he presumed meant his own people, but he needed to speak directly to Ubaid about clarity of action on this point. There was no way he was going to have some foreign contractor running round the facility once they started training.

But the discussion had still talked about Italian contractors. He didn't understand why and looked expectantly to Fuad. "The note," he mouthed. Fuad glanced at Abdullah's hand written scribble in front of him and dutifully raised his hand.

"Mr Chairman," he waited for Ubaid to turn towards him. "I don't quite follow your reference to Italian contractors. I thought we had agreed that this was a secure facility and therefore only local contractors would be involved."

Ubaid looked him as straight in the eye as he could, but the drawn face showed stress and fatigue. "My engineer will explain" he said, without so much as a smile. "Mr Connors, can you please summarise for us?"

Dale wasn't sure where this was going but waded in, nonetheless. "I think there may be some confusion in terms," he was rapidly thinking as he spoke. "We've certainly agreed with the ministry that only local civil and building contractors will be used, but the fact is that most of the equipment used in these facilities is manufactured overseas. And in this area the Italians are world leaders. In fact, all of the Frankfurt installation uses Italian equipment. It's quite normal to use local installation companies but we would expect to use the manufacturer to oversee the final start-up. So, it may be beneficial to use some foreign nationals to ensure that the equipment works as designed, just during the start-up period. Does this clarify the position?"

Fuad didn't have a clue. He could see the logic in what Dale was saying but he was not party to the underlying reason for Abdullah's paranoia over the Italians. He looked firstly uncertain and then towards his boss.

"The other point to remember," Derek was speaking this time "is that in the current climate of sanctions and bearing in mind that this is an extension to a project under the auspices of an Italian humanitarian programme, Italian equipment may well be the only foreign equipment readily importable. They may insist on using their staff as a condition of sale."

Reality had finally struck. "Thank you" Fuad stuttered, "that certainly clarifies the position."

Abdullah sank back in his chair. Not check mate, but nearly. Maybe they could send their own people over to wherever these wretched pieces of equipment were made, train them and avoid the need for bringing more foreigners here. But he knew that that was not ideal. Even he knew that humanitarian projects could stretch only so far. Why, why, why was it always he alone having to think through these problems? Ubaid had not yet established his position regarding the Italians. Abdullah was clearly going to have to do it for him.

He turned to his other preoccupation; speed. The whole damn thing was going too slowly. For him it was very simple. They needed detailed plans of Frankfurt's cargo handing area and also details of the security systems. All this talk about alternatives and options drawn from world-wide best practice seemed like a waste of time to him. Long term reliability and lifetime cost analysis were irrelevant issues for his present purpose. Why could engineers not simply do what they were told and get on with things? Heaven knows they were paying through the nose for these foreigners. All he wanted was a building he could practise in. Was that so difficult? He turned to listen more closely to Derek McCullen.

Something he had said raised a concern for Abdullah and he wanted to be clear in his mind before tackling the issue. Derek knew what he was talking about, and Abdullah grudgingly admitted to himself that in another life he probably would have agreed with him. He tuned in carefully.

"Listening to all the comments we understand that you want to base your new design on the Frankfurt facility." Derek was being careful to repeat himself whenever the initiative was the client's. It was a trick Dale had taught him as it helped establish where all the extra work lay if nothing else. It also flattered the client that he was being given the credit for positive ideas. "We do have a number of concerns with this approach. Let me take you through them." He threw up a new overhead listing four key issues. "Firstly, Frankfurt is showing its age and there have been several security upgrades done over the last few years. They don't affect the structure and logistical movement of cargo, but we will have to pick carefully from the various technology add-ons that have been provided to understand why they were introduced. Getting details of these upgrades may be tricky, although there is a project management competition shortly to appoint a new planning team for the airport. Frankfurt is planning to introduce a wholesale upgrade of their facility, incorporating all the incremental changes they've done so far and fundamentally redesigning their whole handling set-up. Whoever wins that competition will definitely have access to all the current systems."

Abdullah sat up in his chair. A glimmer of an idea had lodged in his devious mind. He listened as Derek continued.

"Secondly, it would be normal practice to review developments in other parts of the world but because of current sanctions we doubt we can do this, especially in the US where sanctions are taken rather more seriously than in some of the European countries. The fact is that the US has been responsible for some of the best recent developments in this field and so to ignore them will probably mean that the facility here is not as efficient as it could be."

Abdullah couldn't care less about efficiency. He was back on the previous issue. For him, time was the issue, otherwise the news from Fayez about the Ruler's impatience would not bode well for him. Why had he not heard directly he wondered? He must try and find out through the Raya and Hasna route. They would know what was really behind the Ruler's thinking. But for now, the message via Fayez had been clear. Get on with things and keep it quiet.

So how could they ensure access to the newer security add-ons quickly he wondered. All he needed was accurate knowledge, but now he needed it soon. Dale had talked about securing past drawings from other engineering firms. Would these cover everything they wanted? Until they saw the first sets they wouldn't know. The certainty in his mind was that their only hope of access had to be through a foreign company, and he had no intention of widening his risk to more than one set of foreigners. By now, Derek was talking about cargo throughputs and had put a dazzling array of numbers on the screen in front of them all. Why can't we keep it simple, he thought, muttering quietly to himself.

"I'm sorry, did you have a question?" Derek had stopped in mid-flight and was looking at Abdullah. "I didn't quite catch what you said, Sir."

All heads in the room turned deferentially towards Abdullah as the most senior-ranking minister present. He stared back at them for a moment.

"Actually, I do have a question," he said at last, his deep gravelly voice defying any reaction. "If you win the Frankfurt competition you say you would have access to all the various updated systems? Is that right?"

Derek nodded his head, but Abdullah continued anyway. "My question is this." He paused. "How can we help you to win?"

Derek looked askance and across to his equally dumbstruck colleague for help.

Abdullah persisted with his train of thought. "It seems to me that this would solve all your problems. If you were to win we would have access to world best practice, through this new Frankfurt planning study you talk about, and also we would be brought up to date about the current state of security at Frankfurt, insofar as it affects our cargo area." he added hurriedly. "Do you see a problem with that?"

Dale stammered his acquiescence. "Not at all" he managed to say, "if we can win."

"Okay, agreed." Abdullah was all business now. "Come and see me tomorrow and we will discuss a plan."

39

Russell was very proud of Wafa. She had been his first recruit in the country, and it was more years ago than he cared to remember. She'd been a student at Hull at the time, on some exchange or other when the governments were still good friends. She was now the information guru at the ministry. Whenever they needed anything she found it. Whenever they wanted something stored away, she did it. She was indispensable to the ministry and in exchange had access to most of the personal files ever produced. She valued her position but priding herself on accuracy and completeness was only part of it. She also enjoyed the secret assignments Russell gave her, such as doctoring his records, and those of his colleagues who had recently come in the country. They still existed but didn't raise red flags anymore, now that he was safely over the three-visit limit, officially vetted and found uninteresting. She once had high hopes of Russell, but he'd always been the professional and she could see that, while she sensed that he may be interested in her, his professionalism always turned him away at the last moment. She could see that the agony of losing his lost all those years ago still hurt. She wanted to help fill the gap, but work was always in the way.

Secretly Wafa yearned for an English lover with Russell's style and quiet civility. She lay at night imagining his English politeness and wondering how this translated into the bedroom. But it was only the stuff of dreams, and so she dreamt. Now at last there was perhaps an answer to her prayers. The new Mr Miles had suddenly appeared from nowhere and she had met him, first with Russell back in October when they'd appeared together, and now several times on her own. They had always met at Russell's rendezvous over the bakery, and she marvelled that they were never seen. But she knew how chauvinistic her local bosses were. They did not see women as a threat and almost never tailed them.

She turned her mind back to Miles. With him she saw a possible opportunity, to escape, to get away. The reality was that she hated her job. Russell might value it, but she had outgrown the tedium and yearned to live where her everyday boss treated her like a human being and also where it was not so damned hot and dusty. Similar age too, she thought as she dressed and redressed for their next meeting. Come on girl, you can do it.

40

Fayez was more than curious when Fuad shared the news about Abdullah's outburst in the meeting. The logic was there but he hated spending more than necessary. They were both now in Abdullah's office and had been through the plan forwards and backwards.

"Well?" Abdullah was brusque this morning. "Anything to add?"

Fayez shook his head. "It's obvious that we have to get the best details about their security systems" he said, "but I'm still concerned about spending more money before we see what Dale brings us by way of drawings."

"Maybe, but I want to speed things up a little, and to ensure their company's success by funding a discount on their bid seems good value to me. The project will start very soon and then we should have all the information we need. It will also bind them to us, even more than now. It's not the sort of thing they're going to tell their competitors."

"But we are still going to build the facility here?" Fayez did not like changes in plan. They reduced his control.

"Of course, we are, but I'm wondering whether we can get our information sooner." He had a gleam in his eye, which bothered Fayez. It meant that Abdullah was having his own ideas, and that definitely worried him. They had agreed on Frankfurt and had agreed on the methodology of planting the device. He'd fed the message about speed, but Abdullah now seemed to be taking him literally. He didn't like changes, especially when it was not clear about what they might be changing, and to what. But he decided to let it ride. He would keep Abdullah under close scrutiny from now on. Abdullah getting involved in running the show was not what he'd had in mind.

Dale was due to join them shortly and Fayez did not wish to take part in any detailed meetings with him. Distance leant gravity to a relationship, and anyway, he had Fuad to rely on for information. He nodded to Fuad and then took his leave.

A few minutes later the expected knock on the door was right on time. Abdullah called for more coffee. He beamed a welcome and waited for his foreign guest to settle himself.

"Did you see the news about sanctions this morning?" he started.

Dale had, briefly, but tended to be sanguine about the proposed timing. "I did," he said. "I'm not sure about the timing though, April seems very optimistic."

"They're always optimistic," said Abdullah, "but what do you think? Are they going to get them removed before you need to import equipment?"

Dale laughed and wondered where this was all going. "That'd be nice" he said, "but I don't think we should plan on it. Knowing how these diplomats work it could be over a year later."

"I agree," Abdullah beamed again "so, all the more reason to get our airport finished so we can benefit when sanctions are removed."

Dale accepted the logic and waited for Abdullah to continue.

"Okay, firstly let's continue from yesterday. Now you see our need for speed. My proposal is that I arrange for Ubaid to subsidise your Frankfurt cargo logistics bid by 10%. This will mean that you can undercut the others comfortably without suffering any losses yourself. When you start the project, you will be able to access all the recent security improvements and we can then benefit from these in our airport design. How does that sound?"

Dale nodded his head. "Sounds feasible" he said, "but we'll have to do a lot more than just have the best price."

"That's your problem" Abdullah's voice was not friendly, "but to help you I'll also ask Ubaid to pay you a 10% win bonus, after you win. You will then use this to fast track our own project." Abdullah's eyes were like flint. Dale had heard he was not a man to argue with. He was beginning to understand why. "The fact is I need your help, and I'm prepared to pay for it."

Abdullah slowly sat back in his chair. He had said what he wanted to say and as far as he was concerned the rest was detail. Why did this foreigner not jump up and down with joy, and thank him? Strange people these Brits.

Dale looked the older man straight in the eye. Why were they so desperate to have the security systems? Maybe the likely end of sanctions did mean something after all. He needed to be careful, very careful. These contracts wouldn't be worth a damn thing if these crazy people did try something. He couldn't afford to expose the firm to more risk, especially of non-payment. He glanced at Fayez, but his face told him nothing – so he didn't bother with Fuad.

"You seem thoughtful," Abdullah was pressing him.

Dale shrugged. "I am," he smiled as he talk-started himself into action. "It's not every day your best client turns up with a proposal for more fees." He had no idea how to raise the question of foreign currency, but he knew he had to. "Firstly, let me say how much I appreciate your offer," he said, thinking rapidly. "I'm sure my company is as grateful as I am. I will have to run this past my boss, Mr Westead, but I'm sure he'll sign off on the idea." Dale paused. He should have remembered the third-party trick in his sleep, but it was safe now, he had the necessary escape route if he needed to say no. "The only thing he may have a problem with is increasing our exposure to local currency. The Frankfurt project will be done entirely in foreign currency and if we accelerate the airport work here it will inevitably cost us more. Maybe I can convince him if the two 10% payments are entirely in foreign currency. I'm honestly not sure."

Abdullah sensed exasperation creeping rapidly upon him. How he hated to haggle. His wife always called him the world worst souk shopper ever. "All right, I hear you" he said, "all offshore. How about the 10% Frankfurt discount paid as soon as you calculate it. If we don't pay then you don't submit the bid. And then the acceleration 10% paid when you sign the contract. Again, no payment, no acceleration."

"And if we don't win Frankfurt?"

"We'll have our discount back, but I don't think that's going to happen, do you?"

"Well, I think I could probably persuade Mr Westead on those terms. Let me speak to him later today." Dale managed to hide his excitement.

"Good, then let Fuad know as soon as you have spoken to him." Abdullah rose from his seat. The meeting was clearly over.

41

Bertelli had calmed down appreciably and was now at least polite. "Ubaid" he chided, "how long have we known each other? Now you tell me that we can't even help you build your new airport. And all you offer in exchange is a few dirty camel houses!"

Ubaid hadn't been looking forward to seeing his friend and had enjoyed the last ten minutes even less. Bertelli had raged histrionically in true Latin style and pointed out the various agreements that Ubaid had reneged on. Ubaid had felt it best to let his anger run its course, but even he was surprised how long this was taking.

"Okay, Okay, I hear you Antonio, but you're not listening to me." Ubaid had had enough. "Stop waving your hands about and listen for a minute. Please."

Bertelli obediently stopped, sat and waited.

"Firstly, they're not houses for dirty camels. They are expensive grandstands plus a tourist complex, with a revolving restaurant and a viewing gallery. In the executive boxes, as well as the restaurant, we are looking for your famous Italian style. Then there's the racetrack itself and the stables. You know Haddad as well as I do. He's fanatical about his camels and Dale's idea for high quality stables was a real hit. Haddad was even talking about air-conditioning the stables until we reminded him that camels are used to the heat. Sure, the fencing is being done locally but all this building work is high quality, has got to be done quickly and will mean the import of lots of foreign sourced fittings and services equipment. My guess is that you will be looking at 80 million dollars of work on this alone. For the right fees I am sure we can negotiate a sensible price. Your bids are already with us, and my advisers tell me that they may be able to recommend your companies. I guess it depends on what special purpose contingencies are added."

Bertelli bowed his head. "I apologise for being hasty," he said. "The last I heard about the camel project was rather different, but you're right, if Finance Minister Haddad is keen then everything will happen. But what about the airport?" Bertelli was still smarting over the backtracking. "You did agree that our contractors would be able to bid for this and now we can't. It makes me look as if we don't know what we're doing."

"Antonio, my friend, you must listen. Who makes the best cargo handling equipment in the world?"

Bertelli nodded. "Okay, I see where you are heading, but we'll still have to compete, won't we?"

"That's up to you," Ubaid began to see how to play with his friend. "You can compete if you insist, but we rather hoped you might negotiate. We've decided to fast track the project and the only way we can do that is using Italian equipment. I suspect too that the only way we can import any equipment is on the back of the Italian humanitarian project, which must add up to quite a good deal for your people.

"So, you're saying you would want to negotiate a deal for this equipment?"

"I believe that's what I just said," Ubaid smiled. "The other thing you should bear in mind is that the equipment we use is likely to be the same at the equipment you supplied to Frankfurt a few years ago. Identical in fact. It could be quite a good deal for your people if all they have to do is reproduce something which they've already supplied once."

Bertelli looked pensive. He was now calm, his Mediterranean hand waving and animation completely under control. "What I hear you saying is very good news indeed," he ventured. "Thank you Ubaid. Is there anything I can help you with, in exchange?"

"Well, there is just one small thing." Ubaid looked mischievous. "Your contracts rely on Dale being able to accelerate his project here, and that depends on him winning the new project in Frankfurt."

"Why?"

"The why is not your concern, but the fact is that he needs to win, and therefore any help you or your government can add to his ability to do that will be very much appreciated." Ubaid was rather proud of this link between the projects and the Italians. He had thought if it all himself and would take great pleasure in dropping the fact to Abdullah when he next met him. It wasn't often that he managed to get one over on his senior ministerial colleague."

Bertelli looked hard at his friend. "Okay" he said, "I'll speak to some people and see what I can do."

Ubaid frowned. "I think you need to do more than see what you can do. No win probably means no negotiation."

Bertelli's face didn't flicker. "I hear you my friend," he sighed.

42

There was no answer and Jim Westead laid the phone carefully in its rest. After Dale's call earlier he had touched base with his old college friend Robert McGuire, choosing to meet at the West London club that McGuire habitually used when in town. The languid club atmosphere had helped to assuage any immediate concerns and McGuire had been careful to put Jim's mind at rest about other possible dangers that might lie in store for Dale and his team.

The extent of McGuire's quiet knowledge impressed Jim. He found out that not only was the British government rooting for them on the Frankfurt project, but also the Italians and Germans too. That, added to the local knowledge Dale had just phoned to him created a curiously worrying situation. Was no one against them? Everything had a price and so he was wondering what price Dale, and maybe he, might have to pay at the end of the day. Were they being greedy? Were the risks manageable? That was a tough question, especially when most were too obscure to state, let alone quantify.

Financially, Dale seemed to have pulled a rabbit from the hat. He had secured a contract paid largely up front in foreign currency, a previously unheard-of feat in this particular country. He had also secured financial support for a prize project in Germany, again up front in foreign currency, added to which, there seemed to be an astonishing array of serious backroom players intent on their success. Finally, young Connors had secured an acceleration fee, again paid-up front in foreign currency, for doing what they had always intended to do, to get on with things quickly. Time cost money, and to be paid double for carrying out a project as they had planned, but not disclosed, seemed like manna indeed. Even if the whole project turned to custard the up-front payments alone meant that they were financially secure. Apart from being polite about the latest news he had been careful not to talk on the phone to Dale, whose paranoia about listeners had reached monumental proportions. Consequently, Jim had taken to taping all his calls linked with Dale, something his PA Gill Browning had initially been worried about but now seemed to actually enjoy. She had even offered to transcribe them in her spare time. Jim knew she had an unfulfilled crush on Dale but surely this was going too far?

He picked up the phone again. It was late but he was determined to do his bit to help Dale win the Frankfurt project. Heinrich was an old colleague and roommate from business school days, and they had since found it productive to share notes rather than secrete them away. Although they competed it was always done in a civilised way, and they had become good friends. The home number in Germany rang and rang. He looked at his watch. 10.35 p.m. Well, I suppose they are an hour ahead, he thought, try again in the morning.

43

Marlena's breath hung in the crisp winter air. She had opted to walk rather than stuff herself into yet another sweaty taxi. Mercedes or not, there was always a distinct lack of freshness as the drivers, be they Armenian, Turkish or maybe even home-grown Bavarians, would invariably pull their leather coats about their ears and turn up the heating. The cars became womb-like, and the fetid smell of past passengers attacked like an emerging skunk as you opened the door. She hated them, and so, she walked, feeling energised with the cold air against her face, and revelling in its sharpness and that penetrating, cleansing sensation which she missed when she was working in the desert.

She looked at her reflection in the shop fronts and smiled to herself approvingly. Her dark green Italian coat, collar turned up against the wind, blended with the masses and her fur hat, its long fluffiness like some misplaced afro hair do, completed the anonymity she desired today.

She glanced at her watch. Good, plenty of time to grab some coffee before they started. The Aviation Authority building loomed ahead, almost directly across the paved roadway. It was stark and functional in its sixties cheapness, the concrete already patched and the thin aluminium window frames looking twisted and fragile. Even in Frankfurt there had been a decade of poor construction, just like the rest of Europe as the post war enthusiasm for technology overtook common sense and a simple awareness of what was good from bad. The Airport Authority was soon to move to new surroundings, out of the city and close to the airport itself. She'd heard that selling the city centre site would almost pay for the new building. The economics made sense to her logical mind, but she had no interest in such mundanities. She quickened her pace to cross the road before another tram bore down on her. It swam down the broad street with swirls of snowflakes eddying behind it. Supposedly a silent form of transport, the brakes squealed, and overhead power wires scraped and showered sparks as if on their last legs.

Marlena sprinted her high-heeled boots over the last twenty metres to where a warm, air-conditioned Starbucks beckoned. She pushed through the door and smiled at her good fortune at seeing that there was a spare red armchair in the far corner. It was opposite a fair-haired man with his back towards her and, as she dumped her shoulder bag into the chair's welcoming softness, she turned towards him.

"Anyone sitting here?" she said in German, and then smiled at the now familiar face.

Dale grinned. "I beg your pardon" he said, "my German isn't very good, but if you'd like a seat, please." He waved his hand towards Marlena's bag.

"Thanks" she smiled. "Can I get you some coffee?"

"No, I'm fine thanks. Just arrived." He held his mug up slightly. He had not expected Marlena at all.

Marlena returned slowly from the counter and sat nuzzling a tall cup of the daily special. They were both silent for a while and then she huddled forward slightly over the table, warming her hands around the cup as she did so. "You're here for the project briefing?"

"You mean the cargo logistics centre upgrade? That's right, it's a decent sized planning study and almost certain to run into programme management. Today's just the formal stuff, presentations by the client, that sort of thing. Everyone goes and no one asks questions. You know how it is."

"No, but I'm learning." Marlena leaned forward, "why no questions?"

Dale looked at her carefully. He had always been mystified by Marlena. Her expertise with languages was a real boon and her logical mind, though frustrating at times, was hugely reliable when it came to detail. But her true background was unknown to him. She had an inscrutable face, and her mannerisms belied some form of training. He had decided long ago that she was not a simple person. There was definitely something mysterious about her. "Well," he said, "simply because any questions and answers will be written down and copied to all the bidders, including those who are not there. I'd rather spend time with the client in private. You don't learn much in general meetings." He paused but Marlena said nothing. "As far as I'm concerned" he continued, "the main purpose of the briefing is to see the level of competition. Frankly, I'd rather not waste my time on it, but appearances are important."

Marlena breathed a sigh of relief. For a moment she thought Dale was saying he wouldn't be attending. "You seem to have a lot of people keen for you to win," she commented, leaning further forward and her voice taking on a confidential tone.

"So, I hear. I'm still trying to get to the bottom it." Dale paused again, this time to down a good half of his coffee. He hated it cold. "How about you Marlena, I hadn't expected to see you here. Are you linked with the project too?"

"Ah, well," Marlena looked away through the window to the light snowfall that had just started. "It's a long story, but I guess the simple version is that I'm being seconded to the procurement team at the Aviation Authority. It's all rather incestuous but I suppose officially I'll be your client, or at least your client's representative."

Dale's eyebrows puckered. There was little that surprised him, but this seemed more than coincidental.

"Assuming we win," he said.

"As I say, there are a lot of people keen that you should. I guess I'm here to help too."

"Help?"

"Sure, help make sure you win."

"You're telling me that you work for the client now, and you're there to help us win?" Dale looked quizzically over the rapidly cooling remnants of his black coffee. "And what about the remaining inputs on the irrigation project? How do they fit in?"

"Not a problem. I've special dispensation to complete those, although they're very minor now. That won't be a problem and it also means I have a reason to keep visiting you, out in the sunny Med!" Marlena laughed at her own joke.

"Not quite how I'd describe it, but never mind." Dale was beginning to see a picture. He wanted to know more. "So, tell me about the project. Winning can't be as easy as it sounds, especially with all these Euro rules about competition."

Marlena took a long time to sip her coffee. She needed to form her ideas before talking, and she hated cold coffee too. She decided to put her cards on the table. "As far as I can see, the combined interests of the UK, German and Italian governments appear to be behind you at the moment, quite apart from your camel racers of the deep desert. Depending who I talk to, this combined support is either unheard of co-operation on the part of my masters, or it's a great example of the new Euro spirit, which has been promoted everywhere since our US friends started going it alone in certain parts of the world. Either way it seems a good thing!"

"So, how does it translate to something useful? Government intentions are all very well, but we still have to win. I always worry when governments get involved. They usually have no idea how to turn ideas onto commercial reality."

"Listen," she said firmly, her Italian mannerisms getting the better of her for a moment. "I've spent the last few days looking at the project seriously and talking to the Aviation Authority people. I guess you have too?"

"Of course," Dale warmed to his subject and sensing more secure ground, "you don't win projects by responding to an invitation. It's all down to finding out what the client really wants, and it's usually not what he writes in the Terms of Reference."

"Good, so what did you find out about the opposition?" Marlena was back in her usual ferret mode. She and Dale both knew she'd be insatiable for information until she had the whole topic sorted out in her mind.

Dale treated her to a brief summary of his findings and quoted the two leading German companies who had done most of the ad hoc additions to the airport over time. They both had stunning relationships with the Airport Authority people and would be tough to beat.

Marlena nodded. "These two are key," she said. "If they were part of your team, I presume it would help to win?"

"Of course," Dale mentally told himself to think of a more imaginative phrase "but so far they've refused to meet me."

"Try again, after today's briefing." Marlena sounded very definite. "I think you'll find that some of their arms have been twisted recently."

"Okay, I'll do that." Dale sat back but then suddenly thought of something. "Tell me, if you're now the client's representative, what would you say the client really wants from this project. If there was one thing he needed to call it a success, what would that be?"

Marlena pondered for a moment. "The aviation people have been told that there is a potential threat to the airport, maybe to the air traffic system itself, even to international travel. But they don't know for sure and neither do we. The Authority's chairman has been told that, if you win, he may have a good chance of averting that threat. What they're all looking for is the best way forward, and they think you can deliver it to them. I guess that's what he really wants."

Dale suddenly felt very exposed and more vulnerable than he had felt in a long time. He began to realise just how much was being placed on his shoulders. He desperately needed to speak to Russell and find out the background to all this. What had started as a 'look and report' exercise now seemed to be much more active and serious. He was not sure he could handle this, as well as do his job, certainly not without a lot more information.

Marlena noticed his quietness. "You've gone pale," she said pleasantly, "seen a ghost?"

"Not yet" Dale replied, "but I'm beginning to think there are some around. I suppose what you just said took me a bit by surprise. You were very direct about what my role might be in all this. I guess I should thank you for that."

Marlena grinned. "Of course, I'm direct," she said. "I'm German," she added proudly. "None of your British 'round the bush' conversations here!"

Dale sat looking at her carefully. "Marlena," he asked politely, "who do you really work for?"

"The German government" she said quickly. "I'm just being seconded to the Airport Authority for a short time."

"And before the government?"

"Oh, just your normal rebellious student." She looked around hurriedly and caught sight of her watch. "Come on," she said. "Show-time!"

Dale smiled at her use of the phrase he used himself whenever they entered a big meeting room. Maybe it was a hackneyed thing to say but it never failed to relax the team. It had been a cause of much explanation and amusement on the irrigation project and he was pleased that Marlena had picked it up. At least she was trying. They pulled their coats together against the snowy cold and walked quickly to the Aviation Authority building.

44

Heinrich Müller rose from the opposite side of the coffee shop and followed them into the building. Signs directed them to the second floor conference room where about forty people were already gathered. Marlena had detached herself from Dale as they walked up the stairs. She now headed straight to the far end, to the head of the table. A large-headed German man was already seated while a young male assistant fussed over piles of handouts. A Japanese computer projector lay in the centre of the table, propped up on a copy of the local telephone directory. Dale noticed and smiled. Things were just the same here as at home. One day there would be a technological improvement on the telephone directory, but evidently not yet. Marlena emptied her shoulder bag and opened up her small laptop computer. Plugging in the power lead she searched around for the stray end of the projector cable then, arching her fingers over her laptop keypad, she pressed three keys at once. Nothing happened, so she swore under her breath and repeated the action. A hazy image began to appear on the screen. She focused and nodded to the chairman. She was ready.

"Jim Westead sends his regards." Dale turned round, startled to face the tall lean faced German beside him.

The thin face smiled. "Let me introduce myself," it said. "I am a good friend of Jim's. My name is Heinrich Müller. And you must be Dale Connors?"

"That's right, but how did you recognise me?"

"Oh, nothing too complicated, Jim just sent me your picture by email."

"Well, it's good to meet you. Are you here for the briefing too?" Dale could have kicked himself. Why else would anyone be here in this desolate building?

"Not directly. We won't be bidding ourselves for this. It's a bit out of our league, but Jim explained to me that you'd be here and thought maybe you could do with some help. I'm the chairman of the German Professional Engineers Association. Maybe I can help with some introductions. I hear you are looking to tie up one or two of our national firms. A sensible plan if I might say so. How can I best help you?"

Dale was becoming dazzled by the array of help on offer this morning. The approach from Abdullah had solved his financial bid and Marlena's suggestions this morning had clearly hinted that there were substantial government interests focused on their success. Now the well-groomed, serious Mr Müller was adding his weight and support too.

"The chairman's an old friend too. Maybe we can meet him after the meeting. I am at your disposal." Heinrich bowed slightly in an old-fashioned sort of way.

At that point, the large-headed chairman held up a glass and rapped it sharply with his pen. Those with a seat at the huge table straightened their papers, while those sitting in the chairs behind squirmed about like young children, trying to ensure a clear view.

"Good morning," the owner of the bear-like head spoke, his voice deep and immediately authoritative. The final whisperings stopped instantly and there was a sudden, complete silence. "My name is Walter Sandler. I am the Director of Airport Development at the National Airport Authority. This meeting is to provide a briefing for the Frankfurt Airport Cargo Logistics Centre Planning and Management Study. We have companies here from several countries and so the languages of the meeting will be German and English. Dale glanced at the array of German, French, Italian, American, British and Japanese engineering forms and smiled. Always in English; the Brits were really very fortunate. He wondered how many briefing meetings at Heathrow were conducted in another language. "My assistant Mr Nagel will make a presentation in German, which will be translated by Ms Kaltenbach."

Dale sat up with a start as he realised that this must be Marlena's family name, Kaltenbach. His German was poor, but it obviously meant 'cold something.' He sat back again while Karl and Marlena took the floor and pedantically ploughed through a presentation of the handouts in front of them, as if no one could read. He used his time to scrutinise the opposition. The two leading German firms were obvious, sitting near the chairman as if already part of the team. They had two participants each and exhibited that sort of bonhomie that was intended, usually successfully, to discourage competitors from venturing too close to their client. Other local companies were close to them, one with a bevy of participants including their own lawyer; but they knew the pecking order and would only be looking to act as subs to the main players. Two Americans, from two separate companies, sat next to each other, huddled for companionship in their foreignness. Expensive, thought Dale, and show me one well-planned airport in the US. The lone Frenchman sat next to the Japanese duo, who apparently represented a consortium of four major Japanese players. As financing was not an issue for the study, Dale thought them likely to be there just to gather information and position themselves for the later construction and equipment work.

To his right was a gaggle of Italians. He had listened to their conversation carefully. Why did so many businessmen always think their own language to be secure? He knew from experience that planning was not an Italian strength. Action was more their style, and he would have dismissed them completely if Italian businessmen were not renowned for developing strong relationships. The other players were all British firms, some with UK nationals representing them and some not. All, like Dale were accompanied by their local office managers and he glanced at Waldo, busy scribbling notes dutifully for appearances' sake, if not for the record. Waldo had done well for them in Frankfurt and this new project would be the jewel in the crown of a promising career for him. The fact that none of the other foreign nationalities had local staff probably meant they did not have local offices. He must remember to ask Marlena to add it to the selection evaluation criteria.

But Dale also had Herr Müller at his side and already he realised that the German engineers, to a man, had recognised him and nodded their respect. Maybe this thing was winnable after all. If he could put together a consortium with the German firms, with promises for all the local engineering work downstream to be done locally, but keeping the lucrative management fees for himself, then he would be happy; and so would they as it meant that none of them would be excluded from basic engineering by having to take the program management lead. Of course, Waldo and their own local firm would also be eligible for local work too if they structured their bid correctly. And the French? He had already recruited the best French airport architect to help them, again with promises of downstream concept work when they reached that stage. He pondered further into the future, with the Italians providing much of the airport equipment. Who hadn't seen their names all over the arrivals boards around the world? He was beginning to see a brightening light at the end of this particular marketing tunnel. Dale smiled, he was doing what he did best, and was enjoying himself.

He turned his attention back to Marlena, who was now taking them through the European competition rules. Knowing German addiction to rules, beating even the Brits into second place on that front, he could not help but be amused at the dexterity with which Marlena was now working. An onerous manual of good practice in her hand, she was no doubt already thinking how to orchestrate events to ensure the team of her choice succeeded.

When the break came for coffee, Heinrich Müller excused himself and was soon speaking earnestly into the Chairman's ear. When he returned he took Dale's arm. "Lunch. When we're finished here," he said confidentially. "Herr Sandler and his two staff, plus the two key German firms. Oh, and bring Waldo, he's paying," he added. Dale nodded his thanks. This is too easy, he thought.

They sat while questions were invited. The two Americans and the two Japanese asked one each, probably just to get their names on the record. In reply, Karl Nagel and Marlena did their best for the next forty minutes to be detailed but not informative and then everyone signed the register and called it a day. Waldo and Dale followed Heinrich to his waiting BMW 7-Series in the basement car park where a driver waited.

"The country club," whispered Heinrich. The big car glided silently out on to the snow-strewn road. And the day is only really starting, thought Dale. He had been to German business lunches before.

45

Helmut jogged along the riverbank. It was early, misty, cold and he was not happy. He was fifty, he was fit, and he was respected, maybe even liked in some quarters. He was certainly successful, but he was not happy, not happy at all. As head of Europe's largest state security organisation, he had literally thousands of people at his beck and call, and he knew more about his German politicians than they would like to admit. And yet he had no idea about how to deal with his son's education. After two daughters, both of whom had excelled at school, how he had managed to bring this long-haired, pseudo-revolutionary into the world was a mystery to him. Every time they met it ended with one or other of them walking out. Every time they talked it ended in argument.

His wife was not helpful either. "Helmut," she would say, "I have brought up your daughters. Is it too much to ask you to deal with your son?" In vain he had remonstrated that this good-for-nothing urchin was her son too, but it was to no avail. Arvin had come to the end of his expensive schooling and had so far failed to gain entry to anything approaching what his father thought of as an acceptable university. In Germany he had to be careful. Exerting influence was all very well, but he needed a good degree of invisibility in what he did, and Arvin was anything but invisible. Arvin, he thought, 'friend of the people.' How did we ever dream up such a name?

A barge hooted mournfully as it churned the filthy water to froth, just beating the stream on its painful journey upriver. The fog was patchy, but the current was strong, and the downstream traffic almost skittered along compared with their colleagues grinding their way upstream. There seemed no right or left side to the traffic, rather the slow up-streamers kept to the sides while the down-streamers flew down the middle, making best use of the river's natural morphology. An upward journey could take a week. A downward one a matter of hours. And all the time the industrial sewage filled its banks as it had done for years. The factory owners would point to measurements of improved water quality while the green-booted environmentalists would point to the paucity of amenity standards for swimming. They had given up on flora and fauna ages ago on this desolate stretch of the national economy. Across the river a few more early-morning exercise freaks trotted along what was evidently the more popular bank.

Helmut coughed as the acrid mist finally caught the back of his throat by surprise, and continued jogging through the morning gloom, his knees beginning to complain. Must lose some weight, he thought otherwise there'll be no knees left soon. Another lone jogger had paused up ahead and as he drew near, he recognised the friendly face he sought and smiled.

"Herr Clark," he said brightening significantly, "you made it! Let's sit out of the wind a little." He indicated an old brick structure set back from the towpath. "Two joggers sheltering from this dreadful weather is perfectly natural. No?"

Russell gratefully accepted the offer of shelter. He found Helmut's insistence on out of the way meetings sometimes irksome and was tempted to respond to Helmut's choice of phrase with a definitive 'No!' but thought better of it. "How are you keeping?" he asked politely instead.

"Oh, well enough, well enough. And you? You're looking well, very well in fact."

"You had a personal request?" Russell was freezing and his teeth were threatening to start chattering. He had been early for the meeting and despite hopping about in and out of the shelter for half an hour he felt as if his legs no longer belonged to him. Wearing shorts without long tracksuit leggings in this weather was clearly a mistake.

"I think you may also have a request, from what I hear" Helmut smiled, ignoring Russell's opener. "I hear you want to promote one of your English companies for our Frankfurt Airport security study, and even have them manage the programme. You know I could stop this in an instant if I wanted. National Security, official secrets, all that sort of thing. So, I'd like to hear the picture from your point of view if I may. I've heard it from our own people, and I must say the reason for calling in the Brits does seem rather fragile."

Russell wondered just how far back to go. "You remember Yemen," he said quietly.

"Of course!" Helmut was all ears now.

"You know that the explosive was traced through East Germany, eventually back to a mining source in Egypt?"

Helmut nodded his head gravely and waited patiently.

"And you recall Atlanta?"

"Vividly!"

"Well, the same route was used for that explosive. There are another dozen or so likely links which we're following up." He paused but Helmut was in a receptive mode and his attention didn't waver for a moment.

Russell ploughed on. "We're getting extremely concerned that there may be a strike against another target. The Egyptian mining source seems to feature too often for coincidence."

Helmut frowned. "Go on," he said

Russell decided to shorten the narrative. He sensed Helmut already knew a lot more than he was admitting. "Global Infrastructure, our UK company, has a number of contracts in Libya, with the Ministry of Construction. We have traced payments for the explosive provided from Egypt. They all end up at this Construction Ministry. It's evidently being used as a front for the government, or someone in the government. Our guess is the Ministry of Security, which houses some rather unsavoury characters, all distinguished by the large chips they carry on their shoulders."

"Fayez Shakari for one?"

"That's right. Well, given the current position regarding diplomatic activity, or rather the lack of any formal presence there, having Dale Connors as our eyes and ears has turned up some interesting facts. We are getting good reports from him almost daily."

"Daily? I thought they were weekly?" Helmut looked up at Russell. "You mean we aren't seeing all the material?"

"Absolutely, Herr Director, you do see it all. But it's collated weekly for transmittal. That was our agreement."

Helmut glowered. "As long as we have transparency," he grunted. Sharing information was a relatively new game for both of them. "And the Frankfurt designs?"

"We believe that they are building their own new cargo facility as a replica of Frankfurt's, in an effort to maximise their information about the airport and maybe have their own training ground. We think they've used this approach before. It all points to something being planned against Frankfurt, but we don't know what, or when. The plan is to use Dale as a courier and give them old designs with in-built faults and incorrect access details. If Global Infrastructure are able to win the Frankfurt study then they'll be in a position to give our Libyan ministry friends more details about the airport's up to date systems. And of course, we, rather than the airport will be providing that information for them. Your people will be essential in this," he added a little too hurriedly. "The whole game is to lead them into thinking they have detailed and secure information and then to intercept their attack before it happens. The fact that they have wrong security details should give them an immediate headache if they ever get as far as entering the facility."

"Why are we sure that Frankfurt is the target?"

"Why is anywhere a target?" Russell decided it was time to switch roles.

"Maybe Frankfurt's just the means to and end? Maybe we're looking at a bomb aboard a flight from Frankfurt. In which case, why Frankfurt? Where do flights go from there that don't go from elsewhere?"

"Maybe, and their focus on the cargo area certainly points that way, but the indications are that they are definitely planning to infiltrate the actual facility. Where they put a bomb then depends on how well they know the layout."

"But there must be dozens of airports with cargo planes leaving every day. Why Frankfurt?"

"I don't know, but actually, if they are planning to put it on a plane as cargo then I guess Frankfurt is a good plan from our point of view."

"Why?"

"Because the old plans show that only small cargo is X-rayed. Anyone planning to target cargo would imagine they can do so unhindered."

Helmut frowned. "We've been well aware of that loophole for some time" he said, "that's one reason we're upgrading."

Russell looked at him in astonishment. "You mean to say that cargo is still not all X-rayed?"

"That's right, and unless we have a small army of hand searchers, that's our Achilles heel. Maybe our bombers aren't so stupid after all. It's not a feature of the airport we shout about."

Helmut looked into the distance. "My own airport people tell me there's no problem" he said, "but I think pride blinds their eyes. I'm more inclined to believe your thesis. I think we have a bigger problem here than we realise." He looked back at Russell. "Give me a minute to think how best to move forward."

Russell pondered on the likely conditions. There were bound to be several, and detailed. That was how Helmut worked.

"Three conditions." Helmut didn't disappoint, but three was modest for him. "One, You deal personally with Mr Connors. No one else controls him, okay?"

"Okay," Russell wondered who had been priming Helmut. This was one of his own conditions anyway.

"Two, we have vetting and veto rights on the product before it leaves Europe, okay?" Russell nodded.

"Three, you share everything, as soon as you know anything."

"If that's two way, then I agree."

Helmut peered into Russell's now blue face. "If you sense any holding back on information from my staff, any at all, you have McGuire contact me directly. And if I hear of anything then I'll be on to him too, okay?"

"Okay," Russell nodded.

Helmut gazed out into the distance. "Now" he grunted, "I need your advice about Alvin please."

Russell smiled. McGuire had briefed him about the wayward lad, and he had been prepared to offer help if it had been necessary to secure Helmut's assistance. In the end it had not, as Helmut himself had raised the issue. Well, that was much better. He listened carefully as his colleague poured out his agony.

"What's he really good at?" Russell had become aware of the cold again and was keen to run some more, straight back to his car heater if possible.

"Worrying about the state of the third world, demonstrating against our American brothers, and drinking away his allowance in the city's worst gossip shops. He's not an idiot but frankly he's not academically minded either, and he isn't interested in technology or the arts. All I want is for him to go to a good university where he can learn to think straight; somewhere with some good examples around him."

"Well, Robert McGuire did discuss this with me and suggested maybe a government scholarship to Cambridge, one of its smaller colleges, nothing too onerous mentally, but plenty of time to debate the state of the world with interesting tutors. His English is very good from what I hear."

"Yes, his English is excellent. Strange, I'd never thought of it as an asset before, but are you serious? If McGuire can manage to organise that, then he'll have my undying friendship for ever. That would really be something. How do you fellows do it?"

"Well, we do have one or two places at our disposal. We'd have to pay fees of course. We can't manage it for free, unless of course we have a brilliant academic on our hands, but then they'd get in anyway. Call it part of a long-standing Government Exchange Programme."

"Just name the price." Helmut was now wide-awake and happy for the first time in weeks.

"Well, that's just it. We aren't allowed to charge for these places. Comes out of operational budgets. You know how it is. Maybe one day we might need a favour in return. You never know. So, if you're happy with the idea, then so are we. We can move straight away."

Helmut knew he was caught, but he could hardly back out now. Damned Brits, he thought. Now he owed them. Well, never mind. It certainly provided the ideal solution for Alvin, and maybe some of the environment of one of the oldest and best-respected universities in the world would rub off, you never knew. He swallowed the remainder of his pride and smiled as benevolently as he could manage in the cold air.

"In that case. Please tell our friend McGuire that I gratefully accept." Helmut knew when to be gracious. "I'm sure he'll want his pound of flesh one day, but never mind; All in a good cause."

Russell did wonder exactly what cause Helmut had in mind but felt he had achieved enough for one frozen morning. "Just wait until you hear from us before announcing it," he cautioned. "We need to do things in the right order, okay?"

"Of course, yes, well now, a good day after all, no?" Helmut's face told all, and he headed out into the freezing wind again, pounding happily up the footpath the way he had come and leaving Russell to make his own way back to the icebox of a car he had abandoned across the fields.

Russell's mind had lightened too, and he was looking forward to meeting up with his Italian counterparts, whose insistence on bending the German service's normally ramrod straight backbone had been unusually determined and persistent. He wondered how far the Italians would go to ensure commercial success. They were certainly more creative marketers than the Brits or Germans and their philosophy towards rules was rather different too. Whereas the Teutonic temperament would look at a set of guidelines with pride and comfort knowing exactly what they had to do, the Latins tended to regard them as advisory at best, and certainly not aimed at them particularly. It always stuck him as strange that the orderly Roman Empire could turn into such a freewheeling society where life and especially style of life were so important. Maybe it was the weather, he thought uncharitably. Certainly, today was a good example where sitting about enjoying life wasn't appealing at all. Oh, for some warm, sunny days. He thought of Como.

He pondered too on the overall layout of events. With false plans organised, and control over the forthcoming new planning work at Frankfurt, he was feeling more comfortable. The good thing, he thought, was that everything was deniable. So essential in his game, the golden rule was always 'don't admit liability.' Relying on commercial firms to wash your dirty linen had its risks, but at the end of the day it was easy to blame errors on commercial interests. People were not surprised when they proved fallible; and with their fallibility lay the trade-off from using them. Politics and security issues could be kept at a distance, visibly far removed from the action and utterly deniable. Overall, he mused, a good morning's work, despite the cold.

46

"This is how you have to tell the story." Marlena had drawn a flow chart on the white board. She and Emanuella were closeted in a small meeting room at Dale's hotel. It had been a revelation to meet Emanuella again and to have her introduced as Marlena's Italian counterpart. It struck Dale that, if the Irrigation Project client had only known who was working on his project, he would have had a fit. There was not much space and Dale was gloomily thinking about the cost per minute. Marlena was becoming repetitive. "You're getting the plans direct from Russell in the UK who will have letterheads and signatures from the previous engineering company who designed Luton, as well as the first Frankfurt facility. The story line is that the airport won't release plans directly themselves and so you're going round the back door to extract a favour from a friend."

Dale nodded. So far this was just recap time.

"The plans themselves will have been checked to make sure that they are covered with Frankfurt references in all the right places. But they will actually be old Luton airport drawings."

Dale's eyes glazed a little. "Why can't we simply use old Frankfurt plans?" he asked. "I thought they were the same as Luton anyway."

"Luton and Frankfurt have exactly the same footprint, so they look identical from aerial photos, but internally they're quite different. You can wander round Luton, especially if you're dressed as a fireman. They seem to have precedence everywhere in England, maybe something to do with the Great Fire of London I guess."

Dale ignored her attempt at humour. "And Frankfurt?" he asked.

"You can't walk round there, even if you've got a map. It's been turned into a maze indoors. Putting it bluntly, there's no way on earth the airport authorities will let out details of the changes they've made."

"If you say that now, about these old plans, what happens if we win this new project? I thought we would have access to all the upgrades too. In fact, I thought that was the whole point of the exercise"

Marlena and Emanuella exchanged looks. "From your ministry client's perspective, it is" answered Emanuella, "and you will have access, but the information you take offshore will be heavily vetted and probably not represent reality too much. I'm not saying the systems won't work, as they certainly will, but they'll probably be two or three improvements out of date."

"So, tell me this." Dale was floundering. "Why are the governments of the UK, Germany and Italy all so desperately keen for us do the Frankfurt job?"

Marlena sighed. "As I mentioned yesterday, I think their main intent is to prevent some sort of incident at Frankfurt. By using your company as the courier of old information we keep control of events as much as we can. To not give information would present a problem as they'd presumably try somewhere else and to allow free access would clearly be a major risk. So, to provide old data seemed a neat way to control things. And meanwhile we keep our ears open for what might be being planned."

"So, you think they'll pull off some stunt at Frankfurt soon?" Dale was back to thinking commercially. Thank goodness he'd secured up-front payments. He must also try to put a large penalty clause in the Frankfurt bid in case it was cancelled. If the governmental support was all it claimed to be maybe that was a possibility. But he was also worried and needed to think through the risks. This was the first time anyone had clearly summarised the plan for false information, and he needed to know what dangers he might be getting himself and his company colleagues into.

"Tell me," he said thinking aloud, "what happens when I hand over these drawings and they say, 'these aren't Frankfurt?' What do I say then?"

"They won't, but if they do you tell them not to shoot the messenger. You know nothing. You've secured the drawings in good faith from the company who did the previous work and the fact that they've asked you to get the drawings anyway means they haven't got access themselves."

"I haven't met the actual company yet. I think I should, if only to be able to talk about the individuals if I need to. Will Russell deal with that?"

"Probably, you can ask him when he comes."

"He's coming here?" Dale's surprise showed.

"Should be. I gather he had a cold meeting this morning. Taking a while to thaw out."

Dale felt somewhat relived to know his friend was expected, but his overall anxiety level was rising steeply.

"Okay, now tell me this. How do I deal with my team on the ground? They're going to be researching Frankfurt's systems, but they'll not be able to pass on what they find. Isn't that going to be rather strange?"

"You'll be using most of your staff from the two German companies, so no big deal there." Marlena was almost offhand. "You'll be the only common link. I guess you'll have your own project manager and management team?" She raised her eyebrows questioningly to Dale.

"Of course, that's the only way we work."

"In which case they'll probably have to sign the official secrets act."

Dale stopped to digest this news.

"And me?"

"You mean you haven't signed?"

"No, should I?"

Marlena laughed. "Better ask Russell."

Dale sat and worried. It was all very well for these girls to play spy games, but it was his career and his company's business that were at risk, not to mention quite a few lives if things turned nasty. The way things were moving sounded too organised and he worried that his clients didn't behave in an organised expected way. Too much was controlled by personalities such as Abdullah and Fayez. He worried some more while the girls chatted about technicalities amongst themselves.

A knock at the door announced Russell. He looked round the room and sized up the situation. "Well," he said jovially, focusing on an unhappy Dale, "I guess I should say 'join the team.'"

Dale returned a look that could have frozen water. "It seems I'm getting into something a lot bigger than I'd bargained for," he said. "When I agreed to be your eyes and ears on this airport project I didn't realise I was going to be the key person in some sort of subterfuge operation involving my client."

"All deniable," beamed a happy Russell. "All you're doing is passing them information in good faith. Maybe you have to live with the fact that I'm a temporary staff member in charge of production at a certain UK engineering firm, but that's all there is to it really. Anything happens, you know nothing; pure as the driven … and all that."

"Well, maybe I'm upset that I wasn't told beforehand. I hate these sorts of surprises." Dale grumbled, more for effect than from any real conviction. The fact was that he felt strangely exhilarated at the thought of doing something 'on the edge' as he would describe it. And 'living on the edge' was what he always secretly liked to do. He wondered how many of the others felt the same. They were all in a very peripheral profession, chasing shadows of their own making most of time, and he guessed that they too felt the need to live out on a limb, mentally and psychologically, if not physically.

Russell seemed to read his thoughts. "Come on," he said. "You're enjoying yourself really. You like a bit of excitement in life."

"Maybe" Dale smiled grudgingly, "maybe." He realised suddenly he was looking at three national security services working together. Was this the new world order, he wondered? And they were all highly professional, even Emanuella had changed from the student image he had of her from their meeting in the university. She looked every bit the fashionable young Italian professional and certainly had the style to pull it off. She was all business and missed nothing. He was beginning to feel a little daunted by these power-girls. What sort of men did they invite into their lives, he wondered? He'd met Fritz and had not been hugely impressed. And his evening with Emanuella had been startling to say the least. How could anyone like this be afraid of sleeping on their own?

"Okay, so where are we all? Have the girls brought you up to date with events?" Russell broke into his thoughts.

"Pretty much." Dale decided he had better take some leadership in things otherwise he would be little more than a pawn in their game. "But I do have a number of things I need to talk to you about, such as when can we meet the UK engineering firm, to start with?"

"Tomorrow if you like, no problem. You and I are travelling back to the UK in the morning, we can go straight there if you wish. I'll call them and make arrangements"

"Okay, and how about the Frankfurt contract. I'm getting the impression that we're mainly here to act as your extended staff overseas. If something happens and all this falls apart in some way, we may be out on our ears. So can we include some commercial safeguards against this sort of thing happening?"

"You mean a penalty clause if Frankfurt pulls the plug. I would have thought so, but Marlena will know better than I do."

"Firstly, there's no way we would have proposed this plan if we didn't have confidence in your firm to manage the project. So don't get any ideas about favouritism will you. That's not the case at all." Marlena sounded as if she was giving a rehearsed speech. "As for a penalty clause, as long as it's fair and not aiming for a windfall I imagine we can do that."

"No, no, nothing exorbitant, just costs plus loss of profit, and maybe a reasonable up-front payment to guarantee cash flow. Something to give Jim some comfort would be helpful."

"All right, let's look at that this afternoon, back in the office. If you come round at about four o'clock I'll try and put something together." Marlena jotted down a few notes.

"And what's all this about the Official Secrets Act?" Dale looked at Russell very pointedly.

"Ah yes, something I'd forgotten to mention. Let's go through that sort of stuff on the plane tomorrow."

47

It was Raheem who tipped her the wink, gave her the nod, or whatever it was he said, to alert her. The corridors of the Ministry of Agriculture were not favoured for covert conversations, but his look and hurried muttering said it all. And whatever he had seen to concern him, and whatever he had then said, it had definitely spooked her. When Ministry of Security people came to visit there was always trouble. Nadia decided to wait until the official summons arrived. She tried to calm her nerves and trawled her memory for what could possibly have instigated this visit. An investigation? These were always on the go. A warning? She was not sure she deserved one. Maybe her relationship with Dale? This was top of her list, but she'd been so careful since that first night that she doubted that they had anything against her. She was sure they were not doing anything illegal. Her own past flashed before her and she hastily pushed it back into the depths of her memory. Changed name, double passports, false work legend from her early days in Italy and the UN. Surely that was all behind her now? Surely these people here weren't capable enough to have caught up with her history. Surely, they couldn't be so interested? Surely, surely. She sat and worried silently, reading and re-reading the report in front of her without a clue what it was about.

When the summons came, she was aghast. Three o'clock. She should be on her way to the airport soon. She had no choice but to ask Fatimah to cover for her. She gave no reason for the short notice, except that she was not feeling well. Fatimah cheerfully took the chance to drive the big Peugeot again and took off immediately. Nadia sighed and made her way slowly up the stairs.

Fayez Shakari had chosen the Minister's own conference room to meet her. He had thought about borrowing the office itself as its owner was away, but the conference room's size and imposing presence was ideal for his purpose. He wanted to impress, and the room's aura would add to her feeling of nervousness. Apart from that it was wired for sound back to his own offices. He could listen again to her answers. They were always easier to analyse without the distraction of visual contact. To ensure maximum effect, he sat with his back to the window that ran along the side of the room. His silhouette black against the morning sunshine. He could have closed the vertical slatted blinds to shield the glare, but he decided to let it pour through. He looked at his watch. She should be on her way now. And as if on cue, there was knock at the door. Fayez stood up and faced away from the table, looking out of the window. "Come in," he said, deliberately lowering the tone of his voice. He heard the door open. "Sit down, please," he added.

There was a silence and then a young man's voice spoke. "I've brought some coffee," it said.

Fayez turned to see Raheem standing with a tray. Behind him was Nadia. He fumed inside as his carefully orchestrated start to the meeting had collapsed in ruins. He sat down, accepted the coffee in bad grace and waved Nadia to a chair across the wide expanse of mahogany. Nadia's face was fixed. She was terrified it might show her amusement. She would be thankful to Raheem for a long time for his neat defusing of the situation. She sat and waited. "You asked to see me?" she said at last.

"You're a pretty girl." Fayez's words struck terror in Nadia's heart. What was he after? Where was this going? Was this a threat? Was he propositioning her? She studied his thickset face, lined and gnarled, as if carved from a walnut trunk directly from the tree. He was a bulky man, and she knew his reputation for bullying and brutality was legendary. She immobilised the expression on her face and said nothing.

"Dale Connors is a lucky man." Her mind had now fused completely. Nothing seemed to be expected in reply, so she said nothing. She hoped her heart didn't sound as loud across the table as it did to her. It was surely impossible for him not to feel her trembling knees.

Fayez pushed a brown A4 envelope across the table and sat back looking at her. "Open it," he commanded.

It was unsealed and obediently she folded back the flap and slid the white paper slowly out from its wrapping.

"And turn it over." Fayez could not hide his anticipation of Nadia's face when she saw the picture. He was not disappointed as she lifted up the edge of the shiny paper and disclosed a perfect view of a tall, longhaired beauty lying peacefully asleep with her head resting on the crooked arm of an admiring, fair haired and fair skinned man. His look of longing and admiration told it all. She left the photograph face up and looked up at Fayez. His grin had broadened to a fully-fledged smirk. She ignored the photograph and studied his face instead, and realised he had a day's stubble showing on his chin. Probably smells too, she thought to herself. She really did not like this man. But she said nothing and waited.

"We have more," Fayez said expansively, "and several at the fort too." He did not say that they were only external shots in the market and coffee shop, taken with a long lens from the van. In fact, this was the only compromising picture they had of the couple. But the effect on the girl was enough. Nadia was clearly stunned. Although she had realised the photo had been taken, it had been a while ago and she'd put it from her mind. But Fayez bringing it up now? That was bad news. Very bad news. She felt numb and even if she'd wanted to speak, she doubted whether she could.

"Keep it" he said, "we always have the original." He paused and looked at her and admired her impassiveness. It crossed his mind that she had either been trained for this sort of eventuality or she was frightened into silence. On balance, it pleased him to think she was just terrified of him. In any case he now had her complete attention.

"Cohabiting with foreigners is not actually illegal," he started to say, but then added "unless, of course, I decide that it should be." He paused again, for effect this time. "But if these photographs were published I can guarantee that you would never work again, never be able to marry here, and in effect would have to leave the country. You would have no means of support. Am I clear?"

Nadia looked at him. It was the first invitation to say something in return. She mumbled an agreement.

"Good, good. So, what I'm going to offer you will probably sound too good to be true, a blessing from heaven if you like. Are you listening?"

Nadia's face shifted a little as her interest rose and the turmoil in the depths of her stomach began to quell a little.

"I'm listening," she whispered.

"It's very simple really." Fayez was now in his stride. "You keep your eyes on young Mr Dale and keep us informed about what he's doing, and we put the photos in our 'never to be opened' file."

"You want me to spy for you?"

"Well, I'm not sure I'd say spy. You've been watching too many movies. Anyway, you need training for that sort of thing. Professionals don't grow on trees you know. No, it's more of a watching and listening, and questioning and reporting. I want to know everything about him, his meetings, phone calls, habits, preferences, friends, everything. You clearly have strong feelings for him. Well, if you really value those feelings then you'll help us." Fayez stopped to gauge the effect his words were having. He could see Nadia's mind churning in front of him. Good, he thought.

"If you do well, then we'll let this relationship of yours continue. But if you fail us, then we can easily send these photographs to his wife, or simply arrange for him to disappear, so when the photographs are published here, you'd have nowhere to run to."

"You'd kill him?"

Fayez was shocked at her temerity in asking such a direct question. He frowned. "No, not at all," he said. "In fact, Dale Connors is very valuable to us. All we're doing is looking after our investment. Taking out a little insurance. Always a good idea to avoid surprises. Don't you agree?"

Nadia's mind was still in turmoil. She was sure Dale had said he was divorced. If Fayez thought he was still married then that explained his reliance on the photograph. But her thoughts were quickly coming back into focus. "So, you're not going to stop us meeting?" she asked.

"Good heavens no. Why would we do that? In fact, we want you to see more of him. Stick to him like another eager wife. How else can you learn everything about him?"

"And how do I report to you?"

"Fuad will come to this ministry every day when Dale is in-country. You will write notes and then discuss them with him. He will brief me on what is happening."

Nadia was not happy with this. She found Fuad creepy and insincere. He also had wandering hands. "I guess I don't have a choice?" she asked, more for the form of saying something than for any other reason.

"No, not at all," smiled a now visibly happy Fayez. "Oh, just one thing I should mention, Mr Dale must not be aware of your assignment. It would be sad for us all, especially you, if he were to give you false information."

"Then I don't want this," she said, pushing the photo back into it envelope and sliding it across to Fayez. "Better not have it on me."

Fayez smiled. "Good," he said. "I can see you're taking what I've said seriously. Come," he added, "it's getting late. I'll give you a ride home." He knew that rides in his official Ministry of Security Mercedes would add to her nervousness. He also wanted to show that he knew exactly where she lived. They left the building together, Nadia looking around her furtively and Fayez striding straight to his waiting car and driver. If Fayez wanted to intimidate her, then taking her home was exactly the way to do it. Nadia resigned herself to her fate and plodded after him.

48

He walked eagerly through the last barrier and looked about him in vain, until he realised that there was only Fatimah standing in the crowd. She smiled and waved as if nothing was wrong, but his heart was already pumping. Where was she? Why hadn't she come to the airport? "I would need to be ill not to come" she had said when they had last parted. Perhaps she was ill. He would have asked Fatimah, but he knew from experience that her English wasn't up to complicated words like 'well' and 'ill.' He would be patient. They made their way out over the sticky tarmac to the waiting Peugeot, corralling the wayward baggage trolley to take more or less the same direction as themselves. He brightened up slightly at not having to use Fatimah's old VW.

His trek through the customs had been unusual today. He had been treated almost like royalty, as if the security staff were on the lookout for him and under orders to be helpful. First, he'd been taken out of his habitual longest line and marched swiftly up to the start of another, newly forming queue as a customs officer was brought on duty especially, it seemed, or maybe it was wishful thinking, to deal with his baggage. Despite the two brown paper wrapped parcels of extra hand baggage, they hadn't quizzed him at all. His preparations of extra adhesive tape in his briefcase had not been needed. Never mind, better not to have that terrible time in Saudi again when the customs officials had taken apart his neatly bound books of bid documents and drawings, all in front of a plane load of curious competitors. Remembering the incident made him shudder and he had expected much the same here. But nothing, almost the opposite, in fact. It was as if the security staff were tasked to ensure the safe passage of Dale with his cargo of brown paper wrapped packages.

He thankfully humped his bags off the unsteerable trolley and into the boot of the waiting car, still clutching his computer and briefcase as if they were glued to his hands. Old habits die hard. He kept his team's package with him too, but he consigned the one for Ubaid with the bags. If they wanted to steal it so be it. The two packages were deliberately contrived to look and weigh the same, although the ministry package had many extra pages of photos, and file extracts which the project team did not warrant. Russell had been at pains to think of everything and had inserted duplicate pages in the project's package, just so they both looked identical. Quite why the packages had to look the same had baffled him, but Russell had insisted that the team not be provided with any more than they needed, while the ministry were to be under the impression that everything they had was real and being used in the design. The logic still defeated him, but he hadn't argued. He felt he was deep enough into this whole affair without taking on any more ownership than he had to. And these were only the first few drawings. The main security details would follow next month.

The car was fast, and the road seemed less pitted and holed than when he'd made this journey in the old Beetle. The Peugeot was also a good deal quieter and, as they entered the city Dale was surprised that time had flown by so rapidly. Maybe he had slept. He could sleep almost anywhere, especially when there was some background motion like a plane or a train. He looked up as they passed the Ministry of Agriculture building. It struck him that he now spent less time there than at the Construction Ministry. It was fortunate too, he thought, that Nadia actually worked for the latter and had been seconded to the former, especially for his project. It had meant that they spent more time together, albeit frustrating to have to put work first all the time. He pondered on his feelings for Nadia. They certainly enjoyed each other's company and they both enjoyed the sex too. But was that all? He hadn't given it serious thought, but he needed to soon. Nadia was something of a mystery to the likes of Marlena and Emanuella and he sensed their slight antagonism to her. He wondered why. After all she was based right in the heart of the ministries and must be able to feed information out through Bertelli that covered much more than his own meagre projects. He realised suddenly that he cared what happened to her. He also wanted to see her again and soon.

His mind was still on her as they rounded the corner of the building and slowed as a ball spun across in front of them. Fatimah braked hard and as he looked ahead beyond the local soccer game he was astonished to be met with the sight of a large Arab climbing into his car, closely followed by Nadia. The car was near to the side door of the ministry and the angle of sight was poor. However, he was sure it was her, despite her cover-all abaya. She was looking around her as if she didn't want to be seen, but it was unmistakably her. He tapped Fatimah on the shoulder, but she had been concentrating on the nearby game, steering carefully round the makeshift goalposts mounted in mid-street. He had not recognised the car or the man, but he was not happy about what he'd seen. Nadia had looked frightened and vulnerable, and he realised he cared. He cared a lot.

49

At the airport, Naiem Fahoud filed his report. He noted with pleasure that the subject had been helped through customs and had passed through immigration procedures in record time. He noted the actual number of minutes carefully and nodded approvingly. Thirteen minutes meant that Dale could hardly have stopped walking from the plane to the airport exit. He was pleased with his team and would make a point of telling them at tomorrow's briefing. He finished off by noting that the subject was last seen heading away from the airport in the direction of the city and yes, he had two equally sized large brown paper wrapped packages with him.

Why his bosses were so concerned about paper wrapped packages carried by some British engineer did not concern him, but they were evidently hot property for somebody in the ministry. Strict orders had been sent along the lines of 'do not challenge' and 'do not open packages' and with the exhortation to dispatch him through the airport in record time, it all added up to something unusual. But it was not Naiem's problem. He had done his bit for whatever cause they'd dreamt up in the ministry this time and now he could get back to his job.

He listed the car's make and number but failed to note the name of the driver. Women were still women to him, and women ministry drivers didn't count in anyone's book. As he signed the record and dated it he noticed that this was Dale's sixth visit and that he would likely be spending Christmas here, not that it made any difference when Christmas was not celebrated. Certainly, it was not a public holiday. Naiem Fahoud, ever the tidy man that he was, added the sixth visit reference to the report. Christmas he kept to himself. He touched a key and the entry vanished into the system. The paper record would make its way to the city later that day.

50

Bertelli was rattled. His man at the airport had just phoned to give him the news about Dale's arrival and he had sent a code stream back to Italy via his contractors' network. Everything on track so far. However, unlike Naiem, Bertelli's eyes on the ground had noticed that Fatimah had collected Dale, not Nadia. That in itself was not too worrying, although it did strike him as surprising, but his close encounter a short while ago had been a real concern. He had been taking a taxi to a coffee shop near Nadia's apartment building and had just paid the driver. Walking across the road he was almost run down by none other than Fayez Shakari's big Mercedes. The car and number plate were well known, and he had not been surprised to make out the bulky shape of the man himself sitting in the rear passenger seat. Even the darkened glass could not hide that shape.

What had blown him away was when the car stopped less than fifty metres away, right outside Nadia's apartment complex. He had been amazed to see his own covert staff member herself open the car door and step out onto the roadway, before hurrying into her front doorway. Taking rides with strangers was something he had always lectured Nadia about and Fayez was worse than a stranger. What was she doing? Fayez did not give rides for free. Was she still safe? Was she now working for the opposition? He crouched down at the nearest café table and watched but the car had sped away and Nadia had not resurfaced. Bertelli began to draft a memo in his mind's eye and would send it later to Russell via the normal routes. He doubted that the Brit would be worried. He never was, he was too phlegmatic by half; but he would have to plan some visits to the ministries tomorrow to find out more.

51

Across the road Nadia lay exhausted on her bed, her mind running through the conversations with Fayez. In the car he had relaxed and had been quite chatty, but he still terrified her. His reach, into the lives of whoever incurred his wrath, was rumoured to be phenomenal, and no one survived to cross him again. Her biggest problem was whether to tell Dale about her predicament or not. Fayez had been very clear, both in the meeting and in the car, but her instinct told her that she needed to be transparent with her own people, and she regarded the Brits, and to a lesser extent the Italians, as her people. Despite her Italian passport, she had a hankering for things north of the channel. At least they were honest and predictable. And if she did not tell them, then how could they help her if things turned nasty. Nasty was not a word she chose to think of when Fayez was around. Today, he had been on his best behaviour. She would hate to see him dealing with someone in anger.

She turned to her feelings for Dale. Were they simply the aftermath of a good time, or did she really care for him? It was a while since she had thrown herself at anyone and not for a very long time had she wanted to hold someone in the same way she needed him to hold her now. And yet the opening given to her by Fayez was, as he had put it, too good to be true. Instead of worrying about being seen and reported back to the ministry, he had actively encouraged her to be with Dale, to shadow him and learn about him. Instead of skulking round the corners of the hotel lobby when they made their way there at night, they could now openly wander about without a care in the world. She had Fayez's assurance on that, hadn't she? She replayed the conversations again. Her problem was that she wanted to believe him but knew that he must be an inveterate liar. She was absolutely sure too that if she did not deliver the goods on Dale, then she, let alone he, would simply disappear to join the ranks of the others who had never existed. She felt the edge of her life drawing very close and the adrenaline building in her bones. What to do? She looked at her watch. Dale should be just about arriving at the hotel now. With her mind made up she bounded from the bed. She would shower, change and make her way there. She had decided she cared. She cared a lot for this man, and she was not going to let him, or her become fodder for the games of these would-be world movers and shakers, no matter what country they represented.

52

Russell's brief had been simple. Research their local files in Libya. Look for inconsistencies, anywhere. Go to the archives in the UK and see what else you can find here. If you can get file copies for the key players then great, but if not then ask Wafa simple questions and let her get the answers, never too many, never too onerous. "Her job's important to us, don't blow it" were his parting words.

Miles looked carefully at the early pages of his notes again. There was no mistake. Raya's records in Wafa's system had a missing period of two years before the paperwork started again about her marriage all those years ago, and her giving birth to Abdullah, now the Minister of Security. Then the record stopped, at the end of a volume. Apparently Fayez now held Raya's files himself and everything covering the last fifty years was in his safe. He suspected that these old file details should also have been removed at the same time, but for some reason they'd been missed. Maybe whoever had retained the two years of papers still had the files when Fayez took over the log.

Whatever it was, the dates matched. In his previous search through the labyrinthine archives of the Foreign Office in London he had been lucky and found what he suspected might be there. It was the story of a highflying young British diplomat who became entangled with a student from Libya. The student's name was Raja, not quite the same but he only had the English version. Her country of origin was the same and the dates fitted exactly. He would need to see the Arabic originals, but he was certain it was the same person.

His later research in the UK had provided more proof. In the archives he had found a copy of the hospital certificate of a baby boy, born fifty-three years ago in London. No name was recorded, but on the next page he had found the answer. Tucked into a pocket was a copy of a registered birth in the names of his own grandparents. His father carried their family name, as did Miles. His father had always known he was adopted but it was only recently that Miles had become aware of it, and this was the first time he'd been able to track anything about his origin. The adoption had been arranged three days after the birth and the address was in his hometown in Scotland. The file had been scant about what happened to the diplomat. He had clearly been persuaded of the error of his ways and the organised abandonment of Miles' father had been meticulously carried out. But as ever in government there was always a file record, somewhere.

Miles looked now at the last page of notes. Raya seemed to have a propensity for losing partners. The diplomat, his real grandfather, as he now knew him to be, had been killed in an embassy bomb blast in Africa many years ago. Miles had found that his grandfather had married an English girl but had no children. Of his grandfather's wife there was a name but no further record. Raya's legal husband, Abdullah's father, had been killed in the coup that resulted in her sister's grandson, the current ruler, taking power. An interesting lady.

I'm related, he thought. What does that mean? He decided to ask Wafa one more request. He had a suspicion this old lady had things to hide.

53

Dale looked through the hotel room's spyhole and opened the door smiling. He could not help himself, despite his concern for her. She almost fell into his arms. He waved to the boy at his desk across the corridor and hung the 'do not disturb' sign before closing and locking the door.

She was still clutching him. "I missed you," he murmured.

"I missed you too," she replied, pulling at the towelling robe that was his only clothing. "Come to bed, now. I need you." She let go, walked past the bed, turned up the TV volume to an almost deafening level and then casually threw her jacket over the top of it. Dale smiled. They were getting good at this counter-surveillance game.

For an hour, maybe more, they made up for lost time, exploring and tasting, reminding and satisfying. Not a word was exchanged. And none was required. They fulfilled a need neither of them had expected, but both recognised. For an hour, maybe more, the world ceased to turn, and their problems were put in abeyance. For an hour, maybe more, they indulged and found comfort in each other, and for a short time they slept.

As Nadia awoke, it occurred to her that she was lying in exactly the same pose as 'the picture.' It was still etched in her mind, and she hated Fayez for putting it there. Her head was resting on Dale's right arm and her hair fell casually across him as well as her. She realised that his hair was exactly like the photograph too, same colour, same uncombed style. The only difference was that he was not looking at her, he was lying flat on his back, gazing into the distant ceiling. The TV still belted out some Egyptian love song or other. She moved her mouth close to ear.

"Dale," she whispered. He turned his head towards. She gently took his chin and turned it back, so her mouth was again next to his ear. "Don't move, just listen," she said. "I'm having a hell of a day, and this is the first time it's begun to make sense."

Dale tried to turn his head again, but she held it firm.

"I'm sorry I had to send Fatimah to pick you up. I had no choice. I was held up in a government meeting."

Dale finally managed to wrench his head free and turning, spoke quietly into Nadia ear. "I saw you, getting into a Mercedes, with a large man," he said hurriedly. "I was worried. Are you okay?"

"You saw that?"

"Yes, we were driving past at the time. You looked frightened. I guess you didn't notice our car."

Nadia took the irrevocable plunge, grabbed his head again and planted her mouth so close to his ear he could feel her hot breath and wet lips against him. "That was Fayez. He sort of ambushed me. If he knew I was telling you this there's no knowing what he might do. I'm frightened. You've got to listen, please."

Dale nodded. "Go on," he said, "take your time."

"Fayez is telling me that I have to spy on you. He wants me to write down everything you do, telephone calls, meetings, everything. He even wants to know what you eat and drink, what sports you play. Everything."

"So, what's the problem? Is he stopping you working with me, or seeing me?"

"No, quite the reverse. He's encouraging me to spend more time with you, quite openly."

"So again, what's the problem? You tell him what we do and he's happy?"

Nadia dragged his ear back to her mouth. "I know and you know that you're involved with the intelligence services. You have too much to lose if they find out. I have a lot to lose if they found out about me too. It's all getting very risky."

"But these people are obsessed with surveillance. Isn't this just another step in their process? You know, I'm surprised they hadn't asked you to report on me before. Russell told me they probably would."

"You discussed me with Russell?"

Dale winced at his mistake. "Well, only before I knew you," he said hurriedly. "But Russell did say he'd be surprised if they didn't approach you to feed stuff back to them. From what you say, it sounds as if we come out of it quite well. We get more time together, officially, and all we have to do is give them some snippets of Dale Connor's everyday life and we're home and dry. Sounds a good deal to me."

Nadia was exasperated. She grabbed his ear again. "Listen," she almost shouted into it "this is Fayez Shakari. He has a reputation as bad as they come and he's a big evil man who you don't upset, at all. He made it very clear that I had to deliver useful and detailed information otherwise … "

"Otherwise, what?"

"Okay, you know the first night we met, we thought a photograph had been taken. The big flash of light, early morning."

Dale nodded; how could he forget.

"He showed me a copy of the photo today and threatened to publish it. He said he would send it to your wife."

Dale pulled away. "But I'm divorced," he said, "three years ago."

"I know that what's you told me, but Fayez evidently thinks you're still married."

Dale thought back to his meeting with Russell and his summary of what Fayez knew. "Well, let him think that. If it keeps him happy then maybe it's all to the good."

"But if he published it here, I would be out of work, out of everything. He also made it pretty clear that if I talked to you about all this then he had the ability to make us both disappear. He's not joking. They may have a high regard for you, and they may need your services like there's no tomorrow, but that's all temporary. He can snuff things out just by snapping his fingers."

Dale realised the TV had quietened between songs. He held up his finger until it started again.

"You're very brave," he said soothingly. "I understand exactly what you're saying, and you don't have to mention it ever again. As far as you're concerned you've told me nothing, only that you had a meeting with some ministry official who gave you a lift. Where did you go anyway?"

"Home," said Nadia "no, not into my home. He dropped me off outside." But everyone knows his car. It would be odd if you didn't hear I'd met him."

"Okay, you tell me you've had a meeting with him. That's why you weren't able to pick me up. I see you outside the ministry and you have a lift home. I don't need to know any more. Maybe you were doing some translation work for them. Security is security. I don't need to know."

Nadia relaxed a little. "You Brits," she said with a smile. "Does nothing upset you?"

"Apart from strange girls pouring out their problems in bed? No not really." He ducked as the pillow flew across the room. "But if you want me to vet your reporting efforts then I shall be happy to do so. Unofficially of course. It'd be interesting to learn something about myself for a change. Mind you, better not make them too accurate. They might suspect something."

Nadia looked relieved and snuggled closer.

"Have you told your Italian friends yet?" he asked.

"No, but I will. I need to remember who I'm really working for." She looked at Dale's horrified face. "I'm joking," she laughed, "but I will tell them anyway."

It occurred to Dale that Nadia might well have been working for the ministry people all along. He remembered the caution from Marlena and Emanuella, and Russell's exhortation to trust no one entirely. "Even you?" he'd asked his friend. "I'm different," Russell had replied, not too convincingly for Dale's fevered imagination.

"Come on," he said to Nadia, "let's go and eat. Are you going to stay here tonight?"

Nadia looked relieved. "Please," she said gratefully, "that Fayez has really shaken me."

Dale's mind had already begun to turn as it sorted the latest information. He let it go its own way. It would be late into the early morning before he finally fell asleep. Tomorrow was another day. He would hand over the packages and they could spend as long as they liked taking them apart. He had his personal life to resolve, and he was not at all sure where to start.

Christmas came and went without a murmur. He took a determined three days leave and he and Nadia visited more antiquities in the desert. Her link to Fayez seemed to produce more benefits than problems. Even her three days away were counted as paid work, all part of her surveillance task. She and Dale dreamt up suitable story lines for each day. It became a game that they enjoyed. One benefit of her reporting was that there seemed to be less need for vans full of watchers everywhere they went, and so life became more normal. It was a fun time for them both, an intimate time too, but with their eyes fixed always, and carefully over their shoulders.

54

By mid-January, Dale was again in Milan, on his way back to the UK, visiting the factories that would likely supply the cargo handling equipment. It was not actually made there, he discovered as soon as he went to the factory. That was in Naples, but all the people who mattered were in Milan. The poor workers of Naples were regarded as people from another planet by their well-dressed, affluent cousins in Milan. After all, as one elegant Milanese woman told him confidentially. "Italy only goes as far south as Rome; the rest is an accident of geography." In conversation the Northern Italians would often compare themselves with Californians, but in terms of wealth only of course. When it came to style, or wine, or women or men for that matter, they knew there was no comparison.

He had spent another chaste night with Emanuella. There was still the same elegant ambiance in her apartment but still the same 'frightened to be on her own' girl when it came to darkness. He had found the bed-sharing something of a challenge until he realised that the bed was bigger than the one he had once had to share with his bearded county manager in Kenya when they found that rooms were in short supply. After this slightly odd rationalisation of the situation, he had warmed to the task and slept like a log. But the enigma of Emanuella still baffled him. The change from the elegant professional to the almost lost soul of darkness was a mystery he had not come even close to understanding.

As they were travelling back from the factories in the east of Milan and made their way across town to Emanuella's apartment near Piazza Amendola they discussed Nadia's recent ambushing by Fayez.

"Do you think she could have been working for Fayez all along?" Dale asked innocently.

Emanuella the professional responded. "No, I'm pretty sure not. When we vetted her she was very solid," she said.

Dale blanched. "Vetted?" He tried not to sound too surprised.

"Of course. When she joined us three years ago we were very careful. She has a very interesting past, as you probably know."

"I'm sure I know very little of her past. She's not very keen to talk about it."

"Italian parents, although the father came originally from desert people. His real background is a mystery. We've never managed to crack that open. He was killed in an oil tank accident in Genoa. Her mother's still around, one of the landed rich in Italy. She spends most of her time drinking the family's assets away in her olive groves. I don't believe Nadia's been home in years. You know that Nadia's not her real name?"

"I beg your pardon." Dale was speechless.

"Born Francesca, after her grandmother. Her father changed her name to Nadia when he took her home for a visit to Libya at the age of three. That's when she got her second passport. And that's why she speaks Arabic too, because of her father. As far as she remembers she's always been Nadia. She knows it was changed and she keeps Francesca as her second name most of the time. Actually, Nadia doesn't appear on her birth certificate. Interesting person."

Dale was curious. "I knew Nadia's father had died when she was fourteen, half a lifetime ago, and that she joined your Italian crowd when she was twenty-seven. Before that, I thought she worked for the UN as in interpreter."

"That's right. That's when she was recruited by the Brits. And she did call herself Francesca then. She wanted to be properly Italian and not have any visible Arab links. The Brits were always on the lookout for bright young things who could make up for their own lack of languages and Nadia, or Francesca as they called her then, was ideal. She had Arabic thrown in too. And she's good. Much better than me at languages."

"So why did she leave the Brits?"

"Some sort of inter-company trade I think. We did a swap I believe. According to her official record she never worked for your people. It was as if they wanted her off their books. I really have no idea why."

Dale tried but failed to get anything more from Emanuella. She had told Dale all she knew, which was what she had been asked to do by her masters. They hoped that Dale would succeed to pry into Nadia's past where they had singularly failed.

"So, you think she's to be trusted?" Dale persisted.

"Oh sure. No problem, just don't tell her what you're really doing for us, and you'll be fine."

"What do you mean?"

"Well, simply that if she doesn't know the details she can't put her foot in things accidentally. It's best to keep the reporting to Fayez as tight and as honest as possible."

"So, on balance, you think this Fayez thing is not such a bad deal?"

"Absolutely. In many ways it shows you off as Mr Clean, and that's what we're all trying to do."

Dale nodded. He had already decided to tackle the issue of Nadia/Francesca's father with her directly. And he might also tackle his secretive friend Russell. He had a feeling that there was much more behind those benevolent eyes than he was aware of.

The taxi shot up another short cut and bounced along a tiny, cobbled street not much wider than the car. They stopped outside an old church. The road sign indicated Vialle Certosa. "Come on" Emanuella was keen to change the subject "let's take half an hour and see Da Vinci's Last Supper." Without waiting for an answer, she leapt from the taxi and shot into the nearby courtyard. Dale paid the taxi and followed.

55

The short hop back to London should have taken two hours but with Milan's famous fog, 'la nebia,' they were shuttled back and forth between Malpensa and Linate airports until finally being bundled off to Genova. Apparently, there was never any fog in Genova and Dale wondered why they had not simply gone there in the first place. The journey took nineteen hours, and by the time he reached London it was snowing; a horrible January wet slush. It was very cold and every taxi seemed to have been taken from the face of the earth.

His meeting with McGuire was not much warmer. Russell had warned him that McGuire was in a prickly mood, not his usual affable, urbane self at all. But he was still the consummate professional and took pains to impress on Dale that he was a welcome passenger, albeit still a passenger in their affairs. McGuire was indebted for his information gathering and his couriering of drawings, and he shouldn't feel in any danger. If there were any problems then he was to contact Russell, no one else please. If there was any doubt at all, Russell was the man, no one else 'please.' Throughout the meeting Russell sat silently listening. He was constantly referred to but never invited to speak, like a witness to a carefully scripted performance. And although the meeting was polite, Dale felt he was being carefully and gently pushed back into his corner and discouraged from trying to play a part in whatever was being planned to forestall events at Frankfurt. He did not feel particularly comfortable as every question he raised was met with a polite but firm deflection. Did McGuire have views on what might happen and when? Did McGuire have an opinion on the likely impact on Dale's projects? If he did he had nothing to say to Dale.

"Marlena has been very helpful," Dale ventured. McGuire's frown did not ease from his face.

"Really, I'm pleased to hear it. She's a competent operator."

"I was a little mystified when she first turned up on the irrigation project, but her Arabic is excellent, and she misses nothing; a very logical person."

McGuire said nothing.

"From what you're saying about only dealing with Russell, should I not be speaking to her anymore?"

"Not at all, regular work, social contact, no problem there. Just anything to do with your intelligence, and anything to do with what we might ask you to help with, please keep to yourself, and Russell. Only Russell, 'please'."

"So, when she talks to me does she represent the German government?"

McGuire's frown deepened, if that was possible. "As I say, any issues, please deal with Russell."

"And the same for Emanuella?"

"Especially the same for Emanuella. Emanuella is another fascinating young lady. She has been driven by a cause since her father died. I sometimes wonder how dispassionate she can be."

Dale was surprised at this sudden openness. "And lastly Nadia? What's her role in all this please?"

"Nadia is an information gatherer. She works for Bertelli. That's all."

Dale wondered whether McGuire knew about Nadia's new contact with Fayez. Russell hadn't been concerned, so he left the matter where it lay.

They parted amicably, but with Dale feeling his enthusiasm dampened and his energy definitely subdued. Maybe that was what McGuire had intended, he thought. After all, he hadn't specifically said 'don't do this or that.' His mind began to replay the conversation.

McGuire watched them leave and waited for Russell to return to the room.

"Well?" he asked, "what do you make of our Mr Connors?"

Russell knew exactly where McGuire was coming from. "Another one who reads too many novels on aeroplanes" he said, "and he's piecing an awful lot of this thing together. It would be nice if he would stay in the passenger role you outlined, and officially that's what we will encourage, but I suspect that we'll find him centre stage as we move forward. I think it's inevitable, and frankly, I don't have a problem with that. We'll just have to keep our eyes open that much more carefully."

"I agree," McGuire stroked his chin, pulling at an imaginary beard. "He seems loyal, which is good, honest, which is also good, enthusiastic, which could be a problem, and inquisitive, which might be his downfall. He's untrained and working in dangerous waters. Keep a good eye on him and have Marlena do the same. Emanuella too, although she has more emotional links to this than she realises. Make sure he sticks to the script if you can."

"When we write it, I will," said Russell.

"That's right, when we write it. At the moment it's a huge melting pot and we're all outside stirring. Poor old Dale is swimming in the middle. As I say, look after him."

"And the Official Secrets stuff?"

"Keep forgetting to get him to sign. We don't want him thinking he represents us in any way. Anyway, as long as he's given good material he should have nothing to worry about. No, best leave it on the side for now."

"What about Marlena's comment, when she said his staff in Frankfurt should be signing?"

"Just betraying her origins. No, let's not tangle with all that."

56

The next week was hectic for Dale. Off to Frankfurt to be briefed on what he could and couldn't say about current security systems, then back again to the UK to visit the engineering company offices and put together another package of Frankfurt data from the Luton records. All the time, Russell trailed him like a dog on a leash. In Germany, they met Marlena, who had obviously been told that Russell was in charge.

There was nothing specific that Dale could put his finger on, but there had been a subtle change in the dynamics between them. Like a soccer match after half time, at least the team now knew who they were and what they had to do. They vetted and checked information and it occurred to Dale that, rather than following McGuire's edicts about sitting back as a passenger, he was being involved more and more as an active participant. He mentioned his thoughts to Russell who laughed and said, "only what you need to know." He wondered what else there was, he did not know.

With two more brown paper-wrapped packages he had set off to Libya again. It was his seventh visit, and he was becoming a regular feature on the airline and at the airport when he arrived. Nadia met him and he felt almost at home. As he leaned down to put his bags in the car she whispered in his ear.

"Fayez seems happy," she murmured, "but he's replaced the listening devices in the car. Be careful."

He leaned across. "And has he wired you too?"

"I'll show you later," she said aloud. As they drove into the city Dale hardly dared speak. What did she mean? Was she wearing a wire now? They drove into the city and to his surprise, bypassed the hotel completely. As they pulled up outside an old apartment block Dale realised that he had never been to where she lived before. They had always met at the hotel.

"Leave your bags in the trunk. Just bring your hand carry." Nadia led them up the stairs to the third floor. Her door opened into a small but immaculately clean one-bed apartment. From its tiny living space, a door opened into a minute kitchen and to its right a glass door opened onto a surprisingly sizeable balcony.

Nadia walked straight into the bedroom. "Okay, watch," she said. To Dale's amazement and delight she casually removed her outer clothes and kept going, until the familiar slender form stood before him, her long hair cascading over her shoulders. "See," she smiled, "no wires."

"And the apartment?"

"No, I had Bertelli sweep it for me. Mind you, wait till they find out we didn't go the hotel! Come here," she said and held out her arms. He needed no encouragement.

Across town the watchers waited. Where was he? Why had he not checked into the hotel? He'd left the airport ages ago, they knew that, so where was Mr Dale? They rechecked the reception desk. They called their man in the project office. Nowhere. Someone called Fuad said "Patience," and then smiled to himself. She's probably following Fayez's instructions he thought, and getting to know him better. He turned his car in the direction of Nadia's apartment. As he drove past he smiled again. Time to get some sound in there; even video he thought.

57

The day was still hot, and the cracked blue tiled pool was inviting. Water splashed lazily from a small hose pipe, still running from when they had topped up the level after lunch and the extra canvas shades, stretched between the barren trees added a civility that was most welcoming. It was Friday and all the team was there, lounging in the lengthening shadows or being energetic in the coolness of the water, now that most of the guests had departed. A dying barbecue sat against the villa wall, just near enough to the kitchen to make life easy. They had debated being cultural for a day, and going to see the desert forts, but lethargy had prevailed. So, a barbecue had been voted instead and the ministry project people had been invited too, being careful with protocol, knowing how easy it was to cause offence. However, it seemed that religious needs were happily met in the morning and late lunches and afternoons were then fair game for all. The difference between what was required in the cautious, veiled public spaces and what was allowed in private was something that Dale no longer felt surprised or concerned about, although the pool was of course carefully shielded from outside view. The fact that Sulaiman and Fatimah had come today, with their children too, made him even more relaxed. It seemed to add a stamp of approval to the proceedings. He was happy about that.

The villa had been a brainwave, though no one could quite remember whose. It was easier living there and they could be a little separate from the city without being too remote. Above all, it kept them out of the hotels, and everyone had a limited tolerance for hotels in the end. Dale reckoned his was four weeks. Others', he knew were shorter. Ubaid himself had been enthusiastic. The villa was owned by one of his numerous relatives and the payment, although in local currency would keep them in tea and shisha for many years after the project was finished.

Even Marlena was there, on a visiting mission for the irrigation project and Emanuella had appeared too, now magically part of the Italian company that would soon to be working with Dale in Frankfurt. They were also providing help on the local project and Bertelli was over the moon at last now that his commercial front was bearing fruit. Emanuella and Marlena had opted to share a room in the villa. No one but Dale knew of their other working relationship.

As for Dale, his project manager had insisted that he not stay at the villa. "Visit by all means," he had said, "but we must keep a sense of status and propriety." So, Dale was stuck back at the hotel. He didn't really mind, his job was differently focused, all marketing and money and he saw more of Nadia that way. He was happy to leave the project in capable hands.

Derek McCullen had proved himself a real asset in organisation and Grant Andrews had joined the villa group from the camel project. He had distinguished himself by forming rock solid relationships with the Egyptian contingent at the ministry. Their subsequent help had materially assisted in getting much of the bureaucracy removed from the system and things had finally begun to hum. Some of the Egyptians had been there today, along with their families. The barbecue had been an inspired idea.

The last group to come had been Raheem and his Palestinian friends from the ministry, again with their families. The overall number of children had added greatly to the fun of the afternoon and Naomi and Ibrahim had showed their friends how to be unafraid of the big foreigners. Raheem in particular had been effusive in his thanks. "It is a wonderful start for the international community" he kept saying, his face beaming from ear to ear.

As the various guests drifted away, Dale called the team together. It was the first time they had properly met in one place, and he used the time to brief them on what was expected from the project. Nothing fancy, no new ideas, just simple modern buildable concepts. He also took the opportunity to warn them again about the prevalence for surveillance everywhere, and counselled their caution, all the time. "We've nothing to hide," he said, "so be friendly to the security people, they're just doing their job."

The ministry appointed members of the team smiled. They liked it that Dale had included them in the warning. It made their role in the project much more open and visible. Everybody knew they had to report back to Fayez and his crowd, so why not be open about it. Yes, they thought, this British guy knows what he's doing. We can see why our boss has such a high regard for him.

Dale was pleased that Fatimah had been allocated to the team as their general driver. He did not broadcast the knowledge about the in-car bug, but he did warn Derek and the foreign staff quietly on their own. "Let them think it's still safe," he said, "we don't want them dreaming up new places to hide microphones."

58

The Italians were happy. Bertelli had reported that contracts for the airport, as well as the camel facilities, were now certain. The revolving restaurant had caught his imagination, but he wondered who would ever use it. But his masters were especially delighted to see that two of their 'staff' Emanuella and Nadia, were now part of the everyday team on the ground. After all, many years ago, Italy had dominated this country. Why not again?

Far away to the north, in a nightmare piece of architecture on the southern embankment of a cold and misty River Thames in London, Russell too was temporarily pleased. Both packs of information seemed to have been swallowed whole. And Dale had a good team safely parked on the site. His German and Italian colleagues claimed to be happy for the time being too. That meant that the preliminaries were all in place. Now, he thought to himself, we have to find out what Abdullah is really up to.

Fayez reviewed his notes on the airport drawings. Overall, he was pleased, in fact delighted. The plan to obtain engineering drawings had been more successful that he could have imagined. As far as he could see they were now the owners of detailed information that their various forays into Europe had hitherto failed to obtain. When Fayez thought of his son's failed attempts during his expensive visit the previous year he shuddered. Brain before brawn, he thought. Always think first, Jamil.

He had been a little concerned when Dale had asked Ubaid about the provision of anti-terrorist measures at the new airport. He wondered for a moment whether Dale was trying to be cute and trap them into saying something but as their conversation had progressed, he realised that Dale was just going through the list of things to be covered. He had replayed the tape and listened more carefully. Maybe they could learn something more from it yet.

He was also impressed by Nadia. She had taken to her reporting chore with alacrity and seemed to spend all her waking, and he suspected sleeping hours at Dale's side. Overall, he was happy. He had his bases covered. Now for some detailed planning.

He turned back to the notes on X-ray procedures at Frankfurt and was happily surprised that larger objects were not subject to scanning. It seemed from the design files that this was common practice, on cost grounds. So, he mused, our plan to do something big is going to be exactly on the right track. He pulled out the water treatment brochures provided by his East German friends. For what he wanted he could see that the Italian company was easily the first choice. Their plant was in Naples, and they were cheap. They probably imported all the heavy stuff from a low-cost neighbour, he thought. The plan was clear in his mind. Maybe they would not need the new airport after all if their information was already so good; but better stay with the plan. Being careful had paid off before. There was no reason to doubt it would again.

He flipped open his phone. "Is Khalid at the fort yet?" he asked.

"Tomorrow, mid-morning," a voice at the other end replied. The phone snapped shut and he sat back to think through his script for the next day. Khalid Abu Nida'a was maybe a magician at his chosen black art but was not known for sticking to plans unless it took his fancy to do so. He always had his own way of finishing an assignment. But, as Fayez knew, he had not failed, ever, and this gave him certain privileges.

The printed flyer was written in Arabic, Italian and English. The timing of the Italian goods and services fair was not precisely stated but was planned to be the first event after the now much talked about lifting of sanctions, planned for April, although no one believed it would happen. Bertelli knew he was jumping the gun but never mind. No one knew yet with any certainly whether the sanctions would really be lifted, let alone when, but he would be first in the queue and he reckoned the kudos it would bring would also help open up the diplomatic avenues later.

Dale looked at the flyer and then back at Bertelli. Since Nadia also reported to him, he had become used to seeing him around rather more than before although always with some construction pretext or other. Today, Bertelli was in jubilant mood.

"Just been speaking with Ubaid," he confided. "More plant on the way from Italy. This time it's high spec water treatment units."

"Where for?" Dale was always curious when clients started spending money. Maybe there was an opportunity.

"Don't know," Bertelli was not in the mood for detail, "all I know is that they're paying for us to import one unit now and then they'll extend the order when they've tested it."

"And this is all under your humanitarian programmes?"

"Of course!" Bertelli managed to sound affronted.

"Why would they want just one unit?" he asked, but Bertelli was off on another tack. "People just don't do that," Dale added.

59

Naiem Fahoud was a troubled man. He had been seconded to advise on the airport security issues from his 'local knowledge and perspective.' He had no idea where to start. These Frankfurt plans were so unlike his present arrangements. To his mind, his airport ran perfectly smoothly, and he saw no need to change. Normally a quiet and careful person, he was now decidedly out of sorts and close to belligerency.

"Maybe we could arrange some visits to other airports?" Dale was just trying to divert Naiem's thought process, "and then you would have some basis for comparison."

Naiem jumped at this thought. Overseas travel was not usually his good fortune.

"Mind you," continued Dale, "with the current sanctions it might be difficult to arrange, but maybe our Italian friends can help. You'll be buying quite a chunk of their equipment after all."

Naiem was already a changed man. The thought of Italy filled him with excitement. Dale left to seek out Bertelli and ask for his help.

Russell sat in his office and worried. He was a troubled man too. The noises he was hearing from Dale and Bertelli were unsettling. Dale had done well to learn about the water treatment unit, although from Bertelli's added comments on Nadia's notes he had gathered that the information had come originally from the Italian. He wondered why Bertelli had not thought to mention it? The fellow was too casual, concerned too much about his contracts. He had gone soft since he left his embassy post.

The latest news about the airport survey trip with Naiem had interested him intensely. Dale and Naiem were departing almost immediately as Bertelli had arranged for them to meet staff in Rome and Naples. The draw of new contracts had proved too much for the Italians and they had opened their hospitable doors wide and willingly. He pondered that the imminent lifting of sanctions was being treated as a foregone conclusion by the Italians. He could see them almost jumping for joy at the thought of being first in line for new trade. But what really caught his attention was the additional news that Naiem had requested that they also go to Cairo. Egypt was an easy destination despite official sanctions, there was an unwritten brotherhood along the north shore of Africa, but he wondered why Cairo. He was desperately in need of some hard data. He now had to wait while Dale did his rounds of the ministries and listened to as many views as he could find about his projects. He also had to wait for the outcome of this jolly around the airports, but at least something was happening. He just wished he knew what.

60

Cairo had not changed since Dale's previous visit years before. The airport was the same and the arrival procedures still unbelievably cumbersome. People meandered everywhere. It was Naiem's first visit, and he was most unimpressed.

"Our Egyptian staff are always saying how wonderful this airport is," he said ruefully. "I believe ours is far superior."

Maybe only if you read Arabic, thought Dale, but did not voice his thoughts. He had learnt long ago never to assume that the other person didn't understand English. In any case Naiem's English was perfectly adequate for their purposes.

They had waited, for ages it seemed, and then met the airport managers to discuss cargo, systems, and security. The conversation was in a mix of English and Arabic and the men were helpful but had no opinions about their airport. Design was someone else's problem. The security chief, Naiem's direct equivalent, was first said to be arriving late, then he was delayed and in the end never arrived. Naiem remained unimpressed.

They departed from the airport with Dale wondering why they had bothered to come at all. He soon found out. As they made their way to the hotel, Naiem spoke to the driver in Arabic. The driver nodded and changed direction, heading off towards the industrial outskirts to the north of the city. Dale was curious.

"Where are we going?" he asked.

"Just a short visit. I have to deliver something to a factory for Fayez."

Things began to click in Dale's mind. If Fayez was involved he would guarantee that this was the reason for the diversion through Cairo. "What do they make?" he persisted.

"Tanks," offered Naiem, clearly struggling with his vocabulary, "big tanks for water."

Dale decided to wait and see and when they pulled into the factory gates, he realised it was a fabrication yard, primarily making steel pressure vessels. A manager appeared and Naiem indicated that he had to excuse himself for a while to attend a meeting, so Dale asked him if he could look around. The factory manager beamed and offered a guide. A few minutes later Dale and a young Egyptian lad were wending their way through foundries, welding shops, paint booths and a modern rubber lining yard where the steel vessels were coated internally.

The young teenager introduced himself "Me Ahmed!" he said proudly.

Another one, smiled Dale. "Pleased to meet you," he said politely, but the lad's English only extended to his name plus 'hello,' 'please' and 'change money?'

They walked into the dispatch shop and straight into Naiem and the factory manager. They were grouped with some workers in blue overalls around a pair of tall vessels and, as Dale approached, they moved away and disappeared up a metal staircase. Dale walked over to where they had been standing. The vessels were over two metres tall and about half a metre in diameter. They had labels attached to them saying 'Naples.' Alongside he saw a set of plans laid out on the workbench. They were annotated in Arabic, which he could not read but the hand-drawn modifications to the diagrams were clear. The vessels appeared to have been modified to provide an extra skin welded into the base of each. More like an internal collar really, the diagram had pencil lines indicating packages in the gap between the steel skins. He wondered why they would need extra internal compartments, if this was indeed what they were. 'Me Ahmed' appeared at his elbow and pointed to the exit. Through the door of the warehouse, he saw the taxi waiting, with Naiem and the manager chatting alongside. He walked pensively through a maze of conveyor assemblies and even a full size half-built baggage carousel, and out in to the sunshine to join them.

The journey back to the hotel was uneventful. Naiem had offered to take him to a Cairo nightspot later in the evening and so he put his concerns for the steel vessels to one side for a while.

At five o'clock the next morning, he was woken by the phone. A 'wakeup call' took on a new meaning when you'd only been asleep for three hours. He mentally calculated the cost of the bed per hour and stumbled into the shower. Why they needed to get up at five o'clock for a flight to Rome at eleven was beyond him. But when they arrived at the airport he understood. If arrivals were busy, departures were positively heaving with people, they had to step over several recumbent families waiting in the main terminal building.

Flights were being called and yet there was no sense of order that he could discern. In the end, he grabbed a passing member of the Alitalia staff, and they were taken round the back of the check-in desk, issued with boarding passes and then personally escorted through the masses to the passport desk and from there to the gate. How the rest of the passengers arrived he had no idea. It was bedlam.

61

Todd Cameron had been out in the desert doing what he enjoyed, reading the landscape. He reckoned that by standing on the top of a hill and merely looking around the horizon he could read the formations of rock and have a pretty good idea about what lay beneath. His colleagues admired his talent, especially as it was almost always correct, and were happy to be part of the proof team, which followed up on his hunches about the state of underground resources. He was officially on vacation again as his company could not strictly speaking be here, but that didn't matter. His first 'vacation' some months before had prompted him to review old geological maps back in London, and now he'd come back to put some of his theories to the test. He had spent several interesting days in the coastal area, visiting forts and poor sea villages and he reckoned that there was something to show for his trouble. If sanctions were removed his company needed to be first in the queue and information was vital. His only problem was that they were an oil company and that was not what he had found.

He looked around the bar and saw the two East German chicken farmers. They were evidently back in town, just as he was. Funny how you always bumped into the same people, time after time. There had been an engineer here when he had met these two characters before. Couldn't remember the name though. He recalled his last conversation with the Germans and decided against joining them. So, unusually, he took a seat on his own, pondering how best to break the news back in his company headquarters.

A hand on his shoulder made him spin round as a well-known voice said, "Dad, what on earth are you doing here?"

Todd Cameron looked at his son Miles, surprise written all over his face. "I could be asking you the same thing. What on earth are *you* doing here?"

They grinned at each other, and Miles sat down and signalled to the waiter for another beer. "As you know, my office doesn't publish my whereabouts," he said, "but how about you?"

Todd was in his usual chatty mood. "I'm here on holiday, well officially anyway," he said, "but between you and me I think I've made a discovery."

Miles looked askance and glanced around. "Then let's take these beers upstairs and finish them there," he suggested. "These walls have ears."

He called a waiter, and they shifted the drinks and the tab to his room. For good measure, he ordered some snacks too. When he had turned up the TV and rotated its face towards the desk, he sat down opposite his father in the room's spacious sitting area.

"Just a minute," he said and sprinted into the bathroom to turn on a noisy shower. "OK," he smiled, "now tell me what you've discovered."

Todd shook his head and waved a hand towards the TV. "Is all this really necessary?" he asked.

"Absolutely," his son responded.

"Then water," Todd was uncharacteristically brief.

"Water?"

"Yes, I was looking at the ground formations and it occurred to me that the shoreline is domed. If we were to dig down in the most arid, unused part of the coast, we should expect to find water. It comes from way inland and there's plenty of evidence to tell us that there's a solid stratum running deep down and all the way from the mountains to the sea. All you have to do is stand on the hill and look."

Miles believed him. He knew his father's reputation and that he had never been proved wrong, but that had always been on oil. "Is water different to oil?" he asked.

"Not really. It's just geology."

"And your company will exploit it?"

"Maybe not themselves but you can guarantee they'll make something out of it. And it will help irrigation too."

Miles' mind slipped sideways a notch. "Irrigation is human-itarian," he said, "maybe you could incorporate it under one of the existing programmes," but his father was already off on an-other tack, recounting a bewildering set of geological statistics.

Miles ignored him and thought about his notes from this morning. He decided to raise what was on the top of his mind. "Dad," he started to say tentatively, "have you ever wondered who your real parents were?"

Todd stopped dead in his tracks. "Your grandparents have always been my real parents," was the careful reply. "I've always known that they adopted me at an early age but they've no idea where I came from and although they asked, they were always told it was unknown. Apparently, I was abandoned," he said rather mournfully, "although your grandfather did find out I was born in Kensington Hospital in London. But that's as far as it goes. He found the hospital certificate, but it didn't have any parents' names on it. I've stopped worrying about it."

Miles was impressed. He hadn't realised that his grandfather had been looking. But what he had heard matched exactly with what he had researched and read. "What if I could tell you who your biological parents really were?"

His father thought for a moment. "I'd be interested, but I don't think I'd tell your grandparents. They're over eighty and I'm sure they'd only worry."

"I'm sure about your father," Miles decided to jump into the news. "He was a diplomat."

"Was?"

"Yes, I'm sorry to say he passed away some time ago. Killed in the line of duty in an embassy in Africa."

"And my mother?" Todd was visibly curious.

"I'm not quite sure yet."

"But you have an idea."

"Oh yes, I have an idea, but I'd rather not say until I'm sure."

"It's someone from here, isn't it?" Todd spoke quietly.

Miles looked astonished. "Why would you say that?"

"Why else would you be here? Come on Miles, you never were very good at hiding facial expressions. Anyway, it would link with the diplomat. My guess is it was someone who lived here, but obviously went to London to have the child. It would also explain the colour of my skin. Even the Scottish weather hasn't removed my ability to turn on the suntan whenever the sun breaks through. You're similar but not so pronounced. And we both have black hair."

"You've been doing more thinking than you admit," Miles smiled at his father. "Is your visit here purely for work?"

"As I say, it's a vacation. And no, I haven't any ulterior motive," it was Todd's turn to smile. "I must say I always feel comfortable when I'm here, despite its problems. The other thing that's always seemed strange to me is that we both learnt Arabic when we lived in Saudi. It was never a chore and I've always wondered whether there was some gene or other tucked away."

Miles knew he was right. His own education, at boarding school in Scotland, had not taken away the language ability he had acquired when he was a youngster living in company compounds on the east coast of Saudi Arabia. Maybe something was hereditary after all. It was in interesting thought to debate another time.

62

By the time they arrived in Rome, Naiem was feeling unwell. The effects of the previous evening had caught up with him and Dale was not sorry when they were extremely brief with their visit to the airport. The meetings were polite but uninformative. They learnt a lot about passenger statistics but little about cargo and nothing at all about security. Oddly enough, Naiem was impressed with their reluctance to divulge their methods.

"I'd do exactly the same," he said with pride, before sprinting to the washroom for the seventh time that morning.

They skipped lunch and Dale parked a willing Naiem in the hotel before graduating to the bar. Two men were chatting there, and he recognised them both. He smiled; his timing was impeccable. He was not sure what Naiem had eaten to put him away for a while, but it could not have happened at a better time.

Grant Andrews had turned out to be a genius in Libya when it came to building relationships. He had patience and did not mind talking and listening for a whole day if it achieved what needed to be done. The Egyptian staff liked him and so did their bosses; but the other man with him today was his new-found soul mate, Jamil Shakari, Fayez's spendthrift son. After their meeting in the Al Hambra, they had soon found a common interest in beer, wine, spirits and conversation about girls. Jamil boasted about his conquests overseas and Grant flattered him with his willingness to listen and swap stories. To Grant it was just business, but he suspected that Jamil was happy to have someone to unload to in his spare time. They had become drinking mates very quickly.

Grant fed back whatever they talked about to Dale. They both knew exactly who Jamil was and what he was capable of and so they were careful. But he seemed a different person chatting and joking over a beer. It was in stark contrast to his tough act when in a formal business setting. When Grant learned of Jamil's trip to Italy and they realised it coincided with Dale's own, Grant had willingly booked up an overdue vacation to the UK routed through Rome. Maybe he could see what Jamil was up to.

Dale had not told any of this to Russell. He felt that the fewer people who knew the better. It occurred to him he was beginning to think like his friend, but he had exhorted him to 'not trust anyone,' so he felt he was only following instructions.

Dale feigned surprise as he walked up to the bar. "Well, what a surprise!" he exclaimed, clapping Grant on the shoulder. "Hi Jamil, I hadn't realised I was being followed here! I should be flattered. I'm only an engineer you know."

Jamil laughed. "But a very tricky one," he said and turned to the bar. "Another beer!" he called to the barman. "No, another three beers!"

"I'm travelling with Naiem," Dale confided, "he's not too well after last night's session in Cairo but I guess he'll be okay to travel to Naples tomorrow."

"Ah, Naiem!" Jamil laughed again, "he can't drink at all. Why are you going to Naples?"

"We're visiting the airport and also Italfabrica, they make cargo handling equipment and I want Naiem to see what he might be buying."

Jamil looked up. "Did you say Italfabrica?"

"Sure, do you know them?"

"I was there yesterday. They're working on another project for us at the moment."

This was news to Dale. "Really, what sort of project?"

"Oh, an industrial plant. They're providing us with some high-quality water plant." Jamil looked thoughtful and then said proudly, "de-min-er-al-is-a-tion. It's a difficult word." He drained his glass in one go.

Dale nodded, his mind jumping as he connected back to the water vessels in Egypt. Could they be the same project? He reluctantly moved onto other topics.

"Come with us," Jamil ordered. "We're going to eat and then find a club. Naiem will be safe in the hotel. Coming?"

It was not a question and Grant and Dale both rose to follow. Dale signed the check thinking that Russell could damn well start paying some expenses, and then joined Grant at the door. The two of them left their almost untouched beers on the bar. Dale sensed they would be having quite a few more as the evening progressed. He began to form some more questions for Jamil, but thought another half dozen drinks would be a good idea first.

Another airport, another poor security set-up. Naples airport had not encouraged Naiem at all. As he summarised for Dale's benefit, "they're strong on heavyweight people standing around the place but they have no method. I could bring a camel through here and no one would notice." But it was the news that the equipment manufacturer in Naples was the same as the one for Jamil's water treatment plant that still ricocheted around Dale's brain. The fact that Jamil was involved increased his interest by several orders of magnitude. Fayez could only be half a step behind.

When they visited the Italfabrica factory he was surprised at the huge amount of equipment being prepared for shipment. X-ray machines were all over the place, all shapes and sizes. They were told that sales of X-ray equipment for baggage and cargo now far exceeded those for basic conveyors and roller tracks. "In these security conscious times everyone is adding X-rays," they told him. The handling equipment itself was now seen as a commodity, to be fabricated locally to Italian designs and specifications or imported from their Egyptian low-cost manufacturing centre.

"And where is your low-cost centre?" asked Dale.

"Cairo," was the immediate answer. "We ship things from there every week or fly urgent items if absolutely necessary. Transport costs are not high these days."

Dale grinned. "Just the cost of processing the paperwork."

Paolo Grenaldi smiled knowingly. "Yes," he said, "there are always certain fees to be found if we want things delivered on time."

"But you still pre-assemble everything here?"

"Yes, we're old fashioned in that respect and like to see it all together before we ship. If something's going to go wrong, we'd rather it went wrong here."

"And then how do you ship?"

"It depends on urgency and money. If a client pays then we'll air freight, otherwise everything's containerised and shipped from Naples, or Rome. Rome's cheaper but slower. There are too many extra fees in Naples"

"And by air? Do you always fly direct?"

"Not at all." Paolo grinned again. He was enjoying showing off his superior knowledge of the transport logistics. "We're dealing with cargo and so keeping costs down is vital. We use a hub such as Milan or Frankfurt. Rome does the same. Frankfurt's cheaper and the paperwork's easier. It's a huge cargo hub and growing."

And from there, thought Dale, to anywhere they like.

The conference had added the final touches to the agreement and details had been worked through in minute detail. It was agreed that the first post-sanction flight would be from Germany in two weeks' time and would carry predominantly German and Italian goods. There had been days of discussion about which airline to use and so a plan had been necessary to overcome the increasing rivalry between the two trading nations. It had therefore been agreed that a cargo plane from Libya's national airline would fly empty to Frankfurt and then return full of goods from the two countries.

The Italians were now focused on making the best of the plan and were keen to be the largest supplier of goods to the new market. They were racking their brains as to how to make up the volume. They had a water plant from Italfabrica and that could certainly be completed and added to the freight manifest, but they needed some more big-ticket items too. Bertelli was in the midst of some tricky discussions with a number of manufacturers. He was a busy man.

The manufacturing plant in Naples had also caught Fayez's attention. When Jamil had called to update him with a carefully worded message and suggested that they could visit the plant as often as they liked if they were following the airport order, Fayez had put two and two together and headed straight to the airport. He needed to talk urgently to Khalid again, but this time he would have to meet him on his own ground. He flipped open his phone and dialled. Two minutes later, he was heading for his car. With luck he would see him that evening and be back in the city the next morning.

As Fayez passed through the airport Bertelli's mobile phone rang. Bertelli listened, cancelled the call and then redialled. "Number 3 is travelling to B," he said quietly. Within minutes Russell had passed on the news to Germany and soon, in Egypt, Basmah and her small team were mobilised and making preparations.

Within minutes Marlena heard that she was urgently needed back in Frankfurt and took the next available flight out. In Frankfurt she did not even pass through customs but headed for the transit desk. She bought a new ticket and flew on to Cairo. Fayez on the move was big news.

63

Wafa had turned up trumps. She had done as requested and looked for possible relatives of Raya and found the file for a lady called Leena. She was Raya's cousin who had had a child on exactly the same day that Raya had given birth to Abdullah. Wafa had also discovered that Raya had been living with Leena when she gave birth. They had obviously been very close. Leena had died in a car accident nearly thirty years before.

"It was another boy," said Wafa.

"And his name?" Miles and she were sitting in the apartment above the bakery.

"Talak. It seems that he and Abdullah were good friends, until Talak went overseas when he was nineteen years old and never returned."

"What do you mean 'never returned?' Where did he go?"

"I don't know, but I guess Italy. There's a note for unpaid fees from Genoa University but then the file stops."

"And Talak was born on exactly the same day as Abdullah? That seems an amazing coincidence."

"What are you going to do?"

Miles looked up sharply. He had not considered the next step in any detail. "Maybe I should meet the lady," he suggested.

"You'll need a good reason," Wafa warned him.

"I wonder what happened to Talak in Genoa," mused Miles. "Maybe I should take her some news of her long-lost son."

64

Basmah and Marlena sat in her small apartment and listened again to the fractured conversation, but it was almost useless. Fayez had been followed successfully from the airport to a small hotel near the gold souk and then he had disappeared from sight. For two hours he stayed in his room, being joined after a while by a striking young lady of 'impeccable credentials' as the hotel manager had politely described her when pressed with money.

At about 10 p.m. he had moved on and been seen entering a night-club where he was seen but hardly heard, holding a deep conversation with a traditionally dressed Arab whose head-dress all but covered his face. They had photographs but the angles were poor and the light worse. Marlena would have to have the tape analysed to see whether the computer could distinguish what they could not. To her it sounded just a blur of noise.

While Fayez had been at the night-club, Basmah's team had continued to watch his hotel room and had managed to get a microphone placed on the outside window. What they had learnt when he returned was an interesting insight into Fayez's sexual proclivities but added nothing to the issue on hand.

Fayez had booted the girl out at 6.33 a.m. showered and then set off to the airport.

"He's probably back in his office by now," said a frustrated Basmah.

Marlena was not so put out. "You did well," she said, "and at such short notice too. It's a pity though, even with your super new German cameras this guy was not very photogenic. You say you had people at all the exits, but he didn't reappear?"

"That's right, we think he changed in the washrooms before he left. It's quite an international type of place. People from all over the world go there – very difficult to see everywhere at once."

Basmah was not to be consoled so easily. She knew the tape would probably offer up more detail when the gurus had been through it, but it still irked her to lose her man. Who was this mysterious stranger, she wondered?

Marlena leaned over to her and put her hand on her knee. "Come on," she said, "it's not the end of the world."

Basmah took the hand and looked up into Marlena's eyes. "Marlena," she whispered, "do you remember?"

"How could I forget?" Marlena lifted their joined hands to Basmah's breast and with her other hand pulled the girls closer together. Marlena's flight was not until early morning, and they had hours to make up for lost time. They took things gently and found that their student passion and recklessness had been transformed into something more mature, something calmer but no less enjoyable and if anything, more sustained. As they lay side by side on Basmah's narrow bed they talked of the past, of themselves and their hopes and aspirations. They dreamt together of living in the same city, and Marlena seriously thought for a moment of giving up her work in Germany and moving to Cairo. But she realised that she was hooked, hooked on the stress, on the secrecy, the urgency, on the people and the fun. Her work stretched her to the limits of her physical and mental ability sometimes and there was no way she could see that continuing if she moved to Cairo.

"It's still fun? This work?"

"Oh yes," answered Basmah, "I wouldn't change it for the world. Every day there's always something that give me a buzz, no matter how small. I couldn't stand a boring life again. When you're dealing with people like Fayez Shakari you know that one slip and he can crush you in his fist. There's an adrenaline rush almost every day. It's like sex."

"But not as good."

"No, not as good." She smiled and the girls turned to each other again. Ships passing in the dark they may be, but she knew they would pass again.

65

Miles sat in the anteroom, wondering whether he was doing the right thing. The palace was old but immaculate and the furnishings had the feel of rather blatant wealth. In the end he had simply telephoned and asked to see Raya, with the pretext of having a personal message from her son. As he was shown into the reception room, Raya sat perfectly still, she knew that the most powerful position was when seated and she stayed exactly where she was.

"Come in young man," she spoke in English.

Miles greeted her courteously in Arabic. She looked carefully at him and then responded as formal etiquette demanded, before offering him tea.

"I understand you have information about my son," she said at last, "I was unaware that you knew Abdullah but I'm all ears."

"It's not about Abdullah, well not directly," Miles had a carefully thought-out script in his head, but it looked decidedly inadequate now, "but I do have the findings of some research in London that I'd be interested to share with you. You may be able to help me."

Raya simply looked at him. She could see that he was not 100% English, and she was impressed by his correct and carefully structured Arabic. He spoke it well and with an educated accent – must have learnt it somewhere in the Gulf, or perhaps Egypt, she thought, certainly not around here.

"Many years ago, you used to live in London," Miles continued. "You were twenty-two at the time; a student learning English. I believe you stayed there for about two years. Also, in London there was a well-regarded diplomat named Gerald Hoffman, an Englishman despite the German sounding name. Until his London assignment he'd been stationed here at the British Embassy. He had a girlfriend. And she joined him in London."

The old face did not move a millimetre. The eyes were steady and her breathing absolutely even. Miles wondered whether he had made a terrible mistake and jumped to completely the wrong conclusions, but he held his ground.

"Fifty-three years ago, this girlfriend gave birth to a son in London. Gerald was his father. The son was adopted almost straight away. It's news of that son that I'm now speaking about."

Raya held up her hand.

"Young man, Mr Cameron," she said calmly. "What you say is all very interesting, but I can't see what it has to do with me."

"The girl's name was the same as yours. The girl was the same age as you, and after recovering from childbirth she returned to this country. All that and more is in the files, and of course the mysterious son exists."

Raya looked hard at Miles. "That's very interesting, but also very circumstantial. Are you really trying to connect this poor young girl with me? What reason could you possibly have to do that?"

"Because that mysterious son is my father."

Raya visibly blanched and then turned bright red as the blood flowed desperately back into her face. "But that means that you are …" her voice tailed away.

"Yes," said Miles calmly, "I believe I am your grandson."

The two of them looked at each other for several long seconds. The silence was overpowering. It felt like minutes, even hours to Miles. He was struck that Raya had not denied his statement. If she had thrown a fit and denied all he would have been lost, but she had not. She merely sat there and looked at him, her face a mixture of amazement and disbelief.

"And your father?"

"Is very well. He's here in town actually, a successful geologist. Spends his time finding oil." Miles had started to gabble but then dried up almost as soon as he had started.

"He's here too? What is this, some sort of family gathering?" Raya had regained her composure and had begun to hit out verbally at whatever was around. But then she leaned forward and looked at Miles closely. "A grandson," she whispered.

"And two granddaughters. I have two sisters."

Raya had finally succumbed to emotion and her eyes glistened. This person from her past had come to confront her and she was not up to the task.

"Why don't you tell me about it," Miles asked softly. "I'd be fascinated to learn a little about my past."

Raya sighed. "Well," she said slowly, "I guess it all started here as you surmised. I was young and Gerald was very dashing. He swept me off my feet really and when he was posted back to London I moved everything to become a student there. In those days it wasn't too difficult. There were all sorts of inter-government grants, and the British Council was very helpful too. I desperately loved Gerald and wanted it to last for ever. You do when you're young. Thinking back, I must have been very young; innocent I suppose. I wasn't experienced with men at all. Gerald was my first love." She paused in contemplation before continuing. Her face changed too. It became severe and hard. Miles was quick to spot the change, it was quite intimidating.

"But when I became pregnant it all changed," she said suddenly. "He became distant and decided it was all my fault, as if I could have become pregnant by myself. He wanted me to have an abortion, but I couldn't. In the end, his father got involved. He was also a diplomat, but well off and so he simply paid for everything to be organised. Hospital, adoption, everything. I was packed off on a paid-for holiday to recuperate and that was the end of it from their point of view. Despicable!" she almost spat out the last words. "Despicable English aristocracy!"

"So, you never saw Gerald again."

"No, never, his father made certain of it. If I'd seen him I'd have killed him. I'm sure of that."

"Gerald Hoffman was killed in a bomb blast in Sudan. He was a senior commercial attaché at the time. The motive for the bombing, and indeed who was behind it, was never established." Miles spoke quietly.

As Raya listened she began to show signs of discomfort.

"But I guess you knew?" Miles wished he had not said that, but Raya's next words made him blink.

"Sometimes revenge must be patient," she murmured, almost to herself.

Miles gaped, Christ, he thought, she had him killed! In as calm a voice as he could manage he pushed gently for Raya to continue.

"I stayed on their paid-for vacation for six months," she said, "six long months, before I eventually came back here. My sister helped me to marry. Actually, we both did rather well. One extra thing I'd persuaded old Hoffman to pay for was to make me a virgin again. It was not easy, but we managed it. That sort of thing is very important here, you can have a figure like a horse and these men wouldn't notice. All they want is a virgin."

"And you had another boy?"

"That's right, Abdullah was born and that put an end to my English history. Thank goodness," she added.

Miles decided to push his luck. "And what about Leena" he said almost in a murmur.

The old lady was instantly on her guard. "What about her?" she demanded.

"Well, she also had a boy, didn't she? Same date of birth too."

Raya looked daggers at him. "How can you sit there and accuse me?" and then her voice tailed away, and she sat bolt upright in her chair. "Leena died many years ago," she said.

"I know, another accident," Miles paused. "But exactly the same date of birth. Very unusual."

"Pure coincidence!" Raya was almost shouting now. "Anyway, the damned woman shouldn't have been so hungry for power. She was never in the same league as Hasna and me."

"And yet you stayed with her from about six months before Abdullah was born? The file says that Leena was infertile. Must be a mistake."

Raya exploded with rage. For an old lady she showed amazingly agility and almost flew out of her chair. "Which file is that?" she demanded. "I have the only files. You're lying!"

But Miles knew he was not lying. Wafa's research had been extensive and finding the local hospital record of Leena had been like a golden nugget. He waited patiently for Raya to compose herself again.

"Please," he said quietly, "I'm not here to criticise, just to find out about my family. It seems rather larger than I'd imagined. Tell me, what happened to Talak in Genoa?"

Raya had collapsed into a little old lady. Her composure had shrivelled, her defiance vanished. She looked helplessly at Miles.

"I have been carried away with emotion," she said finally, "please forgive me. I deny everything and you have no proof otherwise."

Miles pulled the hospital record of Leena's check-up from his pocket. "I believe you are the mother of twin boys," he said at last, "maybe not identical, but nonetheless twins."

Raya stared at the paper for long time. Finally, she sighed and then shuddered slightly. "Okay, I stayed there with Leena for a year in total. My husband wasn't interested in a pregnant wife. He had his other girls to play with. Leena found out about the child in London and threatened me with exposure. That would have finished me, so I gave her my second son to bring up as her own. It was what she'd always wanted, a son of her own. She knew she was unable to have children. He was born three minutes after Abdullah."

Miles waited. He sensed there was more.

"I paid for all his education. It didn't cost her a penny, and yet she still wasn't satisfied. She tried to bleed me dry under the threat of exposure. Finally, Talak went away to Genoa, to learn Italian and become an oilman. Then … then Leena had a car accident."

"Another case of patient revenge?"

"No, actually quite genuine, but it did help, I must admit."

You cold-hearted old woman, thought Miles. "So, tell me about Talak," he said quietly.

Raya's eyes became distant. "He studied engineering at Genoa. Did very well in fact, but while he was there he married an Italian girl. A well-to-do family. Her name was Isabella. Talak was only twenty. You'd think he'd never seen a girl before. She trapped him. She was a witch!"

Miles' mind churned. "You mean they had to get married?"

"That's right. How did you know?"

"Just intuition, I suppose. So, this child must now be what? About thirty?"

Raya thought for a moment. "Something like that, yes, though I have no idea where she is now. Talak brought her here once, when she was three, but Leena had died, and her husband wasn't interested. I met them on that visit, just for an hour, but the shame he'd brought on us all by having a child with a foreigner was too much. We had all become much more fundamental in our thinking. We had to. Even Abdullah was cool. He was well on his way into the ministry hierarchy by then and couldn't afford shadows. So, … he officially denounced him and sent him packing back to Italy with his daughter."

"So, Abdullah isn't aware that he has a brother?"

"No." She paused in thought for moment. "Anyway, after that visit we never saw them again. He became completely foreign to us, even taking an Italian name too."

"And he worked in an oil company?"

"Yes, his father-in-law gave him a job. Kept things in the family. When Talak told me about this on his visit he thought the man was being kind to him. I didn't think so and I think he found that out for himself too. It wasn't kindness at all, just the opposite in fact."

"Why?"

"It was all done to save the family's face and avoid a scandal. By keeping Talak and Isabella safe from scandal he neutralised the problem. Abortion in Italy wasn't an option, and nor was a child out of wedlock. The only solution was to get married, and a daughter in a family like that could only marry a suitable man. So they created him. By giving Talak an Italian name the family looked perfectly normal from the outside."

Raya paused, before resuming her narrative. "He had a good job in the company but as soon as he started, he realised he was always going to be a second-class citizen. He came to hate his father-in-law and his wife too. For him they represented the worst of capitalism. Rich people getting richer while they kept the rest of the world in check. The Italian aristocracy is as bad as the British. His father-in-law was always his target."

"But not his daughter?"

Raya looked hard at Miles. "Your perception does you credit," she said eventually. "No, not his daughter, he loved his daughter. He even gave her an Arabic name."

"It sounds as if you kept in touch." Miles was amazed how much he could keep pushing. There seemed no end to the old lady's story.

"He sent letters through a friend, not very often, but yes, I guess you could say he kept in touch. All that ended sixteen years ago."

"Why?"

"An oil storage tank exploded. Talak and many others were killed. It was an awful mess, there were almost no remains to identify. In fact, they only found about half the bodies in any shape at all. We were never able to give him a proper funeral."

"But he wasn't officially your son anyway, and Leena was dead by then. You mean you would have wanted to see him again?"

"Family is always family," Raya smiled. "Look at us now."

"Did he know that you are his mother?"

She looked dolefully out of the window, to the breeze in the palm tree and the clear blue sky beyond. "No, I was always his friendly aunt who took a great interest in his upbringing."

"And no plans to see the granddaughter again?"

"Absolutely not. If it hadn't been for her family and their oil company job, Talak would still be alive. No, that phase of things is long gone."

The thought that family was not always family crossed Miles' mind. He sat quietly waiting for more, but there was nothing forthcoming.

"Would you like to meet my father?"

Raya brightened a little and smiled. "I'd like that," she said softly. "Do you think he'd want to meet me?"

"We can see," said Miles.

"Young man," Raya voice was now thoughtful and conciliatory, "I have entrusted you with many secrets today, most of which I suspect you already knew. It would do me no good to have these secrets broadcast here, no good at all. It seems you are my grandson; I acknowledge that, but it must not become local knowledge here."

"You have my word." Miles had no intention of publicising anything locally, or indeed making things public at all, but he knew where his allegiances lay. Genoa beckoned. What Raya had told him about the explosion was part of what he already knew, but his own research had met a dead end. Oil companies didn't like admitting that their security had been breached; a dead man with no identifiable remains in an explosion that was shrouded in mystery. He knew there were more answers, but they weren't here with Raya. As an afterthought he turned and asked casually, "what was Talak's name in Italy, Raya?"

The old lady looked venomous. "Ha!" she exclaimed. "You might well ask. They called him 'Fabio' and told him it meant fabulous, modern, stylish, well liked, but he later found out it really meant 'bean grower.' It was a joke, an insult from his father-in-law, and Talak never forgave him."

With that she waved imperiously and turned to go, leaving Miles to find his own way out through the opulent mansion.

66

Russell pulled out the file. With German efficiency it was meticulous, and he had been full of admiration that it had been done within twenty-four hours of Marlena's return to Frankfurt. He glanced through it. It was certainly brief, he thought, but then he began to read the detail.

Analysis of tape provided by Marlena Kaltenbach

Location: Recording made in Cairo (location and date undisclosed)
Method: Directional microphone at distance of about 20 metres.
General comment: There is much extraneous noise including music and many people's voices. Noise from nearby bar often drowns all targeted speech.

Names of Speakers from tape:
1. Arabic man – **Fayez** – other names not heard – Arabic language used. Voice is low in pitch and volume. Difficult to abstract.
2. Arabic man – **Khalid** – other names not heard – Arabic language used. Voice abstracted more readily but only in fragments.

Known names of speakers:
1. Fayez Shakari
2. Not known – referred to as 'Khalid' by Shakari

Translation of abstracted sections follows:
1: … friend Khalid … Naples … (33 seconds of indistinct speech and bar noise).
2: … Fayez, my friend, we have known each other for many years. Since I was a child, and you were like a big brother. Nine years older was a lot when I was half your age … (bar noise 9 seconds) … fees for the university were paid, the drunk

always looked after me ... (bar noise 3 seconds) ... but for you I would have lost contact ...

1: (1.05 minutes of indistinct speech) ... plan earlier. Can you do it?

2: Of course. Have I ever failed you? But there's something you should know. This is my last assignment for you. After this I am retiring... (bar noise 4 seconds) ... the reasons ... (bar noise 13 seconds) ... old man too. He finally died recently. His fortune was in ruins. I did that. It took me years, but I did it. I told him it would be ... (bar noise 5 seconds) ... didn't care... (Bar noise 9 seconds) ... you remember the first time. Oh, how amateurish I was in those days. Now I don't make the same mistakes. That was the only time anything ever blew up in ... (bar noise 3 seconds) ... your friends looked after me, they brought me here to Cairo and put me back together. How long it took. And then how strange to read about my own death and ... (bar noise 5 seconds) ... taught me everything then, but now I teach them how ... (bar noise 12 seconds) ...

1: (3.05 minutes of indistinct speech)

2: There's a change. I'll move from my temporary job at the X-ray plant in three weeks' time and everything will be much more difficult again once that happens. That's why I'm here this week, to make sure we ... (bar noise 13 seconds) ...

1: (24.17 minutes of indistinct speech) ... These people from the UK are new, they've met her twice now.

2: And you don't know what was said?

1: No, it's one of the few places I don't have access.

2: You're slipping my friend. Do you think it's anything to do with her past in London?

1: I don't know, yet ... (bar noise 11 seconds) (13.18 minutes of indistinct speech and noise – nothing abstracted)

2: You leave now, I'll follow. I need to ... (bar noise 9 seconds) (5.22 minutes of indistinct speech and noise – nothing abstracted)

Tape ends

Russell looked back over the transcription. He'd highlighted several words as he read through it, and now he was wondering how they were connected. There didn't seem too much there, but maybe more than was obvious.

'Old friends – contact over long time,' 'like big brother,' 'Nine years older,' 'looked after me in Cairo.' Clearly Fayez and Khalid had known each other for years and more importantly, had been school children together, although they appeared to be nine years different in age. That must mean that Khalid was about fifty, as Russell's file on Fayez had him currently at fifty-nine. Curious, he thought, I'll have to ask Wafa some more questions about the old files. He wondered who had been around forty or so years ago at school and who would have known Fayez at that time too. And also, who was the drunk who paid his university fees? And who were the friends in Cairo who'd looked after him, recovering from an injury? Maybe an explosion? But where? And with a fake death?

'Earlier,' 'Naples,' 'retiring,' 'old man,' 'fortune in ruins.' Were these connected in some way? Who was the old man and why had Khalid ruined him?

Finally, 'X-ray plant.' This really set Russell's mind wondering. Where? Frankfurt? Had Khalid managed to get a job at the airport? Was that how he planned to get into the cargo area? Was that the link they were seeking? He hoped there might some feedback from Dale's visits to Cairo too, maybe they might shed some light. As for the 'her' and London, he had no idea what they were talking about.

67

Miles and Dale had been more of less instructed to get together by Russell. They were to exchange information about their recent travels and researches and Miles was to report back in person after he had visited Genoa. He had been free-range far too long for Russell's liking. The coded emails were taking too long and neither Dale nor Miles was having much luck connecting to the system recently anyway. The internet was always quirky, but they sensed that there was rather more interference from Abdullah's ministry than normal.

The restaurant was the same hole in the wall place where they'd first met, four or five months before. Nothing had changed and, as the evening wore on, the same liveliness began to take over. They began to wish they had not come on their own.

"I've been busy," said Miles. "When did we meet? October, right?

"And right here too. Same table."

"Good memory. How was your visit to Egypt and Italy? What was it, four cities in three days?"

"Four days. I don't think Naiem was very impressed with what he saw though. Only Rome had any security worth talking about. As he said, you could bring a camel through Naples airport, and no one would notice."

Miles laughed. "And Cairo?""

Dale laughed too. "Since Cairo airport's full of camels, I think you'd have to think of something rather bigger."

"So how about the factories. Didn't you go to see the Italian place in Naples that you'll probably be getting cargo handling equipment from?"

"We did, and I think there's a connection," Dale said cautiously. "When we visited another plant in Cairo it turned out to be a low-cost supplier to Naples. The two are all part of the same set up. They make the cheap stuff in Cairo and the expensive equipment, including X-ray scanners, in Naples." He went on at some length to explain what he had seen in both factories and also the comments about Frankfurt being a cheap cargo hub for Italy.

Miles was interested. "You think the water treatment vessels could be how they smuggle explosive into Italy?"

"I've no idea but it certainly looks that way. All the explosive used in those bombs Russell talked about was traced back to Cairo and the funding was then traced back to here."

"Russell told you that?"

Dale realised he had heard this second hand from Nadia, who had sworn him to secrecy about where he'd heard it. "Yes," he said finally.

"So, we have financing from here, explosive from Egypt, a possible route to Naples and a factory making water treatment equipment and cargo security equipment. Russell's going to love all this."

Dale felt his thunder about to be stolen but there was nothing he could do about it. "So, what have you been up to?" he said.

"Oh, nothing much. This and that."

"You look as if you've found the crown jewels?"

"Well, on a personal level, maybe I have. I've just met a re-markable old lady and introduced her to her son. Here, let me take you through it. See if you pick any holes in the logic. I understand you're pretty much one of us now."

Dale smiled at the compliment. He waited and wasn't disappointed as an increasingly emotional Miles took him through his painstaking research. His eyes widened as Miles talked about Talak's time in Italy and the visit to see Raya with his three-year-old daughter. When Miles divulged the name Fabio, Dale was suddenly quiet. "Are you quite sure?"

"Absolutely. I wrote all this up straight away. I wouldn't forget that sort of thing. Why?"

Dale mumbled that it was an unusual name that he'd heard somewhere else. "Nothing special," he said but his mind was churning.

"And you're off to Genoa tomorrow?" he asked.

"That's right. Anything you want me to find out?"

"I'd be very interested to know the family name of Fabio and his father-in-law too. Give me a call will you. If it's interesting I'll share it with you, but I don't want to raise any false alarms. Call me when you find out will you? Where will you start? At the university or the oil company?"

"I was going to take it sequentially in time and start at the University, but from what you're saying, perhaps I'll tackle the company first. I'll call you as soon as I find something."

Dale smiled his thanks. "So, when are you seeing Wafa again?" he asked.

"Oh, not until I come again. If I come again."

"From what you're saying I think you'll be here regularly if Raya has anything to do with it. There can't be too many people from the UK who write 'visiting family' on their visa application."

68

In the Frankfurt afternoon Marlena had also read the transcription, first in English and then in German, both translations of course. She also listened to the scrubbed recording itself and was amazed at how much the technicians had been able to clean it up. Compared with the unintelligible rough babble amidst the clattering night-club noise she had heard the day before, this was almost like sitting in the same room as the two men. Fayez certainly was indistinct, but Khalid's voice at times was clear, although she knew that without many of the high frequencies, it probably didn't sound quite as it did on the cleaned-up tape. She'd also realised that the drunk was a mistake in translation. The listeners probably didn't know that the Arabic was almost the same sound as a name she knew well. She looked at the coded email from Russell. "Take transcript to Dale," it said. She headed back to the airport.

"Fayez was in Cairo? When?"

"Immediately after you were, by the sound of it. I've been trekking from here to Cairo via Frankfurt and back again while you've been vacationing in Italy."

Dale reminded himself to take Marlena's sense of humour in hand some time, but now was not the occasion.

"So, who did he meet?"

Marlena, pulled out the transcript. "Basmah and her team obtained this. They followed Fayez and taped him with his girl-friend too. The guy's name is Khalid."

Dale scanned down the transcript. "How old is Fayez? Fifty-nine?"

Marlena recalled her conversation with Russell before she left Frankfurt. "Yes, how did you know?"

"I'm getting good at guessing. Who's the drunk person and the old guy?"

Marlena looked very pleased with herself. "I listened to the tape myself," she said. "It's a transcription mistake. The Arabic word Rayya means sated with drink, and that's what our translators used for a drunk. I think it's Raya, Abdullah's mother."

Dale looked at her in amazement. "You're sure?"

Marlena was affronted. "Of course I'm sure," she said huffily. "I don't make that sort of mistake. Anyway, what do you make of the rest?"

Dale's mind was teeming with possibilities. "I'm not sure yet," he said lamely, "let me think about it."

"Well, keep the copy. Russell said to make sure you have it. He's already alerted our own people in Frankfurt and they're searching the workforce for employees who speak Arabic."

"Like you?" Dale tried to make light of his comment too him seriously.

"No," she said, "not like me."

69

Khalid Abu Nida'a knew he was up against time. He had agreed with Fayez that they would bring the plan forward but now he had a problem. Italfabrica produced a large number of products and amongst them were several specialist, high-quality water treatment plants for industrial process use. In any month they would ship six or seven to various parts of the world. However, the number of airfreighted units was small and in the near future there were only three that suited his purpose. He had been focusing on his preferred package for some weeks. It was destined for a large oil company in America working in joint venture with an Italian group. They had a pilot programme under way into some creative waste-to-energy project, the sort that sounded too good to be true and probably was, and they were building a new facility near Washington DC. The two sides had blamed each other endlessly for the delays in funding and the schedule had slipped horribly. As a consequence, the project managers were now airfreighting everything to the site in a desperate attempt to have things on track for the Italian President's visit to America in three months' time. The complete plant to supply high quality process water was due to be shipped in a few days' time.

Khalid had been carefully preparing the final product through its final fabrication stages and had incorporated his device so cleverly into the pressure vessel part of the production equipment that it was indistinguishable from the original. His masterpiece had been finished a week ago and had stood ready, waiting for the final elements to be added to the overall skid unit. Now the damned politicians had ordered a switch and the American plant had been put back three weeks so that the equipment destined for Washington could be used as a show piece and sent on the first post-sanction plane to his own country of birth, of all places.

He could hardly wreck his own country and so he had to find another item of plant, another Trojan Horse, and in his discussion with Fayez. he had agreed that he would transfer his device from the water plant to some of the other equipment leaving the factory in two weeks' time. Fayez had been insistent about the actual plant and destination. His preference had been for equipment, which was also destined for America, but entering the country in the north, through Boston. Khalid had argued about the destination but, in the end, had acquiesced.

Khalid had not been happy about the switch. He was a per-fectionist and did not like being rushed into things, especially changes that he had not planned, and his plan was such a good one. He considered his idea of using process water treatment equipment to be flawless. Most plans aimed at airlines failed be-cause the search equipment picked up wires and timers, or simply smelt the residue of explosive, but he was not relying on timers. He was using pressure switches, and these water treatment units, 'demineralisation packages' as they were called, were literally covered in the damn things. It had given him his idea. Who would suspect one of them being linked to a bomb built into one of the main resin containment vessels, where X-rays could not reach anyway, and triggered by pressure switches, which were there for all to see? Okay, he had to change the settings of the pressure switches, maybe even put in a lower pressure one, but who would know? Certainly not some inspector at an airport.

And so his device, which was sizeable, was destined to explode as the air pressure increased, not for the first time, where it was too easy to trace back to where it came from, but for the second time, making tracking of the device almost impossible to achieve. It was brilliant, he thought to himself, brilliant, but now these damned politicians had compromised it. The plant destined for America would soon be on a different path, redirected to form the flagship of Italian commercial pride, to his own country, Libya. He still could not get over the irony of its destination.

So, he changed his plan. As Fayez had ordered, so he had changed, and he was now assembling his creation into the base of another piece of equipment. Ah well, he thought, after this I'm retiring, so good luck to them.

To screen the unit, he had added some refinements, thickening the internal base plate by adding a steel box section to bury his intricate control devices from inquisitive eyes. The water filtration vessels were now history, their carefully planned and sculptured internal compartments redundant. He looked sadly at the new destination labels already attached to the equipment and went on with his work, carefully wiring the pressure switches in sequence and linking the whole affair to an almost invisible metallic seal wired through all but one of the side panels. If the casing was opened, the luckless opener would not exist to tell the tale.

He turned his attention back to the filter vessels and replaced the access hatchway, carefully adding the security seals as before. When you made a bomb, he thought, you always left yourself a way to dismantle it, however obscure that might be. He was cautious and he always left that back door for himself, just in case. He packed away his tools and tidied the fabrication shop. It was 4.30 a.m. No one would know he'd been there. He had worked at nights here for weeks now and had never been challenged, even in the early days when he'd had to climb through the roof panel to gain access at night. In fact, he had earned a reputation as a hard worker, always willing to work long hours and never too proud to take on the meanest job if it needed doing. In three days' time he would make sure that his masterpiece, his 'pièce de résistance' left the workshop and then he would simply disappear. He had been serious with Fayez. He'd had enough and wanted to retire to Cairo.

70

In a nondescript office building in Genoa, Miles looked at the name on the register, and then at the name in his hand. In the end he had followed his original plan and visited the university first. He had no idea where Dale was coming from and wanted to make sure he researched things in the right order. No sense in jumping the gun as he would only have to back track and do it again. But the name Talak Nabayad was there for all to see. He had obtained a good degree in chemical engineering, but that was all. Nothing further could be seen of the university records. So far so good, he thought. He then looked up the name Isabella and found two in the register. When he saw the family names he understood why Dale had been interested.

So now, in the scruffy building that served as headquarters for the Italian branch of a large US oil company, he had wheedled his way into the back office and managed to sweet talk the personnel manager into letting him see the company archives. The record of the explosion was there, with a roll call of the casualties. He moved on to annual reports, listing the board of directors at the time and found the now expected name. He pulled his phone from his pocket and dialled Dale's mobile. A mechanical voice responded. Well, he thought, this is no time for covert codes, and spoke a few brief words into the distant message box. Then he headed for Genoa airport, and London. He made one last call to Russell before he boarded. He did not want any further delay with the minefield of news he now carried.

71

Near Naples airport, in the rear of an Alitalia cargo plane, a small, sealed metal box clicked quietly, once. No one noticed, no one heard. As the plane soared upwards into the sky the small box sat quietly, waiting.

Dale and Nadia landed in Rome late morning, battled their way through the vigilant security staff at customs and made their way to the domestic transfers desk. As they did so, Dale switched on his phone and within seconds a small bleep told him that there were messages. God, he thought, is there no peace in the world?

Their next flight departed in a little over two hours and they bought two economy tickets. "Why do we have to take a day in Naples?" Nadia asked. "Why can't we just go direct to Montepulciano? I thought this was a holiday." She had been delighted at the prospect a long weekend away in her beloved Italy and equally delighted when Dale had insisted on dragging her away at such short notice. It was two weeks since he had returned from the previous Naples visit, and she couldn't see why he needed to go again.

"It's some last-minute details about the contract," he had said darkly, "we won't be there long."

"So why didn't we book tickets before we left? You're normally so incredibly organised. Why not this time?"

But he had left the issue hanging while they waited for their plane, and she had said nothing more. If he wanted to play spy games then that was his prerogative, she thought. Ever since he had met her she had noticed his rising curiosity and enthusiasm for whatever it was that Abdullah and his friends were up to, but she still said nothing. Better not be seen to nag, she thought. It's only one day extra.

Near Frankfurt airport, in the rear of the Alitalia cargo plane, the small box clicked quietly again, just once. As before, no one noticed. As before, no one heard. The plane landed two minutes later and taxied to the cargo hanger. The small box sat patiently, waiting.

It was mid-afternoon by the time they landed in Naples and Dale was in a hurry.

"Come on," he said, "the sooner we get rid of this paperwork the sooner we can go on holiday properly." They jumped into a taxi and sped off towards the Italfabrica plant, the driver brightening at the prospect of a good tip if he took them the quickest way. Nadia resigned herself to a tedious few hours and thought forward to the small hotel she had selected in Montepulciano. It was next to one of the famous wine stores and the local wine there was the best in the world, even if she was biased. Meanwhile, Dale dialled his message box and listened carefully. He pulled out an envelope and wrote a name on the front. He then tore off a few sheets of blank notepaper from his pad, added them to the envelope, sealed it and returned it to his inside pocket. Nadia daydreamed, her head resting on his shoulder. Showtime, he thought quietly, maybe.

Paolo Grenaldi, the factory manager was pleased to see Dale so soon after his pervious visit, but it seemed to Nadia that the meeting was not as essential as Dale had described. Everything seemed so mundane. Why not simply send it by courier? While Dale and Paolo traded pieces of paper she sat in the background flipping through the local business magazines and wondering why anyone would write them, let alone want to read them. So, she pulled out of her bag a well know fashion magazine that she had managed to buy at the airport and happily tuned out of what Dale was saying.

As they finished initialling various pages of the contract Dale asked, as casually as he could. "One of my colleagues apparently has an uncle who works here. He asked me to deliver this." He pulled out an envelope on which was written a name.

Grenaldi looked at the name and then shook his head. "I don't think so," he said, "but let's have a look. We have a lot of people working here." He turned to his computer terminal and punched a few keys. A list of staff came up on the screen and he ran his cursor down the page. "No," he said, "no one of that name. We have three called Fabio but none with that family name."

"That's strange. Maybe I wrote it down wrongly, what are the names of the ones you have?"

"Well, let's see." Grenaldi was helpful but not in a hurry. "The two Castellini names are probably family, father and son looking at when they joined us. Castellini is a well-known local name. Ponte is the other. Fabio Ponte."

"Ah!" Dale rapped the envelope on his knuckles. "Of course, if he's my colleague's uncle he could have a different name anyway. I just assumed they'd be the same. Do you mind if I take this letter to him, or at least see if it's him?"

"Sure, no problem," Grenaldi smiled broadly. "Always happy to help our customers. He works down in the main fabrication shop. I'll take you down there."

"It's okay, I did the grand tour last time. It's just across the way isn't it?" He dragged a reluctant Nadia away from her magazine and they walked down a long corridor and turned left through a small doorway. Before them lay the large fabrication area. It was a tall building, built of steel with corrugated cladding. Floodlights blazed from the walls and roof space. Partially completed skids of equipment lay around the floor in seemingly haphazard disorder. Portable workbenches also littered the concrete paving and silent forklift trucks stood against the far wall, connected by umbilical cables to their battery chargers, to prepare them for tomorrow. High-level rails ran down the length of each wall and the roof area was dominated by two large overhead cranes. One was parked above the main entrance to the building but the other was moving. From its massive hook hung a huge skip.

72

Khalid had been on tenterhooks for three days. After his all-nighter to put right the vagaries of politicians, he had witnessed an extraordinary series of events. On the first day, an air shipment had arrived from Cairo with a duplicate set of pressure vessels. Apparently, the impending lifting of sanctions had released all sorts of roadblocks, and equipment was suddenly arriving from everywhere. The vessels were for the first post-sanction flight and Khalid had volunteered to join the party of workmen putting together the package of water treatment equipment now due to go to Frankfurt in two days' time. It would be added to the rest of the items waiting to take part in the much-vaunted event. It took them all the first day, all night and all the next day, and by the time it was done everyone was exhausted.

The plant was decked out with small flags and special packaging, all done in the national colours of both Italy and Libya. The workshop had been constantly busy, and Khalid had no time to himself. He was still consumed with concerns about the change that had been forced on him and was seriously contemplating the prospect of reverting to his original plan; if only he had the time.

By the end of the afternoon, he had made up his mind. He had one last evening of opportunity and he had to take it, come what may. Never mind that he had not slept for days. The original consignment due for America was already re-labelled, yet again to be air freighted to the US and it sat there, inviting him to reinstall his perfect device. So, he waited, patiently until the workshop was empty. By eight o'clock he had the building almost to himself, apart from the supervisor who would leave in a few minutes. Then he knew exactly what he had to do. It would take a while, probably five or six hours but the original plan, the special delivery to Washington DC was back on track again. He prepared to make his move.

It was early morning and, as the cool March day dawned, several large trucks arrived to haul the various pieces of equipment off to Naples airport. After the exhaustion of the marathon to fabricate Italy's flagship equipment, all the staff were lined up in the factory yard and someone had even dredged up the local brass band. The band's enthusiasm far exceeded its ability, especially so early in the morning, but who cared? The press and TV were there and everyone except Khalid was pushing forward to make sure they were seen and captured for posterity. It was a time that would be remembered and an excuse to stay in the bar for the rest of the day.

Khalid was exhausted and wanted to leave early too, but his supervisor asked him to do him a favour. He was a practical man, and he knew that Khalid had no family, so he asked him to finish clearing away the packaging materials while he sent the married men home for a well-earned rest.

"Tomorrow," he said to a weary Fabio, "take some time off. You've earned it."

The attraction of not having to report for work, and not being missed as a result, was an offer that Khalid could not refuse. He had no intention of coming in tomorrow, or ever again and the greater the distance he could put between himself and the factory the better he would feel. So, he stayed, and spent a couple of hours throwing scrap packaging materials into the huge skip and then climbed wearily into the cab of the overhead crane. He picked up the skip and began to manoeuvre his bulky cargo down towards the big roller shutter side door at the far end of the workshop from where it would be collected early the next morning.

73

Dale looked around him and saw no one. The crane was rumbling overhead, with a massive container of what looked like waste materials swinging beneath its travelling bridge, high in the roof space. Beyond it he saw a long metal staircase leading to a small landing where the crane obviously docked. He took Nadia's hand and walked tentatively toward the stairway.

Then an office door opened behind him and short, fat man appeared wearing a motorcycle crash helmet and huge leather gloves. They looked incongruous against the background of his white, short-sleeved shirt, like somebody about to handle something very unpleasant indeed. He nodded to Dale and walked towards the main entrance of the massive building.

"Excuse me!" shouted Dale. The man turned and waved but carried on walking. Dale ran over to him and lifted the crash helmet's visor. "Excuse me!" he shouted again. The man stopped.

"Yes?" he asked.

"Fabio Ponte?"

"No. I'm Gianni."

"Is Fabio still here?"

The supervisor waved upwards towards the crane. "Up on the bridge," he shouted happily, "like his name."

"Thanks!" Dale did not wait but grabbed a startled Nadia by the hand and now pulled her hurriedly towards the long steel staircase, which led to the upper level. The crane driver's cab would reach the far end of the steel gantry very soon and he wanted to be sure he was in the right place at the right time.

She glanced at her trainers and wondered whether Dale had had second sight when he suggested she travel in something comfortable. They raced up the stairs, back and forth at each landing, clattering on the steps as they went. She glanced down and, even through the holes of the steel mesh treads she could see it was a

long way to the ground. She shuddered and turned her face upwards again as they rushed, panting, to the top walkway. They
were far above the workshop floor and the height was giddying.
The crane drew closer, speeding up as it moved towards them.

And then suddenly it stopped, its huge container swinging
far below, in an upward arc that almost touched the end wall of
the building.

In the crane cabin Khalid grinned to himself, he enjoyed this part
of the job. With an almost childish glee he would accelerate the
massive crane down the length of the workshop and then stop,
just short of the end of the run, allowing the load far below to
continue forward, driven by momentum alone. The trick was to
allow the load to just graze the brickwork of the end wall, but
not to do any serious damage. There were marks all the way up
the bottom half of the wall where he and other crane drivers had
played the same game. The aim was to lay claim to the high-
est and therefore most daring mark. It wreaked havoc with the
crane controls but who cared, that was maintenance's problem,
and they needed something to keep them busy. Maintenance
were a superior bunch who thought too much of themselves anyway. Only once had someone misjudged the distance and the
brickwork had suffered dramatically before it was repaired. The
errant crane driver had been banned from driving cranes for life.

He looked up and saw two people waving to him. A man and
an attractive, long haired young woman. What they were doing
on the gantry he had no idea. He waved back in a friendly way.
In a few minutes he was out of here, for ever. He had no idea
what they could want but it did not concern him. The thought
of leaving blinded him to his surroundings as he looked down
to where the container was swinging in rapidly decreasing arcs.
He edged the crane forward until he was about three metres
from the end of the run and lowered the container towards the
ground. It was squarely opposite the roller shutter door, ready

for the morning and he smiled to himself as it slowly descended. Another job well done.

He looked up. The couple were still there, waving and shouting something. As the container hit the ground he killed the motor, stood up and put his head out of the cab's unprotected doorway.

"What's the matter?" he shouted, his Italian accented.

"Are you Fabio Ponte?"

Fabio shrugged. "What of it?"

"Fabio Ettori Ponte?"

Nadia gasped and clutched Dale's hand. "Dale!" she screamed.

Fabio almost fell out of the cab doorway and then recovered. "Who?" he tried to remain calm.

Nadia gaped and staggered backwards against the railing, her hand leaving deep scratch marks in the back of Dale's hand. He ignored the sharp pain and looked up at her. "Nadia, is it him?" he asked.

"It can't be. He'd dead," she stammered. "It can't be. Can it?"

"Or is it Khalid?" Dale shouted across the void again. "Fabio the Bean Grower who became Khalid the Eternal. Which is it to be, Talak?"

Nadia turned on him, still in shock. "What are you doing, Dale? That can't be Fabio Ettori. He's dead. I went to his funeral."

"When you were fourteen," Dale had his script up and running in his head. He mentally turned a page. "But there was no body. Fabio messed up the bomb, didn't you Fabio, or were you already Khalid?"

Khalid was staring at Nadia. "Nadia? Is that you?" he said hoarsely. "Is that really you? But you're beautiful."

"Papa?" Nadia's eyes were watering rapidly. "Can that really be you too? What … what happened to your face?" Her mind spun as her hand touched the side of her face and her knees began to shake violently and then collapsed against the open space in front of them, her eyes streaming as she wailed in anguish into the abyss. Dale shot out a hand to pull her back. He glanced down and shuddered at the height. There was a safety chain hanging to one side of the unfenced gap and he lifted the loose end and hooked it into place.

Khalid's face was twisted on one side and when he smiled it gave him a ghoulish expression. He wore a dark blue, woollen ski hat pulled down well below the hairline and, lifting his free hand he pulled it off to reveal a patched and deeply scarred forehead. The scars on his cheek were but a small part of the mess. Nadia gasped. She shook uncontrollably as her legs gave way and her sobbing overtook her totally so that she could hardly see through the haze.

"Your friend's right," he said, "the explosion did go wrong. In fact, it was a disaster, a nightmare, and it was all supposed to be so perfect. The old man would have never known what hit him. A beautiful accident to set his family free. Capitalist bastard! It was planned to be triggered when the local mayor and the company directors opened the new tank farm, but the damned politicians changed their minds, just like now, and all my planning was wasted. The mayor changed his schedule and so I had to go and alter the timing. The bomb exploded as I walked up to it. Cheap timer, damn thing went off early."

Nadia leaned over the chain, out into the gulf between them. In the cab doorway Khalid, or was he now Fabio, was lounging against the back of the crane operator's seat. He looked towards his daughter, only three meters away, as she bent her body over the rail towards him. "Why?" she screamed, her chest heaving and tears streaming "why?"

"Why the bomb? Your grandfather hated me," Fabio said, as if it was so obvious it hardly merited a response, "but he hated the idea of you having unmarried parents even more, so he arranged for your mother and me to be married while we were at university. Isabella had to leave; she never got her degree. He wouldn't allow anyone to see her in the state she was. I had to finish the course on my own and hardly saw her until you were born."

"So, when did you change your name from Talak?" Dale was now curious, and Fabio seemed happy to oblige. The unlit gulf between them faded as he focused on the wrecked face peering from the cab doorway.

"The ceremony was held at his family villa, that huge place where your mother now lives. It was only a small family event, not publicised at all. I can only remember about six people being there. I do remember the olive trees covering the hillside though, it was a beautiful place. When I arrived, I found he'd arranged everything for me, new passport, new identity and new name. I became a new person, all in five minutes. I don't know how he did it, the benefit of money I guess. Anyway, I became Fabio Ettori. I was young and I honestly thought he was being helpful. Big family name, big family house, our own apartment in town, promise of a good job when I graduated. At first I lapped it up. I had money, a beautiful wife and an even more beautiful daughter. But I'd forgotten my roots, my own family, and after I'd been working for a year I realised I was trapped. It was Fayez who brought me back to my senses. He showed me it was only so the old man could control me. Even the Fabio name was a joke! I was too stupid to realise."

Fabio gazed at the distraught Nadia. "Fayez was a good friend," he said, "he'd bring me letters from home, and I would write back. He encouraged me to go back, and I did, just the once. It didn't work out. They rejected me because of my foreign wife, because I'd accepted foreign money, especially because I'd adopted a foreign name."

"And you took Nadia, when she was three."

"Whaaat?" Nadia screeched. A myriad of past images flashed through her brain, of a young girl and her father travelling to some distant desert. She half remembered the heat and sand of the visit, but her memory was vague and the faces of the robed figures which haunted her had no form. She began to shake uncontrollably, and Dale held her shoulders tightly.

"Your friend's right again. Your mother hated me for taking you away, but she still refused to come. So, we went on our own, and when we were there I gave you a new name, an Arabic name." He looked straight into Nadia's eyes. "That was when you became

Nadia. New passport, new name, just like your father. I thought it would help get me accepted again back home, but it didn't. I was thrown out, and even renounced to my face by Abdullah. Until then he'd been my best friend, but no longer. Creep!" Khalid spat into the void. They did not hear it land. "That visit was so embarrassing I never talked to you about it ever again. I doubt you even remember you went."

"When we got back to Genoa there was one hell of an argument, but it was you who solved it. It made me laugh, you were wonderful, only three and yet you loved your new name and wouldn't answer to anything else. Wouldn't use Francesca at all, and so it stuck. We changed your Italian passport too. That's why you're Nadia Francesca. Isabella became resigned to it, I don't think she cared, but your grandfather never called you Nadia, only Francesca, after his wife."

Nadia was suddenly calm and quiet. She had no idea now what to say. The comment about her grandfather was one she knew only too well. Her grandfather had always remained distant from her and never ever called her Nadia. Now she began to understand why. She looked at the man she was now being told was her father and studied his battered face.

"But you died in the oil tank explosion. I went to the funeral …" She still had no idea what to believe. Was this really her father, and if so, then what did it mean?

He laughed. "Not quite, as you can see. But your grandfather couldn't wait to get rid of me, so he made sure my name was on the list of casualties. There was no way to tell anyway, most of the bodies were incinerated in the blaze. I read about the funeral much later and I saw his face in the newspaper photographs, he looked really happy. I kept one on my wall for years to remind me. I only threw it away when I learnt he'd died last year."

Fabio became very still. "The only sad face was yours, my daughter. Your tears burnt my heart, but I knew by then it was too late. By then I'd become another person."

"So how did you escape from the fire?" Dale pushed the opportunity to match what he had learnt from Miles.

"I was pulled out of the wreckage by an Egyptian colleague, we worked together at the plant. He and I would often take an evening out, down in the bars around the port area. Isabella hated it but I didn't care, she was always running to her father anyway and if it annoyed him then I was happy.

Anyway, he bundled me into a car and then onto a ship leaving for Alexandria later that day, his brother was the captain. I can't remember much of what happened. I was too far gone to realise what was going on, let alone do anything about it. They patched me up as best they could on the boat and brought me to Egypt, to Cairo first and then out into the desert camp where they literally brought me back from the dead. It took a long time, and I was in bed mending broken bones and having skin grafts for nearly six months. That was when I was given the name Khalid. They decided that I'd escaped death once and so I'd nothing else to lose. I was an easy recruit into their organisation, their cause, and their camp out in the desert became my home. I lived there for three years, training, learning and teaching until I realised that I could use what I'd learnt to take my revenge on Giacomo."

"Giacomo?" This was a new name to Dale.

"My grandfather," said Nadia.

"I chose a new family name too. My name became Khalid Abu Nida'a, 'Eternal' Nida'a. Nothing could touch me. They taught me I was to be a weapon of the people, the one who could never fail, the sword which could never be blunted. I was immortal," he said spreading his hands.

"Nida'a sounds like Nadia. Why?" Nadia was entranced by the narrative, horrified but completely enthralled. Unlike Dale, it was all new to her. Meanwhile Dale was mentally putting in the pieces of his jigsaw.

"Matching my name to sound like Nadia, a sort of anagram was the only way I wanted to link back to the past. If I could have taken you with me, I would have," he added, then paused and gazed wistfully again, across the divide, "but I couldn't. There were more important things to do."

"So, your new-found family was a terrorist group?" Dale was persistent.

Khalid snorted. "It's only the capitalists who define us as terrorists. We are simply putting right the wrongs that the rich and selfish cause in the world. I became their most famous technician, their most creative bomb maker, but all the time I had old Giacomo in my sights. Never for a minute did I let him escape."

"Famous? What do you mean 'famous'? No one's ever heard of Nida'a," taunted Dale.

Khalid looked venomously at the younger man. "Remember Yemen?" he said. "Remember Atlanta?"

"They were both you?" Dale was incredulous although he didn't really know why, but there was one more link he wanted to know about. "So, what about Sudan?"

"The Embassy compound? Ah that was different. In all the others I just provided the bomb. Sudan was personal."

"Personal?"

"For my benefactor. It was to repay all her kindness over the years. That Brit should have known better than to abandon her. He had it coming."

Nadia turned to Dale. "What is all this?" she asked, her face taught with emotion. "Where's this going?"

Dale placed his finger to her lips and turned back to Khalid. "How did you know about her London past?" he asked

Khalid looked puzzled. "Fayez of course! He knew everything. He never found out who the child was, but he certainly knew it existed. It took him a little while to find Hoffman but when he did he let me know. He'd always kept in touch. Sometimes revenge must be patient."

Dale recalled someone else recounting the same phrase, in the restaurant. It had made quite an impression on Miles. "So, he was your paymaster too?"

"Yes of course. They were very supportive."

"They being Fayez, or Raya or the country in general."

Khalid looked quizzically at Dale. "What do you mean?"

"Never mind. Tell me about Raya."

"My aunt? My benefactor, especially after my mother died. She funded my education in Genoa. When I saw her with Nadia she was not especially pleased with us but for some reason she never abandoned me. There was always something between us. I could never make out what, and neither could Fayez. She and he were my only true friends for years. Fayez especially, travelling back and forth as he did. Not like that deceitful Abdullah."

"Abdullah?"

"Yes, Fayez showed me some papers which showed that he'd killed my mother. Something about protecting Raya from blackmail. I never really believed it. What could Leena have against Raya? Abdullah was always vindictive but according to Fayez he's got much worse."

Dale was pensive for a moment. "If Fayez knew so much about Raya," he said, "I wonder why he didn't tell you that she was also your real mother."

Khalid glared at Dale in total disbelief. "What are you talking about? My mother was Leena," he said firmly.

"Leena was barren," said Dale, hoping Miles had been completely accurate in translating the piece of paper he had seen at the restaurant, "and your birthday is exactly the same as Abdullah's."

Nadia's eyes were wide, staring aghast at Dale's determined face. She sat back on an electrical control box. She looked completely stunned. "You mean I'm related to Abdullah, and Raya, the whole lot of them."

Khalid had turned pale and stood rigidly in the doorway of the still unreachable cab. "But Fayez …" his voice tailed away.

"Has been somewhat economical in what he's told you," finished Dale. "Why don't you bring this crane over to these steps and say hello to your daughter?"

But Khalid was dazed, his brain struggling with the latest piece of news. He'd suspected as much many years before and had asked Fayez to look into it for him. Fayez had produced all sorts of evidence to show that Leena was his mother. "Why would he lie?" he asked plaintively.

Dale looked back at him. "Divide and rule," he said quietly. "Can you imagine Raya and her two sons combining forces? Fayez wouldn't stand a chance. My guess is that he knew exactly what he was doing, and carefully kept Talak apart from Abdullah."

To Khalid it all made too much sense. His was momentarily confused, lost for words but then his face flushed red, and his voice became strident, angry, forceful.

"So, all these years I've been working for a so-called friend who had deceived me?"

"Which is why I asked whether the funding was from Fayez, Raya or the country in general?"

"I don't know. Fayez always said he was working under orders, but now I don't know."

"Are you going to bring that crane over here or what?" Dale was not sure what to do next. Khalid was bigger than him, and undoubtedly trained. He looked as if he could look after himself.

"To do what? Give myself of up? You'd like that wouldn't you. Well, that's not going to happen. I'm not going to be locked away just to satisfy you. Nadia," he shouted suddenly. "I am Khalid Abu Nida'a! I am not your father. He died in a fire. Remember?" he screamed, "I am Khalid the Eternal and I'm leaving!"

With that he swung around the end of the cab and began to climb the access ladder to the roof. Dale pulled out his phone and pushed it into Nadia's hands. "Here," he shouted, "phone Emanuella and then Russell. I've got to get Khalid to tell us about the bomb."

Khalid had reached the top of the short ladder and turned. "You'll never find it," he yelled. "I am the best!"

"Then we'll start with the water plant," shouted Dale, looking up at the rails on which the crane travelled. "I saw it in Cairo, remember?"

Khalid looked down at him. "You are too clever my friend, but it's too late. Everything is in motion. It's a pity our politicians are too greedy, otherwise it would have been perfect. But never mind, soon you'll see what Khalid can do." With that he hauled himself onto the roof of the cab and set off on hands and knees across the travelling bridge that spanned between the walls of the building.

Dale took one look at the wall alongside him and scrambled up a pair of loosely bunched power cables. He hoped they were insulated. He grasped the rail track running along the wall and, hand over hand traversed the three metres before he too could reach the small ladder up the roof of the cab. An experienced, if infrequent mountain climber, he shinned up rapidly. Much easier than icy rocks, he thought, and then stood up and began walking, rather than crawling across the narrow steel beam. Even so he was slow. The beam was narrow, and it was long way to the ground. He kept his eyes forward. The distance seemed enormous.

Khalid turned to look at his pursuer and as he did so he felt his hand slip. Looking down he saw he was directly above the skip. He leaned down and grabbed the drum of steel rope hanging on the trolley beneath the beam. He scrambled down on to the drum and grabbed for the steel rope that hung vertically below. Way below, at the far end of the rope was the huge hook, and below that the skip. His brain was in turmoil. If he could slide down, he could escape. But it was a long way.

Dale was right above him now and leaned down to catch Khalid's fast disappearing leg. He held on, his finger nails digging deep into the ankle. There was a shout and a scream from Nadia as he hung precariously in mid-space, then Khalid twisted and Dale overbalanced and fell, pulling the ankle with him. It was the only thing he could hold on to and so he increased his grip.

Khalid slid round the drum and hung onto the steel cable below with as much strength as he could muster. He felt his skin burning as the steel rope ripped unforgivingly through the palm of his hand. Dale's body shot past him, dragging Khalid's ankle and leg, and then the rest of his body with him. Their combined weight was too much for Khalid and his hand shredded itself against the jagged shards of the frayed cable. With a shriek he let go and his body turned a cartwheel as his leg was dragged further by Dale towards the skip below.

They fell together, rotating as if in slow motion, but not for long. As Khalid's head spun outwards, it caught the solid steel edge of the skip, and split, the bone fracturing instantly against the sharp rim.

Dale hung on to the leg and felt himself rammed into the packing material, old cardboard, plastic bubble wrapping and a dirt-ridden canvas tarpaulin. As he sank, crushed into the debris, he felt a gush of blood pour over his face and a heavy body smash down on top of him. He lay still, completely winded and expecting to be dead, or fatally injured at best. Then he opened his eyes and saw the remains of Khalid's face no more than a few centimetres from his own. He retched violently and uncontrollably.

74

Emanuella clearly knew her stuff. No questions, just action. Nadia's relief at Dale's lack of serious injury had prompted tears, but these were now wiped away and she leapt to answer the call to help. Manning the phone, she talked almost non-stop to Russell and then again to Emanuella and also to Marlena. The two girls were mortified at being stuck in the desert but at least their phones were functioning. No 'no network' problems today thank goodness.

As Dale recovered from his fall, and Khalid's bloody remains had been cleaned away from his face and clothes, his brain began replaying the surreal conversation they had had with Khalid. He trawled his memory for what he had also heard from Miles and Marlena. There was a huge amount of information but his gut reaction, like Russell's had been on the phone, was to focus on the location of the bomb. He was sitting in the factory's main conference room where strong coffee had begun to take effect. Paolo Grenaldi had been summoned and was now sitting answering questions from two of the team that had arrived following the first call to Emanuella. Dale listened carefully to the conversation, but while it was interesting, he doubted its relevance. His mind kept coming back to Cairo. Russell had now heard from Miles. They were both at Heathrow and on their way over to Frankfurt where a search had already been started for industrial water treatment units.

"What happened to the steel vessel I saw being manufactured in Cairo two weeks ago?" he suddenly asked. The man questioning Paolo stopped in mid-sentence.

"Why?" he asked.

"Because I think that's the one Khalid was turning into a bomb." The man looked blankly at Dale. "Why?' he asked again.

"Never mind. Paolo, which plant was it?"

"It was planned to be shipped to Washington and then everything was changed last week. The due date was put back and so it was converted to become the unit to be shipped with the post-sanction plane tomorrow morning from Frankfurt."

"So, it's no longer on its way to Washington?"

Paolo looked puzzled. "Everything changed again three days ago. New units arrived from Cairo specifically for the post-sanction consignment. They were specially painted in Italian colours and so the original units were relabelled to go to Washington. They happen to be identical models, both standard units. They come cheaper that way," he explained.

"And where are they now?"

"Well, since they were ready, they all left here this morning to be air freighted to Frankfurt. They'll both be in Frankfurt now."

"Thank you," Dale picked up his mobile and dialled Russell's number. After a swift few minutes, he ended the call. "Russell's just boarding a plane to Frankfurt. They're already checking there," he said. "The post-sanction flight doesn't leave until early tomorrow morning. I've no idea about the Washington plane."

Grenaldi had come to the end of his narrative and Emanuella's men were packing up their papers.

Two severe looking men in black walked into the conference room and put a bag of clothes on the table. "His locker," one of them said and began emptying pockets. Various bits of paper and two empty component boxes were put in a small heap. Dale picked up the torn pieces of cardboard.

"Altimeters," he said, "with alarm contacts." he grabbed his phone and pressed redial. An automatic voice answered. "It's Dale," he said, "call me as soon as you land, it's urgent." Without pausing, he called Marlena. "Your guys in Frankfurt are searching for the water equipment," he said without introduction. "Tell them we've found packaging for altimeters in Khalid's pockets. Maybe this thing's triggered by pressure," he spoke urgently and ended the call. He looked at the packages in his hand. There are two of them, he thought. Why two?

The two men were thumbing through the other pieces of paper, but they only seemed to be receipts from the local supermarket.

"Can I keep these for a day?" Dale had no clear reason why he did that but he signed a receipt for the older man and then put them in his pocket with the component boxes. "Okay, everyone seems done here anyway. Let's go and find somewhere to stay and clean up. I need to think."

Nadia knew him well by now and did not challenge him. They expected Russell to call in a couple of hours or so. It looked like a long night.

Russell called Dale around midnight. "Good news," he said. "They've found both sets of equipment and they've been taken off the airport site for investigation."

"How long will they be?"

"Maybe two or three hours. These things take time. Apparently, the plant due for the US has additional security tags and will take a while to open. They're worried about booby-traps. The other one doesn't seem too secure. Looks as if it was finished in a hurry. We'll find out soon. I'll call you when I know anything."

Dale was still convinced in his mind that something was wrong. Everything seemed too easy. Come on, he said to himself, don't complicate things when it's not needed. Usually, the simple answer's the right one. But he nonetheless pulled out a pad of squared paper and blocked out a three-week schedule.

"Nadia, please help me," he said. "I want you to listen to my logic and tell me where it's crazy." He looked at the timeline he'd drawn. "Now," he said, "if Khalid doctored the US plant he could have done it any time in this period." He waved his hand across the whole page. "Except that Paolo has told us that it had been switched some time ago, and then switched back only recently. If Khalid knew it was going to be switched then surely he wouldn't have used it for his device, would he?" He looked at Nadia for help.

"Go on," was all she said.

"But when it was switched back, then perhaps he could use it after all. I wonder what days he could actually have done something." He started blanking out dates when he knew Khalid had been somewhere else. "Here," he said, "this is when he was in Cairo. It was also the same time that I was here, two weeks ago. And this is when I saw the vessels in Cairo myself. So before then must be out of the question."

"And then there's the comment in the tape. You remember, something about Khalid having a temporary job, in the X-ray plant. Marlena's immediate conclusion, and Russell's too, was that the plant he was talking about was in Frankfurt, at the airport, but now we know otherwise." He paused. "We need to ask Paolo about what his change in job might have been."

"You mean now?" asked an incredulous Nadia. "It's nearly one in the morning!"

Dale looked at the recent dates. "No one had known the US plant would be switched back until three days ago and the new plant for the post-sanction flight only arrived two and a half days ago. So," he said carefully, "if Khalid had altered the new US plant it must have been very recently, maybe last night." He looked pleased with himself. "Russell said something about security tags. I wonder whether that's the indicator we're looking for. Okay," he said decidedly, "they're in Frankfurt and we're not, so first we wait and see what they turn up. Meanwhile," he said as if he'd not heard Nadia's previous comment, "let's see what Mr Khalid's been doing for the last two weeks."

He tried calling Paolo direct but there was no answer from the home number he'd been given, so he picked up the phone to speak to Russell again and then put it down. "No," he said, "let's see what our Italian friends can do." He called Emanuella instead and explained what he wanted her to do. Nadia shook her head and grinned at him.

It took a while, but by 3.30 a.m. he and Nadia were back at the factory, with Paolo Grenaldi and Emanuella's two men in black. They were waiting for the fabrication shop supervisor to appear.

Eventually the man in the motorcycle helmet walked into the room, still wearing his enormous gloves. He nodded a greeting to Dale and Nadia and then turned to Grenaldi. "You wanted me?" he grumbled, looking pointedly at the clock on the wall. He removed his gloves and put them on the table. The helmet followed. Dale was surprised to see he was bald.

"Ah, Gianni, thanks for coming back. As I said on the phone, Fabio Ponte has died in a terrible accident, and we are trying to find out what happened."

It was Dale who took the lead. "Gianni," he said politely, "is the fabrication shop used at night?"

"Not usually, no, not unless we have a rush job like two nights ago."

"Two nights ago, what happened then?"

"The filter vessels had arrived from Egypt, and we wanted to convert them into the plant for the post-sanction flight, so we worked all day and night. We finished yesterday, well, the day before yesterday now, early evening."

"So, until two and a half nights ago anyone could have had free run of the place?"

"Well, no, it's locked at night. Only employees with their swipe cards can gain access."

"And do you know which ones might have used that access?"

"I don't suppose we ever checked."

"Can I suggest you check the record for Fabio Ponte over the last say three weeks.

There was a burst of activity and Gianni hurried away.

Dale turned to Nadia. "What did Khalid say about politicians?" he asked. "I can't remember and yet I'm sure it was important."

Nadia shook her head. The news about her wayward father had hit her hard enough. "Politicians?" she said, "come on Dale, we know where the bomb is now, it's out of your court, isn't it?"

It was an hour and a half before Gianni finally returned. He looked triumphant. "You were right," he said, "look at this. Ponte has been in that shop almost every evening for nearly two weeks and three nights ago he stayed there until five in the morning on his own. What was he doing?"

"That's what we're trying to find out," said Dale. "Why wouldn't he have had access until two weeks ago?"

Gianni thought for a while. "He joined the team working on screening equipment. They work in the other fabrication shops too and so they're issued with security swipe cards. They give access to all the main factory areas. Until then Fabio wouldn't have needed a swipe card as he only worked in the main shop. Mind you it would also mean that he wouldn't have had easy access around the factory, like he would have had with the card. To get in before two weeks ago he would have either had to stay here for the night or find a hidden door somewhere."

"What about two nights ago. Was he here then?"

"Most of the men were, including Fabio. He always liked overtime money. The new plant had come in and we all worked overnight to get it ready."

"Were you here yourself?"

"Not all night, but I did come back last night."

"Last night? You mean the factory was working last night?"

"Well, it was lucky really. It must have been about eight o'clock and I got a call from the trucking firm. They were coming early to collect the shipment for Frankfurt, and they were checking to see if it was ready."

"Ready?"

"I thought they were coming at 5 a.m. to pack and load up, but it turned out that they were expecting everything to be ready. It was an early start. Someone upstairs must have made the mistake. Maybe they didn't know the difference. I had to call some men back to finish the packaging and load the things onto the flatbeds."

"So, there was an unplanned work party?"

"That's right. Fabio was there as it happened. He hadn't left by then, and so I asked him to stay too. After a while, a couple of others came back. It was a long night."

"What time did you finish?"

"Not until about three-thirty this morning, I mean yesterday morning. Then we just lay down on the packing and went to sleep. There was no point in going home."

"And then the trucks arrived, and everything was okay?"

"Yes, they arrived, and then the band and everyone else. It turned out that time wasn't quite as tight as they'd said. They got away late in the morning."

"And then you asked Fabio to stay and clear up the packaging?"

"Yes. But that was after lunch. We took everyone out to celebrate."

Nadia was sitting in the corner of the large conference table, playing with words on a piece of paper. She looked up and spoke quietly. "He said, 'everything is in motion' and then something like 'it's a pity our politicians are greedy,'"

"Otherwise, it would have been perfect." Dale finished the sentence for her and looked thoughtful. He turned back to Nadia. "I reckon that the US package is clean. He had no time to rig anything up. In fact, I reckon they're both clean," he said dejectedly.

It was 5.15 a.m. when Russell finally called. "I've got news," he said.

"Don't tell me," Dale couldn't help jumping in. "They're both clean."

There was a silence. "How did you know?"

"Khalid didn't have any time to modify the plant since three nights ago. I reckon that whatever he did, it was done then. I also reckon that the bomb is designed to explode during the second flight. There were two altimeter boxes in his pocket. If we don't catch the damn thing now, it will still go off, somewhere."

"Okay," said Russell, "take me through the logic." Dale did.

Twenty minutes later Russell asked calmly, "so now what do you suggest?"

"Me suggest? I thought it was you guys who were running things."

"Okay," Russell laughed, "but I'd welcome your advice please. You seem to be having more success than us at the moment."

"Then I suggest we go through the equipment lists here and find out what else he could have been working on. We know it's on its way somewhere, but we don't know what it is. This place produces a huge amount of equipment and there was a lot that left the factory yesterday."

75

The cargo aircraft destined to be the first post-sanction flight stood on the tarmac. It had arrived the previous evening and its extra passenger was at this moment struggling. He had only fallen asleep an hour before and now the alarm clock and the telephone were both attempting to wrench him back to wakefulness. Jamil was staying at the Airport Hotel, and he had had a splendid night. The two girls sharing his bed were now fast asleep, their arms round each other's necks. One was German, the other Scandinavian, from somewhere he had never heard of. They had kept him entertained until he'd cried out in agony. And all his bundle of green dollars had gone, the girls coyly putting it in his own room safe. He did not know the combination.

He looked at the clock, and then his watch. He had swung this trip from his father and Fayez had insisted that when he was there, he had to call Khalid, but the number had not been answered. He had no idea where the guy was. All he needed to know was the flight number of the plane that Khalid had eventually used. Fayez thought he knew, but Khalid had a reputation for not following agreements exactly. There was one they had discussed, but he wanted to be sure, and now Jamil was not looking forward to facing his father, only being able to say there was no answer. Ah well, he thought, looking greedily at the girls, there's always another time. He hauled himself out of bed and into the bathroom. He had to be on the plane in forty-five minutes. Their take off was scheduled for 6.10 a.m.

On the tarmac the last cargo was being loaded. There had been a hiatus over some water treatment units that the customs people had taken way for inspection. In fact, there had been a small army come to collect them, but that was last night and now they were back and safely loaded. The captain looked at his watch. His only worry was whether Jamil would make it in time.

Across from the plane, another aircraft stood being prepped for take off. The captain was in no mood to waste time. He wanted the early slot he had been allocated, not the nonsense that had happened to the Washington flight last night, when a large number of heavies dressed in black flak jackets, with assault rifles and half the German bomb squad had arrived to take one of the skids off the plane. "Just routine," they'd said. Just routine my ass. They obviously had a bomb threat and were over-reacting. The plane had taken off a short while ago, minus its load, which had never reappeared. Ah well, he thought, hope they got the bastard.

The air was clear and there were none of the usual air traffic delays. Frankfurt was ahead of the game for once and flights were on time. The two cargo planes waited patiently at the end of the runway. The first rumbled its way forward before lifting gently into the air, just before the perimeter fence engulfed the aircraft nose. The second, as soon as it was given the go-ahead, revved its engines to full throttle, released its brakes and shot forward and upwards, like a scolded pigeon. Three minutes later, the small black box clicked quietly, for a third time. Again, no one heard. No one paid any attention.

76

Dale and Nadia were poring over papers in Paolo's conference room. There were no less than eight other sets of equipment that had left the factory on the previous day. With Gianni's help they were now listing them and filling out details, including size and destination. It took another half an hour to dig out all the destinations. Dale couldn't understand why there was no single list they could pull from the computer; but everything was on paper, and it took time.

While Nadia took charge of filling in these details, Dale sat with Gianni and had him tell him verbally what he could remember about each equipment order. By the time they had the destinations he also had a rough idea of the scope of each, from a practical point of view, not just what was written down. He put a cross against four consignments. Two were simply conveyors, being shipped to Germany itself. Frankfurt was their end destination. Another was a special X-ray plant for Athens and the last was a set of spares for Istanbul. The other four were to the US and the UK. The destinations were Denver, Boston, London and Manchester. All had large enough components to hide away something the size of suitcase. He disentangled his phone from the charger across the other side of the room and called Russell.

"Okay, here's our top four," he said.

"Four? Oh shit," Russell was dismayed. "Go on then, fire away."

Russell was back on the phone. "Sorry about the delay," he said. "These people are crazy about security. Anyway, Denver and Manchester are still here. We've put a hold on their flights while we check the planes."

"And London and Boston?"

"Gone. They're in the air."

"Shit! So now what do we do?"

"Tell the Brits and Americans that there may be a bomb on board one of their flights, and by the way, don't land the plane to find out because it could go off in your face." Russell was humourless. "What else can we do?"

"How long have we got?"

"I don't know. These planes always carry a lot more fuel than they need, but we've obviously got less time with the London flight. I'll get on to the right people and we'll put together a plan."

Dale had an idea and called Gianni over to him and drew a rectangle on the whiteboard. "Gianni," he asked, "can you show me where the consignments would have been on the factory floor? Which ones were nearest to the Washington filter vessels?" Meanwhile Nadia took the phone over to the far the corner of the room and huddled over it, speaking urgently.

By eight o'clock they were getting nowhere. The equipment location idea had been a good one, but all it had showed was that the Boston consignment had been assembled on one side of the Washington package. This had excited Dale until Gianni showed him that the London consignment had been put together on the other side of the vessels. They were both within easy distance.

77

In the same time zone, far to the South, Fayez walked into his office. He did a double take and then frowned at the two girls sitting in the soft chairs in the corner of his room.

"I wasn't aware I'd left the door unlocked," he said unpleasantly.

"You didn't," said Marlena, "but we had a surprise for you, and we thought you'd like to hear about it in your office, rather than out in the corridor."

"A surprise?"

"We have Khalid," she said simply, "and he's been talking."

"Khalid?" Fayez was stony faced, "who's Khalid?"

"This one," said Emanuella, "the one who's talking to you." She put the small tape recorder on the table and pressed 'play.'

"Fayez, my friend, we have known each other for many years. Since I was a child, and you were like a big brother. Nine years older was a lot when I was half your age." She switched off the tape and returned the tape recorder to the top of her bag. "You don't really want to hear the rest of it do you? We have it all, and also your hotel room. That girl was really energetic wasn't she."

Fayez didn't move. "I was only acting under orders," he said slowly at last. "You have nothing there to use against me or anyone."

"From what Khalid's been saying, I don't think we'll need any. He's confessed to everything and is out there gunning for you now."

"Why would he do that."

"Because he's discovered that you hid the fact that Raya is his mother from him. He really took a dim view of that."

"How did he find out?"

"Because someone showed him the same hospital record from Leena that they showed to Raya. It goes against all the so-called proof you concocted about Leena being Talak's real mother. Why'd you do it Fayez? Scared of what the two bothers might actually accomplish on their own, let alone what they might do with their real mother behind them too. You wouldn't have stood a chance."

Fayez still said nothing. He sighed.

"Qui tacet consentire," Marlena quoted. "Silence means consent." She looked hard at Fayez. "So, who's orders were they Fayez? Who was really supporting these terrorists?"

"Raya," he said, suddenly pulling himself together. "She was behind all this, and yes, that's why I kept the truth from Talak. He wouldn't have believed his own mother would fund such things."

"And the Ruler?"

Fayez, spat onto the ground. "He hasn't got the guts to do anything like that. He's all for putting the past behind us and getting on with world trade, whatever that means. Look at this flight that's coming in this morning. 'Post-sanction special.' That's not how to deal with these capitalists. All it does is play into their hands. You need people like me. We are the only ones that matter. Khalid knows that too. That's why he trained for so long to become what he is. He's an expert. And in a few minutes you will see why."

Raya Al Khayr strode into the room. Fayez gaped.

"Enough!" she shouted. "You're a deceitful liar. There was no way I was funding those terrorist acts. If anyone was, then it was clearly you yourself."

"But the Ruler ..." Fayez stopped in mid-sentence and Hasna, Raya's elder sister entered smoothly into the room. Her wheelchair was pushed by Raheem.

"My grandson is trying to bring his country back into the world," she said. "You're clearly not on the same page."

Fayez looked around him. He was confronted by four very determined ladies, not at all what he was used to. "Well," he said, "maybe you're right, but you can't prove anything."

"Really," said Emanuella quietly. She wound back the tape a short way and put the small machine on the table.

"Well, maybe you're right, but you can't prove anything." Fayez's voice echoed around his office. Fayez hung his head in his hands.

Marlena was not done. "You said a few minutes," she said. "That means it's on the London flight."

Fayez cracked a smile. "Probably," he said. "I told him Boston but he's so stubborn. He wanted London. My guess is that he followed his own decision. That's what he's always done in the past. London should be landing very soon."

"Can you get Abdullah to keep this guy locked away?" she said to Raya.

"My pleasure," said the older lady smiling. She picked up her mobile.

Fayez shrugged his bear-like shoulder and struggled to his feet. There was no way he was staying. But he found himself looking into the muzzles of two small guns. Emanuella and Marlena waved him to sit down again. So, he slunk back to his chair and did as he was told, putting his hand visibly on the desk in front of him.

Raya turned to Marlena. "Thank you, both of you, for coming to see me this morning," she said quietly. "Don't worry, Hasna and I will sort these crazy people out."

78

Emanuella's call to Russell put him into a fit of gloom. It was 8.40 a.m. in Frankfurt and the Boston flight was way out over the ocean. The London flight had been diverted over the North Sea and told to stay high, whatever that meant. They had no idea where any device might be, although he knew in his gut that Fayez was probably right. On the positive side of the equation, the RAF were currently planning to extract the crew from the plane and let it crash into the sea. It was a desperate measure, in effect lowering a pair of parachutes down to the jet's open cockpit window from an air force cargo plane flying immediately over-head. He didn't fancy the chances of the aircrew, but needs must. They only had thirty minutes of fuel remaining.

Nadia put down the phone and walked over to Dale. Emanuella's account of their meeting with Fayez stunned him. "How did they know?" he asked.

"I told them," she said simply, "while you were busy."

"So, we were right," he said, "Fayez is the main problem in all this. What do we do now?"

"I guess we wait," she said. "The London flight has only half an hour or so of fuel, so we'll know either way when it goes down."

"Tell me about your grandfather." Dale was desperately trying to get his mind away from the impending disaster. Nadia was happy to change the subject too.

"My grandfather – after he retired he invested in several new ventures of his own. Almost every one failed, through accidents, fraud, some sort of malpractice or misfortune. He seemed to have an extraordinary run of bad luck, but I wonder now whether it was that at all. After what we heard this evening from Fabio, I would guess that some of it, maybe all, had been orchestrated. That Khalid was a terrible man, not like my father at all." She paused, still willing the memory of the last few hours to be unreal. She preferred her old recollections to those now sprung upon her.

"Anyway, he died a broken man, not ruined financially but his spirit had been shattered. He still had a lot of money in the oil business, but it was much reduced from his family's heyday."

Nadia's mobile rang. It was Bertelli.

"Is Grenaldi there?" he asked. "If he is please tell him I managed to get some more of his plant onto the post-sanction flight. Tell him he owes me."

"Is that all?"

"Yep, that was it. Just tell him that the Brits were real gentlemen."

Nadia put down her phone as Paolo walked back into the room.

"That was Bertelli," she said. "He says you owe him. Something about getting more equipment onto the post-sanction flight."

"Oh, I'd almost given that up as a lost cause," Grenaldi sat down heavily. He was excruciatingly tired. "I wonder who he robbed."

Dale looked up. "Say that again," he said.

"He was talking to some of our clients to see if he could borrow one of their X-ray units, to put it on display when the flight arrives. A sort of Italian exhibition to celebrate the end of sanctions."

Dale jumped up from his seat. "Nadia," he shouted, "call him back, now please!"

Nadia pressed the necessary sequence of keys. "In use," she said.

"Give him a minute. What else did he say?"

"Nothing, just that. Oh, and that the Brits were real gentlemen, whatever that means."

"Maybe it means he borrowed equipment from one of the UK consignments," said Paolo.

They looked at each other. "London," said Nadia.

At that moment, Dale's mobile squawked. He looked at the screen. "Russell," he said putting the phone to his ear. He had the tiny speaker switched on too so that Nadia could hear.

"We got the crew out. The plane's just crashed into the sea," Russell said.

"And there was no bomb was there?"

"Are you psychic of something? How could you possibly know that?"

"We just learnt that Bertelli had some extra equipment put on to the post-sanction plane. We think it came from a British consignment and we're trying to get hold of him now to confirm. I was going to call you as soon as I knew."

Russell sighed. "So, if that's true, then there could be something on the post-sanction plane. When's it landing?"

"Three and a quarter hours from when it took off, if it's the same as the passenger flights." Dale could hear papers being shuffled rapidly at the other end of the phone.

"Christ, that's in ten minutes!"

Nadia was already dialling Emanuella. She handed her phone to Dale as he shut off his own.

79

Jamil had partially recovered from his hangover and was sitting in the jump seat at the back of the cockpit. He was still pondering on what to tell his father about the lack of contact with Khalid. The two pilots were in jubilant mood, they were going home with a cargo of international goods on what was probably the most famous flight their country had ever witnessed. They were exchanging course details with the tower in preparation for landing. They had made up time and were only a minute or so from dropping their undercarriage. The efficiency at Frankfurt airport and the host of Italian and German flags around the plane had rather overwhelmed them and they were now looking forward to being welcomed by their own people. They had no clear idea of the reception committee planned as part of Bertelli's well-orchestrated 'marketing event' but the tower had indicated there were a lot of people at the airport.

The radio crackled. "Alpha Romeo 162 … Alpha Romeo 162 … Emergency change of course, divert right 15 degrees. New course 192 degrees. Hold your altitude until further notice. Please acknowledge." The pilots looked askance at each other. Even Jamil woke from his stupor. The captain flicked off the auto-approach and put the plane in a shallow right-hand turn. His colleague spoke urgently into the radio.

The small black box clicked quietly, for a fourth and final time. It did not realise it had outlived its usefulness, but almost instantly the two innocuous looking fire extinguishers attached to the base plate of the X-ray monitor ignited. As the gases rapidly expanded, each extinguisher split neatly along its weld line and then all hell was let loose.

The extinguishers had been facing in opposite directions and now became white-hot projectiles, one hurling itself forward towards the cockpit and the other rearwards towards the tail. Each was followed by a blaze of fire. As it passed through the main wing section, the forward moving fireball rammed itself into the floor and all cabling, all hydraulic controls and all fuel lines that were safely locked beneath the floor panels were suddenly fused into a single untanglable mass. Its partner missile was more specific, though not by intention, and as the tail section of the aircraft exploded and melted it welded the ailerons rigid, and the shallow turning circle started by the captain became permanent.

80

At the airport everybody was assembled. A carnival atmosphere pervaded the normally subdued airport terminal. The plane had been out of sight when Abdullah's instruction to the tower had taken effect. When Raya spoke, he did not argue. He knew better than that. But he had no way of knowing that Nadia's call to Emanuella had found her walking out of the ministry building and climbing into Raya's personal car as she and Marlena accompanied the old lady back to her residence. As the car sped away from the city Abdullah had merely leaned across to the control tower staff, where he was standing with Naiem Fahoud, and given the instruction verbally. The tower controllers were now looking at him for further orders when they lost contact with the plane.

Fayez was gazing out of his office window, the three armed guards instructed by Abdullah to detain him stationed by the doors. His prestigious office location in the Ministry of Security gave him unparalleled views over the city, and beyond to the inviting calm of the Mediterranean itself. As he gazed, and while his mind was still struggling to dissect the recent conversations, he caught sight of a flash about three miles away. It looked like sunshine glinting off a passing aeroplane. It often happened and usually did not merit a second glance. But this time was different, the flash was continuing, like a white-hot knife of lightning ripping through the shimmering blue haze and, as he watched, the searing light seemed to be turning towards the city. He sat transfixed, mesmerised, as it kept turning, turning towards him until, with an explosive flash of light and a shattering impact that they both saw and later heard at the airport, the plane smashed itself into his own prestigiously placed office, in the Ministry of Security building.

The author

Andrew Wells attended the High Pavement
Grammar School, Nottingham; University of
Cambridge, UK and Harvard Business School, USA.
A restless traveller, Andrew has worked in more
than 60 countries in pursuit of his passion for
all things associated with water, accumulating a
wealth of anecdotes about fascinating people,
local customs and curious situations everywhere.
From the UK, he has also pursued his engineering consultancy career living in Italy, Hong Kong,
Singapore and China, from where, working for his
parent consultancy firm in USA, he has managed
companies and projects in Europe, the Middle East,
India and Asia. Writing keeps him in contact with
the world and the numerous interesting people he
has met over the years.

novum PUBLISHER FOR NEW AUTHORS

The publisher

He who stops getting better stops being good.

This is the motto of novum publishing, and our focus is on finding new manuscripts, publishing them and offering long-term support to the authors.
Our publishing house was founded in 1997, and since then it has become THE expert for new authors and has won numerous awards.

Our editorial team will peruse each manuscript within a few weeks free of charge and without obligation.

You will find more information about
novum publishing and our books on the internet:

w w w . n o v u m - p u b l i s h i n g . c o . u k